OLD THOT NEXT DOOR

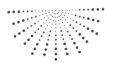

QUAN MILLZ

FOREWORD

Dear Readers,

While I consider this book to be a ratchet soap opera thriller, there are many elements of comedy in this book. Please do not take offense to some of the graphic imagery or depictions of our elders. I mean no disrespect to those who are up in age.

Best Regards,
   Quan Millz

PART I

CHAPTER ONE

***B*ABY! LET ME TELL YOU ONE MOTHAFUCKIN' THANG!** I don't give a damn what you think about me and my age. Yeah, I might be 76-years-old but this big, thick pussy between my toned brown legs don't act like it!

Don't let the gray hairs fool you now!

My name is Vernita Ernestine Washington and I ain't ashamed to admit that I loves to drink brown liquor, smoke good reefur AND most definitely get my fuck on! Uh-huh! You heard that right! Yup! I loves to ride me a big ole black dick!

Age ain't nothin' but a number, baby doll. My body felt like I was still forty. And you best believe I fucked like I was still forty!

If you are blessed to live a long life, you'll see just exactly what I meant.

Now for all you young folk out there, I can let you in on the secret if you were wondering what I did to stay so young and vibrant.

If you thought goin' to the health club every day was my

secret, then you guessed wrong. Now don't get me wrong – I did get my lil workout in at the health club to stay in shape. But truth be told, I really went to go look at them fine young mens they be havin' up in there.

If you think my secret is watching what I eat, then you guessed wrong again. Baby, I gets down in the kitchen. And I shole love me some Popeye's chicken. Baby, give me a two piece dark, spicy with a side of Cajun rice after a good dick down and my sexy ass will be in heaven! And speaking of heaven – no – my secret to being so youthful ain't staying prayed up. Now don't get me wrong – I loved the Lord and I paid my tithes, but I didn't mess with church folk like that. Shit, half of them acted like they were ninety-years-old! And most if not all the people that went to my church were way younger than me!

Baby...let me tell you what my number one secret is.

You ready?

Hold on now! Get a lil closer...

My number one secret to living a long, happy, healthy life was making sure you surround yourself with some young folks. And by young folks, I mean some young dicks! And when I say young, I ain't talkin' fifty or forty. Baby, I'm talkin' YOUNG. Between the ages of twenty and thirty. Call me a nasty woman. Call me a predator if you want to. But riding some young dick is truly what regulates my blood pressure and keeps my cholesterol down.

And that was why I had me not one, but TWO young dicks on their way to my place.

Ding-Dong!

"Whoop! There it is!" That was my doorbell.

"Coming!" I yelled as I hopped off my couch, sprinting toward the front door. Just right on time, 'cuz my pussy was ready to get this party started.

I didn't even bother to put no real clothes on either this

early Saturday evening. I was already in my nice, sexy black lingerie I had ordered off the Amazon. I knew this outfit would mess up Markell's young, gullible mind once I opened up this door, too.

Peeping out the front door's peephole, I took a quick scan just to make sure it was my double dick appointment. And surely it was. Hallelujah! Baby, I was highly blessed and favored to have these two fine lookin' young mens come lay their burden down on me.

I quickly swung the front door to my townhouse open. "Afternoon," I uttered with a big ass smile stretched across my face. Chile, you should've seen how suddenly Markell and this other sexy ass young man looked surprised. Guess they didn't think I'd open the door already ready to get my fuck on.

This sexy ass nicca gasped clutching his mouth. "Yoooooooooo! Damn, it's like that!" Markell smilingly exclaimed, rubbing his hard, muscular hands together. He scanned me up and down, his eyes were glued to every square inch of my body.

"Yoooooo, this who we finne tag?" the other sexy young man chimed in as he too clutched his mouth with his right fist. "Man, she old as fuck!"

All of a sudden I could feel my blood boiling and a look of anger instantly grew on my face. I know they saw how mad I suddenly got. "Old?!? Boy, ya mammy is old! I ain't old."

Markell smacked his teeth and said, "Man, chill the fuck out, Will! Trust me, Ms. Vernita on point, bruh!"

The other young nicca shook his head. "I don't know about this though…Shit, this gon be weird as fuck."

"Can we have this conversation on the inside at least?" I said. "Ya'll lettin' all my cool air out!"

Markell glanced over at this Will friend of his, nodding

affirmatively. "Come on, bruh. Trust me. We finne have some fun...Ms. Vernita a vet."

"Fine," Will reluctantly muttered. And then the two of them walked inside my place.

It was the middle of August, so the sun was blazing although it was nearly six pm. Chicago felt like it was on fire! As long as I'd been living I ain't never felt the city to get this hot. But baby, I wasn't gonna let this hot ass weather deter me from getting what I needed at this moment. I was content with staying in my place and riding these dicks for hours, you hear me!

Both Markell and Will were wearing black tank tops, exposing their tatted up muscular arms and shoulders. They looked like some straight-up gang members. But, ooooh, baby, Ms. Vernita just loved her some roughneck street niggas. Straight out of jail, too! I want that first post-release nut!

Markell and Will had a little sweat glinting from their round shoulders, so I presumed they'd just come back from the gym.

Markell was a lil ole chocolate stallion with Pacific Ocean waves sitting on top of his head. He had broad shoulders, cut up arms and a chest that looked like it was harder than steel. Standing at around 5'10, his young, sexy ass looked like he was a good two-hundred pounds of all muscle. And baby, let me tell you, that dick of his weighed about a good two-hundred pounds, too!

Oohh, chile, I was getting so moist just thinking about the good time I was about to have. This other young man, Will, reminded me of that sexy, fine light-skinded boy that plays on that show that comes on cable. What's the name of it again? Power? Ya'll know what I'm talking about. That drug dealer boy with the beard. GHOST! That's right! That's his name! I almost forgot! Chilllleee, before I forget, I needed to take my fish oil and Ginko Biloba pills. You know, when you get up in my age, your memory sometimes gets a lil fuzzy. I also needed to take my other medication for my leg twitches.

With the both of them in front of me, we marched straight into my living room.

"Y'all sit down and make yourself comfortable," I calmly instructed. "I'm finne go to get the reefur and the Henny. Y'all smokin', right?"

Will's hazel eyes shot wide open out of shock. He looked at Markell. "Is she for real?"

"Yes, bruh! She cool. I'm telling you, bruh!"

Will then looked back at me smiling saying, "Damn, hell yeah I'm smoking! What you got? Some joints or something?"

My brow raised. "Nigga, don't try me! I might be old but baby I smokes nothing but blunts! Backwoods matter-of-fact. I got them Russian Creams in the back." Speaking of cream...I could feel my pussy getting juicier than a fresh pot roast.

"OOOOOH SHIT! GRANNY A THOT!" Will shouted, jumping up and down.

"What did you say?" I turned my face up. I'd be damned if this young nigga was gonna disrespect me in my house!

Markell nudged Will in his shoulder. "BRUH!"

Will quickly got his act together and stood still. "My bad," he apologized.

"That's what I thought...Anyways, I'm finne go run to my room right quick and get the reefur. Y'all make y'all self comfortable!" I said as I spun on my high-heels and sauntered down my hallway to my bedroom.

Now, y'all might be wondering how I met Markell. Well, let me give you the backstory.

I met Markell actually at my fitness club. The LA Fitness right there on 47th street right in Kenwood. That's the

Southside of Chicago. He was the personal training sales manager.

Funny thing was he tried to run game on me and thought he was gonna get me with those expensive ass training packages but bay-baaaay, I wasn't going. Not at all! Yeah, I might be getting a nice lil pension from the DMV, social security and monthly 401k payments but I'd be damned if I was gonna spend no $1200 a month for some personal training sessions.

Shit, I was fine with just walking on the treadmill and doing my calisthenics. However, Markell was a little hustler, so he offered me home personal training sessions on the side...so long as I didn't run my mouth to corporate. He said he could get in trouble if they found out he was training people on the side. So, I agreed. But I only agreed 'cause I could see in Markell's eyes I could make him a victim to my good, tender pussy. And lo and behold, two home training sessions later, I seduced his ass and put this moist pink monkey of mines onto him. Chile, I had to let that young man know Ms. Vernita still had that snapback. Since then, Markell had been my number one boo thang.

Anyways, now that I was back in my room, I quickly made my way over to my walk-in closet. I walked all the way down to where I kept my safe. Although I smokes reefur every day, for some odd reason, I couldn't just have it all out in the open like that. Especially since that stuff was so pungent. That shit would've had my whole entire house smelling foul!

Once I opened my safe, I grabbed my favorite kind of reefur, a pack of Backwood cigars and my lighter.

I dashed over into my bathroom just to make sure I still looked dazzling. Now staring at myself in the mirror, I grabbed my brush off my marble bathroom countertop and lightly ran it through my silver hair. "Hrrrm, I'mma have to call Keisha to have her give me a touch up," I commented to myself. I then leaned close into the mirror and analyzed my make-up. My mascara, foundation and lipstick was still on point. I looked left. Glanced right. "Yes, Lord! I look GOODT! HAHAH!" I chuckled sticking my tongue out.

Quickly dashing out of the bathroom, I heard my cell phone buzzing as it charged on my nightstand. I froze for a moment, tempted to answer it. But fuck it. Baby, I didn't have time to check it. Whoever could've been calling me at this moment was just gonna have to wait 'cause I was ready to get high, drunk and suck some big nigga dicks! And I might just eat they asses today. I was ready to let it all go this afternoon.

I turned my nose up and sexily sauntered through my bedroom with the reefur, cigars and lighter gripped in my hand. "Should've called me earlier," I snickered at whoever was calling on my celly. I then made my way out of the bedroom and now I was back in the hallway.

Now feet away from the living room, I came to an abrupt stop when I saw Markell and Will were now completely naked, sitting on my nice white Italian leather living room couch. Baby, my mouth shot wide open in shock! But it wasn't them being naked that had me stunned! They were making out! Yes! Kissing each other. Tongues all deep down in each other's throat. Their eyes were closed and everything as if they were in love! And they were stroking each other's already hard dicks! WHAT?!?!?! Chile, I was about to pass out! Take me home now, Lord Jesus!

"WHAT IN THE HELL ARE Y'ALL DOING??!?" I screamed to the top of my lungs.

CHAPTER TWO

"**W**HAT IN THE HELL ARE Y'ALL DOING??!?"
Still standing there shocked, I couldn't believe what my wide eyes were observing. These young niggas were crazy as hell if they thought this was okay! I did NOT get down like this. AT ALL! I was still a bit old school!

"Oooh shit!" Markell said, suddenly pulling himself off Will.

But then a gigantic smile came across my face. "Y'all don't need to stop. I loves it! This gonna be very very interesting!"

Guess there was a first time for everything.

Now that was a first for me! I ain't never did no nasty freaky stuff like that before in my life. Two men at the same time? Two bisexual men at that?!? Oohhhh, chile, my deceased husband, Clarence, was probably rolling over in his grave right now if he saw what I did. I felt like I was in one of them pornos!

Baby, let me tell you – I had those young boys scared for

their life, too! Not to be TMI but I did what them young folks call the D-P-D-A: dick in the pussy, dick in the ass! Them fellas thought they was gonna mess me up and have me in the hospital when I suggested we try something a lil different-different.

"I'on know 'bout dat, Vernita. You sure you ready for all that?" Markell said.

"Boy, Ms. Vernita is a vet! All my holes can handle all types of meat!" I spat right back at him.

You know I really hated it when a nigga underestimated me. Now, I cain't lie. Them dicks had Vernita shooketh to a degree. Nevertheless, with that strong reefur and Henny running through my veins, something came over me and relaxed me. Them boys slid right up in me with ease.

Hah! Now that I think about it, Clarence could never! His baby dick was shameful! I can't believe I wasted nearly fifty years married to that. His ass ain't never gave me the sexual satisfaction I needed! I could count on one hand how many times he did something freaky to me. And I had to pull teeth just to get him to try new shit. Ole fat mothafucka.

As horrible as this may sound, I was so glad his ass was dead. I didn't have to be bothered with him no more. He passed away from a stroke about three years ago and since then I've been getting my fuck on like none other! Vernita gotta make up for lost time! And on that note, this was exactly why I was getting ready for hopefully another rendezvous with some young dick!

Some hours later, after Markell and Will did me in and did me right, I was back in my bathroom getting ready to hang out with one of my friends, Alice. She and I used to work together at the Department of Motor Vehicles. At one point, Alice lived next to me when Clarence was still living but now she was living over in Bronzeville while I lived in Hyde Park. I had recently retired from them after a good fifty years of service. Apparently, she was gonna introduce me to one of her cousin's friends. You already know I had to ask how old this dude was. I told Alice straight up I ain't messing with anyone over fifty. I asked to see a picture but apparently tonight was supposed to be a blind date.

After taking a long hot shower, I was now quickly putting on some makeup, getting my face ready for tonight. Some moments later, my face was now beat to perfection as usual and I was ready to show out! I'll tell you this though – Alice had better not be setting me up with some limp dick nigga either or her and I were gonna have it out!

See – one thing ya'll gon learn about Vernita is that I really don't give a damn about anyone's opinions. Life is too short to be caught up on how people think of you. You gotta do you, child! Shit, you got one life to live! Live it to the fullest. Ain't nobody got time to get their time wasted.

I absolutely do NOT do bullshit, so, with that being said, I had to turn some eyes tonight. In the event that this date fell through, oh, Ms. Vernita was gonna be bringing back some dick tonight. You better believe that! That being said, I wasn't one of them types of women that dressed for their "age".

I refused to live up to those old woman expectations. So, I threw on this new black leather Gucci bodysuit and some matching pumps. I made sure to buy this outfit a lil extra tight too because I wanted this nigga to see this fat cat of mine.

With two splashes of Chanel No. 5, I checked myself in the mirror one last time. I grabbed my phone and purse then stepped out of my townhouse, expeditiously making my way over to Paulette, my ruby red drop-top 2019 Ford Mustang.

I chucked up the engine and immediately my favorite music staring blaring through the humid air.

"Do it, baby, stick it, baby

Move it, baby, lick it, baby
Suck up on that clit until that pussy got a hickie, baby!"

I loved me some rap music. Especially City Girls. That song *Twerk* was my jam! Yeah, I already knew what ya'll was thinking. But, baby, I refuse to be some Anita Baker, Gladys Knight, Aretha Franklin-listenin' type of bitch. Fuck that! This right here is the type of music that'll keep you young!

Once I got Paulette on Lake Shore Drive, I sped my way up to 35th street.

The plan tonight was for me to pick her up and then the two of us were gonna head back south to this club over in South Shore called The Dating Game. It was a very popular stepper's lounge.

Knowing that already kind of gave me bad vibes because no one below the age of 45 went to stepper's lounges like that. But Alice gave me her word that this mystery date, was only 47. I really think the bitch was lying to me but we were gonna see.

A good ten minutes later, I pulled Paulette up to Alice's house. She lived in a nice three-story Brownstone. I whipped out my celly and gave her a dial. "Hey, girl! I'm downstairs!"

"Okay, I'll be down in a minute!" she said to me and then hung up.

A minute on the dot later, Alice came bumbling out of her building and walked slowly up to my car. As she got closer I could see she had a weird semi-frown on her face.

"What's wrong?" I had to ask.

"Girl, I said we going out just for a few cocktails and maybe some wings. You dressed like you 'bout to go hang out with my grandbabies!" she huffed.

Alice was about a decade younger than me but I swore she acted like she was someone's damn aunt sometimes! In fact, right now she was dressed like someone's aunty. She could be such a nicer looking woman if she took a bit better care of herself. She kind of reminded me of a thicker Tamala Mann. The only difference was Tamala look goodt! But Alice looked like Tamala's busted down twin that worked at some school cafeteria making six dollars an hour. Alice already knew how I got down and how I rolled when I was in these streets yet she was dressed like she bought her entire outfit off the clearance rack at Wal-Mart! This was actually quite embarrassing! No wonder her husband left her raggedy ass years ago! In fact, I didn't even know why I was hanging out with this heffa tonight! You know what…Let me stop…

ANYWAYS…

"Girl, no, don't do me like that. You already know when I step out of my house I gotta look right. I think you may need to go change your outfit. Girl, you look like you 'bout to go to someone's family reunion! You ain't got nothing better to put on?!?"

"Ug-uh! No! Girl, don't you go there. Don't get mad at me because you over-dress everywhere we go. Girl, just last week when we went to the Red Lobster you were dressed like one of those scandalous young girls! What's really going on with you?!?"

I rolled my eyes. *Going on with me?* Really?

See, now, I was beginning to get mad. I already done told ya'll how I roll and here this chick was making it seem like I was doing the most. The nerve of her. "Ain't nothing going on with me, girl. All I know is these men out here ain't like how they were when we were much younger. They want you to come with it," I said back to her, hoping she realized how raggedy she looked.

I kind of felt bad though for Alice because her husband wasn't no good and he used to beat her ass like a runaway slave. I tried to get her to leave him for years but her self-esteem was so shot that she swore he'd eventually change.

Well, he changed alright. Changed his address. Guess once he realized Alice was getting too old for his liking, he straight up left her for some young nasty bitch. Clarence and I may have had a dull sex life but I'd be damned if I would ever allow a nigga to put his hands on me. The only thing you allowed to beat up on me was this pussy. Otherwise, you'd mess around and buy a one-way ticket to your grave.

"Yeah, they different alright! But a man should like you for your mind and heart, not what you got on!"

"Oh okay! Well, you keep on believing that. All I know is this nigga you hooking me up with better look like Shemar Moore and better have a big ole black dick. I hate getting my time wasted!"

"VERNITA! That is so crude and not lady-like!" Alice shouted.

I shrugged my shoulders. "Yeah, well, it is what it is. I got my tastes, you got yours. And, just to make sure, you did say this man was 48...Not 58, right? And he knows I'm 76, right?"

"Yeah...He knows...But..."

"But what?"

"Nothing..."

"No, girl! You better tell me! Something wrong with this nigga?"

"Chile, let's go and see what this blind date working with. I don't know what I'm getting into either. But I know my expectations are realistic...Unlike others...," Alice said sarcastically.

"Whatever, girl. Watch and see...If this nigga ain't on shit, oh, I'm getting somebody!"

Not saying anything back, she just shook her head. I turned the music up and soon as the City Girl lyrics began to once again fill the air, Alice looked at me saying, "Really? You ain't got no better music? This music is just foul as hell! Put on some Patti LaBelle or something…Hell, even Luther or the Isley Brothers."

"Girl, that's your problem now! You acting too much like your age!"

"And what's wrong with that? I'm 66 not 26!"

"You need to act like you 26! Age ain't nothin' but a number!"

"Nah, girl, I'm good. And you need to be acting your age, too! We eventually all get old…if we lucky enough to live that long."

"Yeah, yeah, yeah. Girl, just sit back and enjoy the music," I laughed, playfully rolling my eyes to the dark purplish skies. "You so tight sometimes. Before I die, I swear I'mma get you right."

"Chile, bye! You got it all messed up. You keep on going after these young guys if you want to. At the end of the day, you can do all the things you wanna do with them, but they'll always run back to one of their peers. Then what you gon do after that? You think one of these boys wanna be laid up with someone who gon be in a home in less than a decade?"

"Girl, enough already! You so negative sometimes!"

See, now, she was gonna make me say something that I was gonna regret. But I was gonna keep my cool. She can act like an old hag all she wanted but not me. I refused to let my age dictate the dicks I wanted. And all the young guys I ever messed with never broke my heart to link up with a younger hoe. Besides, who said I even wanted a relationship? I was married for fifty years! Companionship sounded nice and all but for right now, all I wanted was to just have a good time.

CHAPTER THREE

"Let's go baby to the hole in the wall
I've had my best time y'all at the hole in the wall
3 o'clock in the morning
All the damn clubs are closed
I went to this place y'all
I didn't want anyone to know
I walked into the room
Had my nose in the air
It's 7 in the morning
And I'm still in there!"

*J*ust what I thought. My worse fear was confirmed – this blind date was a hot ass mess!

Baby, I was ready to curse Alice to the high heavens. I just knew this no good bitch was lying her mothafuckin' ass off! We hadn't even been at the lounge for an hour and I was RET TO GO! Baby, I was pissed, you hear me!

Me, Alice, her cousin Samantha and these three other

guys, Nathaniel, Gerald and Robert, were sitting down at a table inside this stiff ass lounge. As all five of them smacked on chicken wings and threw spaghetti in their mouths, I sat there quiet and occasionally sipped on some water. As they conversed amongst each other, I was so terribly disgusted as I stared at my blind "date" Gerald through the corner of my eye. Although he was sitting to my left, I hadn't said a word to him the entire time we'd been here. I swear a part of me was just so ready to pop off on Alice right here but I knew I had to keep my cool. Plus, I didn't get down like that. And perhaps Alice didn't know how this guy looked either. But I had a feeling her big ugly ass knew all along how this nigga looked.

From the moment I was introduced to him, I was completely turned off! My pussy dried up within seconds. Got drier than the damn Sahara! Hah! 48 my ass! Chile, them dark circles and big ass pregnant belly of his let me know this nigga was pushing at least sixty! Maybe about a good thirty years ago he looked good. But his apparent age was definitely a turn off! He reminded me so much of my deceased husband, Clarence. He was light-skinned, had light green hazel eyes and visible streaks of gray throughout his hi-top fade. I caught another quick glance at him and just looking at this slimy ass nigga I knew his black ass wasn't no goddamn 48! Fat mothafucka looked at least 68! Hell, I was damn near 78 and I looked better than his ass!

As this horrible ass Mel Waiters song blared from the club speakers, I sat back in my seat with my arms folded. Silent, I stared off at the thick crowd dancing on the dance floor.

"You mighty quiet over there," said James.

Although he was old as hell, too, he looked like he was in better shape than Gerald. Robert kind of reminded me of Billy Dee Williams minus the permed hair. I was never into

Billy Dee like that. There was always something off about that man. Anyways – I glanced over at James and produced the fakest smile I could. "I'm just taking in the scene. That's all," I replied and then threw my eyes back onto the dance floor.

"You don't wanna eat no chicken? They got good wings," Gerald laughed, smacking loudly on those over-sauced, probably over-fried chicken wings. There was nothing more embarrassing than sitting next to a bunch of old niggas listening to them smack on greasy ass wings and reminisce about shit that happened thirty and forty years ago.

"She just a little tired," Alice said. "Them shots hitting you hard, Vernita?"

I looked over at her trifling ass and said, "Girl, I had half of a shot and this is water I'm sipping on now. I'm fine." I couldn't take the bullshit no more, so I quickly stood up and adjusted my outfit. "I'm about to go use the ladies room for a moment."

From the gawk on Alice's face, I guess she sensed I wasn't in the mood and wasn't feeling this Gerald nigga at all. She looked at me and said, "Yeah, I gotta use the bathroom too. I'll follow you."

"Don't ya'll be in there too long! We got some dancin' to do! I'mma request the DJ to play some Luther," Gerald chuckled.

My eyes suddenly grew big but I had to catch myself and quickly walk off. Luther? Hell to the naw! Somebody better put some Trick Daddy or Future on! Got me all the way fucked up!

Strolling off to the bathroom, I made my way through the thick crowd on the dimly lit dance floor. Although The Dating Game was not that big of an establishment, there had to be at least a hundred people crammed up in here. All black folks – old ass black folks, too. No one looked younger than fifty! "'Scuse me," I politely said when I somewhat rudely cut pass this old ass couple dancing to that stale ass Mel Waiters song that was still blasting from the club's speakers. Although I hadn't said a word to her, I knew Alice was trailing me. Oh, baby, you better believe she was gonna get it soon as we made our way inside the bathroom. And as soon as we made it inside the bathroom, I went straight to one of the sinks and ran the water warm. "You got me fucked up, Alice! You really do!" I spat as I sprinkled some drops on my face to wake me the fuck up.

"What's your problem, girl? Why you acting all funny and shit?!? That is so wrong! Robert is nice-looking and is right up your alley!" Alice said back to me as she stood off to the side. Guilt was written all over her face.

"48? Chile, that man is NOT 48! You played me! You played me big time. I'm so fucking mad at you right now!" I exclaimed as I turned the faucet off.

"Okay, so I lied a little bit!" Alice confessed. "I knew if I told you his real age you wouldn't come out. I'm just trying to hook you up with someone a bit more in your lane! That's all!"

My face suddenly twisted with shock. "My *lane*? Girl, I don't need you to help me find someone in my lane! Truth be told, I only came out to hang out with you and support you. I was trying to help *you* find a man! I don't need no damn man! All I want is dick and that's it! And not no old, limp, need-five-Viagra, shrimp dick either! That man probably can't even see his dick! His stomach is so big, nigga look like he's pregnant with triplets!"

"Ooop!"

I looked in the mirror and saw this young chocolate woman emerging from one of the stalls. She had a huge smirk on her face and was fighting hard to contain her laugh. She walked up to one of the sinks next to me and then said,

"Girl, yo name must be Stella and you must be trying to get your groove back!"

I lightly chuckled. "No, my name Vernita and I need a big peter!"

"Hahah! I know that's right! You remind me so much of my aunty. She was so humorous and whatnot. But you look good for your age, girl! I wanna look like that when I get older!"

A smirk coming across my face, I asked, "How old do you think I am?"

"Ughh, no older than sixty!"

"You hear that Alice? Young girl guessed right!"

Alice huffed and shook her head, not saying anything.

"Anyways," I said playfully rolling my eyes. "I'm gonna leave this boring ass club, Alice. You have your future nigga take you home. I'll be damn if I'm gonna waste my night," I said.

"Yeah, it is kind of dead in here, too! Shit, what club you going to?" the young chocolate sista asked. She reminded me so much of Venus Williams, except she was a bit slimmer.

"Girl, my favorite up in South Loop – Tantrum."

"Well! Shit, let's go together! I'm Denitra by the way!"

"Nice to meet you, Denitra!"

"Well, if that's the case then, I'll holler at you later, Verni-ta!" Alice said in a somewhat angry tone as she spun around and headed out the bathroom.

"That's your friend?" Denitra asked.

"Yeah, she my girl, but she on some other shit tonight. Girl, let's head out so we can get there before ten. You wanna ride with me?"

"Sure!"

Now, any other time I went out, I usually liked rolling by myself. And I didn't fuck with new bitches like that. I was way too old to make new friends. But tonight was gonna be an exception because I was getting good vibes from Ms. Denitra.

We made our way back onto the dance floor and cut through the crowd. This time some R. Kelly song was playing and all the steppers in the club were on the dance floor stepping their old asses off. I caught a glance of Alice and the rest of the group. And just like some typical ass old folks, they were sitting back in their seats looking full and tired from all that food they just devoured.

"Where's your car?" Denitra asked as we made it out into the dimly lit parking lot.

"Girl, over there. I'm in the ruby red drop-top Mustang," I said pointing over to Paulette.

"Damnnnn, sis! That's you!"

"Yes, girl! Paulette is my baby!"

"Paulette?!? You got a name for her and everything?!? Girl, you seem like a lot of fun! I can't wait to see you show out on this club floor!"

I smiled as I was completely flattered. "Watch and see! Baby, I can keep up with you young folks!"

Suddenly I felt my cell phone vibrating in my pocket book. I reached inside and glared at the phone number which I completely didn't recognize. "Who is this calling me," I mumbled to myself. I swiped right on my iPhone. "Hello, who is this?"

"BITCH, WHERE THE FUCK YOU AT?!?" the deep voice replied. All of a sudden I got nervous as hell. "Excuse me?" I replied clutching my chest. "And who are you?!? I think you got the wrong phone number!"

"Bitch! Don't play no fucking games with me! Vernita, you better have your mothafuckin' ass back at the crib in twenty minutes or I'mma kill yo mothafuckin' ass!"

"Okay, I'll be there in twenty minutes! I'm just right around the corner!"

"YEAH! You better be, bitch! GOT ME FUCKED UP!"

I hung up the phone and threw a fake polite smile at Dentria. "Listen, girl, I hate to do this but that was my son on the phone. He got into a bad car wreck and he needs me to come pick him up from the hospital!"

"OH MY GOD! NOOO! I'm so sorry to hear that, Ms. Vernita! Is everything alright!"

"Yeah, he just got a slight scratch on his head! That's all! I didn't recognize his voice at first! He sounds like he needs me!"

"Okay! Well, it was nice meeting you! Maybe one day we'll run into each other again and we can hang out! You seem cool!"

"Yes! Girl! Let's exchange numbers!"

After Denitra and I exchanged numbers, I hopped into my Mustang and expeditiously made my way back home.

Gulping and completely wracked with terror, I had already recognized who this was on the phone. It was my husband. My *other* husband – Percy.

CHAPTER FOUR

Soon as I recognized Percy's voice, I knew I had to rush my sexy ass back home. And, oh God, with what I had on, I knew he was gonna have some words for my ass. Being fully aware of what he was capable of doing to me, I thought possibly of stopping somewhere to change out of my outfit. I usually brought an extra outfit with me anytime I went out, especially if I was gonna snatch me up some new dick and stay at a nigga's house for the night. But at this time of the night, there was absolutely nowhere safe I could stop other than a gas station to change. And I'd be damned if I was gonna do that. I felt kind of bad for having to lie to Denitra. She really did seem like a nice girl. However, I had no other choice but to get back home in a timely fashion otherwise Percy was definitely going to put his hands on me.

Some ten or eleven minutes later, after breaking all the damn speed laws in the city of Chicago, I made it quickly back to my townhouse. I pulled into my driveway and there Percy was, standing there smoking a square, smoke pouring from his nostrils.

My throat and chest both tight, I quickly turned the car

off and got out. I slowly trekked up to him as his beady eyes latched onto me.

"When you got out?" I asked as I held tight to my purse. "I thought you weren't getting released until next month..."

"Bitch, you knew I was getting out today. Why the fuck you kept ignoring my phone calls?"

"I forgot, baby! I swear I did! What's today? Friday? You know I'm up in age and I be forgetting things now!" I lied as I stood there nervous more than ever.

Yeah, I knew Percy was getting out of prison today but I had been avoiding him for some weeks now. He was the one who was calling me earlier before I had my dick down session with Markell and his buddy.

Now ya'll might be wondering how in the hell did I have a second husband. Well, let me explain. See, right before Clarence passed away, I had been creeping around. Percy was actually my first side nigga that I had met some years back. Funny how we met too – he was actually a CNA working for a long-term care facility out in Oak Lawn, a suburb touching the city. When Clarence got ill, the doctors had recommended that he move into that nursing facility to have 24/7 support.

Percy and I started off as friends at first. Although he was a CNA by day, he was a certified street nigga at night. I used to buy weed from on the side to help me deal with all the stress and bullshit with Clarence being sick. Six months later, and as Clarence's condition continued to deteriorate, Percy and I became closer. Well, you already know how stories like this went. One night, after I was in a tiff about some other personal stuff, Percy invited me out to go have a drink with him. And, well, a few drinks later, I was back at his apartment, slurping and riding his big, thick, veiny anaconda. Let me tell you though; CHILE – this boy got some dick-DICK, you hear me!

A year after our little entanglement, Percy's crazy ass ended up getting locked up and served six years down in Joliet Prison for armed robbery. While he was locked up, I was still missing my baby and I made the stupid decision to get married to him. Nobody actually knew about this and now I kind of regretted doing so.

Now ya'll also might be wondering just exactly how old Mr. Percy is. Well – you already know how I gets down. Percy just turned 38. When I met Percy, he was just turning 32. But now that I had the opportunity to get a real good look at him, I was so turned off by his looks. Prison really did age him. Although he wasn't even 40 yet, prison truly did add an additional ten years to him. Thankfully, he still had a nice lil frame to him. He was still tall and sturdy, looking just like my like chocolate Hollywood crush Wesley Snipes. Percy had a gold grill in his mouth and long dreads flowing down his neck. But boy, he must've had some sleepless nights in prison because he had some dark circles under his eyes.

Out of nowhere, Percy lunged at me and grabbed me by my throat. "You cheating on me with another nigga, aren't you?!? Bitch, don't be lying to me!"

"Percy! Let me go! Don't do this right here! You gonna get the cops called on us!" I screamed to to the top of my lungs.

"Fuck the muhfuckin' police! And bitch, I ain't afraid of going back to prison!" he shouted back, his voice echoing down the street. Oh, Lord! This boy was gonna have Chicago Police at my door at any moment if the neighbors heard us arguing. "Calm down, baby! Let's just go inside and talk!" I tried to plea with him. I didn't want any of these nosey mothafuckas up in my business.

"Bitch! Why you dressed like you was out and about trying to get some dick! I'mma knock yo ass out! Let me find out you fuckin' around on me with another nigga!"

"I swear I ain't!" I lied once more and now I was beginning to panic. I was now legit concerned that I didn't do a good job of cleaning up behind the little session I had earlier this afternoon.

Suddenly Percy let go of me and I stood back for a second with my hands in the air. "Percy, you scaring me now! Let's just go inside and I can make you a meal and run a hot bath for you! You just need to relax!"

"Fine! But, bitch, I swear to God I'mma go crazy if I find out someone else been in my pussy!"

My nerves fired up with anxiety, I strolled up to my front door and opened it up. Percy trailing closely behind me, we walked into the dark foyer and I just hoped my house didn't reek of ass, pussy, or dick. Or a combination of all three...

About a half-hour later, Percy and I were sitting down at the dining room table. After going back and forth about him suspecting I was cheating, I managed to simmer his rowdy nerves. So the fuck what I was cheating?!? What was I supposed to do? But, of course, I wouldn't dare confess that to his crazy ass.

I fixed him up a plate of some leftovers and watched him devour the meal as if he was on death row eating his last dinner. After all that fussing and carrying on he was just doing, he better get ready to devour this ass and pussy!

"So, baby, tell me what's the plan now that you are out?" I asked Percy as I observed him continue to get down these leftover oxtails, greens, rice, and cornbread I had made. I was gonna have to whip up another batch 'cause I actually had made these plates for Markell and his friend. I already done forget that other boy's name...

"Shit, I don't know...I was gonna maybe hit up a few car washes and shit. But a nigga ain't got time to be making no minimum wage. Shit, I might just link up with one of the guys and see if I can get back to moving a package. But nothin' too serious you know 'cause a nigga ain't trying to go back to prison," he responded as he stuffed a piece of cornbread in his mouth then took a chug of some homemade peach lemonade.

I huffed and rolled my eyes. "Baby, do you think that's a good idea and all?" I asked. I continued by saying, "You really wanna go back to selling drugs? That is just too risky for that little bit of money you can make. And it's too dangerous out here in these streets now. Every time I turn on the television I'm always hearing about some young boy getting killed and getting killed over nothing! Please don't do that. I'll hold you down until you can get something. I can even talk to—"

"I hate it when you fucking do that," Percy suddenly interjected and smacked his teeth. Anger was laced his tone.

"Hate it when I do what?" I asked, my face screwed into confusion.

"You be on that mama shit with me. You my wife not my mama."

"No, it ain't like that, Percy! I'm just saying—"

"You ain't saying shit. Now let me finish this meal. These oxtails fire as fuck by the way. I'm so fucking glad I'm back out now 'cause that food in the joint is disgusting as shit!"

I nervously smiled. "I can tell. You lost a little weight."

Percy stopped munching and then mumbled, "Yeah... Well, if you would've visited me more, maybe you would've seen the difference."

"Now, baby, you know you were on lockdown most of the time! Don't do that to me."

"Yeah, I was on lockdown alright...," he said. "Go make yourself useful and go run me a hot ass bath. And put some of that Epsom salt shit in the tub too 'cause my muscles aching and shit," he commanded and went back to finishing his plate.

"Alright, baby. I'mma get the kitchen cleaned up first and—"

"Nah, bitch, go run my bath right now! I'mma be done in a minute! I ain't got time to wait! Do as the fuck I say!"

"Okay, Percy! I'm getting right to it!" I said and didn't hesitate in making my way down the hallway and into my bedroom.

Now, anyone could be thinking that I was crazy for putting myself in this crazy, twisted, abusive relationship but Percy was truly a good man. And although he done did some things in the past, I believe he still had a lot of room for growth. I just wished I would've never got married to him because I didn't like being locked down to one dick. But, truth be told, the only thing that kept me in love with this young nigga was that I kind of liked his roughneck nature. I loved me a nigga that would occasionally talk rough to me and put me in my place. That was what a real man supposed to do. Clarence was the complete opposite of that and often in our marriage, I felt like I had to be more of the aggressor. Ohh, chile, I was just getting so wet thinking about this bully ass thick dick that he was gonna give me. That was his only saving grace at the moment. I couldn't lie but I did have a thing for felons. Markell had him a couple of felonies, too.

Once inside the bathroom, I ran the hot water in the jacuzzi tub and poured some Epsom salts and lavender into the tub. I also added in just a tiny amount of bubble bath just to make things a bit more intimate. Once the water filled the tub, I made my way back into the bathroom and changed into some sexy lingerie. I hoped that despite the fact that we had a rocky start to our reunion, he would bless me with some bomb ass dick.

Some moments later, I hadn't heard a word from Percy.

Getting quite curious, I sauntered back out into the living room and there I saw him laid out on the couch, snoring hard. His snores were so loud, they overpowered the ESPN playing on the television. I walked over to him and lightly shook his shoulder. "Percy…Percy…Percy, your bath is ready, babe," I said. He didn't budge. Damn, he was getting some good as sleep. I couldn't blame him. I just knew sleep must've been different when you were locked up. I would've been paranoid 24-7.

Not wanting to disturb him, I retreated back to my bedroom and made my way into the bathroom. Not wanting this bath to go to waste, I slipped out of my robe and then began to take off my lingerie. Damn, with Percy sleep this meant that I wasn't going to get any of that dick.

I exhaled at the thought of knowing my night essentially went to waste. But before I fully got out of my bra, I felt this hot, heavy presence lean up against me. Then I could feel the pulsation of a dick jump between my ass cheeks. "You ready for me to drop this dick off up in you?" Percy moaned into my ear. My eyes instantly widened with shock and I swear this nigga almost made me go into atrial fibrillation. My heart skipped like a hundred beats feeling that anaconda thick dick

"I…I was just gonna let you get some rest," I mumbled. "Sounded like you needed it."

"Nah, I just needed a lil cat nap. But now I'm ready to work this pussy. Shut the fuck up and bend over," he demanded. And just like that, I did what he commanded. I bent over and he pulled off my thong. Before I could even get the damn thong fully off my ankles, I felt his long tongue slither inside my booty hole. "Oohhh! Shit! SHIT! SHIT! SHIT! SHIT!" I groaned aloud! Nigga almost made me have a seizure as I didn't see any of this coming. AT ALL!

Just like I hoped, Percy slurped all of my insides from the

back for the next five minutes. I didn't know how he was able to do it but his tongue magically traveled back and forth between my ass and clit. Baby, let me tell you something – age don't mean ya coochie gon dry up! And I say that 'cause my juices along with his saliva was running all down my leg. Every couple of seconds I had an orgasm. He sent me off even more when he stuffed two of his fingers deep inside my pussy while he sucked on my ass. NONE of my side niggas ever got me right like this! Even Markell's freaky ass! Speaking of which, I wondered if Percy was going to notice my ass was a bit loose. But that fear quickly slipped away into oblivion as he stood me up and turned me around. Percy wiped his mouth and I looked down, staring at his thick ass peter. I gently got down on my knees and began to slurp on that mothafucka like I was five all over again getting a popsicle from the Ice Cream Man. I just loved me a pretty black dick. Now, I done had my fair share of dicks in my life, but this one right here was by far the prettiest dick I'd ever laid my eyes on. And Percy had a big sack of nuts. That turned me all the way on. I loved sucking on a nigga's balls. Ladies, just make sure you be a bit careful when you attempt to put a nut or two in your mouth. Gots to be very very gentle.

"Shit, damn, Vernita, you ain't changed in a minute. Slow that shit down before you make me bust," Percy cried.

Not saying anything, I just continued to devour that dick, stuffing that bad boy all the way down my throat. I let my tonsils dance on that dick head until I took that mothafucka all the way out. A trail of my spit hung from his dick head and before it drooped to the floor, I caught it with my mouth wide open.

"Ooooooh, you's a nasty lil hoe...Damn, stand up. I'm ready to for the pussy now," Percy commanded. And I was ready for the dick too.

On my knees, I immediately shot up from the floor. Percy quickly turned me around and bent me over. He slid the pipe all the way up into my slippery guts and my walls conformed to his veiny girth. "Ahhhh! FUCK!" he groaned as my sugar walls tightened around that dick.

I didn't even hesitate in throwing this pussy back on his rod and I could feel myself cream all over his shaft. Both of our moans together filled the dimly lit bathroom as I hung to the edge of the sink. "You got me cumming so hard!!!!" I cried with my mouth hung wide open, my tongue drooping to the side.

"Yeah, I can see! You creamin' all over the dick!" he said and then suddenly I felt what felt like a finger or a thumb go up inside my bootyhole.

"OOHH! SHIT! YEAH! JUST LIKE THAT!" I cried once more. The feeling of having that thumb up in my ass along with that dick sliding in and out of me had me ready to go meet King Jesus in the air.

My legs shivered and I swear it felt like my pussy was getting wider and wider, allowing more and more dick to fill me up! Now Markell and his friend were working with some dick but this dick right here was damn near giving Vernita a hysterectomy. This nigga was gon bust up all these fibroids I had on my uterus!

BOOM! BOOM! BOOM!

I heard three loud booms coming all the way from my front door and then the doorbell began ringing nonstop.

"VERNITA! VERNITA!" I heard a man's voice call out all the way from the front door. I didn't know who that was. Was that...Markell?

Percy's dick pumps came to an abrupt stop and he pulled out of me. "YO! Who the fuck is that?" Percy grilled as he turned me around and grabbed me by my shoulders.

"Shit! I don't know!" I said back to him, scared as shit!

Please, oh Lord, don't let that be Markell or any other nigga I had been messing with over the past couple of months, I kept thinking to myself.

"Oh, bitch, you mothafuckin' know! I knew you had another nigga up in here! I'mma kill you and that nigga!"

"Vernita! Open up! It's Markell! I forgot something!"

I gasped and my eyes widened with fear.

"Markell?" Percy's eyes' instantly filled with rage.

CHAPTER FIVE

"*M*arkell?" Percy's eyes' instantly filled with rage. Oh shit! I already knew what time it was. I was a dead old bitch.

Percy's arms twitched and that was my que that this situation was about to get really nasty if I didn't think quickly on my feet.

"Baby, that's Markell. That's my personal trainer. Remember, I told you about the young guy who's been coming by to help me out with getting my body toned?" I tried to explain. I hope I sounded believable.

Percy stood there with his fists clenched tightly and his breathing intensified. With his unblinking eyes latched onto me, there was part of me that just knew he knew I was lying my ass off. "Bitch, I swear on my mama's grave you better not be fucking lying to me. I got the blick on me too and if you lying to me, I'mma put a bullet in that nigga's head and your head, too!"

"Blick?" I had to think for a second what exactly he was talking about. You know, sometimes these young folks be using these words and I didn't even know what the hell they mean.

"Blick! My gun! Shit, now that I'm back out here in these streets I gotta stay poled up!"

"Baby! No! It's not that serious!" I tried to plea once again with him. Oh my mothafuckin' goodness! What in the world did I land myself into messing around with this young crazy nigga.

Once Percy quickly put his boxers back on, he rudely shoved past me then stormed out of the bathroom. I grabbed my robe off the chilly bathroom floor and quickly threw it on. Percy by now was already out in the living room. Like a crazy in love bitch, I chased right behind his ass because I didn't want any drama to go down between both of my boos.

Once I made my way out into the living room, I saw Percy rummaging through his sole piece of luggage. He pulled out his *blick* and you already know my eyes quickly grew with terror. "No! Baby, please! Don't do this!" I kept begging.

"Stand the fuck back, bitch! Yo old ass gon die if you fucking lying to me!" he growled and then lunged up to the door and looked out the peephole. "Wait one fucking minute!" he bellowed.

He quickly unlocked the door and tucked the gun in his back waist. "THIS MY NIGGA, KELLZ! I didn't know this was the nigga you was talkin' about!" Percy opened the door and stood there with his arms wide open. "NIGGGGAAAAA! Fuck is you doing around here?!?!?" He then went in to give Markell a hug.

My anxiety simmered a bit and I clutched my chest.

"Damn, Percy! Nigga I ain't seen you in some years! When the fuck did you get out?!?" Markell said back to him with a big smile etched on his face. I stood back a moment just to make sure nothing crazy suddenly started.

"Man, I just got out the joint today. My woman was supposed to pick me up and shit but her ass was tweakin'. Bruh, I ain't know you was the nigga training my ole girl! Come the fuck in!"

"It's cool, bruh! I was just swinging by because I had left one of my dumbbells in the crib and shit," Markell said back laughing.

"Man, come in," Percy said.

Markell stepped in the door, and already knowing protocol, he took his shoes off and made his way near me. "Hey, Vernita, sorry I came over late but I had my left my dumbbells and I need it for a morning session I got at five. I would've called but your phone kept going straight to voicemail," he said as he walked over near the corner of the living room where we kept our workout equipment for when he came by and gave me his "workout" sessions.

"Oh, no worries," I said back nervously. From the look he was giving me and the sudden smirk he had on his face, I guess he already knew what time it was.

"Kellz one of the guys! He and I went to elementary school together! We grew up on the same block. Right there on 64th and Ellis!" Percy laughed as he walked up to me.

It was just so strange because Markell didn't act as if he was at all shocked and what not that Percy would be up in my house this time of the night. Any normal person would've suspected that something weird was going on between us. And obviously, from the look he gave me just seconds ago, he must've already knew I was bouncing on Percy's dick. Shit, he knew how I got down! But, damn, he could've acted a bit shocked to not make it seem so obvious that he was kind of aware of what I had going on with his *friend*. Then again, I could've been making all types of assumptions.

"But, Percy, bruh, let me know if you need a gig. The gym is always hiring and shit. We could use a new trainer on our team. I can get you certified ASAP and have you working out clients and shit like tomorrow," Markell said as he picked up a few dumbbells and made his way back over to the foyer.

"For real, bruh? Hook a nigga up then!" Percy exclaimed. "But only thing is, shit, you really think I could train people?"

Markell laughed and said, "Hell yeah! Man, these folks out here so out of shape, you can make one of these muhfuckas just raise they hands up in the air and their fat asses will be out of breath. You good, bruh!"

"Well, aiight then, I'mma swing by the gym tomorrow! What time you gon be there?" Percy asked.

"Man, just swing by anytime. I'll be there all day after 8 AM," Markell replied and then threw a smile at the both of us.

"Aiight, Mr. Markell. We still on for our session next Tuesday, right?" I asked.

"Yes, ma'am!" he politely responded and then made his way out of the door.

Oooh, chile, that was a close one!

Percy turned and looked at me smiling. "Yeah, that's my nigga....," he muttered.

"Can we finish what we started?" I had to ask.

Without hesitation, Percy grabbed me by my waist and smacked my ass from behind. "Hell yeah!"

The following morning, after a long dick-down session, I was in the kitchen making my man some cheese grits, eggs, bacon, fried catfish, hot link sausage and some pancakes.

It was ten past eight and the sun was shining deep into my kitchen. I had some Shirley Caesar playing from my phone while I whipped up this big, soulful breakfast.

But let me tell you something here, chile! After I get done cooking, Vernita was gonna have to take a hot bath and let this pussy soak in some Epsom salt because I shole was feeling mighty sore. Between Markell and his friend and then Percy, my insides felt like I got skinned like this catfish I was about to fry up to go with these here grits.

Some moments later I heard Percy rumbling through the kitchen. I spun around and noticed he was dressed like he was ready to head out of the house. He didn't even seem fazed by the delectable smells wafting in the air.

"Damn, baby, where you going?!? I made you this big breakfast!" I exclaimed, giving him a somewhat disappointed stare.

"Oh, sorry, bae, but remember I gotta go meet up with Kellz about that job and shit," he explained as he lunged up to the fridge, opened it and pulled out a carton of some orange juice. He took the carton back to the head.

"Damn, you could at least use a glass. Besides, Markell said he was gonna be there all day. Why you gotta leave now! With all of this food I made, the least thing you could do is at least attempt to eat some of it!"

I was really upset. Had I known he was gonna wake up and try to leave the house immediately, I would've just kept my tired ass in the bed. This nigga was really starting to get on my mothafuckin' nerves.

"Sorry, babe, but you know I gotta do what I gotta do. Plus, I was still gonna link up with a few of the guys to see about some other shit."

Huffing, I shook my head. "Please don't tell me you are still gonna try to run in those streets! I already done told you I think that's a bad idea!"

"Bitch, back the fuck off me, like for real!" Percy suddenly bellowed.

"Nigga, don't raise your fucking voice in my house! I'm just trying to help you—"

"Man, whatever! I'm out! I'll holla at you later, Vernita!"

Shaking to my core, I watched this trifling nigga literally toss the orange juice carton back into the fridge and then run out of the kitchen. Seconds later, I heard the front door open and slam shut. I absolutely couldn't believe this right now. What in the fuck was I really thinking messing around with this crazy boy?!? Clutching my chest, I had to sit down for a second in the dining room just to gather my thoughts. This wasn't a good situation at all. Granted, I had a thing for Percy and something in me kind of loved him but being married to him was one crazy, impulsive decision. I let my loneliness get the best of me. Shit, I didn't know why. It wasn't like I couldn't get a man.

As I continued to sit there, I dazed off for a second and suddenly my mind went blank. I was at a complete loss of words.

Who am I?

Why am I here?

What's going on?

My mind continued to fill with this weird sense of emptiness and before you know it I completely blanked out. I stared off at nothing, forgetting everything about myself and where I was currently. What was going on?

Some moments later I stood up and made my way over to the kitchen. Then the smoke alarm inside of my house began to go off. I snapped out of the daze I was in, not realizing how long I had been out of it. "Damn it!" I screamed when I realized I had let the pot of grease cook for too long and now my entire house was filled with the blackest smoke.

BOOM! BOOM! BOOM! Ding-Dong! Ding-Dong!

Suddenly I heard three loud knocks at my front door and then my doorbell kept going off. Getting scared, I tried to quickly gather myself. The entire kitchen was still smoky and now I was wondering if my alarm had set off the Fire department come to my house.

Whoever was at my door kept pounding hard and my door bell kept firing off. Maybe it was one of my neighbors. "Coming!" I shouted as I opened up one of my kitchen windows to let the smoke out.

Once I finally got the window open and the smoke began to quickly pour out of the window, I marched over to the front door and looked out the peephole. And just as I thought, it was one of my neighbors, Mr. Kilpatrick. He was this older white man that I think was probably in his fifties.

I opened the door and greeted him. "Hey, Mr. Kilpatrick!"

"Hey, Vernita! Is everything okay? I heard your smoke alarm going off for a few minutes and I was getting ready to call the Fire department."

"Oh yeah. Everything is fine. I was just about to—"

My mind began to draw blanks again. But this time this intense dizziness came over me.

"I was just about to—"

"Is everything alright, Vernita?"

All of a sudden everything went dark and I fell to the floor.

"$\mathcal{M}$s. Washington…Ms. Washington…How are you feeling, dear?"

I slowly opened my eyes and noticed that I wasn't at home anymore. I was lying in a hospital bed. The sound of all sorts of medical machines were chirping in the background. Glancing around, I noticed I had a slow-dripping IV pumping cool liquid in my arm. I had absolutely no idea why I was brought here. Didn't even know what hospital I was at.

"Where am I? Why am I here?" I said as I kept glancing around. No one else was in the room other than this tall, mahogany-toned man who I presumed had to be the doctor. I didn't have my glasses on me but I squeezed my pupils to stare at his name tag pinned to his white coat. Dr. James McKnight.

I scanned Dr. McKnight up and down and ooh, chile, he was one sexy hunk of a man. I was getting so hot and bothered just thinking of how delicious this boy looked.

"I'm Dr. McKnight, Ms. Washington. You passed out earlier at your house and your neighbor immediately called 9-11," he explained. He pulled out a small flash light from his right pocket and began to scan my eyes with it. The light was very blinding but that didn't distract me from taking in this man's overpowering sexiness. My eyes quickly jetted down toward his lower half and I wanted to see if Dr. McKnight had him a bulge. I was good at analyzing a man's size just based on the bulge. I didn't quite make out a bulge but that was probably because I really needed my glasses.

"Why did I pass out? I asked.

"That's what we are trying to determine," he replied as he checked off a few things on a clipboard gripped in his hands.

"How long I been unconscious?"

"Ahhh, well, you just woke up. We actually had you on a sedative because when you came in earlier, your blood pressure was really low and we didn't know if you had a stroke or not. But based on your vitals, you didn't have a stroke or a heart attack. Actually, your blood tests came back all good. Are you taking any medications or anything, Ms. Washington?"

"No. Not at all."

"When's the last time you've been to a doctor?"

"Well, I just had my annual physical not too long ago. Everything checked out okay," I explained.

"Hrrrrm, well, I think we might need to run some more tests on you. Should I have a nurse try to contact some family members? A husband? Children?"

"I'm not married...My husband passed away," I replied but then just like that I quickly remembered I was technically married to Percy. But I didn't want to bring him up because the last thing I didn't want was for these folks to be judging me.

"Oh, I'm so sorry to hear that," Dr. McKnight said as he stuffed his pen back into his coat pocket. "Okay, well, just let the nurse know if you want us to contact any family members to be here with you. I'm actually gonna order a

CAT scan and some other tests just to check everything out. But, honestly, it just sounds like maybe you just had an unexpected drop in blood pressure. It happens from time to time, especially when you get older."

"Boy, don't put that on me," I said laughing.

"Put what on you?"

"Age...I might be 76 but my body still feels like I'm in my forties."

"Is that right?" Dr. McKnight replied with a smile. "I like your attitude."

"Well, thank you!" I smiled back. "Dr. McKnight, if you don't mind, can you have the nurse dial one of my friends. Her name is Alice. I can give you her number. She also has a key to my place in case of an emergency. I need my reading glasses because I can barely see a thing. My left eye is really giving me problems it seems. Now that I think about it, that usually isn't the case." Now I was starting to get a bit nervous because this was the first time ever I started to notice my vision in my left eye was extremely hazy. Usually I could do fine without my reading glasses but now I felt like I was damn near Stevie Wonder-blind.

"Okay, sure thing. What's her number?" Dr. McKnight asked as he pulled out his ink pen. I told him Alice's number and he jotted it down and quickly made his way out of the room. Some seconds later, the nurse, some young Hispanic-looking girl walked in and said, "Okay, Ms. Washington, I called your friend Alice and told her what happened. She said she's on her way. But in the meantime, Dr. McKnight ordered a CAT scan for you. So I'm gonna get you prepped for that," she said.

"Okay." Anxiety began to rise in my throat and my body grew a tad tight. "What exactly is a CAT scan used for?" I had to ask as I sat up in the bed.

"Well, it's a diagnostic exam that can be used to diagnose

a bunch of things. But don't worry, I think based on your vitals, everything is gonna be fine."

"Okay…" I didn't like the sound of that but I guess I had no control over that at the moment.

"By the way, what hospital am I at?"

"University of Chicago," the nurse explained as she helped me into another gown. Some moments later, another hospital worker stumbled into the room. He was an older black fellow with a shiny bald head. "Mrs. Washington?"

"That's me!" I smiled.

"I'm Donovan. I'm the X-Ray tech that will helping out with your CAT scan," he said. He looked over at the nurse and then said, "I can take it from here."

Some moments later, after both Donovan the X-Ray tech and the nurse got me situated into a wheelchair, I was taken down to another part of the hospital for the CAT Scan. Once we got inside the room, I swear my entire insides filled with a million butterflies. "Is this gonna put a lot of radiation and stuff in me?" I asked.

"Well, yes, but you should be fine. No more radiation than the radiation you get exposed to when you go through one of those TSA scanners at the airport. Those nuke people all the time and people don't even realize it," Donovan said as he helped me out of the wheelchair and then walked me over to a flat table. "Now, lay down on this and hold your hands to your side. The test isn't gonna take no longer than five minutes. I'll have you back in your room in no time, Ms. Washington."

"Okey dokey," I replied with fake enthusiasm. I couldn't help but think something seriously may be wrong with me.

Once Donovan helped me lay down on the table, I laid still staring up at the ceiling of the dimly lit room. All I could hear was the faint rumbling of a machines. This reminded so much when Clarence was in the hospital. All of a sudden, the fear of dying filled my mind and this weird sense of fear gripped every inch of my sexy body. But I had to be calm. *Nothing was wrong with me. Nothing was wrong with me. Nothing was wrong me.* I kept repeating that in my head as I heard the table move and then Donovan said, "Now just lay still and close your eyes." Doing as he said, I closed my eyes shut and just thought about my life and all the things I missed out on wasting my time with Clarence. I thought about the future family I could've had. I thought about the future grandchildren I could've been playing with right now. At the end of the day, although I had a bunch of young guys to fuck around with, I really had nobody.

Trying to hold back tears, there was a part of me that wished that I could pay to hit a button to go back in time. If I could do it all over again, I'd definitely avoid Clarence like the plague. My tears of sadness turned to tears of rage and I was glad I did what I did when he was sick. Some may label me a bad wife but I had to do what was right for me. My sex drive had been bottled up for so many years and I felt repressed.

As I could hear the whooshing sound of the machine circulate around me, the guilt of doing what I did to Clarence escaped. *Good* riddance, I thought to myself.

I got lost in my sea of thoughts and before you know it, I was out of the CAT Scan machine. Donovan walked over and helped me up. "See, I told you it wouldn't take that long," he uttered with a big grin plastered on his chubby chocolate face. Boy, he shole was ugly but he was such a nice man. Bless his heart. Anyways, after he helped me up and put me back into the wheelchair, he wheeled me back to my room.

Soon as he opened the door, I saw Alice sitting down in one of the two chairs inside of the room. "Girl! Oh my God! I was getting nervous for a second! What happened?!?" Alice growled, her voice sounding like she was getting ready to breakdown and cry.

"Girl, calm down. It ain't that serious. I just passed out and the doctor just think my blood pressure dropped too low. I was cooking and I think I inhaled too much smoke," I said as I got up from the wheelchair and laid back down in the bed.

Alice pulled out a pair of my glasses from her purse and handed them over to me. "I stopped by your house by the way because I figured you would need these."

"Thank you, girl. You always looking out for me."

She rolled her eyes and huffed, "I know...I *am*. Like last night..."

"Chile, don't even start. You already know how I feel about men. Don't play me like that."

"Yeah, I know. Well, I am just glad there's nothing seriously wrong with you. Girl, I know sometimes we get into our little arguments but you know at the end of the day you my best friend. I can't let anything happen to my girl. I love you!"

Alice was indeed right. Although we had our occasional disagreements, she was still my friend and she was someone I could count on when things got bad. Hearing her say those words made me a bit emotional and I had to look away to let out a few more tears.

"What's wrong?" Alice asked once she noticed how I quickly went quiet.

"Ohhh, nothing...Just reminiscing...That's all."

"About...Clarence?" she inquired in a somewhat nervous tone.

I glanced over at her. "Yeah."

"You miss him?"

"Honestly..." I paused for a second. "Yes," I lied. "Miss him every day." Of course I couldn't let her know how I truly felt about that nigga.

"Yeah, sometimes I wonder what life would've been like if I had a husband for that long who I truly loved and cared for like that. Clarence was a good man. Just count yourself lucky you had someone like that for such a long time. Not everyone is blessed to have a long-lasting, happy marriage," she said dozing off into space. Although I was cringing at every word she said, I understood why Alice felt the way she felt. Hell, I'd be feeling the same way too if I wasted my time being with a nigga who knocked me across the head every now and then for not making his meatloaf right.

Some moments later, the door to my room opened and Dr. McKnight strolled in with his lips pursed. He had this weird, solemn look on his face. "Excuse me but I can I have some privacy with Mrs. Washington?" he asked Alice.

"Sure thing. I'll be outside," Alice said as she quickly stood up and made her out of the door. Once the door was shut, Dr. McKnight's sexy ass coolly strolled over to my bedside and rumbled through some papers on a clipboard. He reminded me so much of Blair Underwood. I loves me some Blair Underwood…except when he was knocking that lil light-skinned girl out in that Tyler Perry movie.

"Unfortunately, I have some bad news, Mrs. Washington."

Now billions of butterflies filled the empty pits of my stomach and I felt like the walls inside the hospital room were closing in. "What's that?"

CHAPTER SEVEN

"*Y*ou have brain cancer."

"Huh?"

My face twisted with confusion. I had to have him repeat what he just said. I just knew he didn't say what I thought he said.

"Yes, Mrs. Washington...Unfortunately, we suspect you have brain cancer. The radiologist detected a large growing tumor on the right lobe of your brain. It's spreading to the point where you are becoming symptomatic...which might mean you might be at stage three or possibly four."

My eyes widened with fear and I clutched my chest out of shock. "Cancer? Like cancer-*cancer*?"

"Yes...Cancer..." He continued, "I'm sorry to have to tell you this,"

"So...Does this mean I am going to die soon?"

"I don't know," Dr. McKnight muttered.

Laying there, I didn't know what else to say. So many thoughts flooded my mind that I couldn't even squeeze out another question.

"Well, based on the CAT Scan, we think there is hope for

a treatment. We're gonna refer you to the top oncologist here. Cancer is not always a death sentence. We have newer treatments—"

"But at my age," I interrupted. "I'm in my late-seventies... What kind of real treatment is out there that would really work for someone in my age bracket. Is it even worth it?"

"You never know, Mrs. Washington. The best thing you can do right now though is remain optimistic." He continued, "But anyways, I'll leave you some time to process everything and I'll go ahead and get into contact with the Oncology department to have an appointment set up for you as soon as possible."

"Okay," was all I could respond with as the doctor made his way out of the door. Alice then strolled in right after him. "So, what's wrong?" she asked.

I looked dead at her and said, "I have cancer...Brain cancer."

Alice suddenly clasped her mouth and her eyes widened to the size of two big moons. "Cancer?"

"Yes...Cancer...."

"No! No! NO!" She exploded into tears as she made her way over to me.

"This ain't right! This ain't right!" she kept repeating herself as she leaned in to give me a hug. "We gotta get you to another doctor ASAP! I mean, how do they even know for sure you got cancer! They could just be telling you anything. You should get a second opinion!"

"Alice, calm down," I said trying to assure her but I was nervous and scared just as she was. "The doctor said he's going to refer me over to an oncologist. Hopefully, I can get an appointment first thing in the morning."

As Alice managed to calm herself, she and I continued to talk until the doctor came back into the room. After running a few lighter tests, the hospital discharged me and Alice took me back home. As we hit the city streets, it was so crazy how such a beautiful sunny Sunday gave birth to such sad news. My life was coming to an end, ya'll. Sitting in the passenger seat and staring out of the window, I just wanted to explode into tears but I had to hold myself together. Although the doctor told me to remain optimistic, there was no way in hell I had it in me to survive something as horrible as cancer.

Alice pulled her Camry into the driveway of my townhouse and as the two of us got out, I could hear some loud, bass-heavy music rumbling. Alice threw a look of confusion at me and asked, "What in the hell is that noise?!?"

I threw a glance of shock right back at her and shrugged my shoulders. "Hell, I don't know!"

"I'mma call the police!" Alice shouted as she quickly rummaged through her purse.

"Wait, don't do that! I forgot...That's my sister's son. I forgot I left him a key."

Confusion suddenly swamped Alice's face. "Your sister's son? You got a sister? I thought you only had a brother?!?"

"Girl, I got a half-sister that I didn't really tell anyone about. My father was a rolling stone. You know how that goes," I fibbed. I had to make some shit up quick.

"Oh...Damn...," Alice mumbled then got quiet. She trailed me as I made my way up to the front door. Once I unlocked the door and opened it, a plume of smoke escaped the front door. The smoke was thicker than molasses and it reeked of weed. "PERCY! PERCY!" I screeched out. "Cut that goddamn music off! WE GOT COMPANY! THE HELL IS WRONG WITH YOU!"

"Girl, is everything alright? You sure you don't want me to call the police?" Alice asked as her voice turned high pitched and filled with nervousness.

"No, don't do that. I'mma get his ass right!"

I couldn't believe Percy was doing this to me right now. I

hadn't even been gone the entire day and this trifling nigga was already turned my house into a pig sty. The music was so loud and when I made my way past the foyer and into the living room, I noticed it was playing from my television and the speaker system hooked up to it. I didn't even realize those damn speakers could even get that damn loud! "PERCY! BRING YO ASS OUT HERE RIGHT NOW!" I yelled.

"Calm down, Vernita! You don't wanna get yourself too worked up!" Alice pleaded but her words went through one ear and out there. I was ready to kill this nigga! This was just entirely too disrespectful. From the way he'd been talking to me to him not wanting my breakfast. Then to add fuel to the fire, I was now walking around with a mothafuckin' tumor in my head that could kill me at any moment. Although he'd only been out prison for less than a day, I wanted his ass gone already! First thing I was going to do once I left the doctor's office tomorrow morning was to run my ass down to a lawyer and get this marriage annulled or serve this crazy nigga divorce papers!

"PERCY!" I yelled again to the top of my lungs when I lunged over to the television and cut the music off.

"WHAT, BITCH?!?!" I heard him yell as he stormed out into the living room without a damn thing on his body! He was fully naked and his big ole dick was hanging down to his knee caps.

"PERCY! PUT SOME CLOTHES ON!" I screamed.

"OH MY GOD!" exclaimed Alice as she clasped her mouth and spun around.

"I'm so sorry about that!" I apologized feeling so embarrassed that this was happening right now!

"Man, who the fuck this bitch is?!? Why she up in my house?!?" Percy screamed as he stood his naked ass there with no shame. "She act like she ain't seen a dick before!"

he laughed. "Maybe she ain't seen a big ass black dick before!"

"PERCY! HAVE SOME MOTHAFUCKIN' RESPECT OR YOU NEED TO PACK YOUR SHIT UP AND GET THE HELL UP OUT OF MY HOUSE! THIS IS NOT YOUR HOUSE, NIGGA!"

"Look, I think I should just leave, girl. I'mma holler at your later," Alice said as she quickly made her out of the door.

"I'm so sorry about this, girl! But thank you for helping me out! I'll call you later. I need to get this bastard straight!"

"Okay, well, holler at me and call me if you need anything," she muttered as she zipped out of the front door.

Pissed, I dashed down the hallway and made my way into my bedroom where I saw this nigga casually putting some clothes on.

"Why in the fuck do you got my house smelling like this?!? And why did have that music blasting to the high heavens?!? Who do you think you are?!? Nigga, this is MY house! MY HOUSE! I paid the mortgage for this mothafucka!"

"Bitch! You must've forgot! I'm married to your ass! So this means this my house too!"

"NIGGA, YOU LOST YOUR MOTHAFUCKIN' MIND! This is not your house! Let's get that straight right now, partner!" I screamed to the top of my lungs. Why was I even continuing to bother with this fool?!? No, fuck that! He needed to get ALL of his shit and leave immediately. "In fact, you know what, I'm done!" I yelled throwing my hands up in surrender. "We don't need to be married. You don't have the slightest respect for me and what I've done for you! You need to pack up all of your shit and get the hell up out of my house! NOW, NICCA!"

Suddenly, without hesitation, Percy lunged at me,

grabbed me and slammed me up against a wall. "Bitch! I'll kill you! I ain't going no mothafuckin' where!"

"LET ME GO!"

"OLD HOE, I AIN'T LETTIN' NOTHING GO! SHIT, YOU LUCKY I'M EVEN FUCKING YOUR OLD, WRIN-KLED ASS! DRY ASS PUSSY AIN'T EVEN THAT GOOD ANY DAMN WAY! NOW GO IN THERE AND FIX ME SOMETHING TO EAT, OLD BITCH!"

Old bitch?!?

First this nigga disrespects me by talking all types of shit to me. Then he put his hands on me? Not to mention, he even disrespected my friend?!? But even worse, you called me an old bitch??!? I didn't know what came over me but all I saw was red.

"YOU HEAR ME, OLD BITCH?!? I SAID GO FIX ME SOMETHING TO EAT! A NIGGA IS HUNGRY!"

"Alright...Alright, I'mma fix you something. Just calm down," I said softly.

Here I was, standing in front of this man, and didn't even bother to ask me where I'd been at all day. I was fresh out of the hospital, freshly diagnosed with brain cancer and all he wanted was some food.

I got his food alright.

"So you not even gonna ask me where I been at all day?" I had to ask before I left out of the room.

Smacking his teeth, he growled, "No. I don't give a fuck. You was probably out playing Bingo or some shit. Now hurry up and go fix me something to eat so I can put this wood up in you so you can get off my fucking nerves."

Just like that, I already knew what I had to do. I coolly strolled into the kitchen and noticed how the breakfast I had been making earlier was all still out. The kitchen was an absolute mess. I spent the next hour or so cleaning up before I started whipping up a quick lunch. I already had the perfect meal in mind too. Shrimp and grits. I just knew Percy was going to love them.

I pulled down a box of grits, measured out two cups and then threw them in a pot of boiling water. Once they finished, I gently stirred them then set the oven to low. It wasn't going to take long to make the shrimp, so I went back into the bedroom to go run to the bathroom right quick.

Percy was laying down in the bed watching ESPN while he smoked on a joint. "My food almost ready yet, woman?" he asked sternly.

"Yes, baby. It's almost done. I just gotta tinkle," I replied as I strolled into the bathroom.

"Okay, good, 'cause I got other shit to do tonight."

Once I closed the bathroom door and locked it, I rummaged through the medicine cabinet and pulled out an old bottle of some medicine I had last year for my blood pressure. I quickly checked the bottle to see how many pills I had left. Too many too count but enough to put Percy in his rightful place. I closed the bottle and stuffed it in my bra. Once I took a tinkle, I made my way back into the kitchen and pulled the bottle out of my bra. I took out my food processor from the cabinet in front of me and threw the entire bottle of pills into it. Once I crushed the pills up into a fine powder, I stirred it gently into the grits and then added some seasonings and other spices to cover up the taste. Some moments later, I finished making the Cajun shrimp and bacon medley to go on top of the grits. I scooped out a generous serving on top of the grits and then sprinkled some chopped green onion on top of it. "Percy! The food is ready," I called out with a big smile on my face. Not even a half minute later Percy came strolling into the kitchen. "FINALLY! A nigga is hungry as fuck!" he groaned and sat down at the dining room table.

I sat the heavy bowl of shrimp and grits before him.

"What you want to drink? I can make you a lil nice cocktail to go with those shrimp and grits?"

"Like what?"

"I can take this leftover peach lemonade and mix it with the whiskey and some vodka. It'll calm your nerves down really good."

"Well, fix me one but don't add too much vodka 'cause I said I got some shit to do tonight," he grunted and then dived right into the food. "DAMN! This shit is good! Your old ass is good for something still!"

"Yes, I am! I sure am...," I smiled.

CHAPTER EIGHT

ix months later...
It's crazy how life can suddenly turn and turn for the worse. Just when I thought I was living out my best life, I got hit with cancer. And then my love life started to go into shambles. Crazy thing was after I tried to put Percy to sleep for good by putting a bunch of my blood pressure meds in his grits, that nigga just slept it off and woke up the next day feeling like a thousand bucks. Soon afterwards, like the trifling nigga I kind of always knew he was, he left me after he told me he got some young girl pregnant.

I can't say I was devastated when he told me what he did. After all, I wanted him to leave anyways. But I was truly broken knowing that I wasted time messing around with some young kid who treated me like dirt and made his mission to constantly remind me that I was nothing more than a piece of old ass, shelter and a home-cooked meal. That truly hurt, especially now that I was living with this cancer and I had no real man who really loved me to look after my being.

To make matters worse, soon after Percy left me to go be

with his lil young pregnant bitch, Markell decided to up and leave Chicago for Atlanta. Guess he wanted to be in a space where he felt a bit more comfortable with his real *self*.

The day after I found out I had brain cancer, I ended up going to an oncologist who told me that I had an inoperable tumor and that there was nothing I could do other than potentially try some experimental treatments. But the doctor told me that at my age those treatments might end up doing more damage than good. So, left with no other choices, the doctor told me that the cancer was terminal and that I had no more than a year, two at the max, left to live...

Honestly, I can say since Clarence died, I had spent the few years after his death trying to make up for lost time. And it was a good run...But now, as I stood here in my bathroom mirror, looking at my poor old self begin to slowly deteriorate, I just knew it was a matter of time before my health would take a much more serious turn.

The one thing that I can say I truly regretted was not taking heed to Alice's advice and actually settling down with a man who was right in my age range. Gosh she was so right. I should've just stayed in my lane and found me an older man who was more mature and had his stuff together. I would've had me somebody right now to look after me. I was so lonely. Crazy as it may seem, shortly after my cancer diagnosis, Alice ended up finding her a man and now she was living her best life. She lost a hundred pounds, got an entire makeover and now she was looking better than ever. I, on the other hand, was beginning to look like a dried up prune that nobody wanted. Some of my hair was beginning to fall out. My muscles ached damn near every day. My bones felt so brittle and every time I went somewhere, I had to pause just to catch my breath. My oncologist had me taking a few prescriptions to manage the vertigo and occasional nausea I'd have. He told me though that within a few months I should expect my condition to get worse and that I better start getting my affairs in order. He even told me to consider checking myself into a hospice where I'd have 24-7 support and I could make some friends as I began to transition...

There was a part of me though that still couldn't believe any of this but I guess I had to realize that at the end of the day we all have to meet our eventual end. Life isn't forever. We all have to die one day, I guess...But damn, why did I have to go out like this? I always imagined I'd go out in my sleep, soft as cream. But no, I had to suffer in this agony and any day now I was just expecting myself to further devolve into absolute pain and horror of cancer.

It was late December and snow was falling hard from the skies. Although I'd been in my house all this week, I could feel that it was so somberly gray outside. It was something about this weather that just made me so sad. I used to love Winters so much. Now it was just a bittersweet reminder of how eventually I'd one day end up frozen in a morgue some-where, getting ready to be buried in some grave.

Alice called me earlier and asked me if I wanted to hang out. Although she had been coming by occasionally to check on me, her new relationship had occupied a lot of her time. I honestly thought she would've been a bit more supportive in helping me out but then again, could I blame her? This was the first time in her life she truly felt loved. I was so happy for her but at the same time so envious. One thing I came to realize was that although I'd had my fair share of young mens, none of them actually *loved* me. They just wanted me and my sex. They just wanted my money. Wanted my cook-ing. None of them wanted my heart. None of them wanted my love. And all I wanted was their love. Their affection. All this time I'd been living in delusion.

Anyways, I had to get myself out of this funk though because life obviously was way too short. As I finished getting ready, I wanted to put on one of my sexy outfits just for old times' sake. I wanted to prove to myself I could still get it. I had no idea where Alice was taking me though but she wanted to tell me she had a big surprise for me.

Some moments later, after I got finished doing my hair and putting on my makeup, I put on one of my sexy dresses and sprinkled some of my favorite perfume all over my body. "Damn, I look good!" I congratulated myself for looking so marvelous but deep down I was truly a mess. I had to stop myself from crying. "Get it together, Vernita. Don't do this right now. Everything's gonna be alright. God is still in control. Everything's gonna be alright. Just breathe." I took in a deep breath and exhaled. "Breathe in, breathe out." While I tried my best to simmer my nerves, I still couldn't help but let out a single tear. As it quickly escaped the corner of my left eye, I grabbed a tissue and gently wiped the tear away so I wouldn't ruin my makeup. Then I heard my phone vibrating on the edge of the bathroom countertop. That had to be Alice so I quickly yanked the phone and answered, "Hey, girl! You almost here?"

"Yeah, girl! I'm just pulling up!"

"Okay, I'll meet you outside then," I replied and then hung up. I grabbed my purse, phone and turned off all the lights. Soon as I got outside I saw shiny black, brand-new Lincoln Town Car pulling up into my driveway. My mouth flung wide open. I saw Alice in the driver's seat and then she waved at me.

Once I got into the passenger seat, the smell of a fresh new car filled my nose. Oooh, I just loved the smell of a new car. "Girl, when you bought this?!?" I had to ask.

"Girl, I just got this yesterday. Lamar gave me the down payment for it and everything!"

"Oh, wow! I see you and Lamar getting really serious!"

"We sure are!" she replied with a big, ecstatic smile

stretched across her face. It was so amazing how losing all that weight made her actually look younger. Looked like she took about twenty years off her face. Whatever she was doing I had to do too! I had to commend her because she was doing such a wonderful job. "You looking good, Alice! Girl, I need to do whatever you doing!"

"Oh, stop it, Vernita!"

"No, but for real! I'm so proud of you! Girl, you look like a million bucks!"

"Well, thank you," she bashfully replied. "You still looking good yourself though! I would never even think you had cancer! How's everything going with that though? Are you still going to at least try out the other treatment options that the other doctor told you?"

I sat there silent for a second. I honestly didn't know how to reply. "Probably not. I don't think I should proceed. It just seems like the cons outweigh the pros. Besides, even if the treatment does work, what's the point of even living anymore. I lived my life."

"Oh, no! Vernita, please don't say that! No! You have a lot to live for!"

"Like what?"

"Like me! I want you to live. All of your friends want you to live. Your family wants you to live!" Alice cried. "You gonna make me really cry! Please don't give up hope!"

"Yeah, well, speaking of which, seems like I ain't got no more friends or family. You got a man now and you are living your best life. I don't really talk to my own blood like that. Never really did."

"Oh, no, Vernita, is that how you really feel? I am sorry I couldn't be any more supportive but you know I am always going to try my best to be here to help you out! Now, you know you need to get out of this funk right now because it's just not healthy. It ain't right and it ain't gonna do you no good thinking this way!"

"Yeah, well, how can I help but to feel any different?" I didn't want guilt-trip Alice and, truth be told, she was right to an extent. If I kept thinking this way, I was going to hasten my demise. But how could I not feel depressed? How would you feel if a doctor told you that you had less than two years left to live? Every day I had to walk around knowing this very bitter fact.

"You know what though...You're right. I'm sorry. I'm just a bit in a tizzy right now. I just feel so down because I never thought six months ago my life would suddenly turn for the worse like this," I explained, my head hung low. Once again, I tried to keep myself from crying. But suddenly this burst of energy filled me and I shot my head up. "But you're right. I can't keep thinking this way. Sorry I even sound down like this."

"No, it's okay. You gotta get it out."

"Yeah, well, just forget I'm even acting this way. I just wanna hear this surprise of yours! Where are you taking me?"

"Girl, well, I wanna take you to this seafood spot out in the suburbs called Pappadeaux's! You ever been there before? Lamar took me there a few weeks ago and it was so good. They got good shrimp!"

I chuckled. "Yeah, I've been to Pappadeaux's before. I love their drinks."

I had to laugh because I remember one of my lil dips used to work there. Terrence was his name. He was a lil sexy yellow thing. Reminded me of Shemar Moore, just a bit brawnier. And I'll never forget how he tossed my salad in the backseat of Paulette in the parking lot.

As Alice and I continued our conversation, she pulled out of my driveway. We hopped onto Lakeshore drive and I swear my mood shifted. The sun began to peak through the thickness of the gray clouds and I had a glimmer of hope that perhaps things would be a bit different. Perhaps I should get a second opinion about my health. In fact, now that I think about it, I'm gonna do that first thing in the morning. Find me a new doctor. I didn't like that cracka of a doctor I had any damn way.

*a*n hour later, after a long journey on the highway, we had finally made it out to the restaurant. I swore Black folks loved them some seafood. And I said that because it seemed like every nigga and their mammy was at this damn seafood restaurant. Pappadeaux's was like a fancier Red Lobster. Luckily, Alice got us reservations, otherwise we would've been waiting for what seemed like a good hour just to get a table.

It was just twenty past noon, and she and I were sitting down at a table eating some bread and butter. She was strict about counting her calories so she was eating tiny bits of bread but I was devouring the entire loaf by myself as I sipped on this huge drink called the Swamp Thing. It was a mix of all different types of liquor, and baby, as that alcohol began to swim in my veins, I was starting to feel mighty different. I hadn't felt this way in a while and I swore I was beginning to feel like my old self.

Shit, now that I thought about it, maybe that was just what I needed to do to relax my nerves – have me a nice cocktail here and there. That doctor told me not to drink but hell, what did he really know! Besides, if there was nothing else I could do to cure this cancer, why not have a drink?!? Fuck him! I'mma live my life!

"So, you need to go ahead and tell me what this big surprise is," I mumbled to Alice as I stuffed a big piece of bread in my mouth then took a gulp from my drink.

"Well, you already know Lamar and I are getting really serious." She took a deep breath and I already knew what she was about to say. "Well, last night, Lamar proposed to me!" Alice confessed.

My eyes widened. "Girl, congratulations! Why you had to wait to tell me this! I'm so happy for you!" I quickly looked at her hand and didn't even realize she had this beautiful, big ass ring on her finger. How did I not notice that earlier?!? Gosh, I was so out of it!

"I'm surprised you didn't notice my ring," she then said as she held her left hand toward me and showed of what had to be at least a three our four-karat ring! "Wooow! This Lamar got some money! Girl, you struck gold I see! Everything is lining up for you!"

"Yeah, well, here's the other surprise…," she said and then her smile went a bit flat.

"What's that?" My brow raised out of curiosity.

"Well, I know this might not be what you wanna hear, Vernita, but Lamar wants to move to the Bahamas. He bought some land down in Nassau and built this nice house. He wants to move in a month or so," she said.

"So…You're gonna move out of Chicago…For good?"

"Well…That would be the plan, so yes…But…"

"But what?"

"I just don't know."

"Know about what?"

"Well, you know, our friendship and with everything you

got going on. I don't know how I feel about just upping and moving, leaving you here by yourself."

"Chile, listen, do not worry about me!" I said smacking my teeth. "Don't let what I got going on hold you back! You gotta do you, boo!"

"But, Vernita, I just wanna be here for you. I mean, we just talked about friendship in the car and whatnot and how important it is...You really gonna be okay with me just moving away like that?"

I didn't want to come off as crass and be selfish. But, to an extent, I was feeling a certain type of way that she would just drop all of this on me. But what would it look like being so upset that she was getting married and then moving away? I should be elated that my friend was finding true love and happiness.

Among the laughing, conversations and clinking of dishes inside of the restaurant, I started to feel nauseous and my vertigo began to kick in. My stomach rumbled a bit and I wondered if I had too much to drink. Suddenly I hung my head low and went quiet.

"Everything alright, Vernita?" Alice sounded very concerned as she leaned in and rubbed my back. "Girl, I think you may have had too much to drink," she said.

"I'm fine...I just need to use the bathroom right quick," I replied as I slowly stood up and leaned against the table for a moment.

"Is everything alright, ma'am?" I heard our waiter say from behind me.

"I'm fine...I just think I had too much to drink," I said as I stood myself up. "I just need to use the ladies' room. Where is it at?"

"It's over near the far end of the bar, ma'am."

"You need me to help you, Vernita?" Alice asked. "She has

brain cancer and I think some of her symptoms are beginning to flare up," she said aloud.

My eyes instantly grew wide with embarrassment and slight rage. Why in hell would she reveal my damn medical history to this gay-looking white boy! How dare she! There was a part of me that suddenly wanted to grab this plate of bread and smack her across the head with it!

"No! I'm fine, Alice! I'll be right back," I said back to her, my tone a bit angry.

Making my way through the crowded restaurant, I flew inside the ladies' restroom and then made my way down to the handicap stall. I quickly locked it and began pacing inside the stall, punching the air.

All types of rage filled my mind and honestly, I wasn't doing good right now. I wasn't dizzy or anything from cancer. I was dizzy because I couldn't believe that ex-fat ass bitch was getting married and moving away. Fuck her! I was supposed to be the one getting good news, not her! The bitch made all sorts of stupid decisions in her life to stay with a crazy, abusive ass nigga that cheated on her and beat her ass. But no! Here I was, the one dying from cancer, and this flabby arms-having bitch was getting all the good news. And yeah, I lied to her mothafuckin' ass. She didn't look good at all. She looked like pure shit. She looked like Bozo the Clown did her make up. And that cheap ass wig she had stitched in her head was a pure mess. She probably let that ratchet ass daughter of hers do her hair and makeup. Got her out here embarrassing me and shit.

Quickly trying to get myself together, I took a few deep breaths as I clutched my chest and closed my eyes. "Calm down, Vernita…Just calm down… You doin' the most right now. You got yourself all worked up," I said to myself, hoping my words would soothe this inner rage.

I made my way out of the stall and strolled up to the sink

just to sprinkle a few drops of water on my face. Ooh, chile, I was so red in the face! Nah, this couldn't be the way I was gonna go out. Fuck that! I needed to get my mothafuckin' mojo back. Yes, ma'am! I was gonna die riding me a big black dick.

Chuckling at myself as I stared in the mirror, I couldn't believe I was getting so envious of Alice's newfound happiness. But fuck her though. Fat ass bitch. Yeah, she was my friend and she was being supportive, but I didn't want any friends right now. I wanted me a man with a big heart, big pockets and most important a big ass dick. If Alice could find someone and be happy, well, damn it, if I had two years left to live, I needed to find the same!

The doors to the bathroom opened and lo and behold, Alice stumbled in scanning me up and down. "Vernita, is everything okay?!? I was getting worried for a second!"

"Yeah, girl. I just vomited a little. But I took my medicine. I'm fine now. Ooh, chile, I almost thought I was gonna have to call 9-11!"

"We can still go to the hospital if you need to!"

I shook my head. "No, girl. I'm fine. I just need to not have another drink," I said.

"Okay, well, do you wanna get the food to go and just go back to your place and relax?" she asked.

"No, we can eat here, girl! Don't worry about me. I just wanna learn more about your plans," I said as I turned the faucet off and wiped my face with a piece of paper towel.

The two of us strolled out of the bathroom and made our way back to our table. The waiter came moments later, took our orders and then she and I went back to talking about her future plans. "So, you know, I still have yet to meet this Mr. Lamar. When am I gonna have a chance to finally meet him?"

"Well…" Alice grinned hard and then said, "I was hoping

we could all go out maybe in a few days! I think you will really like him!"

"Yeah, well, I wanna see for myself. I can't just let my friend marry any and everybody! Don't wanna make that mistake twice," I said winking.

"Yup, you right! You and I both know that for sure!" she said back to me. Although I kept smiling, all I kept thinking was I couldn't believe this heffa had the nerve to compare my marriage to Clarence with that low-life nigga she was married to. Clarence may have been a bust when it came to the bedroom but at least he wasn't beating my ass and fucking every fast-tail hussy in Chicago.

I was already over hearing about Lamar and Alice's joy, so after our food came, I made up some bullshit and told Alice I wasn't feeling well and that we should just get the food to go. And that we did. Less than two hours later, I was back at my house and I didn't even want her company anymore.

"Alright, girl, thank you so much for everything. I just need to take me a nap. I'll call you when I wake up," I lied.

"You sure you don't want me to stay behind just in case?" Alice asked.

"Nah, girl. I don't wanna bother you," I replied as I got out of the car with my food in my hand. I didn't even want this over-fried, nasty ass shit anyways. I'd rather get me some catfish from Chicago Chicken and Waffles than eat this bullshit.

"Alright, well, give me a call," she said. Once I got out the car, she quickly took off and I made my way back inside.

Now that the old Vernita was back, I needed to get this back cracked. This tender pussy ain't been touched or ate in nearly half a year and it was definitely time to get my fuck on! I may have had two years left to live but that didn't mean I couldn't go out with a bang, no pun intended.

I sexily sauntered through my kitchen and threw the food

straight in the garbage. Fuck this moping and complaining. I was gonna live it up until the wheels fell off this pussy, so with that being said, I dashed into my bedroom and began looking for a new outfit to put on.

Although it was Sunday and the streets were a bit quiet, Vernita was gonna go out tonight and snatch me up some dick. A part of me wanted to call up Percy and tempt him with cash so I can just get some quick dick, but fuck that, I wanted some new dick. I wanted to see if I still had it in me to make a nigga crave this body.

Although it was dead in the middle of Winter, I rummaged my closet looking for something that reveal all the curves I still had left in my body. After a few minutes or so, I found the outfit I was exactly looking for – this all-black, thigh-high slit gown to reveal these sexy, succulent toned brown legs of mine. Oohh and baby, the neck to the dress was open to reveal these nice firm, titties that I worked so hard to get – thanks to Markell.

Although my hair was starting to look a bit patchy, I had the best wig to make a nigga's head turn. I had this blonde bob wig with china bangs. It was now approaching two PM and I didn't want to hit the streets until around nine or so. So, in the meantime, I was gonna lay down, relax and get me in a nice nap. In fact, before I did that, I wanted to smoke some good ass reefur to get my mind right.

I pulled out my phone from my purse and called up one of my dealers. Twenty minutes later, he came through and dropped me off a big bag of that reefur.

Once I rolled me up a nice blunt, I laid down and took a sip of some Hennessey I had left over from months back. Tonight was gonna be nice!

CHAPTER TEN

"…STILLETO PUMPS IN THE CLUB
WHOEVA THOUGHT THAT THESE GIRLS WILL GET
CRUNK?!?
WE ROCKIN' STILLETOS HOE!
WE ROCKIN' STILLETOS HOE!"

*C*lub Sanctuary was one of these young folks' nightclubs over in the West Loop, which was like west Downtown Chicago. Although it was Sunday night, surprisingly the club was packed to the brim!

Bitter cold air swam through the air but my sexy ass was protected by this heavy chinchilla fur draping down to my ankles.

This tall, big, thick security guard nigga who was darker than midnight checked me for weapons. Then, like the cocky, bad bitch I was, I sauntered through the doors of the club as the loud music blasted and rumbled the walls and floor.

Sparkling orbs of neon light illuminated the entire night club.

A bad bitch could feel so many eyes on me, however, I didn't know if the stares were good or bad. But I didn't give a good god damn though! Baby, I was just here to have me a few drinks, meet a couple of niggas, and of course, hopefully bring some young dick back to my place of residence.

This song blasting from the speakers sounded a bit dated but it sure was giving my ass life! Why? 'Cause I shole did have my stilettos on!

My pumps click-clacked against the floor as I made my way over to the bar. I eyed an empty seat next to this man. Guessing he felt my presence, the young gentleman looked over his shoulder and then quickly pulled an empty seat back for me to sit in.

"Oh, thank you, darling!" I said to him with the biggest grin on my face.

"No problems, ma'am," he replied as he scanned me up and down. With the weird smirk on his face, I knew he had to be curious about who I was and what I looked like under this fur coat. And just like that, I slipped out of the fur coat, revealing to every curious nigga in the club what I had on. I was bedazzling, you hear me! I had my pearls and diamonds on too!

"Damn, lady, you really showing out tonight," the young man replied as he kept that same smirk on his face. And, oh chile, he was just what I was looking for tonight. He was this tall, yellow fellow that reminded me of that actor Terrance Howard. He had these glowing blue eyes, this chiseled face, and these full lips that were making this cat of mine roar like a lion! He looked athletic too. Perhaps he played basketball for the Bulls. Maybe even football. Hell, I didn't know but I was gonna get to know. He wasn't dressed like the rest of these guys in the club though. He had on this nice crème-colored Ferragamo suit. Boy looked like he made a million dollars a year! What was to him? I wondered…

"This music is a bit…. aggressive," I said to him as sat down in the chair. The bartender, this chubby brown guy, strolled over and asked, "What are you having tonight, ma'am?"

"I'm having some coke and Hennessey. On the rocks. Make it a double shot, too," I replied.

"It's on me," the young, sexy gentleman next to me said to the bartender. He then glanced at me and said, "It's on me. I'll treat you since you came here dressed like the Queen."

"Oh my! Thank you so much!" I grinned. "And what's your name?"

"Terry. Terry Franklin." He stretched his hand out to shake mine. "I'm Vernita. Vernita Washington. Nice to meet you, Terry," I said shaking his hand. I quickly glanced down and noticed his hands were manicured. Oooh, chile, I just loved it when a man took good care of his hands. His hand wasn't too soft or too hard.

"Nice to meet you as well!" he replied then he took a sip on his glass.

"So what are you drinking?" I had to ask.

"Some vodka. I'm about to have some Patron next."

"Oooh, you mixing them liquors together. You gonna get a headache!"

"Nah, I'm a pro," he laughed shaking his head.

Terry and I talked for some time and kept having drink after drink. By now, I was so tipsy and ready to see if I could transition this casual conversation into a dick-down session. But, for some odd reason, it just seemed like Terry wasn't going. I didn't know what it was, but if he was truly wasting my time, then I needed to scour the rest of this club for some potential dick. I ain't got all the time in the world to be wasting it on some nigga who just wanna be friends at this point. He told me all about himself. He said he owned an IT consulting firm and was just in town for a convention. He told me he was from Los Angeles. That was good because for right now I truly preferred to not fuck anybody local.

Some moments later, out of the corner of my eye, I saw some lil young red bitch stroll up to Terry and put her hand on his shoulder. "Hey, baby! I wanna dance!" she said.

Baby?!? Damn it! I knew it was something about this nigga! The whole time he had me thinking his ass was single and this nigga had a whole entire girlfriend in the club with him. I had it in me to throw this drink all over him and ruin that outfit he had on. Fuck nigga!

"Vernita, I want you to meet my friend, Lacy," he said. He then looked at her and said, "Lacy, this is Vernita."

The young bitch extended her hand to shake mine. With a fake smile etched on my face, I extended my hand and shook hers. "How are you?" I asked with fake politeness.

"I'm great, actually! I just wanna dance!" she said. She seemed kind of ditzy.

"I'm sure you do too! Well, ya'll have fun!" I said, slightly rolling my eyes. "It was nice meeting you, Terry. Thanks for the drinks." As I was about to get up from my seat and grab my coat, he gently grabbed my arm. "Where you goin'?"

"To leave you and your girlfriend be...Nice meeting you," I said.

"Nah, she ain't my girlfriend," he said. "She's just one of my *friends*," he seemingly tried to explain but I wasn't falling for that bullshit. AT ALL! I already knew this nigga was lying. I was just shocked he'd do that right here in front of his face. Either he was lying or this nigga was a scammer. Whatever it was, I wanted no parts of it.

"Yeah, no, we're just friends, Vernita," she chimed in.

"Just sit down and relax, Vernita. I still wanted to get to know you," he said politely.

"Look, I'm fine. I wanna get around the dance floor anyways," I said.

"So, you wanna dance, too?"

"Something like that," I kind of lied. Truth be told, I just wanted to meet other niggas because I was just getting shady vibes from this fool.

"Well, I guess we all can dance," he said. "Come on," he said as he grabbed my hand along with Lacy's! "Ohh, we are about to have some fun!" she bellowed in a roaring laugh.

I tensed up a bit, slightly embarrassed because I didn't want folks staring at me. Terry noticed how tight I suddenly got. "I'm good, Terry. I really am."

"Oh, don't be so uptight! Just relax and live a little! Life is too short!"

"I'm just a bit too old to get down on the dance floor like that! I was kind of lying about wanting to dance," I confessed.

"So what?!? Who cares! You ain't that old. What? You are like fifty or something like that? Shit, I'm 42. You ain't that much older than me!" he said chuckling.

And just like that, hearing him say that I was fifty gave me all the confidence I needed to shake off the negative vibes that were just swarming my mind. I didn't know if he was just saying that just to fuck with me, but it did fuck with me – it made me feel good again. "Fuck it! You're right! One life to live!"

"Good! Now let's go dance!" he replied and then yanked Lacy and I toward the center of the dance floor. Nicki Minaj's Truffle Butter, which I knew by heart, came on and this zest filled me to the core. I felt like I was truly back to my old self. The lights on the dance floor turned purple and pink and the three of us danced our asses off together, having the time of my life. I hadn't experienced this type of fun in a long time. I began to get super-sweaty and I could feel my makeup running down my face. Although I couldn't get down like I used to, I sure was working every muscle and bone in my body to the best of my ability.

The DJ had a remix of the song playing and it continued playing for another minute or so. As Terry grabbed me and started grinding up on me, he leaned and looked dead into my eyes. "You wanna have some real fun?" he muttered.

"Sure," I said, trying my best to gather my breath.

He then reached into his pocket, pulled out a small pill and put it on the tip of his tongue.

My eyes widened. What in the world was that?!?

He then looked at me, leaned in closer, and began kissing me all over my neck. Although I was wracked with fear about what the hell that was on the tip of his tongue, this deep sense of lust overpowered me. My pussy was beginning to get so moist as those kisses sent me into a frenzy. He pulled back a bit, looked me in my eyes again, and then leaned in and kissed me on my lips. I gave in. The two of us made out on the dance floor. As his tongue wrapped around mine, I felt the bittersweet pill dance in my mouth. I then swallowed it, not even knowing what it was. But who cared?!? Whatever it was, I just hoped it made me feel good.

As the three of us continued to dance, it seemed like I sweated away all of my fears, doubts, and dreadful thoughts about my age and having cancer. Nothing at the moment mattered other than this very moment.

I felt so good.

Felt so alive!

Felt like I was twenty all over again and was starting my life.

Terry's grinding felt so good and next thing you know I found myself getting so moist and loose. I was ready to jump all over his dick…if he was willing to give me some.

I closed my eyes and saw all of these crazy visuals and patterns I ain't never seen before in my life! What in the hell did this boy put in my mouth?!? "What did you give me?" I asked Terry as I leaned into his ear. "I gave you a good time," he replied with a devious grin painted on his face. "Now let's take things back to my hotel room." "Most definitely," I said as I smiled back. Yes, Lord! Finally! Vernita still got it ya'll!

"I'm coming, too, right?" I then heard Lacy say as I looked over at her. She ran her finger down my chest and then tickled my nipple. My eyes exploded open with shock and surprise. Oh no! I was strictly dickly! This heffa got me fucked up if she thought she was gonna be a part of this situation!

"Yeah, you can come, too," Terry muttered into Lacy's ear. The entire time we were dancing, I kind of muted her ditzy ass out but now I was back to feeling a bit annoyed again.

"I don't know about all that," I said.

"Don't know about what?" Lacy said. "Just relax, Vernita. I won't bite. I promise you." She leaned into my ear and then said, "Besides, I bet you I can fuck you better than Terry." Without hesitation, she leaned into my neck and licked my earlobe. Chills shot down my spine.

But honestly…

It. Felt. Soooo. Gooood. Okay, now I was sold. Fuck it! You only live once, right?

"Okay, let's go. I'm horny as hell!"

"That's what I thought," Lacy replied with the same devious mile Terry still on his face.

Without caring about my car, let alone what in the hell I was about to do with these two, some ten minutes later I found myself in the backseat of a Taxi. Seated in the middle, I had both Terry and Lacy kissing all over my neck. Both of them ran their hands between thighs and I swore I was gonna cum right here on these seats. I felt a bit embarrassed because the African cab driver kept looking back. But I didn't give a fuck. I felt so good right now.

Some moments later we arrived at The W, right in the heart of Downtown. Terry paid the driver and then the three of us quickly made our way to the elevators. Moments later, we were now on the fiftieth floor, expeditiously making our way to Terry's room. Once inside, I took my coat off and tossed it off to the side. "Lay down and make yourself comfortable," Lacy commanded from behind me.

Not saying a word, I did as she said. My skin was tingling with this pulsing joy and the more I looked at her the more attracted I was to her. She was so thick, sexy, and angelic all at the same time. All I could imagine at the moment was her head in between my thighs sucking on my clit.

Laid out on the bed, I closed my eyes again, and those same psychedelic visuals were etched into my eyes. I truly felt like I was in a different universe. This boy gave me something and I didn't quite know what it was.

Once I opened my eyes again, I didn't even realize it, but I was now completely naked. I must've dozed off for a minute while Terry and Lacy got my dress, bra, and underwear off. Both Terry and Lacy stood there with nothing on. Her body was gorgeous. Terry's was too. He was cut up from head to toe and his dick was harder than a brick. Lacy then got into the bed and crawled in between my legs. She gently pushed them wide open then buried her head deep between me. Without hesitation, she began to suck on my pearl. Chile, I couldn't believe I was letting another woman eat me out. If I died tomorrow, I was going straight to hell! No questions asked! But I did NOT care!

I never would've thought in a thousand years that a woman knew how to eat the cat better than a man. Whew, chile! My pussy was gushing juices left and right as she worked that throbbing clitoris of mine.

I was so enraptured in my own bliss I hadn't even realized that Terry was pumping all types of dick up in Lacy as she continued to eat me out. Then again, the room was a bit dark and I could barely see.

Some moments later, Terry pulled out of Lacy and strolled over to me. He slapped his pussy juice-covered dick in my mouth and I began to relentlessly suck on it like a lollipop. Baby, if you would've told me I died and went to heaven, I would've believed you. What a crazy way to end this day…Vernita was back ya'll!

CHAPTER ELEVEN

I didn't know what time it was but I was suddenly awakened by the sound of loud laughing and constant thumping piercing my dark bedroom. My hazy eyes slowly opened and I glanced over at my alarm clock and saw that it was nearly three PM.

Chileeee, I didn't know what the hell came over me but I shole did do some crazy shit last night! That was the first time ever I had an experience like that. The crazy thing was most of the night now was a blurry memory. But the one thing that I still had stitched in my mind was how that young girl ate my juicy box out like none other!

I was still curious about what Terry gave me but the more I laid in my bed, the more I realized that boy probably gave me one of those XTC pills or something like that. I ain't never messed with nothing like that before in my life and I didn't know if I would ever do it again. I did have some fun but that was just a bit too much for me. All of those crazy visuals almost had Vernita thinking she was about to go meet Clarence, my mama, my daddy, and all of the rest of my dead peoples up in The Upper Room.

I didn't know how I managed to make it back home but after I woke up, Terry helped me get a ride back to my car. From there, and by the grace of God, I drove straight back home although my head felt like it was about to explode. The heaviest fatigue drenched my entire body so as soon as I got back to my house, I went straight to sleep.

"What in the hell is all that noise?!?" I mumbled to myself as I wiped my eyes and crawled out of the bed. With nothing on other than my bra and my underwear, I strolled over to my bedroom window and peeled the curtain back. I looked down next to the unit next to mine and saw a big ass U-Haul moving truck and three Mexican-looking men moving boxes in an out. Guess the vacant townhouse next to mine finally got sold and a new person was moving in. I'd always wondered when someone was gonna buy that place because it had been on the market for quite some time. My nerves frazzled, I was getting a bit irritated because I truly didn't want to wake up but now that I was up, I figured I'd go take me a long, hot shower and clean myself up. Chile, I didn't even know if I let Terry cum up in me. Although I was pretty much dying, shit, I still didn't wanna get any diseases and shit. Ain't nobody got time to be getting AIDS and shit. Especially when yo ass already got the cancer. Uh-uhh. No, ma'am!

These Mexican movers were making a lot of noise and I had it in me to go down there and curse them the hell out for being so loud! Outside in the middle of the damn fucking cold speaking that Spanish and shit! But the more I thought about it, the more curious I became as to who exactly was moving in. I sure hope it wasn't these three amigos because, baby let me tell you one thing, them Mexicans were notorious for partying and carrying on. Baby, them Mexicans will be up to three AM in the morning drinking coronas and fucking up piñatas, even during the middle of the goddamn winter.

"Ughhh!" I grunted as I rolled my eyes and quickly pulled the curtain back. "Got me fucked up!" Now I was too nosey and I had to go see who my new neighbors were gonna be. Deciding to take a shower later, I threw on a pair of jeans, a shirt, and a coat. I made my way outside and put the biggest, fakest smile on my face. "Excuse me! Excuse me!" I yelled out to get their attention as I waved at them.

"Good afternoon, ma'am! How are you?" one of them said. He was a short pudgy man with a thick ass mustache.

"I'm doing fine! Ya'll my new neighbors?" I asked myself I stood there beginning to shiver. These temperatures were beginning to drop. Felt like it was twenty degrees outside.

"No, ma'am! We're just the movers," he replied.

"Oh, okay! Where are they? I wanna meet them!" My nosey ass replied.

One of the other movers, some tall and slender young man, said, "They went to the store. They should be back short-ly." I took a good look at him and, oh my, this Mexican boy was very handsome! Although it was so frigid outside, this boy had on this tight-fitting black t-shirt that snugged every muscle on his upper body. His biceps were the size of pineapples and his shoulders were so thick and broad. He had a well-shaved beard that wrapped around his chiseled light brown face. I looked deep into his eyes and felt my heart almost skip a beat. "Damn," I replied with my mouth flung wide open. I took a quick scan at his legs and he had on some gray sweat pants. My eyes instantly flashed wide open when I realized this boy had a burrito of a dick print bulging right in front of me! Soon as I saw that dick print I swear my pussy started having multiple seizures. "Damn, damn, damn," I said then clutched my mouth in surprise once I realized I had zoned off.

"Excuse me?" he said with a raised brow. Suddenly the air felt awkward and I said back to him, "I'm sorry, I just…. I'm just a bit up in age and I'm a bit hard of hearing. What you say now, baby?"

"Oh, no worries," he said smiling, revealing the whitest, prettiest teeth. "I just said they went to the store and they should be back shortly. They left out about ten minutes ago." This boy had to have been a model or something because he just looked so damn exotic. Child, let me make sure I made that doctors' appointment ASAP because this Mexican boy was giving Vernita a reason to live, you hear me!

"Okey dokey! Thank you so much!" I said reaching my hand out. "I'm Vernita by the way. Do you have a card? I might need y'alls moving service one day."

"Yes, ma'am. My name is actually Juan and I'm the owner. These two other guys are my older cousins," he said. I looked at the two other older men and nodded at them and threw my attention right back to Mr. Juan. He pulled out his wallet then pulled out a business card and handed it to me. "Thank you," I said to him smiling. "I'll give you a call later on this week. I have another house out in the suburbs that I got some stuff in that I wanna move."

"Cool beans. We offer great discounts," Juana said.

"Thanks! We'll be in touch." I spun around and made my way back into the house.

Chile, I came out here ready to curse these men out to then meeting some new possible dick. Mexican dick at that. Baby, I was gonna stuff that burrito down my throat as soon as possible!

Back inside, I stormed straight to my room and peeled the curtains back again and watched Juan and his two cousins chop it up as they moved furniture and boxes from the U-Haul truck inside the house. Although I had a raging headache, I suddenly mustered up the strength to wanna play with my pussy as I fantasized about Mr. Juan. Baby, this sex drive of mine was really flaring up. If I didn't get my shit together, my pussy was gonna fall up out of me and die before I did.

I jetted into my bathroom, popped a few aspirins, and then expeditiously made my way over to my bed. I took off all of my clothes and got completely naked. Once I laid down, I rummaged through my nightstand and pulled out Mr. Cummings, my favorite high-powered vibrating dildo. Mr. Cummings had been resting comfortably in the darkness of the nightstand, collecting all types of dust. I ain't used this bad boy in a hot minute!

Once I plugged into a nearby wall outlet, I powered it on, spread my legs, and let that mothafucka work this big clit of mine. Now you'd think this pearl would be a bit sore from last night but it shole wasn't! This lil pussy of mine still had at least twenty or thirty orgasms left in it for the day!

Closing my eyes, I plowed Mr. Cummings in out and of me. He was about a good ten inches long. My snatch could handle that mothafucka too. As my hips and ass gyrated in the bed, my moans filled the dark bedroom. I visualized Mr. Juan fully naked as he laid on top of me and thrust his big dick in and out of me, his big nuts slapping my ass.

"Damn, damn, damn! Shit, baby!" My groans were getting louder and by now I had already came twice. I wasn't gonna stop until I squirted. I wanted to squirt so bad. I wanted to drench these sheets up! "FUCK ME, JUAN! KEEP ON FUCKING ME! FUCK THIS PUSSY!"

Buzz. Buzz. Buzz. Buzz.

All of a sudden, my eyes shot wide open and I was immediately distracted by the sound of my phone vibrating on my dresser. Trying my best to ignore the phone call, I closed my eyes, and once again I saw Mr. Juan back on top of me, pumping that burrito in and out of me. But the goddamn cell phone kept vibrating and the noise of it was now overpowering the sound of Mr. Cummings. I figured whoever it was calling me would get the mothafuckin' cue that a bitch didn't want to be bothered right now and that they would just need to call me back later. But the phone kept vibrating!

"Ughh!" I grunted and snatched the dildo out of me and tossed it off to the side in the bed. I hopped out of the bed and dashed over to my phone. I didn't quite recognize the phone number but I quickly answered, "Hello?!? Who is this?!?"

"MS. VERNITA! IT'S SHARDAY!"

My face scrunched in confusion. "Sharday?!?" I shook my head. "I don't know no damn Sharday! Wrong number."

"MS. VERNITA! STOP IT! THIS ALICE'S DAUGHTER! SHE HAD A HEART ATTACK! SHE IN THE HOSPITAL!"

I suddenly clutched my chest. I guess I was too tired and horny to realize that this indeed was Sharday, Alice's daughter. She occasionally did my hair. "Lord! Chile, I just woke up and I was confused for a second! Wait a minute?!? Alice had a heart attack?!? Is she okay?!?"

"I don't know! All I know is I got a call from one of my cousins telling me they found Mama passed out in the house and they called 9-11. That's all I know and I ain't got nobody to come pick me up!" she cried. Her sobs were so loud and intense that I knew this wasn't no joke; reality set in and I began to panic. "Okay! Let me put my clothes on! I'mma be at your apartment in fifteen minutes! Oh, lord! Please let everything be okay!" I sobbed. "Please hurry up!" she begged. "I'mma be there. Just calm down, okay?" "Okay," I heard her mumble, and then she hung up.

Tears running down my face, I didn't want anything bad to happen to my friend. Although I was feeling jealous about Alice and her new love life and all the newfound happiness, I truly didn't want anything bad to happen to her. She didn't deserve it. Once I had my clothes back on, I zipped out of the house and made my down to Sharday's apartment. From there, we zipped to Rush University Hospital. God, please just let my friend be okay. Don't do her like this. I was supposed to go first…

CHAPTER TWELVE

*S*itting in this cold ass hospital room, I was completely devastated.

The doctors had informed us that Alice had suffered a major heart attack and that she had been placed into a medically induced coma for the time being.

This was so gut-wrenching because just as my friend was beginning to celebrate the start of a new life, she was now unconscious and probably in a lot of pain.

As I sat by her bedside, I rubbed her stiff, cold hand. I was trying my best to fight back these tears but Lord knew that if the doctor came in and delivered us some more devastating news, I was just gonna break down.

Alice had all types of tubes and shit running in and out of her mouth, nose, and arms. The constant chirping of all of these machines was reminding me too much of when I first learned I had cancer.

This was so traumatizing and a part of me wanted to get up and get some cool air just to simmer my nerves. But I had to stay; I had to be here for my friend. I leaned over into her ear and whispered, "Everyone's here baby. This is Vernita.

We love you so much. We need you to get better. Please don't die on us," I lowly sobbed.

I closed my eyes and said a small prayer, hoping God would reverse this situation. But then as I sat there, something strange hit me.

Where in the hell was her fiancé at?

This Mr. Lamar. It seemed pretty strange that he hadn't been here. Did anyone tell him what happened? Then again, did anyone have his contact information?

I looked around the room and Sharday along with her nieces and nephews just sat in silence. They were all devastated too.

"Did anyone get into contact with Lamar?" I had to ask.

"Yeah, I did," said Mitch, one of Alice's grandsons. "But he ain't pick up his phone though."

Alice had three children. Janice, Paul and Sharday. Unfortunately, Janice died some years ago. Paul was currently incarcerated. So Sharday was pretty much Alice's only child who was still around to help her out here and there. Gosh, I just felt so bad for that child.

"You tell your dad what happened?" I asked Mitch.

"Not yet. He on lockdown."

"Oh… Oh okay," I simply replied and threw my attention back to Alice. Continuing to rub her hand, I got lost in my own dreary thoughts and thought about my own looming mortality. This wasn't right at all. I was supposed to be the first to go. Not Alice. None of this was sitting right with me. Starting to feel a bit nauseated, I proceeded up out of my chair and looked at Sharday. "Come and let's go smoke a cigarette. We need to have a break. We not gonna know anything until a few more hours," I said.

Sharday agreed then stood up. The two of us exited the ICU. A good five minutes later, she and I were out in the dark, gray early evening in the designated smoking area of the hospital. Although I didn't smoke squares like that, I sure did need one right now. Some nicotine, a shot of some brown liquor, and even some reefur was what I needed to simmer this damn headache and fatigue I had going on.

Sharday pulled out her pack of Newports and handed me a cig. She slapped one in her mouth, lit it up, and then passed me the light.

As we stood there silently taking puffs on the cigarette, the chilly air somewhat provided relief to this lingering headache. Although I was quite certain it was still from that damn XTC pill or whatever it was that nigga gave me last night, I had to be conscious of the fact that I had a ticking time bomb growing in my head. Maybe this was it. Maybe the tumor was going to finally grow and start to really begin to send my health on a decline.

I took another drag from the cigarette hoping the nicotine would calm my nerves but it did nothing but amplify my anxiety. Having spent the last couple of hours by Alice's bedside was a bittersweet reminder that one day I was going to be in that very position. Unlike Alice though, I didn't have grandchildren and others who would be there to surround me. And that was exactly why I needed Alice to live. She was the only one who at the end of the day truly cared for me and I knew who would be there once this sickness really began to take over my body. Knowing all of this, I felt so bad and guilty knowing that just yesterday she expressed how she was more worried about me and concerned that her new love life would distract from our friendship. A long, cold tear dripped my eye, and once again I found myself fighting back the urge to breakdown and cry.

"This is so just messed up. Mama was so happy. This was the happiest I'd ever seen her in years. This is just so fucked up. I'm mad as hell right now. Like, I just wanna hurt somebody," Sharday sobbed.

"I'm mad too but we just gotta be thankful that at least she is still alive right now. We don't know what is gonna happen but we just gotta pray that the doctors have some good news for us," I told her. I truly felt bad for Sharday was exceptionally close to her.

Sharday was a bit on the ratchet side and lived in some housing project over in Bronzeville. She was once a cute girl but life seemed to have gotten the best of her lately. Although she was a hairdresser, her hair was an actual mess. She had a patchy short afro. The darkest circles were painted around her jaundiced eyes. Her mouth was filled with a few rotten, crooked teeth. She had a tooth missing here and there. In so many ways, she took on Alice's weak nature and let men run all over her. In fact, with all the stories Alice used to tell me, seemed like Sharday was like Alice on steroids. You know they say the leaf don't fall to far from the tree. Well, shit, in Sharday's case, the leaf was still on the mothafuckin' tree.

Shaking her head and wiping her face free of tears, Sharday took a long drag from her cigarette and then tossed it into a light blanket of snow on the sidewalk. "I'mma go back inside. Thank you, Ms. Vernita, for being there for Mama. You know you her number one row dog," she said cracking a faint smile.

"Alice my girl. I gotta be there for her no matter what," I said smiling right back at her. I tossed the half-smoked cigarette into the snow then trailed Sharday back into the hospital and to the ICU.

Making our way past the nurses' station, from afar I had noticed a few more folks were standing around Alice's room door. Those must've been Alices' peoples and word was probably spreading quickly that she was in the ICU. Wow, this hospital sure did have a very relaxed visitor's policy though. Although these were Alice's kinfolk, I didn't like the sight of this at all! She didn't need all of these damn people up in her room like this. "Damn, they just gonna let everybody come up and visit her?" I grunted to myself. Sharday heard what I said and then looked back at me saying with wide eyes, "I don't know who any of these people are."

We got closer and then Sharday said, "Excuse me? Who is ya'll?"

"Oh, we are Mr. Hawkins' security. Sorry for the disturbance but we got clearance from the nurses that we could be here."

Sharday looked back at me and then back at the two fellows standing near the door. "Security? Why Lamar got security?" One of the men who was this tall chocolate fellow scrunched his eyebrows and said, "Because, umm, he needs security..."

Who in the hell was this Lamar figure?!? I was so thoroughly confused. Damn, I kind of had the idea that this Mr. Lamar had some money but security? I threw a nervous gawk at the gentlemen and then strolled into the room. But, baby, I swore once I entered that room, I almost had a heart attack my damn self. Once my eyes set onto Mr. Lamar, I realized God was playing a really big ass joke on me. I had to blink twice just to make sure this is who I thought it was. But it surely was him just by that shiny baldhead and goatee of his. I knew this Mr. Lamar. Knew him pretty well actually.

I fucked this nigga. Yes, chile! I was bouncing all over his dick. No rubber either.

I met Lamar some years back when I went on this month-long Caribbean cruise. I was so ashamed to admit to this at this very moment but, baby, he was some good vacation dick too!

Lamar was sitting next to Alice's bedside holding her hand and he hadn't noticed me yet. With millions of butterflies filling my stomach, I quickly tried to dash back out of the room because I didn't want him to recognize me.

Immense guilt once again filled me and I didn't know how to navigate the hell out of this crazy, precarious situation. Lord, Lord, Lord! Why were you doing this to me?!? I suddenly thought to myself as I dashed back out of the room and zipped down the quiet ICU hallway. I had to get to a bathroom immediately because I was going to vomit all over the place. I had fucked my best friend's fiancée!

Scrambling near the elevators, I asked someone who looked like a nurse where the closest bathroom was at. And once they pointed me in its direction, I took off running and dashed inside.

I found the closest stall, locked it, and began to puke all over the place. I barely had anything in my stomach but what I did have came all the way up. The walls felt like they were closing in and my chest tightened. My ass was gonna die tonight!

I heard the doors to the bathroom whoosh open. "Ms. Vernita?!? Is everything alright?" That had to be Sharday. She must've noticed I zipped out that room like a track and field athlete.

"Ye-yeah," I stammered. "I'm fine. Just these meds got me a bit nauseous. I probably should've never smoked that cigarette," I lied.

"Oh, okay. Well, just let me know if you need me to get a nurse," she said.

"I will..." Then I heard her leave out of the bathroom.

I plopped myself up off the floor of the stall and exited out, making my way over to the closest sink. I splashed some water on my face just to make sure this was all still real.

Wow! Wow! Wow! I fucked my best friend's man!

Now how in the world was I going to explain this to her?!? The more I thought about it though the more it dawned upon me though that Lamar was rolling in some big money.

Staring in the mirror, I tried my hardest to remember what he told me did when we met on the cruise but my memory was so shot by now. I think he told me he did something in real estate or construction. However, my mind kept shooting blanks. I had it in me just to dip out of the hospital and take my trifling ass back home! But if I did that, everyone would be concerned. Besides, if and when Alice woke up from her coma, I was going to eventually have to *reconnect* with Lamar. How in the world was I ever going to explain this to Alice?!?

CHAPTER THIRTEEN

*C*hile, ain't nobody got time to be caught up in some bullshit, so rather than go back into the room, I snuck out of the hospital and jetted the fuck right back to Paulette.

Once I chucked the engine on, I sped out of the parking lot and zipped right back home. A minute later, my phone began ringing. I looked down and instantly recognized it was Sharday's number. I wonder why she had this new phone number. Then again, it was probably because her broke ass probably had got one of them new government phones. Broke hoe.

"Ms. Vernita, where are you? You still in the bathroom?"

"Nah, girl, I'm sorry but I had to zip back home because I forgot my medicine," I quickly lied. "And I also think I left my stove on! I'mma be back up there maybe later tonight. Is everything alright?"

"Oh, dang! Why you didn't come back to the room to tell us?"

"Girl, I had to leave immediately. I gotta take this medicine at a certain time. But I'mma be back up there. I promise," I lied again. Ain't no way in hell I was gonna meet Lamar again. Not now. Not never! If Alice ever found out what happened between us, I just knew she'd be devastated. And then she might have another heart attack and die...if she survives this one.

"Oh, alrighty then, well, call me once you come back up here. I may need another ride 'cause you know I ain't really getting along with my nieces and new like that," explained Sharday. I instantly rolled my eyes. Bitch better get on a bus or something because I shole wasn't running my ass back up to the hospital. At least not anytime soon. If I went back, I was gonna have to make sure that Lamar's ass wasn't there. "Okay, I will," I said then hung up.

Minutes later, I got back home, jetted right into my house, and made my way straight to my bathroom inside of my bedroom. I needed a hot ass bath with lots of Epsom salt and lavender. It was just too much bullshit going on. TOO MUCH. Just when I was getting my mojo, it seemed like life was throwing me some more bullshit to deal with.

After I had fixed my bath, I had now found myself laying in the tub sipping on some Hennessey and smoking me a big joint. If Sharday called, I was just gonna ignore her calls and then text her in the morning that I got super-sick and fell asleep.

I laid in the tub for about good two hours, damn near drifting off to sleep. The combination of the weed, liquor, and bath worked some good magic on me because I didn't feel as frazzled and nauseated anymore.

Although I was still a tad upset about Alice's condition, I was just gonna have to let that go and let God. Besides, there was nothing I could do other than just hope and pray everything would be okay. Yeah, a part of me felt very guilty for storming out of the hospital and abandoning my girl and her family in a time of need, but hey, it is what it is. I just needed to come up with a way to make sure Lamar never recognized me. But that just seemed impossible at this point.... I was gonna have to eventually meet this nigga face to face.

But just thinking about that cruise years back, chile, I was getting so moist thinking about it all over again. Lamar was such a gentleman, too. Too bad I didn't really wanna take things further with him. At the time I just wanted a good dick down and nothing else. Ironically, he wanted us to continue talking after the cruise ended but I wasn't going for any of that. Well, seemed like Alice found her a good catch... if she survived.

The following morning I woke up and at seven am on the dot and gave a rang to my oncologist's office. I wanted to book an appointment with this white man ASAP because I was going to tell him to his face I was going to get a second opinion about my cancer.

Ain't no way in the hell was I gonna be content anymore with just not doing nothing about this. I wanted to live. I had to live. Shit, I had too much in me to just let my life end this way. Like I told ya'll, Vernita wanted to go out soft as cream in my sleep. Ain't no way in the hell was I gonna allow myself to die a painful death. Cancer just seemed so depressing and grueling. No, ma'am. I wasn't gonna speak that into my life.

The receptionist luckily managed to squeeze me into a nine AM appointment. So, I quickly hopped out of the bed, took a shower, threw an outfit on, and made my way out of the door. But before I walked up to my car, I looked across the lawn and saw a neon Dodge Charger parked out in the front. My curiosity was immediately piqued as there was one thing I knew about those who drove Chargers – usually a nigga with the biggest dick came with one. A roughneck, felony-having, thug nigga, too! And ya'll already knew how I just craved me some felon nigga dick!

There was a part of me that wanted to quickly jot over and see if anyone was home to introduce myself. I just had to know who my new neighbors were. "Girl, if you don't stop with your crazy ass!" I mumbled to myself then chuckled. Shaking my head at my craziness, I just kept laughing to myself as I hopped in Paulette, chucked up the engine, and made my way to my oncologist's office.

The doctor's office wasn't too far away from my townhouse, so about seven minutes later I pulled into the parking garage, parked, and made my way inside. Once I checked in with the receptionist, I was escorted to an examination room and was told the doctor would be with me shortly.

Damn near thirty minutes went by and this old honky still hadn't come in yet. Shortly my ass! Didn't even peek his head in just to tell me he was running behind. This was exactly why I was gonna change my doctors. This white man had me all the way fucked up if he thought I had all the mothafuckin' patience in the world to wait on his ass. I had other shit to do today! And just like that, the door cracked open and to my surprise, some Asian man bumbled through the door with this weird smile on his face. "Mrs. Washington...Pleasure to see you. I'm Dr. Chang-Li?"

Slightly rolling my eyes to the ceiling, I replied, "I'm fine, doctor. Doing just well. I never met you before. Why are you here?"

"Well, I don't know if the nurse made aware but Dr. Newman had a sudden medical emergency and he's going to be out the office indefinitely," Dr. Chang-Li explained as he sat down and fumbled through some paperwork on his clipboard. "But, oddly enough, before you came in, I've been going over your scans, tests, and whatnot and I am so thoroughly confused..."

"Well! I'm glad you are confused because the reason why I came in today was just to let Dr. Newman know I am gonna be going to another doctor to get a second opinion about my diagnosis. I am not satisfied with his level of care! He just pretty much told me there was nothing much I could do but just let time go by and from there consider different pain treatments. I am not ready to die!"

Dr. Chang-Li pursed his lips and didn't say a word. He looked back down at his clipboard, rummaging through the thick wad of paper clipped to it. "I understand. Well, I, umm, I think before you do that, we should run a few more blood tests right now just to check on a few things. I, umm, I think getting a second opinion is a good thing but before you do that, I think we should just run a few more tests just to see what's the progress of the tumor."

My face screwed up into disgust. "The hell for what?!? Uh-unh. No. Hell no. Ya'll just trying to keep me. All ya'll care about is money!"

"Mrs. Washington…I, umm, I don't know how to explain this but I think it's very important that we go ahead and run another battery of tests on you just to—"

"Just to confirm what?!?" I said, but this time my tone was a bit loud and angry. I was so sick of their shit!

"Well, I think there is a remote possibility that there have been some small mix-ups in your files. I just wanna make sure that before you run and get that second diagnosis that you hear it from us first…"

All of a sudden, this feeling of confusion swarmed me. "What in the hell are you talking about?"

Dr. Chang-Li then said, "Well, Dr. Newman has been getting up in age and his vision has been a bit muddled. There is a possibility that your cancer may not be as advanced as we initially thought. In fact, you may not necessarily have cancer at all…"

My eyes widened with shock! "Excuse me? Say that again?!?"

"Yes, unfortunately, there may have been some serious issues with how Dr. Newman diagnosed your tumor. I have a feeling that you may have just developed a small, benign, non-cancerous mass. It's actually very common but Dr. Newman may have misread some of your charts and scans and diagnosed you with an advanced form of cancer."

"YOU HAVE GOT TO BE FUCKING KIDDING! So, you mean to tell me all this fucking time I didn't have cancer!"

"Please, ma'am, I'm sorry. I know this is very alarming and we are combing through all of Dr. Newman's files to see if this has happened to any other patients," the doctor tried to explain. However, by this point, every mothafuckin' thing this man had to say went through one ear and out the other! I'd be damned! For the last six months or so I had been walking around here thinking that my days on earth were numbered and that I'd soon be going on to glory! But, no! Lo and behold all this time I was fine. But I was still confused. "So, wait one damn minute! If I didn't have cancer then why in the hell do I have these dizzy spells and why is it that my vision goes in and out?!?"

"Well, that's very common symptomology associated with these types of benign tumors," he explained. He continued, "Vertigo. Dizziness. Loss of vision. Headaches. Sometimes these symptoms run congruent with worse tumors but nonetheless, in time, tumors like this stop growing, and sometimes they just go away altogether. That just might be the case with your situation."

I shook my head in total disbelief. A part of me was definitely relieved to a degree, that's if this doctor was telling the truth and he wasn't misdiagnosing me. But there was another part of me that was fuming with rage. "I oughta sue the hell out of ya'll! Ya'll could've killed me!"

"I know. I'm sorry, Mrs. Washington. I really do."

"I was walking around here with all types of anxiety and depression!"

"I completely understand, Mrs. Washington," Dr. Chang-Li said as he looked back at his clipboard. "This is a very unfortunate situation but the good thing is once we run these blood tests, we can make a final confirmation that everything, for the most part, is fine. But I have to ask, Mrs. Washington."

"What's that?"

"Well, going through your medical history. Some years ago, you were prescribed a medication called Mirapex. I believe your GP or family physician may have given it to you to help you with restless leg syndrome."

"Yes, I still take that from time to time. Especially when my legs get really bad. But it doesn't bother me. Why do you ask?"

"Are you aware of some of the other side effects of this drug?

My eyes boomed wide open once again. "No...What kind of side effects!"

Dr. Chang-Li cleared his throat and said, "Well, I don't know if your GP explained to you exactly how this drug works. Mirapex is the brand name but it's commonly known as Pramipexole. It's what we call an anti-Parkinsonian dopaminergic."

My mouth flung wide open. "Huh? What? All of this is over my head. Break it down in layman's term."

"Yes. Sorry." He cleared his throat again. "Well, Mirapex is usually prescribed to people who've been diagnosed with Parkinson's disease. It's supposed to help them with their twitches because their nervous system is failing. But sometimes it's used for people with restless leg syndrome. However, the drug is currently under a major investigation by the FDA because it can cause the growth of these types of tumors you are experiencing right now. Also, a lot of patients who are prescribed this drug end up...Umm...Well, they end up developing hypersexuality."

"I'm confused. Please, just get to the goddamn point! Ya'll done already made me mad!"

"This may seem like an inappropriate question but have you been sexually promiscuous since you started taking this drug?"

I didn't know what to say. "Ummm...I, ummm..."

"It's okay. I'm sorry I asked but you don't have to answer. But if you may, let us run the necessary blood tests so we can clear you and then my recommendation is that we switch you to another medication for your restless leg syndrome as soon as possible."

"I...." My mind was drawing blanks. "So, you said this medication can cause people to be promiscuous? I mean, I still have sexual relations every now and then but...But, umm, is that necessarily a bad thing?"

Dr. Chang-Li shrugged his shoulders. "I guess it depends on how comfortable you are with how the medication makes you feel. These types of drugs often turn people into compulsive sex addicts and gamblers. They feel like they are losing control. They often end up engaging in very risky sexual behaviors."

"Even in my age?"

"Yes...Even in your age."

"Wow...Okay...This is a lot! This is just too much! I'm gonna talk to my lawyer about all of this mess!"

"I understand completely, Mrs. Washington, but please, in the meantime, please let us run these additional tests."

"FINE!"

I had enough and I just wanted to get the hell up out of this office. This was just too much for my mind to handle.

Way too much shit was going on and now it seemed like the one thing that was for sure going to kill me was all this anxiety and panic. These doctors were straight-up reckless! I should've known better and tried to find me a black doctor because these white doctors I swore were on a mission to kill us black folk!

I agreed to let this damn new doctor run all the necessary tests on me. I had to stay behind an extra hour or so for them to quickly get the results. And lo and mothafuckin' behold, I was indeed cancer-free. Never even had it from the very beginning! Once I was done, I stormed out of the office and headed back to my car. Inside, I just sat in the driver's seat staring at the steering wheel wondering who was I really?!?

I couldn't believe that a medication could make me the freak I was.

Nonetheless, the more I thought about it the more it all made sense. I started taking that goddamn medication right around the time Clarence was admitted to long-term nursing after his stroke. This explained so much! I started taking that medicine and I turned into a whole ass sex addict! But, truth be told, I loved it. Yeah, there were moments where I felt out of control.

But, baby, I loved it! I absolutely loved all of it.

I'd be damned if I was gonna stop taking the medicine if it made Vernita fuck like a beast!

CHAPTER FOURTEEN

*I*t was a sunny yet cold Friday morning.

Ten am flashed on my alarm clock on my nightstand.

Ever since I had learned that I didn't have cancer and that this medication I had been taking all these years had been messing with my sex drive, I couldn't go anywhere.

For the last three days I had been holed up in my house, mainly sleeping in my bed. Although I was so tempted to continue taking the medicine, I realized I had to slow my roll. I didn't know what other side effects might result if I continued to take it. Thank God the tumor turned out not to be cancerous. However, the more I thought about it, the more I realized the doctor was right. I needed to think about getting off that medicine so it wouldn't cause me to have any other issues.

Sharday had been blowing my phone up asking me if everything was okay. I told her I was severely under the weather and that I didn't know if I was gonna be able to make it out to the hospital to be by Alice's side. She told me she would keep me updated about Alice's condition. She was still in a coma apparently. By the grace of God, the doctors had said that Alice didn't sustain that much injury to her heart or brain. However, they were keeping her heavily sedated to allow her body to heal as much as it could while they kept her under observation.

Now that I had been weaning myself off this medication, this weird depression set in and I was feeling so unmotivated. I tried to use some other herbal supplements to see if that could help me out with my energy levels, but nothing worked. I was zapped.

"Shit," I grumbled to myself as I managed to crawl out of the bed and made my way into the kitchen to fix myself a pot of coffee. That wasn't helping either but it was doing a good job of at least getting rid of the headaches I was experiencing from withdrawing from the medicine.

All of this completely made sense now that I had time to myself to really contemplate the last couple of years. Especially these last six months. When I found out I had cancer, I scaled back on taking the medicine and my sex drive went out the window. However, soon as I had started taking that medicine again when my leg twitching really got bad, it just so happened that I started to feel like my "old" self again. No pun intended.

After I fixed myself a cup of coffee, I sat down in my living room and returned back into a slump on the couch. I turned on the television and flipped through channels. Once I landed on one of these crazy court shows, I went into a daze.

My mind filled with so many dreadful thoughts and I really started to feel like I was really in my upper-seventies. Oh Lord, this heavy feeling was just too much. As some minutes passed, I just sat there with my eyes latched onto the television. But I wasn't paying attention at all. Everything just seemed like one big blur. Suddenly, a weird urge bubbled up in me. I had to take that medicine. I just wasn't feeling right. I needed it. It made me feel so different.

All of a sudden, I got up from the couch and like a zombie-walked back into my bedroom's bathroom. I went through my medicine cabinet and pulled out the bottle of Mirapex. I popped the cap open and took a deep stare at the sea of pills. I was prescribed to take two a day but I had it in me to double up. I was so damn drained that I probably needed the extra pills just to get my energy levels immediately back up. Anxious, I tapped four pills in my left palm and stared at them for a moment. Then, without hesitation, I threw them back in my mouth and swallowed them. I ran some cold water in my bathroom sink and then cupped some water in my palm to wash the pills down.

Hopefully, those pills would kick in soon. I couldn't waste any more of my day lounging around the house and I started to notice I was becoming very flabby. I needed to get into the fitness club ASAP! So, I took my robe off then hopped in the shower.

Some twenty minutes later I was in my gym attire. By now it was approaching eleven AM and as I made my way out of the door my phone started buzzing. I whipped it out of my purse and saw I had got a text message from Sharday. "Ms. Vernita! MAMA IS AWAKE!" she texted me.

My eyes beamed with excitement when I read her text message. "Thank God!" I clutched my chest and wanted to suddenly bust out with tears of joy. I quickly shot her a text back telling her that I was going to be at the hospital soon as I got done with my running my errands.

I threw my phone back in my pocketbook then pulled out my keys as I strolled up to Paulette. However, before I hopped in my car I heard the rumbling of that green Charger parked in my new neighbor's driveway. The windows were completely tinted so I couldn't make out if someone was in the driver's seat. Since it was very cold out, it could've been that whoever my new neighbor was had a remote ignition and started up their car while they were still inside the house. But then just as I was about to open up my car door and get in, the driver's side window of the Charger rolled down and I saw what looked like an older chocolate woman sitting behind the steering wheel. That caught me by surprise! Damn it! Chile, I just knew that car belonged to a roughneck nigga in possession of a big dick.

"Hey! You my new neighbor!" the woman shouted out as she flashed a huge smile, revealing a mouth full of gold teeth. Now that really took me by surprise!

"Hey there! How are you?" I smiled back as I waltzed over to the car. However, the closer I got the more I realized this woman had to be at least in her late-60s if not early-70s! Shit, she could've been my age! "I'm Vernita Washington," I said extending my hand through her window. She reached her hand back out. "I'm Rhodessa! Nice to meet you!" she exclaimed through a discernibly thick southern accent. She sounded like she was from Memphis. Maybe even Mississippi. I had to ask. "I saw you just moved in a week or so ago. You from Chicago?" "Naw! From Memphis. Me and my husband just moved here not too long ago. Well, he's actually from Chicago." My assumption was confirmed.

Rhodessa and I continued to talk for a few more minutes. She told me she and her husband, Ricky, had owned a number of businesses back in Memphis. They wanted a change of scenery so they sold them and decided to get into real estate flipping or something like that. Chile, I had no idea what all of that even meant. I was just so caught up in the fact this woman had a mouth full of gold teeth! Then the outfit she had on. Chile, she was dressed like she was about to go to one of those hood nightclubs on the South Side. Although it wasn't extremely freezing outside, I wonder if this woman knew just exactly how cold it got in Chicago. She was dressed like we were in the middle of an Atlanta winter. Chile, you know folks down south swore forty degrees was cold. Hell, that's a spring in Chicago. Anyways... Rhodessa's complexion was dark chocolate but this woman had this voluptuous purple weave stitched into her head. To top it off, her entire face was covered in the thickest makeup. Where in the hell was she going?!? Had to be a strip club! I was almost certain! Whew, chile, the ghetto!!!!

"So, yeah, Ricky and I have been flipping houses like I said for quite some time now," she continued talking about real estate and her other hustles. "Speaking of which, I wish this mothafucka would hurry up!" she roared smacking her teeth. She started honking her car horn. "Slow ass boy!"

"Well, anyways, Rhodessa, it was nice to meet you! I'm gonna go ahead and head to the health club," I said, trying my best to quickly end the conversation.

"Oh, it was nice meeting you too, Vernita! Maybe one day I can invite you over for some drinks and shit. My husband used to be a bartender! He can make some decent ass drinks, girl!"

"Sure, why not!" I said back to her although if she was seriously going to invite me I'd probably decline the invitation. She just seemed a bit too hood for my liking. Now, I ain't got anything against hood folks. Hell, I was born and raised in the ghetto. But soon as I got married to Clarence, I moved the hell out and spent a good chunk of my life living around nothing but white folks. Granted, Rhodessa was much older and probably didn't keep up no mess but I was just floored to meet someone who was in my age range who acted like they were much younger. Then again, who was I to judge? Hell, I pretty much had been doing the same thing. But hell, I was classy with mines. This chick just looked like she was doing the most. Although it wasn't my business to ask just exactly how old she was, I just knew from them wrinkles in her neck and those moles on her face that she was pushing at least seventy at the minimum. I had it in me to ask but I really wanted this conversation to be over already.

"FINALLY!" shouted Rhodessa. "Slow ass nicca!"

I turned around to make out who this Ricky that Rhodessa was married to. But babbyyyyy, let me tell you something! When my eyes latched onto Ricky, I almost collapsed right in the goddamn driveway. This was one fine specimen of a man! My pearl was thumping in my panties and if I didn't control myself, my juices were gonna freeze up in this cold.

Ricky was tall and thick. I mean, really thick. Not fat. But thick! He stood at least seven feet tall and had long dreadlocks running down his back. Although he was still feet away from me, from afar I could see he had piercing greenish hazel eyes. They were Asian-like, too! This boy had to be from somewhere. Probably some island in the Caribbean. Had to be! Oh and his skin! This nigga had a bronze glow, you hear me?!? A GLOW! He had this broad, chiseled face with this well-trimmed beard wrapped around his face. He walked up to me and I just stood there in shock. "Ohh, chile, this your husband?!?" I had to say to Rhodessa. "Yes he is!" she laughed.

Now, I hated to be that type of woman but as Ricky walked up to me, I was trying my best to figure out how this old ghetto hag could snatch up a fine ass nigga like this! Ain't no way hell! Rhodessa obviously had to be the breadwinner and this boy was just mooching off her. Shit, he could mooch off me too! Mooch off this fat cooch! But you know what – that was another thing – this boy looked like he was no older than thirty! How in the HELL did she get with a boy like this? Now if she invited me over for some drinks, I was definitely going to take up that invite!

Standing inches away from me, I couldn't help but stare at this nigga. I gave him a quick up-and-down scan. The boy had on these gray sweatpants, so you already knew the first thing I noticed was that elephant trunk-dick sitting right on the side of his leg!

My palms got sweaty and I felt the hair on the back of my neck rise. That medicine was now really kicking in and my ovaries were ready to explode! If I was thirty years young, Vernita would definitely be trying to have his baby! "Hey there! You must be our neighbor. I'm Rich but everyone calls me Ricky. Nice to meet you," Ricky said as he extended his hand. I reached my hand out and slowly shook his head. And oooh chile, his hand was so big, thick and hard. I usually hated it when men had fucked up hands and fingernails but when I felt those calluses on his palm, that sent me into a deeper frenzy. That meant this nigga could lift some serious weight. And if he could pull and push some serious weight, that meant he could he toss my ass right! Oh this ain't right! This ain't right at all! That medicine was really going into overdrive and there was a part of me that wanted to instantly fall to my knees and get to sucking that dick in the most expeditious manner. I wanted to drain them nuts of every sperm cell up in there. Baby, I wanted to suck the lining of his dick and ass!

Clenching my fists hard, I had to suddenly snap myself back into reality. I was making it way too obvious that I was feeling a certain type of way about this man. "You're a handsome man," I said as I pulled my hand back and then looked at Rhodessa. "Girl! Chile! Honey! You better be careful out here in these Chicago streets. One of these young bitches might try to throw themselves at your man!"

"Oh no! He know better! I'll fuck him up if he even think to look twice at one of these ratchet ass hoes," she laughingly roared. "Besides, no offense, but these Chicago girls are a bit rough around the edges. Dirty as hell too!"

Not saying anything back, I just shrugged my shoulders. But then I said, "Well, that's any city. I'm pretty sure they got some rough ones in Memphis, too!" Now I knew this old, washed up trick wasn't talking about folks. Her ass looked a hot mess with that crazy wig and outfit on.

"Shit, you ain't lying," Ricky commented.

Just like that Rhodessa's facial expression went from that of laughing to rage. She smacked her teeth then shouted, "Boy, get yo ass in the car. We already running late for this fucking meeting!"

"Bruh, calm down! I had to send off that e-mail!" Ricky said as he walked over to the front passenger door. Sensing the tension, I simply said, "Well, I'll catch up with you all later and let me know when you wanna have those drinks." "Yeah, I will," Rhodessa replied but this time a faint smile was on her face. I could sense the shift in attitude. Guess when I rebutted her and Ricky agreed she didn't take well to that. She rolled her window up and then quickly pulled out of her driveway. I spun around and then sauntered back over to my car. "Can't believe I got an old thot living next door to me. Hell, I thought I was the old hoe. Guess I'm beat!" I said to myself shrugging my shoulders. What a world we lived in. I wondered if her ass was on some medication, too.

CHAPTER FIFTEEN

he health club was virtually empty and that was exactly how I liked it. I hated working out when everyone and their mammy was here. It had been quite some time since I stepped foot in the gym but it shole did feel good to be back. Lord knows it did!

I was down on the main floor in the cardio section. I loved walking on a treadmill for a good hour while I listened to my music before I hit the weights.

As some Cardi B played into my earphones from my phone, I dance-walked on the treadmill. Baby, these thighs needed to get back to shape. And truth be told, once I got done walking on this treadmill, I needed to run over to the leg extension machine to work on my quads. My knees were starting to give me some issues. Perhaps I should look into getting me a personal trainer. However, when I walked in earlier and took a peep around for the trainers that were currently working here, none of them piqued my interest. And by piquing my interest, what I really meant was that none of them niggas looked good and I didn't want to waste my time getting worked out by some young stank heffa. I'd just continue to work out using the little knowledge I still had from when Markell used to work me out. I sure did miss that boy from time to time. Aside from the good dick, he was also a good conversation. We used to talk about everything!

Deep into my treadmill workout, I had my eyes laser-focused on the calorie counter. I was gonna make sure I burned at least four hundred calories. I closed my eyes and held onto the machine. My imagination went off thinking about nothing but dick. That medicine was starting to go into overtime in my body. Tomorrow I better scale back and go back to only popping two pills. All of a sudden, my eyes popped wide open when I felt a few taps on my shoulder. I glanced over my right shoulder and lo and behold, it was Mr. Juan! I immediately stopped the treadmill and yanked my earphones off. "Mr. Juan! How are you?!? You work out at this gym?!? I've never seen you here before!"

"Yes, ma'am!" he confidently answered with the biggest grin on sexy ass face, revealing those pretty ass teeth. Chile, I swore this Mexican man was soooooo delicious looking. I wanted to ride his face. Shit, he could ride my face! "I see you are getting it in! You look good for your age!"

"Oh my! Thank you so much for the compliment! You look pretty good yourself." Ooh chile, I just knew I was blushing. This pussy was blushing, too! Blushing and gushing!

"Gracias!" He grinned once again then licked his lips. Bitch, my knees were gonna buckle and I was gonna have to run to the bathroom and play with my pearl if this man didn't get immediately away from me.

"So, what kind of workouts do you do?" he asked as he started stretching. The boy had on nothing but a tight-fitting black tank top that revealed all of these tattoos running down his cut-up arms. So many veins were running all over his forearms. Chile, I could only imagine how many veins were running all over that dick of his. And he looked like he had a big ole pretty dick. But then as I thought about it, you know them Mexicans don't be circumcised. And uncut dicks was a huge turn off for me. Vernita does not like to pull no damn dick skin back. That's just nasty!

"Well, it depends. My workouts vary but I try to do exercises to keep my legs toned and what not. I don't wanna push too much weight because I'm not trying to look all butch. I'll leave that to young guys," I said chuckling.

"Yeah, I feel you. Well, I do light workouts too. I try not to lift too many weights because it affects my boxing."

My eyebrow raised. "You're a boxer?"

"Yeah. Golden Gloves champion all throughout high school!"

"Wow!" Oh yes, hunny, Juan was gonna have to pound on this pussy then.

"Not to infringe or anything but you said you were gonna call me about some moving needs. Were you still shopping around?"

"You know, I've been caught up in some other stuff that it totally slipped my mind that I was supposed to call you," I told him. "One of my good friends is actually in the hospital and I've been stressed out about that situation along with some other personal stuff."

"Oh, wow, I'm sorry to hear that."

"It's okay though."

"Well, perhaps I could give you a call later on tonight..." Juan hesitated then said, "Or maybe can I come by and we can talk in more detail?"

My eyes immediately shot open out of surprise. Come by my place? Hell, sign Vernita up! Baby, you can come and CUM anytime you want! "Oh, okay, well, I'll be free later on tonight. I just gotta go check on my friend because I just found out she's doing better. What time works for you, Mr. Juan?" I threw him a seductive grin.

Mr. Juan scrunched his face then licked his lips. "Sure. Perhaps...I'm free after five PM."

"Cool. Well, I need to finish my workout and then head out to the hospital. I still have your business card so I'll tell you when I'm free. How does that sound?"

"Sounds great, Ms. Vernita."

"Oh, you even still remember my name and everything, huh?"

"Of course," Juan said as he flashed another sexy grin then licked his lips. He rubbed his goatee and his eyes turned to curious slits as I noticed he quickly scanned my body up and down. Oh yeah! He was definitely feeling me! And I was feeling him too! Wow. You know...It must've been something in this medicine that had these boys all over me. Maybe this medicine made my natural smell waft in the air and these boys could pick up on it. After all, I know my pussy got a delectable smell and flavor to it. And I knew that for sure because anytime I sucked some dick after I let a nigga knock these sugar walls down, I just had to get a taste of myself.

"Excuse me, ma'am? Is everything okay?"

"Huh?" My face scrunched into utter confusion. In the blink of an eye, Mr. Juan had disappeared, and now standing in front of me was one of those ugly ass personal trainers. "What are you talking about?" I asked as I suddenly got annoyed. Damn, where did Juan just jet off too? What the hell just happened?

The personal trainer, who was short and kind of chubby, just stood there holding his waist with this look of confusion plastered on his face. "Well, you had been talking to yourself for quite some time. You were having a whole ass conversation as if someone was standing next to you or something. Is everything okay?"

I smacked my teeth and rolled my eyes. "Boy, get away from me. Let me guess. This is your way of trying to get me to sign up for them personal training sessions ya'll selling. Well, if that's that the case, I ain't interested. I already have a personal trainer!" This boy needed to get the hell on before I smacked the fuck out of him. But damn, where did Juan go! I looked around and didn't see a single trace of him. How in the hell did he just disappear that quickly?

"No, ma'am. Actually, my schedule is already booked and I'm not certified to work out senior citizens. Mr. Ron is the trainer with that type of expertise," he replied with a concerned raised brow. "But, like I said, I'd been watching you for a minute now and you were talking to yourself. At first, I thought you were on the phone."

"Please! I don't have time for the mothafuckin' games! Get the hell away from me! You know good and goddamn well I was standing here talking to someone! He was just standing there! He probably went to go lift some weights."

"No, ma'am," the trainer replied again shaking his head. He pursed his lips and walked off.

This strange feeling overcame me and then I immediately hopped off the treadmill. I scurried over to the weights section and looked for Juan but the entire area was clear. Literally nobody was in the gym.

Getting nervous and wondering how in the hell he just zipped off like that, I made my way over to the check-in desk because I had to ask the receptionist if she'd seen Juan.

"Excuse me, miss," I announced. She spun around in her seat and looked at me. "Yes?" she replied with this annoyed look on her face.

"One of my friends was just in the gym and I was wondering where he went. He was a tall Hispanic young man who looked no older than thirty. Very handsome with a nice beard. You seen him?"

"No, ma'am. You are actually the only one in here at the moment. Noon is a dead time and the only other people who came in were two people looking to get a membership," she replied then threw her eyes back onto her phone.

"Are you sure?"

"Yes…I'm sure. You're literally the only person here right now, ma'am."

Rage suddenly filled my core and I was ready to explode. "I think you lying to me. All of you mothafuckas are lying to me! Where is my friend?!?"

The receptionist girl, some young yellow fat girl with microbraids, shot me a look of concern. "Ma'am! Calm down! What's the problem?"

Just like that I snapped back into reality and clutched my chest out of surprise that I just had an unexpected meltdown like that. What in the hell was happening to me.

"Ma'am, is everything okay? Do you need me to call someone?" the receptionist asked again.

"No, I'm sorry, dear. I…I just, umm, I'm just a bit confused right now," I said as I rubbed my temples and I started to feel dizzy. Damn, the medication was kicking in big time. I began to feel a bit loopy and everything around me seemed like a faint blur. Was this the tumor though? I had no idea but all I knew at the moment was that I needed to head back home. I quickly spun around and dashed into the women's locker room to get my belongings. Rummaging through my locker, I stuffed my gym bag like a manic then slammed the locker door shut. But the second the door shut, standing next to me was Juan! My eyes exploded with fear and surprise. "What in the hell are you doing in here?!? You can't be in the women's locker room! Boy, are you crazy?!?" This boy was absolutely out of his mind for sneaking in her like this! But something wasn't right! How in the world did that girl at the front desk not know he was here?!? Then again, that heffa was so caught up looking at her damn phone that she probably didn't even notice him stroll in. And then that personal trainer was full of hot bullshit. Got me out here thinking I was crazy!

"I wanna fuck you, Vernita. I wanna be your Papi Chulo!" he seductively groaned then without hesitation grabbed me and slammed up against the locker.

"Boy, let go of me! Are you crazy?!?" I shouted to the top of my lungs.

"You want me! I knew it from the moment I met you! Stop resisting me!" He leaned in and started planting all types of kisses all over my neck. Then he slithered his tongue up to my earlobe and whispered in my ear, "I wanna get you fucking pregnant. I want you to have my baby!" He then looked me deep in my eyes and instantly my pussy began to quiver uncontrollably.

"Yes! FUCK ME! FUCK ME, MR. JUAN! FUCK IT!"

"Before I do that, I want you to ride my face," he said and without hesitation, he got down on the locker room floor and beckoned me to come sit on his face. I couldn't resist. My mind was racing with so many nasty thoughts. Not even the fear of getting caught fazed me. I didn't care. This was exactly what I wanted. What I needed in this very moment. He was playing a game on me and he was playing it well! I pulled my gym shorts and panties down in one swoop then tossed them off to the side. My light shaven kitty was now out in the open. My clit with throbbing and jumping. Juan licked his lips and growled, "Give it to me, Mamacita. That culo looks juicy!"

"Oh, I'mma give it to you alright!" And just like that I jumped right on his face and started gyrating. Holding onto his head, I felt his tongue slither between my clit and ass. With his thick lips, he sucked the shit out of my pearl. Tightening my thighs around his head, I felt his beard tickle my inner thighs. My eyes rolled in the back of my head and I knew I was gonna squirt all over the place. "YES! SLOB ON THAT CAT! GET IT NICE AND WET FOR THAT DICK!" I groaned.

"Piss all over me!" I then heard him mumble.

"You want me to do what?!?" I shouted back to him.

"I said piss all over my face. I wanna drink your pee! DO IT!" he commanded.

Now that right there was a whole level of freakiness! As I felt him continue to devour my juicy guts, I succumbed to his nastiness. I drowned him out with my urine. "Yes, Mami! Don't stop!" he begged as he tried to drink up as much as he could. I glanced down and saw a puddle beginning to grow on the locker room floor around his head.

"MA'AM! WHAT ARE YOU DOING?!?"

Those loud words pierced me back into reality. My eyes widened with shock, I stared at the manager of the club standing there looking mortified along with some other health club employees.

As I continued squatting on the ground, I glanced down and saw that Juan was once again gone. But I kept pissing all over the floor. "I…umm…I….LEAVE ME ALONE!" I screamed.

"Yo! Someone go call the police! This old bitch is FUCKING CRAZY!" the manager, a tall and slender black fellow, screamed. "Bitch fucking pissed all over the goddamn floor!"

CHAPTER SIXTEEN

*S*itting in the back of a police cruiser with handcuffs slapped on my wrists, I was distraught. The cuffs were so tight. I ain't never think in a thousand years I would get arrested, let alone get arrested for peeing all over a gym's locker room floor! That medicine obviously had me hallucinating and I was terrified that I was seeing things that just simply weren't real!

Truth be told, I didn't even know if Juan was a real person. Was I imagining him all this time? Who else did I imagine? Shit, I truly had no idea and the thought that I was losing my mind had me wracked with so much dread and terror. Lord knows soon as I got back home, whenever that was, I needed to throw that medicine away and talk to the doctor about what was going on.

I was so disturbed by everything that went down. As I sat in the back of the policeman's car, tears ran down my cheeks. "Lord, I can't believe this is happening to me! I don't know what's wrong with me!" I sobbed and my body shivered.

"Ma'am, please, just gather yourself and calm down," the burly white officer said as he sat in the driver's seat of the squad car. We were parked in the parking lot of the gym. There were four other cop cars surrounding us. Blue police lights flashed all throughout the parking lot and I knew this was creating a scene. As curious gymgoers passed by, some of whom I'd recognized, they caught a glimpse of me in the back of the policeman's car. I just knew folks were gonna be gossiping about me once they found out what had happened. Lord, this meant I was gonna have to probably move out of the neighborhood.

Some moments later, another police officer walked up to the car I was sitting in. The police officer who was in the driver's seat rolled down his window. The other officer, a taller older black man, leaned in to the window and said, "the manager doesn't want to press charges, so she's free to go. However, they've banned her from coming." He then threw his attention at me and said, "Ma'am, you are free to go but you cannot step foot on the gym's premises ever again. Your membership has been officially canceled."

"Officer, I'm so sorry! I truly am! I don't know what came over me. I believe it's the medication I am taking," I tried to explain as tears continued to drench my cheeks. I wanted to wipe my face so bad but I couldn't because my hands were behind my back.

"Well, if that's the case then, you need to get into contact with your doctor and let them know what's going on. In fact, we can take you the hospital if you feel like you're experiencing some sorta psychiatric distress," the officer explained.

"All of that isn't necessary! I just need to get home and just sleep off this medicine. I took too much this morning and I believe it really caused me to have these hallucinations!" I exclaimed. "I'm really sorry. All of this is just so embarrassing."

The officer walked over to the back passenger door, opened it, and then pulled me out. As a few more gymgoers passed by, I looked at a few of them and they shook their heads out of shame. The officer took the handcuffs off me and I immediately massaged the stinging pain out of my wrists. They were hurting so bad. They had me in the back of that car for at least a good hour.

"Now, please ma'am, as I stated before, please leave the premises immediately and you are not to return ever. Just count yourself lucky that the gym manager isn't pressing charges against you," the officer said then escorted me over to my car.

Once I hopped in my car, the officers trailed me back to my townhouse. I quickly got out of my car and made my way inside the house. My heart racing with anxiety, I felt like I was going to pass out at any moment. That medicine was working overtime all over my body. As crazy it sounded, even when I was in the back of the squad car, I kept seeing visuals of Mr. Juan. My insides were fired up and although I didn't have the ability to touch myself while I was in the back of the squad car, I kept having orgasm after orgasm! What in the world was going on?!? I didn't realize this medicine was this potent!

I dashed down the hallway and made my way into my bedroom's bathroom. Once inside, I flicked the light switch on but I exploded into a scream when I saw Rhodessa staring at me in the mirror! "HOW IN THE HELL YOU GET INTO MY HOUSE?!?" I screamed to the top of my lungs, almost ready to fight this old, crazy bitch! But when I quickly gathered myself and stared at the mirror, Rhodessa was just standing there. I didn't see myself at all in the mirror. As I raised my right hand to my face to check to see if I was even real or if I was hallucinating again, I saw Rhodessa raise her right hand as well. Then I raised my left and Rhodessa did the same. I stormed closer up to the mirror and began to poke and prod my face. And that was when it hit me. I was

Rhodessa. "WHAT IS GOING ON?!? Why do I look like this?!? I'm going crazy! No! HELL NO! I do not look like this?!?"

Freaked out, I stormed out of my bathroom then flew toward my bedroom window. Pulling the curtains back, I looked across the lawn and saw that the townhouse next to me still had a "For Sale" sign up on the lawn.

Was Rhodessa even real?

Was her fine ass husband Ricky even real?

Was I hallucinating all of this?!? Baby, this was just too much for me to handle!

Just to make sure I hadn't fully lost my mind, I stormed back into the bathroom and saw my real self in the mirror. "Ohhh, chile!" I clasped my chest out of relief. Without hesitation, I rummaged through my medicine cabinet and pulled down that horrible medication. Once I popped the lid to the bottle open, I threw all the pills down the sink and ran the faucet. "Pills got me fucked up!"

Back in the bedroom, I pulled out my cell phone and gave that Dr. Chang-Li a call! He had to know about what was happening. I needed help immediately. Some seconds later, the receptionist at the office picked up and I asked her to put the doctor on the phone. "Good afternoon, Mrs. Washington. Is everything alright? How are you feeling?" he asked once he answered the phone.

"Doctor! That medicine! I took it again and I think I took too much of it and I've been hallucinating! That medicine got me going crazy!" I cried into the phone. My breathing was rapid and I tried to control my fluttering heart rate.

"Calm down, Mrs. Washington! I'm so glad you gave me a call because I was worried you'd continue taking the medication. We need to get into contact with your GP now and I'm going to explain to them everything that's happening," he explained. "If you still need to take a medication for your restless leg syndrome, we might have to switch you over to a new medication, but you need to throw away that medicine now! Hallucinations are one of the main side effects of the drug!"

"I know! I get that now! I was hallucinating all this morning!" I said back to him as I shivered. It seemed like the medicine was hitting me waves. My insides were once again quivering and I just had every urge to get the hell up off this phone and go find some quick dick!

"Mrs. Washington, has this been the first time you've hallucinated!" Dr. Chang-Li asked.

"Yes! I am quite certain! This was the first time ever something like this happened."

"What exactly happened?"

I went silent for a moment. Then I said, "I'm too embarrassed to say but it is bad! Very bad!"

"Okay, I understand. Mrs. Washington, we may also need to bring you in for some additional evaluations just to rule out that it is truly the medicine causing these hallucinations. The mass on your brain may be causing these issues as well."

"Why?!?" My face scrunched out of disgust. "I'm tired of all these goddamn tests! You said I don't have the cancer no more! I done did enough of these tests now! NO! Hell no! I can't! I can't do any of this anymore! I gotta go! I threw the medicine away! I can't handle any of this anymore!"

"Please, Mrs. Washington, please just calm down. You sound very manic right now. Do you need me to send someone by to check up on you? We can have you admitted to the hospital!"

"HOSPITAL! YOU GOT ME FUCKED UP! I AIN'T GOING TO NO MOTHAFUCKIN' CRAZY HOUSE! I SAID I THREW THE GODDAMN MEDICINE AWAY! Now don't fuck with me!"

The walls were closing in. Everything around me was spinning.

"No, Mrs. Washington! Not that type of hospital. Please, just try to calm down and get yourself together for a moment. What I mean is I think it's important we admit you to run these tests just to rule out any possibilities that the tumor could be causing these hallucinations along with any other personality change."

"NO! I SAID NO!" I hung up the phone and tossed it off to the side.

I shot up from the bed and began manically pacing my bedroom floor. I wasn't going crazy! Ain't nothing wrong with me! It was just this medicine fucking with me! That was it! I'd be damned if I was gonna let these doctors keep messing with me!

Needing to immediately soothe my nerves, I stormed out of my room and made my way into the kitchen. I pulled down an unopened bottle of some Courvoisier, twisted the cap off, and took a huge swig. The liquor burned like hell as it ran down my throat but within seconds a sense of calm came over me. Hell, I needed some reefur too!

I stood in the kitchen for a few more moments just to gather my thoughts then I marched back into my bedroom. I grabbed my cell phone off the bed and saw I had a missed call from Sharday. And just like that I had forgotten I was supposed to go to the hospital since Alice was now out of her coma. I shot her a text message and told her that I'd try my best to make it up there but I was still feeling under the weather.

I needed to just sleep off this medicine and hope my life would return back to normal. My only fear though was that I'd slip right back into depression and not have the motivation to do anything. But at this point, I'd rather take depression than going crazy.

❄

A week had gone by and once again I found myself holed up in my house. Absolutely drained, I couldn't muster up not a single iota of strength to get up out of the bed. When I did, it was only to tinkle or to get something to eat from my kitchen. And I was barely eating. I'd have an apple or an orange here and there. For the past few days, my stomach had been in knots. Withdrawing from the medicine had been working something serious over my body.

A few people had been calling me over the last few days to check in on me but I wasn't answering anyone's phone calls. I was way too out of it. I did feel bad though that I hadn't checked on Alice yet.

It was Tuesday morning and as I looked over at my alarm clock I saw that it was almost noon. Since I had been off that medicine I had been sleeping for almost twelve or thirteen hours every damn night. It was like my body was trying to make up for lost sleep.

Just as I was about to slide out of the bed and take a shower, my phone starting to buzz. I looked down at the screen and recognized the number. It was the doctor's office. "Oh, Lord, what in the hell do they want with me now?!? I done told them I don't want no more damn tests done on me!"

Reluctant to answer the phone, I sat there in the bed as I watched the phone continue to vibrate. But something told me to answer so I quickly yanked the phone of its charger then answered, "Hello?!?"

"Mrs. Washington! How are you? This is Dr. Chang-Li! I'm just checking in on you."

I rolled my eyes. "I'm fine. But I can't talk long."

"Okay, no worries. I know the last conversation we had

was a bit rough but I just wanted to reach out and let you know that we are here to help. I know everything has been pretty brutal this year but I just wanted to let you know that I've been thinking about you and I am just concerned about the tumor."

"What are you concerned about? You said that it's not cancerous?!?"

"Right. But that doesn't mean that the tumor still may not have some sort of impact on your brain health. It could also possibly grow and then cause a hematoma which may lead to death. This is a very serious matter. Especially considering how long you'd been on that medication," he explained.

Silent, I sat there for a second trying to quickly conjure up a response. But hearing him plea with me made me realize he was right. Absolutely right. What was I doing?!? This man was a doctor trying to save my life. I was being absolutely hard-headed. "Okay, doctor, you got me. I'll come in and do the tests. I've just been feeling so funky though."

"That is understandable. I'm glad you've had a change of heart," he replied. "As for the depression, it's my recommendation we get you to talk to a psychiatrist to do an eval and from there you could be prescribed an antidepressant to help with everything that's going on. Sometimes those dopaminergic drugs have very bad withdrawal and can leave patients worse off."

"Okay, that can work but just to let ya'll know, I'm still very upset about how this entire situation unfolded. I'm very disappointed in the level of care and I will still be filing a complaint against Dr. Newman and I will still be consulting with my attorney about this type of medical negligence. I'm a senior citizen and you all should be very aware of the fact that every health decision at this point in my life matters!"

"Understandable. Do what you have to do. But in the meantime, please just give me a time when you can come in so we can get those additional tests going," Dr. Chang-Li said as I could hear him ruffling through some papers.

"I can come in this afternoon. Does that work?"

"Yes! Two PM!"

"Good!"

I hung up the phone and went straight to the shower. Later that afternoon I went to the doctor and let Dr. Chang-Li perform all the tests he needed. That same day he referred me over to a psychiatrist. The following day, after talking with a psychiatrist, who just so happened to be a very smart young sister, I was put on a new medication to help me deal with the depression I was experiencing. Hopefully, this medication didn't have any crazy side effects.

CHAPTER SEVENTEEN

*T*wo weeks flew by and just as it was the start of spring, I was experiencing a start to a new life.

I was back to feeling like my old self. But not my sinning self. I was filled with so much joy and energy, and by the grace of God, I was feeling a thousand percent better!

GOD IS STILL ABLE!

Now that I was getting my health together and feeling like a new woman, I finally had the strength and energy to finally get around the neighborhood. Most importantly, I had enough strength to finally pay Alice a visit. That was actually what I had planned on this sunny, windy afternoon.

Sun rays pierced through my bedroom blinds. I stood in my bedroom finishing up this Yoga exercise DVD I had playing on my television.

You know I never would've thought in a million years that a medication could have that type of impact on you. But, honey, let me tell you something – I was somewhat relieved to have been delivered from that demon of sex addiction!

Now I was truly free from that crazy drug, I realized that stuff had been driving me crazy all these years and had really changed my personality. That stuff turned me into a nasty, scandalous woman and I never wanted to go down that road again.

While there was a part of me that still craved companionship and to an extent enjoyed all of my sexual relations, I felt so guilty knowing that I was out there running those streets like that. That was just not me.

The more I had time to let my mind, body, and soul heal, the more I realized how I really missed Clarence. While we didn't have the best marriage when it came to sex, he was a good man and really took good care of me.

Sure, there were times where I wanted to leave because I wasn't able to start a family. But our marriage definitely had a lot of happy moments and I would be forever grateful for all the good times he gave me.

I just couldn't believe that while he was down and out in that nursing home, I was out there messing around with all of these young boys. But that was the past. Let bygones be bygones. It was time to move forward and clean up what I messed up. I was starting my life over again. I had made up my mind I ain't hoeing no more 'cause a whore can't make it through the door! So, the first thing I had to clean up was my friendship with Alice.

I finished my exercise and then went straight to my bathroom to get ready. After hopping out of the shower, I threw on a light outfit and then took all of my medicines. There was still a part of me that was so apprehensive of having to take all these medications given all of what I went through. However, baby, I was just so thankful that Dr. Chang-Li didn't give up on me and saw that I received excellent medical care.

After he ran a few more tests on me, it was determined that the non-cancerous tumor growing on my brain wasn't having any real impact on my health and that it would soon shrink down due to this other medicine I was currently taking.

Also, I had now started talking via phone to my psychiatrist and therapist, Dr. Kimberly Jackson. She was a wonderful young woman and I was so relieved that I had me a black doctor who could help me get my mind right. She was helping me manage my mood.

Now the only thing that had me a tad concerned was that she did tell me that there was a possibility I'd experience some weird side effects from taking the medication. But, baby, let me tell you something right now! If I started to feel any type of funniness going on in my mind, I was going to stop taking that mess. At that point, I'd just have to rely on prayer and some of my herbs to help me through. I had to say though that the one thing that had me relieved was that the hallucinations I'd been experiencing being on that Mirapex drug weren't as bad as it could've been. Dr. Kimberly told me that those drugs could've turned me into a full-blown psychotic!

After I got done taking my medicine, I made my way out of the house and hopped in my car. Strolling down the avenue, I pulled out my phone and dialed Alice to let her know I was on the way. She had been discharged from the hospital a few days ago and we finally spoke by phone last night. We talked at great length about everything that had happened. She was such a true friend indeed and told me that even when she was down and out, not knowing whether or not she was gonna live or die, she was still worried about me. Her saying that made me feel so bad and I felt like such a bad friend for not having the courage to visit her. But the fact that I had messed around with her fiancée some years ago still bothered me. But it was time to fess up to her to tell her everything if our friendship was going to survive.

✻

"Vernita!" Alice cried when she swung the door open and lunged at me! Hugging her back tightly, we both cried in each other's arms. "Girl, it's sooo good to see you!" I sobbed as we rocked each other.

She planted kisses all over me and then tugged me inside her house. Quickly walking over to the living room, we both sat down on the couch. "Girl, you still looking good!" I commented when I noticed she was still in good shape and didn't even look like the heart attack did anything to her.

"Sis, stop it! The doctor told me I had lost like fifteen pounds when I was in the hospital," Alice said smiling. "But I'm just glad to be alive by the grace of God!"

"Yes, I am too! I am so glad you made it, girl! I don't know what I would've done had you passed on," I said.

"But I am still so happy to know how everything turned out with your cancer. That would've been more devastating, Vernita. See, God is working some miracles throughout the world."

"Chile, tell me about it! You ain't lying!"

She and I spent the next hour or so talking about all of our health woes. "It's just so crazy how everything just went from good to bad to now being back to good it seems," she commented.

"Yeah, well, that's just life, I guess. We just gotta do our part and get closer to God's will. I've been reading my Bible more and trying to get right with God," I said. I was being completely honest, too! I had been missing going to church. "I need to find me a new church home though," I said.

"Why? You don't like Pastor Meeks? He's such a wonderful man!" Alice said as she flipped through some television channels on her TV.

"Yeah, he just be having folks up in church too long. I love the Lord but I can't be up in no church for no eight hours. I just need to hear the word and leave," I said shaking my head. I couldn't tell her but the real reason why I didn't want to go back to Mt. Plymouth, my old church, was because I had slept with the Pastor. Don't judge me. Anyways...

"But yeah, I'm thinking about going over to Pilgrim Baptist on 115th."

"Oh yeah! I loves Dr. Franklin. Now, he's a good preacher," Alice said then started laughing. "This is so hilarious though. I would've never thought you and I would be having a conversation about church. Seemed like just months ago we would've been talking about nothing but men."

"Yeah, you right! But things gotta change. Vernita gotta slow her roll," I nervously laughed. Now was the time I had to tell her the truth. Butterflies filled the pits of my stomach and I didn't know exactly how I was going to roll out this confession. But I had to get it off my chest. I had pretty much concluded that although I felt guilty for messing with this man years back, she had no right to hold a grudge against me because she wasn't dating him then. They hadn't known each other at that point. At least I didn't think they did. I simply went on a cruise, met him and we did our thing. There was nothing more to it. Hell, he was so adamant that we have a relationship but I didn't want one. And now I was glad that didn't happen because, truth be told, Alice would've never had a chance to meet him and now experience true happiness.

Just like that our conversation had shifted to the topic of Lamar. "Lamar is such a good man though. I'm so glad I met him."

Before I confessed, I just had to make sure that I wasn't going crazy and that this indeed was the same Lamar. I was pretty sure it was though. He had a face I'd never forget. Even with me taking that crazy medication I could still vividly remember the good time we had on that cruise. Oooh, chile, just thinking about it had me getting so moist. But just like that, I quickly deadened those Jezebel-ish thoughts.

"So, what exactly does this Mr. Lamar do again?" I asked. "You know, it was crazy because when you were in the hospital, he had his security with him. He must have some money…"

Alice's beaming smile suddenly turned flat and she pursed her lips shut. She cleared her throat and then said, "Well, I didn't want to tell you this but, umm, Lamar used to be a big-time basketball player back in the late 70s," she said.

Now, I never knew exactly how old Lamar was but I knew he had to be in his late 50s or early 60s. He didn't look like it though. Didn't fuck like it either. Oh, hell! *Stop thinking nasty, Vernita!* Ya'll excuse me but I just couldn't help but to think about just how he handled my body those nights on that cruise!

"So what are you trying to say? You acting all weird about it and whatnot," I said back to her.

"Well, he's a multi-millionaire. But I didn't want him to flaunt his money around nobody. That just ain't my style, you know?"

"What?!?" I was shocked but then not really. Something even back then told me Lamar had to have some money. But damn! Millions? "When you say multi-millionaire, what exactly do you mean?"

"Well, I didn't want to ask him but I just had to know… He's worth at least twenty million…"

My mouth flung wide open! "Girl, you hit the damn jack-pot! 'Scuse my language!"

"I know but.."

"But what?"

"I just…I just know our lives are gonna change. Honestly,

I didn't even know why he was so interested in me. I mean, we hadn't even had sex yet…He's been moving pretty quickly, too!"

Damn, no sex?!? Now I was feeling even more guilty. Oh, God, this was gonna be bad. I had it in me to suddenly not tell her anything. But then I heard a voice tell me it was still the right thing to do. I had to tell her. *Don't hold back, Vernita. It is what it is…*

"Well, I'm so glad you found a man who is gonna treat you right and treat you like a Queen, girl. You deserve it!"

"Yeah, I'm just still so nervous. We are actually supposed to have dinner later on tonight to talk about our wedding. He wants to elope too. Get married in Mexico."

"Then do it! Why you wanna have a big wedding any damn way?!?"

"I just want all of my friends and family to be there!"

"That is a good point but still…Take advantage of it! Especially considering everything that happened."

"Yeah, well, that's a good point indeed."

The two of us got quiet and then stared off at the television. Some court show was blaring on the television. Then the voice sounded off in my head again – *Tell her Vernita…Tell her…*

I glanced over at her and gently placed my hand on her shoulder. "Alice, I got something I need to tell you. Please, I do not want you to be mad at me."

"Tell me what?" Her face twisted with confusion.

Anxiety bubbled deep down in me.

I closed my eyes and took a long breath. "Well…It's complicated but…"

"But what?"

I went silent. Lord, please, I didn't have the strength to do it. But the voice said again, *"Just do it. You need to let go and let God…"*

I exhaled… "I…Well, remember years ago when I went on that cruise?"

"Yeah?" Alice's brow raised out of curiosity. "Please… Vernita, just tell me what's going on. I don't like surprises like this…"

"Well…"

Suddenly Alice clenched her stomach and squeezed her eyes shut. "Hold that thought," she muttered. She sounded anguished.

"Everything alright?" I asked sounding concerned.

"You got me nervous now my stomach is hurting." All of sudden Alice blasted up from the couch. "I need to use the restroom. I feel like I'm gonna vomit…"

"Is everything alright though? Do I need to call someone?"

"No, I'm fine…It's just this medicine the doctor got me on sometimes causes extreme nausea. I'll be right back," she said as she then quickly made her way toward the staircase. I followed her up the staircase and feeling very concerned, I asked, "Are you sure though, girl?"

"I'm sure," Alice said as she labored up the steps.

"Here, let me help you," I said as I got to her side and helped her upstairs. Lord knows she didn't need to be running up and down the stairs like this. I was pretty certain the doctor would agree with me as well. "Take your time, Alice!" I told her then once we approached the door of the guest bathroom, she flew inside, closed the door, and locked it. I had to stand by and listen just to make sure she was okay.

Although I wanted to listen to this voice and tell her the truth about everything, another voice told me to back and down. This wasn't the right time. This would be absolutely devastating to her. Hell, she just got out of the hospital. This type of confession would surely break her heart!

Still standing guard near the door, I leaned against the door and listened to see if she was okay.

"Ohhh, shit!" she bellowed and then I heard the sound of what had to be diarrhea blasting out of her rectum and into the toilet. Then a bomb of farting went off. My eyes widened out of disgust as I did not need to hear all of that. What kind of medicine did the doctor have her on?!? Her bowels sounded very loose. Now that I thought about, shit, maybe I needed to ask her what the doctor gave her because my bowels lately had been a bit clogged up. Chile, I haven't used the bathroom in nearly two days. I tried everything. Prune juice. Fiber. Hell, I even took me some milk of magnesia and nothing was working. Perhaps that was a side effect of these new medications Dr. Kimberly and Dr. Chang-Li had me on.

Some moments later I heard the sound of her spraying air freshener in the bathroom. Then the sound of the toilet flushing along with the faucet running escaped the door. Thank God nothing was seriously wrong. Just sounded like whatever she was taking just gave her the runs.

The bathroom door flung open and I took a few steps back because I'd be damned if I was gonna smell what came up out of her.

"Sorry about that, chile! Oooh, Lord, sometimes that medicine got my colon doing jumping jacks!"

"It's okay. I need me something like that 'cause my bowels are locked up," I said.

We both exploded into laugher then slowly waltzed over near the staircase. We began to head back down but then Alice turned around and said, "Please…Just go ahead and tell me what happened? Did you catch something on that cruise?"

"No!" I snapped. "Why would you say that?"

"Well, what else could it be?"

I took another deep breath then exhaled. "I slept with

Lamar." I just let it out. I don't know why it came out that way but it did.

"Excuse me?" Alice's face suddenly turned sour. "What did you say?"

"Girl, please don't be mad at me but I had messed around with Lamar while I was on that cruise."

Alice stood there for a moment. This empty look filled her gaze at me almost as if she was staring at her dead mother. "Wait, I just need you say what I thought you said. You did what now?"

"I said I slept with Lamar, Alice. Damn, now, please don't make me say it again!"

"WHEN!?!? HOW?!? You lying!" she roared, her angry voice echoing all through her house.

"Please calm down, Alice! You're gonna put too much stress on yourself. Let's just go downstairs and let me explain everything!"

Rapidly shaking and waving her finger no at the same time, she said, "Nuh-uh! No! You need to tell me every moth-afuckin' thing about this bullshit right now! This is probably the real reason why your lousy ass didn't even bother to come by and visit me! Isn't it?!?"

"Alice, please! Let's just sit down and talk about this!"

"No! I ain't got nothing to say about it! I should've known! SHOULD HAVE MOTHAFUCKIN' KNOWN! I just knew this was all too good to be true!" she cried. "My own damn friend fucked my man! The only man who ever really loved me!"

"Alice!" I cried as terror and dread filled my body. I damn near was about to vomit myself. See, I knew something told me not to say anything. I didn't know why I listened to that stupid ass voice going off in my head!

"DON'T SAY ANYTHING TO ME! JUST GET THE FUCK UP OUT OF MY HOUSE!"

"Alice! Don't do me like that. This was years ago! On the cruise!"

"I don't trust a GODDAMN THING you are saying! You gon come up in my mothafuckin' house and tell me some bullshit like that?!? Bitch, are you crazy?!?" Her face turning red, I could see she was becoming extremely flustered and I really needed to calm her down before she ended up having another heart attack."

"Alice, please, let's just go downstairs and talk about this before you get yourself all worked up. Just calm down, baby! I can explain everything!"

"DON'T SAY SHIT TO ME, YOU NASTY OLD BITCH!" she thundered. "BUT YOU KNOW WHAT! NOW THAT YOU TOLD ME WHAT YOU DID! I'M GLAD I DID WHAT THE FUCK I DID YEARS AGO! I DON'T REGRET ANY OF IT NOW!"

My brow raised out of absolute confusion. "What are you talking about, Alice?!?" I cried back to her as my body shuddered out of control. I damn near had to sit down myself to get myself together.

"Hah! I guess this is all karma! I'll be damn! You fucked my man! Well, guess what, honey?!? I fucked your man! YUP! Baby, I FUCKED CLARENCE! I WAS FUCKING HIM FOR YEARS. AND GUESS WHAT! HIS DICK WAS GOOD! He used to complain about your dry ass crotch all the time! Baby, he was dicking me down and eating me out so good!"

My eyes widened with absolute surprise. I clutched my mouth. "You're lying! Stop lying! You're just saying that! That is a horrible thing to say! How dare you?!?"

"BITCH! I am not lying! I FUCKED CLARENCE. BELIEVE IT, BABY! Yeah, he may have had a shrimp dick but, bitch, he knew how to work that little dick of his! And his tongue. He used to eat my ass every night and would still go home to kiss your raggedy ass! All them years you were kissing him, bitch, you were tasting my ass and my pussy! YEAH, BITCH!"

"NOW STOP IT! STOP IT RIGHT NOW, ALICE! I DONE HAD ENOUGH OF YOU! YOU STOP THIS RIGHT NOW! YOU ARE LOSING YOUR MIND!"

"NAH, BITCH! I AIN'T LYING! YOU WANT PROOF? BITCH, I KNOW CLARENCE HAD ONE TESTICLE! HE ONLY HAD ONE BALL! HIS RIGHT BALL! AND I USED TO LICK ON THAT EVERY NIGHT TOO! AFTER HE GOT DONE EATING MY ASS, OF COURSE!"

My heart completely stopped! Right then and there I knew she was absolutely telling the truth. Clarence indeed only had one testicle. And it was for that very reason we could never conceive. We tried for years to have a child but it never happened. Two years into our marriage, Clarence was diagnosed with testicular cancer. At the time, the doctor told him he had no other choice but to remove his left testicle. After the surgery, we were told that our chances of conceiving were still pretty high but it never happened. We tried everything for a decade until I became too old to have children. Hearing this almost induced a heart attack and I could feel my chest tighten.

"HAHAH! Yesss, bitch! Gon' come in my mothafuckin' house and try to spill secrets. Well, take that!" she shouted at me as I fell into what seemed like an asthma attack.

"You ain't right!" I cried. "Yo ass ain't right! Why would you do that to me! All these years and this how you do me?!?"

Hurricane-like tears fell out of my eyes and all I wanted to do was just fall out and die. Lord, this was too much to handle! Why were you doing this to me, God?!?

"OH, and another mothafuckin' thing! Yo ass may have not had a kid! But guess what, bitch, Clarence shole did have one! BY ME! AND HER NAME IS SHARDAY!"

I gasped. "You're lying! STOP IT!"

"NOPE! NOT LYING! BITCH, I STILL GOT THE DNA TEST!"

"STOP IT! JUST STOP IT!" Panicking, the walls began to close in and dizziness overcame me.

"Bitch, fuck you! Just get the hell up out of my house!"

"CLARENCE WOULDN'T DARE!"

"Baby! Clarence was lying to you! The reason why he couldn't have babies with your ugly, raggedy ass is because after he got pregnant with me, he got a vasectomy! Now get the hell up out of my house!" she bellowed as she pointed down the staircase toward the door.

Those words instantly triggered me. Everything around me turned red. "YOU FAT BITCH! I'MMA KILL YOU!" I didn't know what came over me but without hesitation, I lunged at Alice and pushed her down the staircase!

"AHHHHHHHHHHH!" she screamed as her body tumbled down the long staircase. Everything happened instantaneously and before I had a chance to process every-thing she was now down the floor. She didn't move at all.

Still standing at the top of the staircase, reality set back into my mind and I saw Alice sprawled out near the foyer. "Alice! ALICE!" I cried out as I quickly made my way down the stairs. However, as soon as I got close enough to her, I saw she had a puddle of blood leaking from her head... "OH, NO! ALICE! WAKE UP! OH, LORD, LORD, LORD! WAKE UP, BABY!"

PART II

18

VERNITA

I kept screaming to the top of my lungs as I panicked seeing Alice on the floor, her body completely motionless.

Baby, my body was filled with so much heightened terror. I didn't know what came over me. However, the moment her ass hit me with that bombshell revelation, something in me just compelled me to attack her. But I really didn't mean to push her down the stairs. It all just happened so quickly!

Continuing to look at her laid out on the floor, my entire body shivered, and if I didn't get myself together, I was gonna be laid out on this floor too! I had it in me to call 9-11 but something stopped me. Something told me don't do it. Just leave. Get the hell out! I ran over to living room couch, grabbed my purse and keys and then flew back into the foyer. She still wasn't moving. "ALICE! WAKE UP!" I yelled one more time but the voice in my head told me to leave again.

I closed my eyes, took a deep breath and then stormed out of the house. I hopped in Paulette then took off.

On the highway, tears swam down my face and my hands

were shaking so bad that I couldn't even hold tight to the steering wheel. If I didn't get my shit together, I was gonna lose control over this car and crash. I just couldn't believe this though! I killed my best friend. I pushed her to her death. Oh Lord!

Traffic was somewhat heavy but suddenly I swerved over to the side of Lake Shore Drive and began sobbing uncontrollably. "LORD! WHY?!?! WHY, LORD?!?? I KILLED MY FRIEND! LORD, I KILLED HER!"

Pounding the steering wheel, I just had it in me to swerve this car back into traffic and let someone hit me. I had to die! This was just too much for me to handle! I was ready to go!

"STOP IT! STOP IT! JUST SHUT UP! STOP IT RIGHT NOW!" I snapped, instantly checking myself back into reality. "GET IT TOGETHER! FUCK THAT HOE! SHE FUCKED YA MAN AND HAD A BABY BY HIM! FUCK HIM AND FUCK HER! GON' FUCK MY MOTHA-FUCKIN' HUSBAND AND HAVE A BABY BY HIM?!? BITCH YOU GOT ME FUCKED UP! FUCK THAT! DIE BITCH!"

I kept punching the steering wheel until my knuckles became red and tender. If I didn't stop, I was gonna give myself arthritis and I didn't even have no damn aspirin or reefur back at the house to alleviate the pain swelling in my hands! "FUCK IT! SHE DID ME WRONG! I DID WHAT I HAD TO DO GODDAMNIT!"

As cars flew by me on the highway, this weird calm suddenly came over me. Fuck it. It is what it is. She should've never fucked with me! The pulsing anxiety running through my veins and nerves dissipated and I made my way back onto highway.

A good ten minutes later, I made it back home. As soon as I parked, I dashed into my house, went straight to my bedroom and collapsed into the bed. I had to get everything that happened out of my mind!

Trying my best to squeeze my eyes shut, I just focused on the darkness I now saw. But the more I tried to blank everything out of mind, the more I kept seeing flashes of what happened. I really pushed her down those stairs and watched her possibly bleed to death. Everything from what she told me about her and Clarence to me pushing her down the stairs kept firing off in my mind.

Some minutes later after realizing I wasn't going to be able to sleep off all of this craziness, I shot out of the bed and began to manically pace my floor. I was never a nail biter but now I had both of my hands in my mouth.

Shaking uncontrollably, I had it in me to just call 9-11 and head back over to Alice's place but if I did that I just knew I was gonna end up in jail for murder! Ain't no way in the hell I was going to jail though! I'd be damned! As those dreadful moments kept replaying in my mind, I tried to reconcile within myself that I didn't mean to do that. It was just impulse. She made me do it. She didn't have to say any of that shit! Why would she tell me something so crazy like that and not expect me to react in such a way?!? I mean, anybody would've had the same reaction, right? Could you imagine if your best friend told you out the blue one day she sleep with your husband? And even worse, she then told you she got pregnant by him knowing good and goddamn well you couldn't get pregnant!

That fat bitch had me all the way fucked up and the more I ruminated on how everything went down, the more I realized I was justified in doing what I did. She made me do it. I told her to calm her ass down but she kept egging me on.

Although tears of guilt began to escape from the corners of my eyes, I wiped them away with the absolute quickness. Fuck Alice! Fuck Clarence. And FUCK SHARDAY! "YEAH!

FUCK EM ALL, GODDAMN İT! I DON'T EVEN GIVE A
GOOD GOD DAMN! FUCK THEM ALL! ROT IN HELL
BITCH!!" I roared so loudly that my voice probably pierced
the walls right into my neighbor's house. But I didn't give a
fuck anymore. I did what I had to do!

Still shivering, I realized I needed to take me a hot ass
bath to cool these nerves, chile! So I rushed over into my
bathroom to get a bath going. However, before I got my bath
started I stood still for a moment. My finger tapping my
chin, a sudden thought came over me. Hrrrm. Now that I
thought about it, I probably needed to get some reefur and
some liquor to knock me the hell out. I hadn't got drunk or
high in a minute, but Lord knows I needed something right
now to get this crazy shit out of my mind!

I ran the hot water in my tub and threw in some Epsom
salt and lavender. Then I marched back into my room to call
up the young boy who used to sell me reefur. I grabbed my
phone out of my pocketbook and hoped that I still had
Hakeem's number locked in my phone. And lo and behold,
after scrolling through my contacts, I landed on his name!
Thank God! But just as I was about to dial his number, my
phone began vibrating and I saw Sharday's name flash across
the screen. My eyes exploded with fear as I knew what she
was calling me about. Had to be about her no good ass
trifling mama who I just pushed to death...

I hesitated in answering the phone because I didn't know
if I was quite prepared to hear what she was going to tell me.
But I already knew what she was gonna say. *I found Mama
dead!* I just knew she was gonna be crying and carrying on
and then I would have to pretend like I had no idea what
happened.

Gripping the phone hard, I suddenly became filled with
rage and all I could hear sounding off in the back of my head
was Alice telling me how she fucked Clarence and got preg-

nant by him. Worse of all, this bitch calling me right now was his mothafuckin' child. I just had it in me just to explode and throw my phone against the wall, not caring that it would break into a million pieces. The phone kept vibrating. "Fuck it," I grumbled to myself and then answered the phone. I quickly threw on a fake smile and then said, "Hey, girl! What's going on?"

"Hey, Ms. Vernita...," she sobbed in a low and slow tone. Yeah, she must've found her mammy laid out on that floor! My heart began to beat fast and I clasped my chest to anticipate what she was about to tell me. Her sniffles echoed into my ear and at any second I just knew what her uglass was gonna tell me.

"What's wrong? Why do you sound like that...?"

"Mama...It's about Mama...," she continued to sob. "She... She...AHHHHHHHHHHH!"

19

VERNITA

"*C*alm down, Sharday! What is wrong?!?"

"Mama is cutting me out of her will!"

Suddenly my face twisted with confusion. I went silent and my mind was drawing many blanks. "What are you talking about?"

"I just came back from Mama's house and she and I had a huge fight. She told me she's cutting me off and that I won't be in her will no more because she said I don't know how to act right! Ever since she got with Lamar she's been acting funny!"

I didn't know what to think at the moment but I had to play along as if I was truly concerned about what Sharday was telling me. "What well what happened? What did you all get into a fight about?" I had to ask but so many questions began to fill my mind because how in the hell did she just get off the phone with her Mama when I was just over there and then I pushed the woman to her death?!? Sharday cleared her throat and began to explain what happened but then I interjected. "Wait a minute! You just came from over your mama's place?"

"Yeah! She was so nasty to me! I ain't did nothing to piss her off!"

Shaking my head, I paced my floor wondering what in the world was really going on?!? But then I thought to myself that perhaps this entire time I had been hallucinating. Did I even leave my damn house?!? "What time is it?!?"

"It's noon. Why?" Sharday replied then quickly asked, "Is everything okay, Vernita? You sound kind of under the weather. I'm sorry I called you. But I just needed to vent and I wanted to see if you could talk to Mama for me! I don't know what's come over her. It's like I feel like Lamar is putting a lot of ideas in her head!"

"Umm...I'm fine. I think...," I replied. "I just think this medicine I've been taking lately is messing with me. Oh, chile! I must've dozed off or just woke up and didn't even realize it!"

Nervousness came over me as I began to twitch all over. Lord, Lord, Lord! Why were all of these medications messing with me?!?

I just had to pinch myself just to make sure I wasn't caught up in another crazy hallucination. I glanced over at my alarm clock sitting on my nightstand just to confirm it was truly noon as Sharday said. If that was the case, I was still scheduled to go meet up with Alice. And, lo and behold, it was noon! I slapped my forehead mumbling, "Lord, Jesus. I need to go to my doctor." "Look, I'm supposed to be going over there soon anyway. I'll talk to her to get a rundown of why she's acting this way," I told her.

"Okay, thank you so much, Ms. Vernita! I really appreciate it! You already know how I feel about my Mama and I would never do anything to disrespect her," she said. "Alright now, chile, just relax and I'mma see if I can really figure out what's going on. I hope this man ain't influencing your Mama to make crazy decisions," I told her. "Thank you so much, Ms. Vernita. If you need anything, just let me know," she said. "I will, chile!"

Once we hung up, I threw my phone on the bed then stormed back into my bathroom. I'd be damned if I was gonna let these pills make me go crazy all over again, so without hesitation, I quickly opened up my medicine cabinet, took down every pill bottle I had, and emptied everything into the sink. I ran the faucet and made sure the gushing sink water washed down every single pill. I had enough! I truly did! I'd be damned if I was gonna end up in some mental hospital!

Feeling a bit apprehensive, I rushed back into my bedroom and then dialed up Dr. Jackson. Once I got her on the phone, I was going to tell her everything that happened.

"Hey, Vernita!" Dr. Jackson answered. "How's it going? I wasn't expecting to hear from you until our session. Is everything okay?"

"Dr. Jackson, everything is not okay! I just had one of them crazy hallucinations!"

"What happened?"

I made my way over to my bed and sat down on the edge as I began to shiver once again. "I'm feeling very funny and I've been having these weird cold chills. But I had hallucinated I went over to my friend's place and she told me some nasty stuff! Then I pushed her to her death."

"Oh no! Are you at home right now, Vernita?"

"Yes, I am!"

"And have you left your house?"

"No, I haven't!"

"Are you sure?"

"I'm quite sure! I just got off the phone with my friend's daughter and she told me she had just spoken to her. So I know I had to be hallucinating!" I explained to her as I sat on the bed, rocking back and forth. I was an absolute mess.

"Okay, well stop taking the medication and in the meantime, I am going to seek out some alternatives to help manage your anxiety and leg twitches."

"I don't want no more of this stuff! No more, Dr. Jackson! I can't be walking around here like a crazy woman! I don't ever wanna have any type of thoughts like that ever!"

"Vernita, just try to relax. I think we also need to consider whether or not it's the medicine causing you to have these hallucinations or the tumor. Also, now that you are up in age, we might want to consider booking you an appointment with a neurologist to screen you for Alzheimer's or Parkinson's Disease. The type of psychotic hallucination you had sometimes is a symptom of neurodegenerative diseases like Alzheimer's and Parkinson's!"

I didn't like the sound of any of what she was telling me! Parkinson's? Alzheimer's?!? It just seemed like any time I had any issue and I spoke with these doctors, they were so quick to want to diagnose me with some shit. I done had enough of it! "I ain't got time to be fooling around with you doctors! Every time something go wrong with me, ya'll wanna say I got this and that! I'm sick of this shit!"

"Oh, no, Vernita! Please, just calm down!" Dr. Jackson tried to assuage my concerns but like I said, I wasn't here for any of this bullshit today. "I threw away that medicine and I bet you in a few days I'm gonna be fine! Watch and see!"

"I understand, Vernita. I completely understand. Sometimes some of these medicines can have really crazy side effects. But, please do understand that not all medicine is like this. It's necessary for a lot of people," Dr. Jackson tried to explain but once again I just wasn't feeling anything she was gonna say. "Look, baby girl, you might be a doctor, but Jesus is my *real* doctor and he writes out all my prescriptions. I'mma stop taking this bullshit and just let my body and mind heal from this foolishness!" "Okay, well, am I going to still see you in a few days for our appointment?" Dr. Jackson asked. But I responded with, "I'mma have to think about it!" then abruptly hung up. These damn doctors had me ALL the way fucked up if they thought I was gonna let these medicines continue to poison my mind.

I needed a really stiff drink right now, so I stormed out of my bedroom and into my kitchen to see if I had at least a bottle of something hiding away. Searching cabinet after cabinet, I couldn't find anything. "Damn it!" I grunted but just settled on drinking some iced tea I had in the fridge. Once I managed to soothe my nerves, I went back into my bedroom's bathroom and took a long hot shower before I headed over to Alice's place. Chile, I am just so relieved to know that was all a hallucination. Before I hopped in the shower though, I just had to confirm once again I wasn't trapped in one of my crazy, manic moments. I sent Alice a text message just to confirm if she was still fine with us meeting up this afternoon. Within seconds she replied back and joy instantly filled my heart. "Thank God!" I gasped, wiping my brow clear of anxious sweat beads.

After I got out of the shower, I threw on a light outfit, put on some makeup, and then made my way outside. It was such an extremely pleasant day and I was so relieved that none of that crazy hallucination was actually real. Chile, I didn't even know if I had it in me to just snap like that. I hopped in my car, hit the highway, and some minutes later I got off 35th street. As I made my way down the street, from afar I could see that Alice's block had been cut off by a plethora of cop cars, a fire truck, and an ambulance. "Damn it!" Someone must've gotten shot or killed. I really wished Alice would get out of this neighborhood. Although Bronzeville was on the up and up, these young men around here were still up to no good. Hopefully, she and Lamar would get married quickly, and then they would get the hell up out of Chicago.

But speaking of Mr. Lamar though –

I still had it in me to tell Alice the full truth about the brief sexual relationship I had with this man. However, something told me to just keep everything to myself. That hallucination was all too real and the last thing I wanted was for her to drop something crazy on me to then make me snap. It was just so funny though how the mind could play games on you. Baby, let me tell you something though. Clarence and I may have not had the best sex but I knew one thing for sure. Clarence would never have slept around on me. My nookie was too good and he knew it too. And when he was alive, he often made side jokes about Alice's appearance and weight. I used to have to chastise him for talking about my friend but he couldn't help but always make slick comments about her.

As I got closer to Alice's house, a policeman was standing guard directing traffic to go around. A small line of cars formed at the intersection and as I peered closely I noticed that the cop cars and ambulance were all surrounding Alice's house. My eyes bugged out of their sockets and suddenly dread filled my core. Once I got near the policeman, I rolled down my window and asked, "Excuse me, Officer! What's going on?!? I'm supposed to be visiting my friend! She lives right there on, about two houses down."

The officer, who was a nice-looking young black man with a small afro, looked at me with such a serious face that I knew something was wrong. "Ma'am, unfortunately, we have this entire area roped off because of an active investigation. Which address are you trying to get to?"

I told the young officer Alice's address and just as the address rolled off my tongue his eyes turned to slits and he pursed his lips. "I'm sorry, ma'am, but the person you are trying to visit suffered a serious medical emergency."

I clutched my mouth. "Alice?"

"Yes, ma'am."

"NO! Can't be! I just—"

"Yes, ma'am. I'm sorry to tell you this but she's currently en route to the hospital right now."

"OH MY GOD! Please, Lord! No!" I cried as my hands trembled as I held onto the steering wheel. "Which hospital is she going to?"

"I believe Mercy right up the street, ma'am!"

"Lord! What happened?!? Did someone break into her house or something?!?"

"I don't know the exact details, ma'am, but if you don't mind, you are currently blocking traffic. Just pull over to the side."

"OH LORD!" I scrambled to then pull my car over to the side street. I parked, got out of the car, and dashed down the block toward Alice's house. A small crowd of neighbors formed outside and as I got closer to her house, the entire area had been roped off with yellow tape. Tears falling out of my eyes, I couldn't believe what was going on. I searched the crowd of onlookers hoping I'd recognize someone who knew exactly happened. Then I spotted Marla, one of Alice's close neighbors who I also knew in passing. "MARLA! MARLA!" I called out to her as I dashed over to her. She appeared to be so visibly distraught that I already knew something bad had to have happened. "Marla! What happened to Alice?!? Where is she?!?" I asked her as I lunged to her side.

Sniffling and wiping her eyes free of tears, she replied, "She apparently had another heart attack and fell down her stairs and hit her head pretty badly!"

"WHAT?!?" I yelled out shaking my head. "Who found her?"

"One of her grandsons," Marla replied sobbing as she wiped her nose with a piece of tissue.

"Is she okay?!?" I asked, my eyes beginning to water.

"I don't know. But the EMTs had to do CPR on her when they came. I hope she made it. This is just too much! I just knew she'd bounce back from her heart attack. Oh, Lord! Poor Alice!" Marla cried shaking her head.

Clutching my chest, I damn near was about to faint. Everything around me began to spin and I had to quickly gather myself. This was all too surreal.

20

VERNITA

*S*eemed like the entire world was falling apart before my very own eyes.

I stood next to Marla in complete shock. *I did this. I just know I did this.* I kept thinking to myself that I was responsible for all of this. Shivering and in total fear, I didn't know what to say or what to do.

"Okay, well, I'm gonna head to the hospital!" I told Marla as I took off running back to my car. Once I got inside, I whipped out my phone and went through my recent calls. I didn't see a phone call at all from Sharday. Then I went through my text messages. My eyes exploded with angst when I saw I hadn't even sent a text message to Alice. "Lord! Lord! LORD! I'm GOING CRAZY!" I cried, my scream echoing out onto the street.

My hands still trembling, I quickly started up Paulette and headed down the street to Mercy Hospital. Baby, I didn't give a fuck about running through no stop signs or red lights! Mercy Hospital wasn't that far away from Alice's house so about a good five minutes later I swiftly pulled into the parking lot. Once I parked, I ran through the lot like a madwoman, catching the attention of a few folks passing me by. I rushed through the double sliding doors of the emergency room and then jetted straight toward the receptionist girl who was sitting at the check-in desk.

"I'm here to see my friend, Alice! She was just brought here not too long ago!" I panted, trying my best to gather myself.

"Calm down, ma'am! Just relax. What's her name again?"

"ALICE! ALICE BROWN!"

The receptionist, some portly, dark-skinned girl with a short afro, quickly typed away on her computer as she searched for Alice's name in her system. "Okay, well, she was just admitted, ma'am. And right now no visitors are allowed. Just please wait in the lobby area and then if the family grants permission then you can visit her," the receptionist said.

"Bitch! That's my friend! YOU GON LET ME SEE HER!" I suddenly exploded as I got close up to the girl's face.

"Ma'am! Please calm down! Get out of my face! What in the hell is wrong with you!"

Out the corner of my eye, I saw a security guard running toward me. "Hey! Hey! HEY! What's going on over here?" he said. "Calm down, ma'am!"

"I am here to see my friend and this fat ass hoe won't let me!" I just knew my face filled with reddened rage.

"Ma'am! Please calm down or we are going to have to ask you to leave!" the security guard barked back at me as he tried to pull me away from the desk.

"Let me go!" I snapped as I slapped his hands off my shoulders. "Fine! I'mma sit and wait but you gon' let me see my friend!"

I didn't know what came over me but I was quickly losing all my marbles. Everyone inside the emergency room's waiting area had their eyes on me. Then this sudden sense of embarrassment and regret came over me. Quickly finding a seat all the way over in a quiet corner, I sat down and held my head in palms as I began crying. I just kept thinking to myself how I was responsible for all of this! I had to be. But the problem was I just couldn't quite remember how any of this transpired?!? Nothing was adding up at all! Baby, I couldn't even put together the right sequences of events of how this entire day transpired. Everything was all muddled and jumbled together. Honestly, at this point, I was more terrified of me losing my mind than Alice's condition.

Some fifteen minutes later I saw Sharday along with a few of Alice's grandbabies frenziedly rush through the doors of the emergency room. "Where my granny at?!?" Charles, one of her grandsons, screamed at the top of his lungs.

I suddenly flew out of my seat and ran over to them. "Sharday!" I called out to her.

Sharday suddenly rushed into my arms and began crying her heart out. "Where's Mama?!?"

"I don't know! That heffa wouldn't let me in the back!" I angrily spat looking straight at that rotten ass girl sitting behind the check-in desk. "I've been waiting for what seemed like an hour!"

"Ms. Brown's family?"

I suddenly heard a soft voice pour into my ears. I spun around and some white blonde nurse looked at us with this stiff look on her face. "Yes?" Sharday managed to squeeze out as she wiped her face free of tears.

"Please follow me…," she said holding onto a clipboard.

"Where's my mama?!? Is she okay??!?" Sharday cried out, her entire body shuddering.

"Just, please, follow me. The doctor would like to speak to you all…," she said as she then lead us out of the waiting area and into the actual emergency room.

I gulped out of fear that we were about to get delivered

some horrible news. We followed the nurse in a solemn fashion. She then escorted us into what was another waiting area, but this one much smaller and private. This was just bad. So bad I didn't know if I was going to be able to handle all of this. My stomach quivered and this horrible, dreadful nausea came over me. Immense guilt baptized my mind and I just knew at any moment the doctor was going to walk in and tell us that Alice had passed.

"Why won't they just tell us what happened?" sobbed Belinda, another one of Alice's grandbabies.

As I sat there taking in the somber moment, the door to the private waiting room opened. I glanced up thinking it was going to be the doctor, but it wasn't. It was none other than Lamar himself. My mouth dropped open a bit when I scanned him up and down. Completely frozen, he looked at me. Our eyes locked together. This was not how I wanted to have a *reunion* with this man. Oh Gosh, I could only imagine what he would think if knew that I was the one responsible for what had happened to Alice.

"Hey everyone...Sorry I'm late. I just got a call and found out what happened? Did we get any updates from the doctor?" Lamar asked as he scanned the room looking for an immediate answer.

"No...We just got here and we were escorted to this room," Sharday said. "We're still waiting for the doctor and we have no idea what's going on!"

"What exactly happened?" Lamar asked as he walked into the room and stood almost right in front of me. My heart was beating so fast and this intense nausea began to bourgeon deep down in my stomach. Gosh, this man was so sexy. If we weren't in the situation we were in right now, I'd pull his pants down and began to suck that dick with the quickness, you hear me!

Stop! Stop! Stop thinking that! That is horrible! I thought to myself, trying to quickly stamp out those crazy thoughts. Lamar stood there holding his chin looking very concerned. I cleared my throat and just as I was about to say something to him, the door to the room opened and this time some Arab-looking man with a white coat on strolled in. "Hi, everyone, I'm Dr. Abdul Aziz…"

"Where's my mother?!?" Sharday bawled.

"Sorry for the delays…" He cleared his throat. "Unfortunately I have some bad news…Ms. Brown didn't make it. She passed away a few moments ago…"

"NOOOOO! NOOOOOOOOOOOOO!" Sharday screamed as she suddenly fell out onto the waiting room floor. Alice's grandchildren, too, exploded into tears. Nothing but loud, thunderous wailing filled the entire room. I sat back shaking my head no as I couldn't believe any of what I was hearing.

"Where is she at?!?" Lamar sobbed. "Where in the fuck is my fiancée!"

"She's upstairs in an ICU unit. We tried our best to revive her but she suffered another major heart attack and a major concussion to her head. We believe she went into cardiac arrest while she was walking down her stairs."

"I kept telling Mama not to go up and down them stairs! I just kept telling her!" Sharday cried.

I couldn't handle the combination of grief and guilt any longer, so without saying a word, I immediately shot up out of my seat and stormed out of the room. Feeling the urge to throw up, I had to find the closest bathroom. I was so nauseated that as I tried to find the closest bathroom I almost fell out.

Trekking through the bright, chilly corridor of the emergency room, my hazy gaze landed on a small women's bathroom. I stormed in and immediately locked the door. I flew over to the toilet and threw up every single thing I had in me.

Baby, I didn't care who just sat there funky ass on this seat. My entire head was submerged in the toilet bowl.

Some moments later, once the nausea and vomiting subsided, I managed to get myself up off the floor. Limping over to the sink, I stared in the mirror and began to cry uncontrollably. *I killed her.* My mind kept dwelling on the horrid fact that I was a murderer. I did this.

Now I had it in me to go back into that room and explain just exactly what happened. I couldn't live with this type of guilt knowing that I probably had some weird hallucination because of that damn medicine and ended up killing Alice.

Running some cool water in the bathroom sink, I washed my face and hands. Once I got done, I slowly made my way out of the bathroom, and anxiously walked back to the room. However, as I got closer, I saw a group of police officers huddled around the room. Lamar was standing by them talking to them. But as I got closer, I must've caught their attention. Then they all looked at me with such serious faces. Oh, Lord. They must've figured everything out! They caught me. I didn't know how but they must've found out I had been over Alice's place earlier.

21

VERNITA

My y heart racing fast like a horse at the Kentucky Derby, I approached Mr. Lamar along with the officers standing guard. "Lord, Jesus, I can't believe all of this happened. I feel so bad! Feel so horrible," I mumbled clutching my chest out of angst. "Is everything alright?" I then asked one of the officers standing in front of me.

"Are you Mrs. Washington?" the tall, slender Black policeman asked looking straight at me.

I stood silent for a moment. "Yes...Yes, I am," I then nervously responded as I knew exactly where his line of questioning was going to go.

"I'm one of the first responding officers who was on the scene. I have a few questions to ask," he said. "If you don't mind, I'd like to talk to you in private."

I could feel Lamar's eyes burning into me while the officer asked to speak to me in private. I looked at Lamar and then he looked at me with this curious yet concerning gawk. Yeah, eventually he and I were going to have to *talk*. We had much to discuss, especially our past entanglement. "Sure thing, Officer," I said to the policeman and then he escorted me off to a quiet corner of the emergency room.

"I'm so sorry to hear about everything that has transpired. I am sure that Ms. Brown was a wonderful woman," the officer said as he pulled out a small notepad and pen from his shirt's front pocket.

"She surely was. She was a wonderful person," I replied, my voice low and sad. Shaking my head I said, "I just can't believe all of this happened. I just…I'm just shocked by all of this. None of this just seemed real to me!"

"I promise my questions won't take long," replied the officer. "I just have some questions surrounding how the entire day transpired."

I gulped. "Okay. No worries. Ask away…"

Oh, Lord! This was it! The police were gonna put two and two together and then arrest my ass for killing Alice. Lord, I wasn't built for no damn jail!

"From what I gathered from another office on the scene, you were in the area to go visit Ms. Brown when you found out what happened to her. Correct?"

"Yes…Yes, that's correct…."

"Had you talked to her previously that day?"

"I…umm…I don't recollect. I don't believe so. She and I had spoken the night before. We had planned to have lunch together earlier this afternoon…"

"Okay…Cool…" The officer continued, "Do you know if she had any issues going on with any of her family members? Do you know if she expressed any concerns about her safety?"

My brow raised out of confusion. "No…Not that I can think of. Alice just got out of the hospital recently. She just had a major heart attack and was currently in rehab for it, I believe. That's what she told me."

"Okay…," replied the officer as he continued to jot down a

few more notes. Then he said, "I'm only asking these questions because one of her neighbors said that she spotted your car earlier in the neighborhood. This was obviously before Ms. Brown was found unconscious. Why were you in the neighborhood?"

I was riding around??? Huh?

I kept thinking to myself as I couldn't even recollect leaving my house. Oh, Lord! All of this was so confusing. I just didn't know what to say or do at this point other than just go ahead and tell the officer the full truth about what happened. "I think I was…I don't know, Officer. I just don't feel right. I did something horribly wrong," I said with my head lowered.

"What happened, ma'am? Were you there when Ms. Brown fell?"

I looked up at the Officer and tightened my lips. Something deep down inside of me told me to go ahead and let the young officer know exactly what happened and that it was all just a horrible mistake. I didn't mean to kill my friend! Lord knows I didn't! I felt so ashamed that I let my mind slip away like this. All of this over me taking these crazy medications! Clutching my mouth with my trembling hands, my lips parted open as I got ready to confess what happened. But just as I was about to 'fess up, another officer came storming down the corridor. "Hey! We got a suspect!"

I was shocked! Totally shocked!

This whole entire situation had been nothing more than chaos.

A few hours later I was now back at home in my living room. As I sat on my living room couch, my mind kept replaying all of the hallucinations I had earlier. Thankfully they were just that – hallucinations. And while I couldn't help but to feel a sense of relief, I still couldn't shake this intense remorse about how everything panned out.

Apparently, I was hallucinating so bad that I did somehow make it out of my house and was in Alice's neighborhood. However, she and I never actually met up. I had sat in her driveway for a few minutes before I backed out and made my way back home. All of these weird details were told to me by the officers once everything had been pieced together.

Apparently, they had camera footage of me from a few neighbor's houses. Also, Alice's house had a security camera as well. On the footage, somehow or another, I managed to make it back home. I must've been so zoned out that I probably went straight to bed and then continued on hallucinating, thinking that I was still at Alice's house having a whole ass conversation with her.

Nonetheless, while I spazzed out thinking I was the one who may have harmed Alice, it truly wasn't me. As crazy and coincidental as it sounded, some young thug broke into Alice's house while she was still there. The police said a fight must've ensued and the young boy pushed her down the stairs. Luckily, Alice had a few cameras inside of her house and once the police went back and retrieved the footage, they saw how everything went down. Poor Alice.

Alice's story was so horrifying and tragic that it managed to make the nightly news. And that was what I was doing now in my dimly lit living room – getting ready to watch this news report rehash everything. "This is Dale Harrington with ABC7 Action News. I'm reporting live from the Bronzeville neighborhood where we have an unfortunate story that transpired earlier this afternoon. Police have in custody Jarquayrious Miller who is a suspect in the death of a long-time Bronzeville resident, Alice Brown. Police say that Jarquayrious Miller, 22-years old and also a resident of Bronzeville, broke into Ms. Brown's residence this after-noon. Not realizing she was home, Mr. Miller engaged in a fight with Ms. Brown and then pushed her down a staircase in her house where she suffered a fatal head injury. We've learned that Ms. Brown recently suffered a major heart attack and had been recently released from the hospital. From what we've gathered, a concerned neighbor who went to go check on Ms. Brown's well-being found her uncon-scious and immediately called the police. She was taken to Mercy Hospital where she was pronounced dead on arrival. Initially, police suspected her death was completely acci-dental due to a fall in her house. However, after retrieving security footage from inside of Ms. Brown's home, police were able to capture in vivid detail all the events that led to Ms. Brown's death. Mr. Miller, who prosecutors now say will be charged with first-degree murder along with a host of other charges, was easily identified on the footage and taken into custody. Mr. Miller has yet to confess to the crime, however, Ms. Brown's family, friends, and neighbors are relieved to know that justice was immediately served. However, this is just a devastating blow to the Brown family. Back to you, Chuck…"

Now that my mind was starting to get a grip again on reality, I had come to the full, bittersweet realization that Alice was gone. Yes, all of this was real. My sweet Alice was gone ya'll! I didn't even get a chance to see her at the hospital. And truth be told, I didn't even know if I was prepared to see her lying dead in a hospital bed. Oh well. Poor Alice. I just wondered at this point who was gonna get the body. Lord, I just hoped they didn't send her down to Bates Funeral Home because they did a horrible job on Clarence!

Tears falling down my face, I had to cut the television off and get this craziness out of my mind. "Ohhh, Alice, chile, I'm so sorry this all happened to you!" I kept sobbing and shaking my head. Truth be told, I wish this was all just one big hallucination. "Why, Lord, WHY?!? Why are you doing this to me?!? I just don't know how I'm gonna make it!"

I needed something to cool my nerves down immediately. And the only thing I knew that would calm me down and help me sleep tonight was some good ole reefer. Funny how I had hallucinated that I had called my dealer up earlier to get me some green. But, chile, I knew I definitely didn't have any in my house because that stuff would've had my house smelling so loud!

I made my way into my bedroom where I had my phone charging on the nightstand. I ran through my contacts hoping I still had that young boy's number saved. Hakeem was his name. I swore I deleted his number but I was blessed to see that I still had it! Thank God! But just before I was about to dial his number, my doorbell began going crazy. "Who in the hell is that?!?"

I dashed out of my bedroom and then made it to my front door, immediately looking out the peephole. My entire gaze widened to the heavens when I saw none other than Percy standing there with his arms folded. He then began pounding on the door. "VERNITA! Open up! I know you in there!" he yelled.

"Percy! What in the hell are you doing over here?!?"

"Just open up! I need to talk to you!"

I stood there frozen wondering what in the fuck he wanted with me. Ain't no way in the hell was I gonna open up this damn door. Not now. Not never! Especially after all the shit he put me through. "Percy, I ain't got time for your bullshit! I ain't in the mood. Just leave. Go run back to wherever the fuck you came from!"

"Vernita! Please! I miss you!" he cried.

I continued looking out the peephole watching him damn near look like he was about to break all the way down. "Please, baby, I know I fucked up! Just let me in because I really need to talk to you. I've been going through some things! Please!"

"PERCY! NO! NO, NO, NO! I ain't got time for any of your mess. I'm not feeling well and my friend passed away today! So, please, just go home!"

"Vernita, please!" he cried. "You know you miss me. I missed you. I've been thinking about all these months. I missed your smile. Your smell. I missed the way you used to tell me everything was gonna be alright when I was locked up. I'm in a bad place right now and I just need someone to talk to!"

He kept begging and begging but I just wasn't ready to hear any of his goddamn bullshit. The more I thought about it, the more enraged I became. I had it in me to really let this nigga know how I really felt. "PERCY! Get the fuck away from my goddamn door right mothafuckin' now! How dare you come over here this time of the night begging me to come in and talk! Nigga, are you crazy?!? You got some mothafuckin' nerve, especially after you went off and got some young bitch pregnant! HOW DARE—"

"Bitch! Open up this mothafuckin' door now or I'mma go run and tell ya lil secret about Clarence!"

I gasped, my eyes shot open with surprise. I didn't know what to say or honestly how to respond. Flustered, I slowly moved my hand to the doorknob, still hesitant to open up the front door and let this trifling, no good ass nigga into my house! But he sounded so serious and I didn't want to take a risk of him running his mouth. "Fuck!" I grunted in a low tone to myself. I then unlocked the front door and opened it.

He stood there for a second and produced the biggest smile of life. He scanned me up and down. "Yeah, I knew that would get your mothafuckin' attention. But damn, baby, you still looking good, I see…"

22

VERNITA

"**G**et yo ass inside!" I roared yanking him inside then slammed the front door shut.

He waltzed into the foyer looking around. "Damn, baby, smells good up in here. What kind of candles are those? You know my baby mama make candles now…"

As he continued to stand there, I instantly grew disgusted with every aspect of his appearance. Why on Earth did I ever get involved with this fool?!? Oh! I forgot! That medicine! Goddamnit! Last time I saw Percy he was looking a tad rough but now he just looked like complete shit. He even put on a good fifty or sixty pounds! This nigga looked like he hadn't even been to sleep either in over a month. The circles he had under his eyes were even more pronounced! To top it off, this nigga had on old ass faded black t-shirt riddled with holes, some faded jeans and a pair of Sneakers that looked like he had borrowed them from some homeless mothafucka on the streets. Even worse, now that I was only feet away from him, he reeked of shit, piss and alcohol! He knew he was foul as fuck for coming up in my house smelling this way!

"PERCY! Enough of this shit! What in the hell do you want to talk about?!?"

"Well, since I did a favor for you them years back," he said rubbing his hands together. "It's time to for you to do the same for me..." A devilish grin came over his face as he made his way over into the kitchen. Without even asking, he opened the fridge and pulled out a carton of orange juice.

"What favor are you talking about, Percy?!?" I played dumb. I didn't want to rehash old memories.

Percy slammed the fridge door shut then strolled back over to me in this very cocky fashion. I just had it in me to go grab my phone and call the police on this nigga. But knowing that Percy was probably very serious with his threat, I didn't want to take that risk. Besides, I didn't believe in calling the cops on black men. Especially someone like Percy.

"Bitch, don't really stand there and play fucking stupid. You know exactly what the fuck I'm talking about. You old and you might be losing parts of your mind, but you not that old and forgetful to suddenly forget about how you killed Clarence..."

"PERCY! I have no idea what you are talking about! Now you just need to get out of my house right now!"

"Bitch, if I didn't know what the fuck I was talking about then why the fuck did you let me in?!? You obviously know what the fuck I'm talking about!"

Standing there shivering, I pointed toward the front door. "Leave! Now!"

Percy let out a light chuckle. "Fine then. I'll just run over to the police station and confess to everything." Still holding onto the carton of orange juice in his hand, he suddenly tossed it off to the side, spilling juice everywhere.

"Oh no the fuck you didn't! CLEAN THAT MESS UP RIGHT NOW! And then GET THE FUCK OUT OF MY HOUSE!"

"Bitch, you got more to worry about then orange juice on your carpet," Percy laughed. Then he stood there and placed a finger on his chin. "But now that I think about it, you do gotta worry about your carpet. The carpet between ya legs. Yeah, bitch! That shit finne get took when you get locked the fuck up. Then again, who the fuck wanna munch on some old ass pussy other than a desperate bulldagger bitch!"

"FINE! What do you want, Percy?!?" I gave up. I had to! I just wanted to do what I had to do to get this nigga out of my house and out of my life for good. "It just better not be anything crazy!"

"I'm tryin' to hit a lick but the nigga I'm trying to get at is pretty hard to get to!"

My eye brow raised out of confusion. "What does that mean, Percy?!? Now you know I don't know any of these words you young folks be using and shit!"

"It means I'm trying to rob a nigga! That's what the fuck it means!"

"Rob?!?" Shaking my head furiously, I wasn't down to be a part of any of Percy's foolishness. This nigga was absolutely out of his mind if he thought I was going to help him rob someone. "PERCY! Do you hear yourself? You wanna rob someone?!? Nigga, you just got out of jail not too long ago for this same mess?!? Do you wanna go back?!?"

"BITCH! I don't give no fucks about no goddamn prison! I just wanna get back at this nigga for playing me!"

"AHHH!" I threw my hands up in the air out of frustration. "PERCIVAL! I'm about to be 77-year-old and you want me to help you rob someone?!?!? Why can't you just do right for once in your life and get a job and save your money?!?" I lunged up into his face and continued yelling to the top of my lungs. If I didn't lower my voice I just knew I was going to attract the attention of some neighbors. "But see, you always wanna get this fast money. Selling drugs. Robbing folks. Stealing cars. Who in the fuck really raised you? Some damn banshees at the zoo?!? Your rotten ass mammy oughta be a shamed of herself!"

Out of nowhere Percy's fist came crashing right into the middle of my face. I instantly blacked out and collapsed to the floor. All I saw was glittery stars cast among darkness. I slowly opened my eyes and as hazy as my vision now was, I clearly made out Percy hovering over me.

"Bitch, don't you ever in your mothafuckin' life ever bring up my mama again!" He leaned down then whipped out a gun from the back of his waist. My eyes instantly widened even more when he aimed the barrel right at my forehead. He leaned further down then growled, "Now open your mouth, you old, nasty ass bitch!"

"Pe-Percy...," I stuttered as tears escaped my eyes. "Why are you doing this to me?!? How in the hell am I even gonna help you?"

"Bitch, You're gonna help me as I see fit. And if you don't, I might just skip all the putting ya dark secrets out there and will just blow your mothafuckin brains out. NOW OPEN UP YOUR MOUTH!" He jammed the gun to my lips and I slowly opened his mouth. He then shoved the gun deep down in my mouth, damn near choking me. He yanked me off the floor then dragged me over to the couch, still keeping the gun shoved down my throat. "Now, you feel that? If you keep giving me mouth, I swear to God I will pull this trigger and splatter your brains all over this damn couch!" He continued, "Now this is what the fuck we gonna do. You're gonna go get yourself cleaned up and then fix me something to eat. I ain't had a nice, homecooked meal in a minute. I want oxtails, yellow rice, greens, macaroni and cheese, corn bread, and something sweet on the side. Then, after you get done cooking, I'mma fuck your brains out. Then, after we get done fucking, your gonna shower up, put on a nice outfit and then we're gonna drive out to Orland Park where this fuck nigga is at. I'll tell you more details when we get out that way." He pulled the gun out of my mouth then wiped the barrel on the couch. "Now get to it, bitch...I'm hungry as fuck."

Trembling and crying, my face all the way down to my lower torso filled with intense pain. My stomach bubbled nausea from all the anxiety. "Percy...I wanna help you. Lord knows I do. Can I just give you the money?"

"Nah! You ain't got the money to even get close to what the fuck I'm trying to get out of this nigga."

"Percival, please, I am going through a lot right now. My friend, the one you scared away that one time, died today and I am dealing with a lot!"

His eyes turned to slits. "Well, I'm sorry to hear that, but that ain't got nothing to do with my money." "Besides, like I said, I just know you ain't got the cash to help me out. And you shouldn't have to give it to me either."

"Percy, please, baby, just tell me what happened...What did this man do to you?" I begged.

"This clown ass nigga stole from me. I gave this nigga like two hunned-k to flip for me and he stole every single penny from me and now won't give it back!"

"Why?"

"'Cause that fuck nigga is a liar! I know he is! I should've known it was something dirty about that nigga. Even my BM told me to just stick with what I know. But noooo! I wanted to do shit the legit way. I trusted that nigga and this how he did me in?"

"Who is this man? How did you even meet him?"

Percy smacked his teeth. "This nigga who used to be a retired basketball player for the Bulls. This nigga named Lamar Speights. That fuck nigga into real estate and investing and shit!"

My eyes widened with surprise. Did he just say what I thought he said. "Lamar Speights? He's bald and got kind of like dark brown skin? With the goatee?"

"Yeah! That nigga! Fuck nigga owns an insurance company or some investment company. Some shit like that! I gave that nigga my money to flip. He said I could make a mill in a few weeks! But then he ran some game on me and then told me something happened in the stock market and all my money went away!"

I couldn't believe what I was hearing. This was just too much for me to handle! Too much of a coincidence! "Percy... I...That was my friend's fiancée..."

Percy suddenly became enraged again. "WHAT?!?"

"Percy! Look, just calm down! This is too much of a coincidence! But that was my friend's fiancée! She died today!"

"How?!?"

"Some young boy broke into her house trying to rob the place. But he didn't realize she was home. She was there and they got into a fight. He pushed her down the stairs and she hit her head pretty badly. She had just came home from the hospital too for a heart attack!"

"Nah! This shit don't sound like some mothafuckin' coincidence!" Percy's eyes suddenly amplified with rage. "This shit sound like you in on it, too! You and that nigga! You must've fucked this nigga, too!"

"Percy! Please calm down!"

"Bitch! You fucked him! Yes, you did! I can see the fucking guilt written all over your face!"

"NO I DIDN'T, PERCIVAL! Now stop it and lower your voice!" I yelled at the top of my lungs. Oh, Lord! The neighbors were going to for sure hear all of this fussing and carrying on we were doing! Yeah, I was lying, but I'd be damned if I was going to admit to that!

"Stop calling me that, bitch!" Percy then, without hesitation, yanked his gun back out and aimed it right at my head! Immediately frightened, I threw my hands up in the air. "PERCY! NO! STOP IT!"

"Bitch! FUCK YOU! LYING ASS HOE!"

"Percy, no! You gotta stop this right now! You're losing your mind! JUST CALM DOWN!"

"BITCH! YOU IN ON IT WITH THIS, NIGGA! THIS MAKES ALL THE FUCKING SENSE NOW! YO ASS SET ME UP!"

I had no idea what this boy was talking about! Like I really didn't it! Tears mixed with sweat drenched my face as I continued begging Percy to calm down and get the gun out of my face.

"BITCH! I swear to God I'll kill you on my mama's grave if I find out you fucking that nigga!"

"PERCY! Please! I swear I ain't mess with that man!"

"I DON'T BELIEVE YOU BITCH!"

"PERCY! NO!"

POW!

23

VERNITA

I literally saw my entire life flash before my eyes. Baby, I swore I had already made it to the pearly gates!

But within seconds, my strained eyes slowly opened and there Percy was standing before me, his gun still aimed at my face. "Bitch, the next bullet I fire is going straight into your brain. Now get the fuck up and go fix me something to eat! I'm tired of playing fucking games with you!" He grabbed me by the arm then snatched me off the couch, dragging me into the kitchen.

"Percy! I don't have no oxtails and other ingredients. I gotta go to the store. And everything is closed now!" I told him. This boy was absolutely out of his fucking mind! Who in the hell even expected that type of dinner this late at night?!?

"Bitch! Muhfuckin' Jewel-Osco is open 24-7! And Wal-Mart still open, too!"

"Percy! It's almost midnight and I'm too tired! I will cook for you tomorrow!"

Percy once again aimed the gun at me, and this time I

ducked down on the floor and covered my face. I knew now he was certainly going to put a bullet in me. "BITCH! DO YOU THINK I AM PLAYING WITH YOU?!?"

Boom! Boom! Boom! Three loud pounds came from the front door. "Vernita! Is everything okay?!?" My eyes widened with fear as I knew that had to be Mr. Kilpatrick from next door. I wasn't quite sure but I was certain that was him. Only his nosey white ass would Goddamnit! I just knew someone was going to hear that gunshot!

Suddenly both of our heads turned toward my townhouse front door. We were obviously caught by surprise when we heard what I knew had to be Mr. Kilpatrick continuously banging hard on the door. "See! I done told you all this screaming and fussing was gonna get the police called on us!" I yelled at Percy.

"FUCK!" Percy then lunged at me, grabbed me off the kitchen floor and dragged me toward the foyer. Feet away from the front door, he pulled me close into his face and said, "Answer the mothafuckin' door and tell whoever the fuck it is that everything is okay..."

"O-Okay," I muttered back to him crying. Following his stern instructions, I quickly put on a face of fake calmness, wiped my face and then coolly sauntered over to the front door. I looked out the peephole and saw that it was Mr. Kilpatrick. He kept pounding the door. "Vernita?!? Is everything okay?!? Are you okay in there?"

"Mr. Kilpatrick! I'm fine! I just...I just dropped some pans. That's all!"

"That sound didn't sound like a pan! Sounded like a gunshot! Are you certain, Vernita?!? I can call the police if you need me to! I heard some loud arguing as well!"

I looked over my shoulder. Percy was standing a good two feet away from me. He growled, "Tell that cracka to get the fuck away from the door or I'mma blow his head smooth off!"

Shivering, I looked back into the peephole. "Mr. Kilpatrick. I promise you everything is fine. Just go on home now."

"Alright, Vernita...," Mr. Kilpatrick responded and within a few seconds he strolled away from my door. I took a deep breath and then exhaled. However, my nerves were still running high with anxiety. Percy then lunged at me and dragged my ass right back into the kitchen. "Now get to cooking, hoe! A nigga is fucking starving!"

"Percy! I just told you I don't have that type of food up in my house right now!"

"AHHH! GODDAMN IT! FINE! Just go to the room and get naked 'cause I want some pussy!"

"Percy! Please, I'm just not in the mood for any of this right now, baby! Can we please just simmer down, maybe have a drink and go to bed or something?!?"

"No! BITCH! I want some pussy! Now go before I go the fuck off again!"

"Fine..." I didn't want to keep going back and forward with his crazy ass.

Percy smacked his teeth. "Yeah, better be fine...Raggedy ass old hoe. Probably was missing this dick anyways."

Just as I was about to walk down the hallway and make my way into the bedroom, I froze for a moment and pondered on something...I looked at Percy and said, "So, you would really go to the police and tell them what I did, huh?"

Percy looked me up and down in a very nasty manner. "Yes the fuck I would. In a mothafuckin' heartbeat." He shrugged his shoulders. "It is what it is..."

I shrugged my shoulders right back at him. "If you say so. If you say so..."

"Yeah..." He chuckled then began taking his clothes off

right there in the living room. I was disgusted seeing how flabby he'd gotten.

"Well, let me run and take a quick bath just to wash up," I said and made my way into the bedroom.

Just before I was about to make my way to the bathroom, I froze when my eyes landed on something on my nightstand. I smiled knowing that this one thing would immediately get me out of this crazy, fucked up situation with Percy.

I stood in the mirror, checking myself one last time before I made my way into the bedroom. If I was going to fuck Percy, then chile, I was gonna do this the right way! Hell, why not make the best of the moment, right? Makeup was on point. Had my hair put up in a nice bun. Pussy washed, sanitized and shaved. I was ready to get this shit over with, so I quickly slipped into my robe and sprayed some light perfume on my body. Thank God I took a quick shower too because I had been out all day and the last thing I wanted was this nigga to complain that my coochie stunk.

I sauntered into the bedroom and there I immediately saw Percy already laying in the bed completely naked.

I stood there for a second and threw him a nervous smile. Then I took the robe off, letting it slip quickly to the bedroom floor. Now I stood before him completely naked. His eyes widened. "Yeah, you still lookin' right! Old ass hoe. Now come jump on the dick," he commanded.

Slowly making my way over to the bed, I kept smiling at him not saying anything. Once I got in the bed, I crawled on my knees toward him. He slowly parted his legs open while he played with his soft dick, trying his best to get it hard for me. But I was about to get it hard for him so he can enjoy this pussy for one last time. And just like that, without even saying a word, I began to suck on his soft dick until I got it super-hard. Stroking up and down on his shaft, I began blessing him with the wettest head of life. Sucking dick was truly a talent of mine. I just loved the way a dick tasted in my mouth! "Ohh, Oooh!" Percy groaned as he pulled my head back, trying put a swift break to my head game. Holding his saliva-covered shaft, I looked up at him smiling not saying a word. "Oh, you back to that nasty shit I see," he moaned. "Yeah, well, now I want you to eat my ass!"

Nigga, what?!? Oh hell no! I thought to myself but obviously at this precarious moment I wasn't going to lose my life protesting eating his ass. So, without hesitation, I began to suck on his dick again, then I slowly made my down his shaft toward his balls. I licked on them for a few seconds before I migrated my tongue down his taint. I closed my eyes and wasn't quite ready for what I was about to possibly smell or taste next. Percy spread his legs open and then slightly tooted his ass up in the air. Oh, God! Save me! But then I had to do what I had to – I suddenly dived my tongue in his ass and began to slobber all up around his booty hole. Fighting back the urge to want to throw up, I was somewhat relieved to know this boy didn't smell like shit...nor did he taste like it.

"Oh shit, yeah, keep eating that ass, you nasty bitch! Just like that," Percy moaned as he grabbed my head. "Stroke my shit while you eat my ass!"

He pushed my head deeper into his ass and I just let go and went to devouring that ass like it was my last meal before dying.

A good minute later (although it felt like twenty), he pulled my head up out of his ass. "Now come jump on the dick!" he said as he gripped my arms, pulling me closer to him. I saddled on top of him, spread my legs and let his dick slide up in me. I couldn't lie. I hadn't had some dick in a minute and although I was fucking him under strange, dangerous circumstances, his dick was feeling mighty good up in me. A part of me felt relieved from everything that had went down earlier. However, I still couldn't get flashes of Alice out of my head. As I bounced on the dick and Percy dug deeper and deeper up in me, stretching my walls out, I tried to blank all of the craziness. But by now all I saw were flashes of red. Everything around me became completely blood red. *Do it, Vernita. Do it, girl.* This horrid anxiety bubbled up in me but the voice in my head kept urging me to go ahead and do what I had to do.

With his eyes wide open, he stared deep down into mine. The intensity of the dick down ramped up he gripped my waist. "Why you ain't saying shit?" he groaned as he kept digging my guts out.

But I didn't say anything back.

A big smile stretched across my face as I kept bouncing on the dick. I could feel myself creaming all over his shit. I slightly leaned down and planted my head toward the side of his face. He grabbed my ass and kept pounding me out. "COME ON! I KNOW YOU FEEL THAT SHIT!" he screamed. "TAKE THIS DICK, BITCH!"

Grabbing my ass even harder, he kept fucking me hard, damn near tearing into my uterus! I was slightly moaning but I didn't want to get to ecstatic. And that was because unbeknownst to Percy, I was about to kill his mothafuckin' ass. While my head still rested on the side of his as I rode him, my eyes were glued to the letter opener I had sitting next to some pieces of mail on my nightstand. I slowly extended my hand out and grabbed the letter opener. "FUCK ME HARDER, BABY!" I screamed out to distract him. And then in a flash, I shot up and without hesitation drilled the letter opener right into the side of his neck! I took the opener out of the gash and kept stabbing him in the same spot and then tossed the letter opener off to the side.

"AHHHH!" Percy cried out as he grabbed his throat, blood spraying all over the place.

I was so zoned out that I wasn't even nervous anymore. As I sat on top of his quaking body, he held tight to his neck with both hands as he choked on his own blood. "See what you made me do! You done fucked with me!" I yelled at him as I watched him bleed out from his neck.

Yelling and screaming, blood continued to gush all over the place. His blood even splattered all over my face and torso, dripping down my titties.

"You...You b-bb-bitch!" he painfully muttered as blood continued to drain out of his body through the big gaping hole in the side of his neck. A huge ocean-like puddle of blood formed in the bed, drenching my entire white Egyptian cotton sheets.

I simply smiled. "Rot in hell, mothafucka!"

I carefully climbed off his now motionless body then hurried into the bathroom. Soon as I flew through the bathroom door, I was hit by a bloody reflection of myself in the mirror. "Wow!" I groaned under my breath. "I really snapped!" My entire body was damn near painted in blood.

Although my heart was racing, damn near ready to explode out of my chest, I was so damn calm. Hell, I was serene. Satisfied that I finally had the chance to get rid of this nasty, low life mothafucka. I couldn't even believe this nigga would threaten to spill all of my secrets. This nigga was really out of his mothafuckin' mind if he thought he was going to come up into my residence and force me at gunpoint to get down with his nonsense he had going on with Lamar. Shit, I didn't know if he was even telling the truth! But see, now I was gonna have to look more into whatever shenanigans he had going on with him.

I debated whether or not I should hop in the shower but I just kept staring at myself. I was still so enraged that this nigga came up into my house and then threatened that he'd run and tell the police what I did to Clarence. See, baby, what you is not gonna do is fuck with Vernita in that type of way! I took good care of his ass when he didn't have shit and then this was his way of trying to get back into my life?!? Nah! Fuck that! Fuck him and fuck Clarence!

Yeah, so, the fuck what I killed Clarence! He had to go! And if I had it my way, I'd dig him up and kill him all over the fuck again! Matter of fact, I'd kill any nigga who would dare cross me the wrong way. And I mean that!

Nothing but the constant flashing of blue police lights filled my living room as I sat anxiously at the edge of my living room couch. Biting my nails, my entire body quaked with deep fear. Crying and sniffling, I was trying my hardest to mutter out the chain of events that led to me defending myself against the armed and dangerous intruder-rapist, Percy. "…And next thing you know. He just stormed in and told me to get naked. I…I resisted and tried all I could to defend myself but he just overpowered me."

"Oh wow. I'm so sorry to hear all of this ma'am. This is truly unfortunate but thank God you managed to survive," the detective who was interviewing me said as he rubbed my knee. He kept consoling me, telling me that everything was going to be alright and that there was no need to worry anymore.

"Thank you so much, Detective. I'm just really…Really terrified at all of this. I just don't know why he would do this to me," I said. "He was always such a nice man to me."

"Understandable…" The detective, who was a light-skinned, slender young man with a nice fade, continued to jot down notes in his notepad while an army of police officers scoured my entire townhouse for evidence. Some moments later, I saw the workers from the County Morgue rolling Percy's lifeless body through the hallway. He was zipped up in a shiny black body bag. I looked over my shoulder, instantly getting nervous all over again as I saw them slowly push his body toward the front door. For a moment, I stared at the bag and saw COOK COUNTY MEDICAL EXAMINERS OFFICE written in blocky white letters on the side of the body bag.

"Well, Mrs. Washington," uttered the detective, breaking me out of my horrid trance. "I am done asking all the questions I have for right now. But, we are going to need to take you to the hospital for a full medical exam. We are also going to need to collect a rape kit for evidence. The paramedics are outside waiting for you...."

Hospital? The fuck for what? "Can you all just give me this test right now? Why do I need to go to the hospital for that?" I asked as I didn't want to leave my house. Why though? I told them everything they needed to know and furthermore, it wasn't like Percy *really* raped me.

"No. We need to make sure you are totally fine. Besides, we would want the doctors to run a battery of tests on you just to confirm there wasn't any transmission of sexually transmitted diseases and whatnot," the detective explained.

I winced. "Fine...I just...I'm just really still so upset about my friend. I don't know if I can go back to another hospital." Shaking my head, I let out some fake tears. "This is just all too much for me."

"I understand," replied the detective. "But we really gotta run those tests...It's standard procedure."

"Fine...." I huffed. "I just need to take a shower to get this blood off me," I told him.

185

"Cool. And when you change out of your clothes, please leave them behind so the evidence technicians can also bring those with them," said the detective, who arguably was a very handsome man. He then patted me on my shoulder and stood up. He helped me up and then escorted me to my bedroom. Before I entered, I turned to him and planted a fake smile on my face. "And what was your name again, Detective?"

"Detective Colvin." He smiled and then said, "I'll meet you out front and then escort you to the ambulance."

"Fine by me," I replied then went inside my bedroom to grab my shit. A few police officers were standing inside the bedroom taking pictures of my bedroom. Seeing them snap photo after photo kind of enraged me but I had to keep my cool. "Can you gentlemen give me a moment while I change clothes and grab some of my belongings?" I politely asked them. "Sure thing, ma'am," they both said in unison. They were both chunky, older looking white men with thick mustaches. Eww! I couldn't stand no out-of-shape man, especially no damn police officer. I didn't even know why in the hell the Chicago Police would allow these two fat motha-fuckas to be on the force. Shit, if I was really in distress, I wouldn't trust these two at all!

Now by myself, I rummaged through my dresser, grabbed a pair of jeans and a shirt. I made my way over into the bathroom and quietly closed the door. Now standing in the mirror, I finally had the chance to relax a bit and stop putting on a goddamn performance! Shout out to all the women who could really act cause, honey, let me tell you something right now; putting on this act for these officers truly was a hell of an Oscar performance!

Now, don't get me wrong...I was a bit frazzled and fucked up in the head from everything that went down with Percy. What really disturbed me the most was his drama he apparently had going on with Lamar. I didn't know how I was going to do it, but I needed to get to the bottom of their situation. Earlier when that Detective Colvin was asking me a million questions, I almost told him what Percy told me about Lamar. However, something inside of me told me to not say shit. *Let's see how everything plays out...*

I closed my eyes just to clear my head. Then I took a deep breath.

But soon as I opened them, I saw Alice standing behind me. "You killed me! Bitch, you mothafuckin' killed me!"

"AHHHHH!" I screamed so loud that even my own ears cracked from my piercing wail.

"This ain't real! This ain't real!" I shook my head, hoping I was just imagining Alice. "Bitch! You killed me! Pushed me down them damn stairs! You damn murder. You three for three now! Clarence. Me. Now Percy! Bitch, you goin' straight to hell!" Alice's voice, demonic sounding, kept firing off. "YOU AIN'T REAL!" I yelled, shaking my head to the point where my neck was gonna snap in half! I shut my eyes and squeezed them tight. Once I reopened them, Alice was gone. And so was her voice. I quickly scanned the bathroom hoping that this was just a mere hallucination. "Alice... Alice...," I mumbled, my entire body quaking with fear. "I didn't kill you! I swear I didn't!"

"Is everything alright in there?" I heard a voice of what had to be an officer shout out.

"Yeah...Yes, I'm fine...I...ughh. I just saw a roach," I lied. Still standing in the mirror, I was coming to the full realization that I was quickly losing my grip on reality.

Although I was a bit apprehensive about going to the hospital, I had to get the hell up out of here! I wasn't one of those types that believed in ghosts and spirits, but I'd be damned if I was gonna become a believer today. I hopped in the shower and let the beads of hot water clean this blood off me. Once I got done, I hopped out, changed into a fresh outfit, and made my way back over to Detective Colvin. "Ready?" he asked. "Yes, sir." He led me outside where I was instantly struck by the number of people standing outside. Guess word was spreading around the neighborhood because several of my neighbors were huddled up staring at me. Officers continued to comb in and out of my house. A few of them were also standing guard on my front lawn, talking amongst each other. As Detective Colvin escorted me over to the back of the ambulance, I paused for a moment and looked up to the deep dark skies hoping my dark secrets wouldn't get revealed.

4

INTRODUCING DETECTIVE MIKE
COLVIN

"*I*t's something about that lady…I don't know what it is but there's something off about her…" I took a sip of my cold coffee as I continued to scan my interview notes. I was sitting inside of my police car. The ambulance just took off with Mrs. Washington strapped in the back. My gut got that weird feeling anytime I knew something was off. That feeling that was like a combination of tightness and nausea. Like, you just knew some shit was not right…

"Why do you say that?" my partner, Jake, asked huffing. "Colvin, I swear you always got these weird hunches. Remember the last time what happened. Your *hunches* almost got you wrote up by the Lieutenant."

I rolled my eyes. "Yeah, whatever, motherfucker. I wasn't *that* off with my last hunch. I'm usually 90 percent right."

"Yeah, but since you were ten percent off the mark the last time, you almost let a killer have their way with a five-year-old."

I shrugged my shoulders. "Police work is complicated, man."

"Okay, so what's your hunch with this lady? Man, she's an

eight-year-old who was just raped by some crazy ass guy. What's more complicated than this?"

"Yeah, I get that. I am not denying that. But…Something is just off. I don't know what it is…It's like she's telling the truth but lying at the same time. And those marks on her face and arms."

"What about them?"

"They are bruises. But they don't look like real punches." I went silent for a moment thinking about Mrs. Washington's recap of what happened. "But I guess we'll see once we get some pics back of the rest of her body."

"Man, what in the hell do you mean by they don't look like real punches…"

I shrugged my shoulders. "I don't know. Our suspect is… well, *was*, a pretty heavy man. Huge hands. But the marks on her face looked like she'd gotten into a fight with a kid or something…"

"Ughhh! Colvin! Just stop. Stop right fucking now. There's no need to dig this deep. Look, the man broke into her house, he held her hostage, tried to rob her and then he raped her. Then, she out of self-defense managed to kill the crazy motherfucker with a letter opener that just so happened to be right there on her nightstand. Case closed. Please, let's not make this extra work."

I looked over at Jake and saw his chubby face getting redder than Mars. He was fuming. He absolutely hated it when my hunch had me digging too deep. When I felt a certain type of way about an investigation, I couldn't help but let my intuition guide me down a path that others didn't want to trek. I enjoyed being a detective. Every aspect of a homicide investigation was a fucking orgasm to me. I'd been on the force now for nearly two decades and half my career was spent in Homicide Investigations. I lived and breathed this shit. Hell, I had nothing else to do but work. My wife left me years back. My only kid, Brianna, was off away at college. And even then, she and I barely spoke. So, when I had hunches, I truly had them because nothing else held my attention but work. And I had to pursue every last one of them to feel satisfied. Being satisfied with my work is what kept me alive.

"Brother…Listen…I know you don't have a fucking life. But I do. And right now it's nearly midnight and all I wanna do is go home to my wife, drink a beer, and then sneak away into the bathroom and jack my fucking dick to some of the pinkest pussy pics I can find on the web."

"Well, if that's what you wanna do, then, by all means, do you," I said back to Jake as I sat behind the steering wheel still going over my notes. "But I'm gonna do me."

"You always do…motherfucker."

My *hunch* was firing off. I felt like something was pulling me to go right back into that house and find exactly what the fuck I was looking for. Now, you could call me crazy and obsessed, but when I could sense something was wrong about your mothafuckin' ass, I was gonna dig deep until I found out the truth. I didn't give a fuck if you were eight or eighty. Wrong is wrong. This old bitch wasn't tell me the full truth about what happened. Was I trying to say what happened to her was justified? Of course not. But what I've learned over the years is that in all of these cases you should never ever take someone's word at face value. Even if the victim was some church-going, soul food-cooking grand-mother who could recite every single Bible verse like it was nothing, that didn't absolve them from the possibility of doing wrong. Everyone was capable of some shit. Even me.

"Be right back," I told Jake as I quickly hopped out of the car. "Where the fuck are you going, Colvin?!? God-mother-fucking-damnit! Get your ass back in this car now so we can finish up this report and go the fuck home!"

Without saying a word, I proceeded to walk off and tossed a birdie toward Jake as I walked up the still-crowded driveway of Mrs. Washington's townhouse. The first thing that struck me by surprise though was the car she had. What type of woman damn near eighty-years-old drove a fucking muscle car? Now, I get that people of all ages had a thing for cars. Especially men. Old ass men who were trying to live out their remaining days usually used sports cars to attract young pussy. Hell, if I had the cash, I'd be riding around in the city in a Corvette. But the more I stared at this red drop-top Mustang the more my interest in Mrs. Washington grew. Granted, I could be making all types of erroneous presumptions about this old chick but the nigga in me knew one thing: old ass black women never drove cars like this. Cadillacs. Beemers. Benzes. Lexuses. That was what the fuck I would expect out of a woman who wanted to spend some extra dollars on a nice whip. But a fucking Mustang? This wasn't even the type of car to have in Chicago. Especially during these crazy ass winters. I just knew her old ass had low iron levels and her ass probably complained all the time about being cold.

"Nice car, ain't it?" an officer on the scene asked me. I glanced over at him and then immediately threw my attention back to the car. The license tag was even crazy as fuck. PAULETTE. This lady had to be character… "Yeah. Yeah, it is," I said to the fat ass white officer. This motherfucker needed to lose weight. I couldn't stand seeing fat ass cops. Gosh, the force was going to shit. "Just blown away at the fact that this woman is driving a V-8 engine."

"No, buddy! This is a V-12. This is a special edition Hemi. Mrs. Washington definitely knows her cars."

Instantly an eyebrow rose out of suspicion. *V-12?* Yeah, no, this old bitch was definitely up to no good. "That's crazy," I simply replied and began to make my way back inside the house. By now, officers had begun to clear out of the house. Evidence technicians were done taking photographs and collecting evidence. In most cases, a homicide detective assigned to a case like this would've already had a report ready for their Lieutenant to sign off on and close out the investigation. But not me. I was gonna be diligent about this shit. And I didn't even give a fuck of Lieutenant Daniels gave me some push back.

"You all almost done?" I asked one of the evidence technicians. "Yup," she said as she pulled off a pair of latex gloves from her hands and tossed them into a garbage bag she had in one of her hands. "This lady is gonna definitely need to hire a maid service ASAP to get up all that blood. Her entire bedroom is ruined."

I chuckled then made my way into the bedroom. I froze in the middle of the floor and took a deep scan of the entire immaculate bedroom despite the fact that blood covered damn near half the room. This was a nice ass townhouse. And given we were in the middle of Hyde Park, one of the most exclusive areas on Chicago's South Side, I knew this place had to be worth at least a million. Then and there I wondered what Mrs. Washington did for a living. Soon as I got back to my desk, I was going to research the shit out of this woman. Hell, I was gonna research her deceased husband as well. I was gonna get all up into this woman's shit.

"You find what you're looking for yet, Colvin?" My eyes rolled when I heard the voice of my annoying ass partner from behind me. "No...But I have a feeling I'm close."

"Dude, just give it the fuck up, please. You are getting way too above your pay grade," said Jake, his tone sounding as if he was annoyed.

"Give me two minutes I swear I'm gonna find something that's gonna make you rethink everything."

"Please don't. I don't wanna rethink shit. We have the case wrapped up. All we gotta do is finish the fucking paperwork and take our overworked asses home!"

Ignoring Jake, I waltzed through the bedroom toward the bathroom. I pulled the door back and then strolled in. Even the goddamn bathroom reeked of nothing but luxury. You would've thought you were in Buckingham Palace. I could sense Jake trailing me and the moment he walked in, the first thing that came out of his mouth was, "Italian marble. Damn. This woman is rolling in some cash."

"Exactly," I replied. "Lots of it. That's a V-12 parked out front by the way. Special edition one of the officers told me."

I looked over at Jake and he raised a curious brow. "Really?"

"Yeah…"

"Damn, this lady is something else then…What in the fuck is she doing with a car like that?"

"Exactly," was all I said and I knew from the tone of Jake's voice that even he was beginning to get a tad suspicious. So I presumed…

I stood in the middle of the bathroom for a moment. With my hands gripped to my waist, my eyes turned to inquisitive slits, I contemplated my next move. *Come on, hunch. Come on…*I looked over to my right and saw a clothes' hamper filled to the brim. That struck as a bit odd. Despite the fact that Mrs. Washington's living room was a tad disheveled from apparently was a fight and that her bedroom was now a murder scene, the bathroom was entirely clean. But the hamper…Clothes were literally spilling out and I couldn't imagine that a woman up in age who kept her house tidy would allow clothes to spill out of a hamper like lava pouring down the sides of a volcano.

"See that?" I said to Jake pointing toward the hamper.

"See what?"

"The hamper…"

"What about it?"

"That doesn't strike you as odd?"

"No…It's just clothes."

I chuckled then strolled over to the hamper.

"Motherfucker, please do not tell me you are about to go through this woman's clothes! The fuck is wrong with you?!?"

"Every aspect of this house is a crime scene, you lazy fuck. Including the hamper."

"OH WOW! So now an old woman's shitty underwear is a part of our already closed homicide investigation! Un-fuck-ing-believable! You are a sick fuck! Let me guess?!? This is just a fucking excuse for you to swipe a pair of her panties so you can sniff on them all fucking day and night?!?"

"There are websites for that actually…," I laughed.

"What?!?"

"Yeah, there are websites where you can buy used panties from women. Big business apparently!"

"You sick fuck! Why on God's green earth did I get fucking partnered with you?!?"

I pulled back the lid to the hamper, a tad apprehensive about going through Mrs. Washington's clothes. And yeah, I couldn't lie. Perhaps if Mrs. Washington was no older than forty and looked like someone I'd wanna fuck, I'd lift a pair of her panties for keepsake. But I'd be damned if I was gonna get off on the smell of an 80-year-old woman's crotch. I had my interesting fetishes but dicking down old bitches definitely wasn't one of them.

Without hesitation, I dug my hands into the hamper and started tossing clothes off to the side, not giving a fucking if I was making a mess. I could easily stuff the clothes back in the hamper and Mrs. Washington probably wouldn't even notice that someone hunted through her dirty laundry.

"Damn, you could at least put on a pair of gloves if you're gonna do all that, you grimy motherfucker!"

Ignoring Jake, I continued to toss clothes out of the hamper onto the floor. I hoped my hunch was right because as I dug through, getting closer and closer to the bottom, I wasn't finding anything. But once I yanked out and tossed a pair of denim jeans, my eyes landed on something interesting…

"Look at this," I smiled as I pulled up a pair of stockings stuff with lemons and tangerines.

Jake's mouth dropped. "What…Oh wow. That…That's can't be…"

"That can't be what?"

"Those…Those *punches.*"

"Bingo."

25

VERNITA

The smell of the hospital was permanently fixed in my nostrils now that I had been up in this place for what seemed like a good six or seven hours. The doctors ran all types of tests on me. The police were constantly in and out of my room, taking a million pictures of my entire body. I felt so embarrassed but I knew I had to do this just to get this investigation over with.

I didn't even know what time it was. Felt like it was close to five AM or something like that. I was laying in the hospital bed, dressed in a single gown. An IV was pumping fluids in me along with some medication to make me feel relaxed. Although I was still annoyed for having to be here, this drug they had running up in me had me on cloud number nine.

Some moments later, one of the doctors, who was this fine ass young Arab-looking man, came into the room with a clipboard in his hand. "Okay, Mrs. Washington, we ran every test we needed to and you are in good health."

"Oh, thank God!" I exhaled, clasping my chest. "Lord, this is just all so much for me to handle but I thank God for you. You are such a wonderful doctor."

The doctor smiled. My eyes latched onto his wide, muscular chest and saw his name, "Dr. Talal Aziz", written in cursive blue stitching. He stood at good seven feet tall and had this dark, well-kempt beard wrapped around his chiseled face. His hair was curly. His eyes were piercing green. Chile, I didn't know these Arab mens could be so fine. Although I was high as hell on whatever drug they had running through my veins, baby, my loins were starting to get so damn moist. If I had the energy in me, I'd hop out of this damn bed, lock that damn hospital room door and then get on my knees to stuff that dick of his down my throat. I quickly glanced down at his pants and saw his print. My eyes instantly exploded with utmost surprise. That dick was like a baby anaconda just resting on the side of his leg. I bet you he had some big, long balls too.

"Is everything okay, Mrs. Washington?"

His deep voice instantly snapped me out of my daze. I looked up at him and said, "Yes, I'm sorry. I just dozed off for a moment."

"No worries. Yeah, that lorazepam can make people feel very relaxed. Nonetheless, I'll go ahead and have the nurse ready your discharge paperwork so you can head back home. I do believe the police may still have some additional questions and even some paperwork for you to fill out, he said with the biggest smile stretched across his sexy ass face. Child, his ass was having me forget about every crazy thing I had going on at the moment. All I could think about was getting me some dick. That was gonna be a true relaxer for me. Some Henny, dick, and weed was what I needed to put on my mothafuckin' menu right now! And when I got done, I'mma slide up to Wing Stop and get me a fifteen lemon pepper flats fried hard! Baby, I loves me some Wing Stop ranch, you hear me!

"Oh, so, that's why I am feeling this way. Makes total

sense now. I was wondering why I was feeling so relaxed," I told the fine ass doctor. Some dick in my ass would make me even more relaxed right about now was what I really wanted to tell him.

The doctor gave me some brief discharge instructions and then made his merry way out of the room. Back to being alone all over again, I patiently waited for the nurse to come in with this discharge paperwork. The silence was now beginning to annoy me so I flipped on the television and landed on CNN. While the morning news played I drifted off again, thinking about all the crazy shit that happened. I was definitely going to have to see Dr. Jackson to help navigate me through all of this mess.

Some moments later, a nurse bumbled her way into my room. "Alright, Mrs. Washington. I got everything cleared from the doctor and I spoke with the police and they said you are free to go. Did you want me to arrange some sort of transportation for you? Or call some family members?"

"I'm fine...I'll call for a cab," I told the short white nurse.

She walked over and began to take out the IV line running in my arm. After she bandaged me up, she handed me my discharge paperwork. I quickly signed off on the thick wad of papers so I could get the hell up out of here with the absolute quickness. I slowly began to make my way out of the bed to put my clothes back on. The clothes I wore to the hospital were inside of a bag sitting on top of an adjacent countertop inside the room.

"Okey dokey then! You're all set!" the nurse said as she made her way out of the room.

It didn't take me long to put my outfit on. Once I squeezed into my shoes, I began to make my way toward the door. Once outside, I pulled out my cell phone and dialed for a yellow cab. Five minutes later, my ride came and I was quickly taken back home.

❄

As the yellow cab pulled down the street, I saw that red police tape still sectioned off my house. "Where are we going again, ma'am?" the cab driver asked in his thick foreign accent.

"The house with the red tape…"

"Oh…Wow…" The African cab driver was just as stunned as I was at the sight of the red tape. I couldn't believe those officers would leave that shit, making my house stand out like a sore thumb. By now it was nearly 10 AM and everyone who passed by now knew my residence was the obvious site of a horrible tragedy!

"What happened there?" the cab driver asked.

"Mind your own damn business," I spat back to him and he didn't say shit back. He just kept his beady ass eyes on the road. Nosey ass mothafucka. I had it in me to report his ass to the immigration authorities. Black ass mothafucka. I was so mad right about now and this Cab driver amped me up even more!

Some seconds later, this nigga drove up to the entrance of my driveway. I threw him a $20 bill I already had in my hand and got out of the car without saying anything. This nigga was so musty and stank, too. I couldn't believe this nigga had the audacity to have the entire cab smelling like old, raw onion. Nasty mothafucka.

Just as I was about to slam the door shut, I heard him mouth off, "Nasty old bitch!"

"WHAT?!? WHAT DID YOU SAY TO ME, NIG-GUH?!?"

Before I could get into that ass, his punk bitch ass took off down the street. "YOO SON OF A BITCH! I'MMA CALL TRUMP ON YO MOTHAFUCKIN' BLACK ASS! NIGGA, YOU GOT THE RIGHT ONE TODAY, BITCH! HOE, YOU DON'T KNOW ME! I'LL KILL—"

"Vernita!"

I immediately froze when I heard the sound of what I knew was Mr. Kilpatrick standing not too far away from me. I cautious spun around. "Mr. Kilpatrick! How are you?"

"Vernita…How are you? Is everything okay? I've been so sick and worried about you. I am so sorry about everything that happened!"

"Oh, I'm fine now, Mr. Kilpatrick. I'm hanging in there. Just blessed to be alive."

"I really don't even know what to say. All of what happened seems so surreal. I just wish…" He paused for a moment, looking like he was holding himself back from crying. "I just wish I could've done more. I'm really sorry…"

"It's not your fault, Mr. Kilpatrick. It truly isn't…"

"Well, I'm just glad to know you are okay," he said as he leaned in and tried to give me a hug. I quickly jumped back though, not wanting this old ass peckerwood to put his fucking clammy paws on me.

"Sorry," he quickly apologized. Guess he realized if I was a victim of rape, the last thing I wanted was for a man to put his hands around me.

"You're fine, Mr. Kilpatrick. Thank you for checking up on me though. I appreciate it."

"Okay, well, umm, if you need anything, just let me know. I'm here for you. Just give me a ring if you need anything, Vernita" he said through a nervous grin and then walked off.

Soon as he walked off I couldn't help but grimace. Why in the fuck were white people so mothafuckin' nosey?!? He needed to mind his own fucking business! Mind the business that pays you, cracka! All up in my shit. Punk ass didn't even come and save me when he heard Percy cussing and carrying on. I smacked my teeth as I yanked my house keys out of my purse. "All of this fuckin' red tape around my shit! They couldn't even have the courtesy to remove this shit! Got me out here lookin' crazy!" I yelled at myself. I didn't give a fuck if the whole entire goddamn city could hear me going off either. I was mad as FUCK. "Shit make me wanna kill someone."

"You already did that three times…"

What the hell?!? My eyes shot open with fear again. I quickly looked around when I swore I heard the voice of Alice. I didn't see her though. I closed my eyes. "It's just a hallucination, Vernita. Just a hallucination. Calm down. Calm down."

I grabbed my chest. My heart was pounding so damn hard. As I quickly tried to unlock my door, my hands quaked with sudden anxiety. The hallucinations, the voices, the flashbacks – everything was beginning to really drive me fucking crazy. I got inside the house, slamming the door shut and quickly locking it. I stood there in the foyer for a moment, silent and frozen. "Alice," I mumbled.

"What you want, bitch?"

My eyes once again exploded wide open. "Where are you, Alice?"

"Bitch, I'm right here." I heard her voice to my left and I quickly spun in that direction. And there she was, standing there holding her neck as if she had immense pain radiating from it. She had a visible gash above her eyebrow. She began to move closer to me, limping as if she'd broken her ankle or foot.

"GET AWAY FROM ME!" I screeched. "BITCH! I'LL KILL YOU!"

"I'm already dead, bitch! How in the fuck can you kill me again!"

"NO! NO! I DIDN'T KILL YOU! STOP LYING ON ME! I WOULDN'T DARE!"

Everything around me began to spin and it seemed like I was in the middle of a violent earthquake.

Suddenly I took off running in the middle of my living room, making my way toward the bedroom.

"Don't run, you old ass whore! You lying ass Jezebel!" I heard her shouting from behind me.

"GET AWAY FROM ME! LEAVE ME BE! I AIN'T DID NOTHIN' TO YA!"

"YES THE HELL YOU DID!"

Once I flew into my bedroom, I came to an abrupt stop when I realized my entire room was still a wreck from when I killed Percy.

"YOU KILLED ME, VERNITA! WHY?!? WHY DID YOU KILL ME?!?"

I gasped when I heard what sounded like Percy shouting at me. I turned to my right and there he was standing there. The side of his neck was gushing with blood. "NO! THIS IS ALL FAKE! JUST IN MY HEAD!"

"NO IT AIN'T, BITCH! YOU FUCKING KILLED ME, YOU RAGGEDY ASS BITCH! I'MMA GET YOU—"

"No! Don't put your hands on my wife, nigga!"

"Cla-Clarence?"

Was that...Was that Clarence?!? I spun to my left and there Clarence was, walking slowly up to me looking like a Zombie!

"WHY YOU KILL ME?!? ALL I DID FOR YOU!"

"NOOO!" I kept yelling as I flew over to my closet. I had to get my hands on my pistol expeditiously so I could shoot these motherfuckers!

Knock! Knock! Ding-Dong! "POLICE! OPEN UP!"

"The police?" I suddenly becoming immobile when I heard the sound of someone saying they were the police pounding at my door and then the doorbell began ringing.

Taking deep breaths, I closed my eyes. "It's just all in your head, Vernita. All in your head." I re-opened my eyes and the ghosts of Alice, Clarence and Percy disappeared. "Lord! Lord! Lord!" I cried, shaking my head furiously.

"IT AIN'T IN YOUR HEAD, BITCH!"

"NO! NOOOO!" Oh, Lord! These voices! This was just too much!

26

DETECTIVE MIKE COLVIN

*S*leep deprivation was a motherfucker. But being deprived of hours of sleep was worth it if I can get the truth out this woman.

"Where the fuck this bitch at?" I grumbled to myself as I kept pounding on Mrs. Washington's front door, wondering if her shady ass was home.

I looked around and almost had the urge to go next door and ask a neighbor if they'd seen her all this morning.

I yawned – I was tired as fuck and I wanted to get this shit over with already.

I stood back for a moment and took in the scenery. Wow. Hyde Park was an amazing ass neighborhood. This townhouse complex was off the fucking chain. I always wanted to live in Hyde Park. The area was now booming and this luxury townhouse complex was built not too long ago.

Anyways –

I had just got off the phone with one of the nurses at the hospital where Mrs. Washington had been taken to after what happened last night. I was told she went straight home. Nurse said she flew straight out of the hospital and took a cab. Now that was pretty strange. I wondered why she didn't have a friend or a family member come pick her up. That seemed pretty odd given that she was just in a fucked up situation. Hell, if a nigga broke up into my shit and raped me, I'd be afraid to even go back home.

I kept knocking on the door. "Damn, lady, what the fuck?!?" I was getting very pissed.

As seconds turned into a minute I was just about ready to give up and head back to the station. Still standing at the door, I put my hands on my waist and exhaled wondering where this woman could've been. Then again, perhaps she did go over to a friend's house or something. I paused for a moment when I heard what sounded like faint screaming. Sounded like it was coming from inside of the house. "The fuck?!?" My eyebrow raised, my face twisted with confusion. "Damn, someone's in there…"

I began pounding on the door again. "Police!" I yelled out. "Mrs. Washington?!? Are you in there?"

Just before I was about to try to bust the door open, I heard the front door unlock and there she was standing there with the biggest grin on her slightly bruised face. "Hey there!" she greeted me enthusiastically. "Detective Colvin, right?"

"Yes, ma'am…" I paused again for a second as I scanned her up and down. I swore – for a woman who was just violently attacked, raped and then ultimately had to kill her rapist, she seemed to be in a somewhat festive mood. Nothing, and I mean absolutely *nothin*, at all made me think this woman was just a victim of a horrendous crime less than twenty-four hours ago. "I, umm, is everything okay? I wanted to swing by to check up on you. I just called the hospital and they told me you were home. I had been knocking on your door for quite some time." I let out a weird, nervous chuckle. "…I think I may have even heard some yelling going on."

Mrs. Washington exploded into laughter. "Haha! Child, I was just in there singing to myself with my earphones on. I was just trying to get myself together and get my mind off of everything that happened."

"Okay…," I replied, and then we both stood there staring at each other in complete silence. Shit was starting to get super-weird so I broke the uncomfortable silence by saying, "Well, I have some more follow-up questions."

She simply replied with, "Okay," and suddenly that smile of hers turned partly flat.

"Can I come in?" I politely asked. I didn't want to stand outside. The weather was a bit chilly. That was one thing about living in Hyde Park. The neighborhood was right off the fucking lake and the winds that rolled off the lakeshore were nasty, especially during this time of the year.

"My house is very much still a wreck. I got these folks coming over soon to clean up the place," said Mrs. Washington.

"Well, I can just ask a few questions here then," I said. "If you don't mind."

I could tell I was getting on this woman's nerves already. Her ass was probably super-suspicious that I had an inkling about her lies.

"No…No, I don't mind. Ask ahead," she said tucking her hands under her arms as she leaned against the frame of her front door.

"So, once again, I just want to say I know all of this is very devastating to you and I deeply apologize that something like this happened. I just wanna make sure before I send my final report over to my lieutenant that I got all my facts straight."

"Ok, no worries, sweetheart. Ask away…"

"Cool…" I quickly pulled out a notepad and a pen from my jacket pocket, flipped open to a blank page and then asked, "So, those punches on your face. You said the suspect, when he broke into your house, began punching you around until you fell out on the floor."

"Yes, that is correct," she said.

"Wow, you must've put up a good defense because in any other circumstance you could've easily sustained more damage to your face. I'm surprised you didn't get a broken jaw or something…. Especially considering your age."

Yeah, I went there. I knew it was borderline disrespectful to bring up a woman's age. But hey, it is what it is…However, I guess my statement must've rubbed her the wrong way. Her eyes briefly broke their attention away from me and then she smacked her teeth. "My age? Now what is that supposed to mean, Detective?"

"No disrespect," I said flashing her an instant sham smile. "But you're a bit up in age and the suspect was in his forties I believe. Actually, late thirties. I'd have to double-check." I paused for a split second. "But that brings me to another point. This suspect…You said you knew him from years back. How was that?"

"He was my husband's caretaker at the nursing home he had been staying in before he died."

"Interesting. Okay. And how exactly did he know where you lived?"

"Well…" She paused and then took a deep breath as she clutched her chest. "…We remained friends…" Mrs. Washington took another long, deep breath as she lowered her head. "I don't know what to make of it all. I just…I never would've thought he would do something like this to me. He was such a nice young man to me."

"Wow. Yeah, that is crazy. And you said this was over money?"

"Yes…He kept mentioning this man named…I forgot… Started with an L. Lawrence or something."

"Okay…Well, I'll keep this in mind."

"Any other questions, Detective? I really hate to be short but I got a lot of stuff on my plate right now and I need to get to my doctor. Also, my friend's funeral is coming up pretty soon and I'm still so devastated by that. I gotta help the family with funeral arrangements."

"I understand. Well, yeah, that is all the questions I have… for right now. And you have my condolences."

"Thank you, Detective…"

"No, thank you!" I replied, giving her the biggest grin I could make. But then I knew this next question would throw her for a surprise. "By the way, do you prefer the taste of tangerines or oranges?"

Her unassuming eyes instantly became large with fear and I could tell she was fighting hard to stop herself from producing a scowl. Then she smiled, which I knew that was nothing more than a fraudulent smirk masking her unexpected nervousness. "Huh? Excuse me?"

"Nevermind. I just have a hankering for something sweet and tangy. I saw the lovely fruit bowl on your kitchen countertop earlier. Sorry…Just random question," I told her as I quickly put my notepad and pen back into my jacket pocket.

"Ohh…Hrrrm. Okay then…Well, I prefer tangerines," she replied. "I love to put them in my morning smoothies. But anyways, Detective. I gotta get going." She looked over my shoulders. "The cleaning folks just arrived."

I turned around and then saw a white Ford minivan pull up. Two Mexican-lookin' muhfuckas hopped out. Both of them had on white jumpsuits and N95 masks wrapped around their faces. As they began walking up the driveway, I looked back at Mrs. Washington and reached my hand out to shake her hand. "I'll be in touch, Mrs. Washington."

She cautiously shook my hand then pulled away as if I was some pervert or some shit.

By now the two cleaners were a foot away from us. "Hello

there. We're here to clean up the house," one of the cleaners said.

"Yes, come on in," uttered Mrs. Washington to the cleaners but she kept her eyes glued on me. Guess now she knew I *knew.*

I spun around and made my way back to my car. I chuckled knowing that I was inching closer and closer to the truth. This old bitch was telling all types of lies and I was going to get to the bottom of it.

Once I hopped in my car, I checked my cell phone for any missed calls or text messages. And lo and mothafuckin' behold, I saw that I had five missed calls – all came straight from my Lieutenant. Then I checked my text messages. Boss even sent me a text. Seemed like I was in trouble. I opened the text message and I was hit with, "BRING YOUR STUPID ASS BACK TO THE STATION! NOW!" And on that note, I quickly chucked up the engine to the cruiser and headed back to the station.

Back in the station, my partner Jake and I were sitting in our lieutenant's office getting our asses handed to us.

"PLEASE, PLEASE, PLEASE explain to me why you are letting this low-life motherfucker run wild?!?" Lieutenant Daniels was literally foaming at the mouth, screaming directly into my partner Jake's face. "I'm not gonna hold him accountable. Because I already know he's a prying piece of shit that doesn't know how to mind his own fucking business and just go with the facts at hand. So I'm blaming your ass, Jake! I can't believe you all are going to pull this shit! An old woman gets her house broken into and she's raped. She defends herself. CASE CLOSED! What more else is to this?"

Jake cleared his throat. "Lieutenant, with all due respect, I tried to tell him to back off and close out the case but we—"

"BUT WE WHAT?!?" Lieutenant interrupted Jake and threw his hands up in the air. Before Jake could finish his statement, the Lieutenant continued, "I don't give a good goddamn what this asshole over here thinks. You need to push back and hold him responsible." Then Lieutenant Daniels' big, black and menacingly ugly ass stared directly at me. "And you...I swear on my dead mother's grave that if your clearance rate wasn't as high as it is – because I must admit you are a pretty good detective – I would have your ass working evidence. Better yet, I'd have the fucking commander assign your punk ass to traffic. Stick your ass out somewhere on the far Northwest side. And you know those senior citizens out there obey every fucking traffic law in the land."

With a small smirk on my face, I was confident once I told the Lieutenant of my little discovery, he'd back the fuck off and let me do my thing.

Slight silence filled the room for a moment.

"Why aren't you saying anything? Say something, moth-erfucker! Say something or I am going to write you up for insubordination!" screamed the Lieutenant as a few of his spit speckles landed on my forehead. Gross.

Without saying a word, I reached into my jacket pocket, pulled out a few photographs and placed them on Lieu-tenant's desk, gently sliding them in his direction.

"What's this?"

"Look closely...," I replied and sat back with my arms folded, anxiously awaiting his reaction. "I took these with my phone then printed them out a moment ago."

Lieutenant's face was screwed with confusion. "I'm not quite understanding what the fuck I'm looking at, Detective...All I just see a pair of stockings with some balls stuffed in them. What the fuck is this shit?"

"Sir...those aren't balls," I said.

"Then what are they?"

"Those are tangerines," I replied.

"Okay, and?"

I snapped my fingers trying to remember the woman who played that crazy ass chick in that movie. "You ever seen the movie *A Thin Line Between Love And Hate*. That nineties flick with Martin Lawrence and the chick with the big forehead?"

The lieutenant's eyes widened as if everything clicked in his head. "Lynn Whitfield. And yes, I've seen that movie. But...No..." The Lieutenant shook his head with fervor. His entire body language instantly became fluent in disbelief.

"See...I told you...Case ain't closed," I said laughing. Jake took a quick glance over at me and then shook his head. I didn't know if he was shaking his head out of embarrassment or shock that I persuaded the Lieutenant. However, the boss stood there for a moment, wrapped in deep silence. Guess he was trying to put everything together.

"Colvin...," the Lieutenant said in a tone that had me convinced he was convinced.

"Yes, Lieutenant...," I replied.

"Get this shit out of my face. Throw these pictures away. I'm tired of your shit. END THE FUCKING CASE, YOU ZEALOUS SON OF A BITCH!"

"But Lieutenant! This doesn't seem shady—"

"I DON'T CARE!" Lieutenant interrupted. "Close out this fucking case now! Have the report on my desk by five PM or I am writing you up for insubordination and I will put in a request to transfer your ass to Traffic! NOW THE TWO OF YOU GET THE FUCK OUT OF MY OFFICE!"

With that being said, I nodded at Jake and then we proceeded to stand up. "Well, Lieutenant, it's your squad and

I will follow orders," I said. "I'll have that report on your desk ASAP."

"And close my mothafuckin' door when you two assholes leave," yelled the Lieutenant as Jake and I walked out of the Lieutenant's office. And following his stern instruction, I gently closed his door. Jake and I took cautious strides toward our cubicles while the rest of the detectives on the floor gave us awkward stares. They must've heard all the screaming and cursing.

Once we made it back to our cubicles, I sat down at my desk and a wave of fucking anger came over me. Jake sat down then rolled up to me in his chair. "Listen, brother…You know sometimes I'm just fucking joking with you. Man, you're a great detective. You've solved a bunch of cold cases. But this one right here; just drop it. There's absolutely nothing going on with that old woman."

"That's what everyone says every time," I said turning on my computer monitor. I booted up my PC. "I'll finish out the report…But that doesn't stop my investigation."

"What are you talking about?" Jake angrily asked. "Dude, just fucking drop it! Unless you seriously want out of Homicide! And if that's the case, you can commit career suicide by yourself! I'm gonna do what the fucking Lieutenant says."

"No…I'm not committing career suicide. I'll do my *job*. But that won't stop me from finding the real truth. And when I do, I'll put money on it that this was a much bigger story."

Jake smacked his teeth and said, "Okay, well, you do that." He rolled back over toward his desk.

Once my PC got started up, I logged in, quickly opened up Microsoft Word and began to finish my investigation report. Truth be told, I had an inkling the Lieutenant would rip into me and threaten to write me up for not closing out the case much earlier. So, that being said, most of my report had already been completed. My ass worked on it all fucking early morning soon as I left the crime scene.

Although I was running on zero hours of sleep, nasty ass McDonald's Black coffee kept me fueled. But now sleep was truly setting in and once I got done with finalizing some of these notes I was going to head straight home. I had the next two days off, so I figured I'd use those days to start doing my own off duty investigation. I wasn't going to let Mrs. Washington get away with a crazy ass lie.

Just before I was about to get to typing, I heard a knock on the side of my cubicle. I glanced up and saw it was a beat officer in full uniform. He was a younger dude, looked like he was new to the force. Black, too. "Wassup?" I said and looked back at my monitor as I began typing.

"Hey, Detective. I was told to come see you," he said.

"About?"

"Last night…or early this morning. The rape-murder case over in Hyde Park."

I looked back up the young officer. "Yeah. What about it? It's a closed case already?"

"Yeah, well, okay. Well, I don't know if you know this but that old lady…"

I paused for a moment and I could find my intuition begin to fire up. Please let this young dude have something good for me. "What about her?"

"Something's off with that chick."

"What do you mean?"

"Well, just a few weeks ago, we caught her having a full-on psychotic breakdown in the women's locker room at the health club on 47th street."

"What's your name, Officer?" I asked the rookie. "You must be new."

"Yeah, I am. I'm Officer Harrington. I've been on the force now for about six months."

Guess what Officer Harrington just said caught the attention of Jake. He rolled over in his chair next to me and now we both were giving Officer Harrington our full attention. "Okay, so tell me about this psychotic episode."

"Well, we were called to the gym sometime in the mid-afternoon. When we got there, she was literally squatting down and pissing all over the floor." He paused for a moment then cleared his throat. "But that's not the crazy part…"

"Shit, then what is?" asked Jake in what I knew was his typical sarcastic ass tone.

"She was pretending like she was having sex with someone. It was almost as if she was squatting over someone's face and someone was performing oral sex on her."

Jake and I instantly looked at each other. "Told you," I laughed.

"Just drop it," Jake huffed and then rolled over to his desk.

"Well, thanks for that info, Officer Harrington. But like I said, the investigation is closed. Crazy story but it ain't none of our business. Besides, did she get arrested for anything?"

"No. We just let her go. Felt kind of bad for her," the rookie said. "But anyways, considering what happened earlier this morning I figured you all should know that…"

"Okay, cool. Well, let me get back to this report and you get back to your beat," I told the rookie. He wandered off and I went right back to finishing up this report.

I definitely wasn't going to sleep now…

27

VERNITA

*T*ANGERINES?!?
What the fuck did that motherfucker mean by tangerines?!?

He must've gone through my shit! I just KNOW it!

Why else would that nigga mention tangerines?!? Yeah! He went through my hamper! That was exactly he thought he was being all cute and shit talking about tangerines! That nigga must've thought I was dumb!

Rage instantly brewed down within me when that no good, rotten ass Detective thought it was a tad funny to make that snarky ass joke about tangerines.

I stood in my door, watching his ass make his way back to that raggedy piece of shit cop car. Low life mothafucka. Gone come and try get under my skin. I was just a rape victim, nigga! Yeah, I knew exactly what the fuck he was doing. He came over to my house to ask me some "follow-up questions" alright. Nah, nigga! You think you on to something. But I'd tell you right now, nicca! Yo ass ain't on to shit! You ain't gonna solve shit over here, buddy! GOT THAT FUCKING RIGHT! *Okay, calm down, Vernita. Calm down. Don't make a scene. Do NOT make a scene, girl. Maybe the man really did see the fruit bowl sitting on top of the kitchen countertop? Yeah, that was it! Had to be. Why else would he go through your clothes like that?!? Girl, you tripping! Haha!*

I had to keep reassuring myself but I just had this inkling that nigga went through my shit. I couldn't help but swim down that vicious stream of thought. And the more my anxious mind kept dwelling on it, the more I could feel my pulse thumping on the side of my neck. My blood pressure was up. Felt like I was about to have a stroke and nervous meltdown all at the same time.

Like a ticking time bomb, I was ready to explode but I had to keep my calm as I kept my eyes on the detective. Then I heard the engine to his car start up. While he idled on the street for a moment, my gaze then wandered over to the two cleaners standing in front of me. I stared at them for a moment but my mind was drawing blanks. "Mrs. Washington?" one of them asked. "Yes…," I responded but my eyes were now back onto the detective's car. I clenched my fists tight. *Calm down, Vernita. Calm down. He don't know shit. You're overthinking this shit.*

Within seconds, I manage to subside the paranoia within me but I couldn't help but think that this detective was trying to figure me and my shit out. Gosh I was so mothafuckin' mad right now. Chile, I swear I just had it in me to go and cuss that punk ass nigga out. How dare he! You know what?!? Soon as I got back into the house, I was going to call up the police station and ask to speak to his motherfuckin' supervisor! How dare he come over to my house unannounced and try to ask me all of these intimidating questions! Punk ass bitch! AHHHHHHHH!

"Ma'am?" one of the cleaners asked, breaking me out of a deep trance.

Oh shit! I realized I had dozed off as I watched the detective speed off.

"Sorry about that. Ya'll come in. I'm so glad ya'll were able to come down as soon as possible," I quickly apologized to the cleaners and then let them inside the house. Side note – it was such a nice day outside. Might have to take me a walk later on. Seemed kind of windy though…

I quickly slammed the door shut and locked it once the two gentlemen were inside. I led them into the bedroom and showed them what needed to be cleaned up.

Thank God I was able to stop those crazy hallucinations though. Ever since I had come back from the hospital, I kept getting haunted by visions of Clarence, Percy and even Alice. They felt so real but I knew they weren't. At least that is what I had to keep telling myself. But, honey, I really needed to call Dr. Jackson as soon as possible and really figure out what the fuck was going on with that goddamn medicine she had me on! That shit was way worse than that other damn medicine. Praxamil. Paracemil. WHATEVER THE FUCK IT WAS CALLED! Chile, I done forgot!

Shit, truth be told, only thing I missed about that medicine was how horny it made me. Ooh, chile, Vernita could shole use some dick right about now. But, baby, this new medicine here that Dr. Jackson had me on – it definitely was worse than that other shit 'cause I was seeing all types of crazy stuff. But, baby, let me find out that damn medicine was making my tumor worse! I'd run down to that damn doctor's office and wrap my hands around that little stank bitch's throat! See, I done already told her I didn't want no goddamn medicine in my body that was gonna have me going fuckin' crazy! She knew how I felt about putting that stuff in my body that was going to make me loopy!

This was all too much! JUST TOOO MUCH! Especially considering everything that happened with Alice and now with Percy! Lord, Lord, Lord! I had no idea why you were doing all of this to me, Lord, but I didn't deserve it. I ain't deserve not none of this here! *Okay, Vernita! Get it together! Get it the FUCK together!* I had to snap back into reality before I scared away these two nice men.

The two young Mexican guys stood a few feet away from my blood-soaked bed, assessing the amount of work they were probably gonna have to do. They were speaking in Spanish amongst each other, and every few seconds or so, they would look at me with this weird ass look. They were probably wondering what in the hell happened. I didn't give them that much detail when I had called them an hour ago. I just told them that a crime had been committed inside of my house and I needed someone to help me clean up as soon as possible. One of them looked at me strangely again and I was just about ready to pop off on him if he kept giving me that weird ass stare! Yeah, yeah, yeah, mothafuckas. Someone died up in here! Yes! I killed someone! I was so mad too because these mothafuckas were charging me an arm and a leg. Six-hundred dollars plus an additional two hundred for the rush job. Fucking ripoff. They kept talking to each other in Spanish and as time flew by I was getting ready to cuss them the fuck out. "Umm, excuse me, but when do ya'll plan on starting 'cause I got some things to do. Do ya'll have everything you need?" I asked not trying to sound annoyed as fuck but baby I was annoyed! "We're just trying to figure out exactly all the chemicals we need. That's all," one of them said back to me. "Oh...Oh okay," I said as I stood back for a moment wondering once again why in the fuck that damn detective made mention of tangerines.

I just couldn't quite shake what that nigga said out of my mind. I just knew he had to have gone through my hamper. I knew he did! I could feel it. Why else would that nigga make mention of that shit?!? No, he was fucking with me. He must've easily figured out that Percy didn't really put his hands on me like that. "I'll be right back," I told the cleaner as I marched over into the bathroom. "Ya'll excuse me," I said with a phony smile on my face as I gently closed the bathroom door.

Soon as the door closed, I flew over to the hamper and tossed the lid back. I paused for a moment, wondering if I could notice if someone had been running their claws hands through my shit!

And indeed my suspicions were confirmed! The hamper looked like it had been toyed with! I could just tell. I just didn't throw my shit in the hamper any ole way. YEAH! Something was definitely off! I could tell! GODDAMN IT!

I saw a pair of jeans sitting on top of the pile inside the hamper and that was my sign right then and there that someone had been through all my shit! "I KNEW IT! THAT NUCCA IS FUCKING WITH ME!" I spat aloud but then quickly clasped my mouth. I forgot just that quick I had company. "Okay, calm down, Vernita. Calm it down, girl. Don't go crazy now. Just calm down. It's all in your head. Just in your head." Baby, I had to keep repeating that in my head just to get my nerves together. I kept taking deep breaths to simmer the rage once again brewing deep down in my core.

I began pulling out clothing item after clothing item from the hamper until I got damn near the bottom. Soon as my eyes landed on the tangerine-filled pair of stockings, I yanked it out and took a good gawk at it. "Yeah, he knows... He knows. This nigga thinks he's slick. Think he gonna try to figure some shit out. Okay, mothafucka! BRING IT, NUCCA! BRING IT! I want you to try me, hoe! TRY ME!"

My breathing once again intensified to the point where I was damn near hyperventilating. Felt like I was about to have a full on asthma-attack.

"YESSSS, BITCH! He's onto your shit now!"

My eyes exploded once again with terror when I heard the voice of Alice over my shoulder.

I quickly turned around but she wasn't there.

"DON'T FUCK WITH ME! I GOT COMPANY, BITCH!" I couldn't help but yell out but I had to cover my mouth again. "Fuck, fuck, fuck!" I grumbled then began pacing the bathroom floor like a manic. You know what – these crazy ass visions were all I needed to know that I had to get the fuck up outta here and just let these Mexican boys clean my shit up. Truth be told, I didn't even know if I could stay at my own damn house tonight, let alone for the next few days. I had to get the fuck up out of here!

Without even bothering to put the clothes back into the hamper, I stormed out of the bathroom. The two cleaners, who looked like they were in the middle of moving furniture around, immediately stopped what they were doing. "Is everything okay, Mrs. Washington?"

"Ooops!" I covered my mouth like some little girl. "Ya'll heard me??? Yeah, umm, yeah, I'm fine! I was just on the phone talking to one of my good ole friends," I lied with the biggest smile etched on my face. "I'm gonna let you boys do your thing. I'm just gonna pack up a bag of some clothes and find me a hotel where I can stay for the next few days?"

"But how are you going to lock up your house?" one of the cleaners asked while I noticed my phone was actually charging on my nightstand. Damn, now it was obvious I had told them a lie! I ran over and grabbed my phone. I then ran over to my jewelry box sitting on one of my bedroom dressers. I yanked out a spare house key then rushed over to one of the Mexican boys. "Ya'll ain't some thieving ass moth-afuckas, are you?" Chile, you just know I had to ask 'cause see these Mexicans be known to break into yo shit and clean your place the fuck out!

"No," one of them, who was a tad short and stubby,

responded. He seemed very weirded out by me. "Why would you ask that?"

"Well, I'm gonna leave you all a key. The alarm code 445529. Do what ya'll gotta do. Have my shit looking like it's a brand new house and I'll throw ya'll an extra *somethin'-somethin'.*" I grinned. "Can you do that for me?"

A brief moment of awkward silence filled the room.

"Sure...but how much is this extra somethin-somethin?" one of them asked.

"How about another $500? Does that work? How about five-hunned each?" Hopefully that would get them to just shut the fuck up and get to work.

Both of the Mexican boys looked at each other with enlarged eyes and then they both stared back at me. "Sure," they said in unison. Guess they didn't have to speak in Spanish to quickly say yes to my proposition. Although this was now gonna cost me thousands of dollars to get my place back together, at this point, I didn't give a damn! I just needed get the hell up outta here and get my mind right! This was just all too much! Too much, I tell you!

"Okay, great! Just charge it to my card!" I quickly exclaimed as I dashed over to my closet. Once inside, I grabbed the first piece of luggage my eyes landed on and then began stuffing it with as many clothes as I could grab off hangers. I stormed back out of the closet and went to one of my dressers where I kept some more clothes. I had no idea what the fuck I was putting in my bag, but all I knew at the moment was that I needed to get the hell out of here. If I needed something, I'd just have to run my ass to Target or some other department store.

28

DETECTIVE MIKE COLVIN

*S*oon as I submitted my case report over to the Lieutenant, he shot me back an e-mail telling me I needed to take the rest of the week off. Told me I need to stop thinking about work for the next few days or so. This wasn't the first time he dished out one of his lectures to me about work-life balance. He always told me I needed to stop being so obsessed with trying to figure everything out and that I needed to learn how to set boundaries. And so now that I was doing – taking my mind off work and I figured there was no other way to do that other than drill deep into some pussy.

"Yeah, fuck me! Fuck me harder! FUCK ME!"

I just wished this bitch would fucking nut already so I could get the fuck on with the rest of my day. I thought busting a nut would at least help me sleep, but I couldn't even fucking let one go.

I kept gliding in and out the pussy, but I honestly just wasn't in the mood at all. Truth be told, I was only even fucking this broad just to get her off my nerves.

Lisa's hands were gripped to my back and she stared deep

down into my eyes as if she was trying to read my soul. "Are you cumming yet?" she asked in this porn actress voice. I hated it when she did that. It was so fucking annoying.

Gyrating deep inside of her, I almost found my corner deep up in that puss but something was just off. I closed my eyes and began to fuck her harder and harder. The headboard thumped against the wall. I wondered if the next door neighbors heard us. Then again it was about one pm on this seemingly sunny Monday. Usually around this time no one was home.

"Come on! FUCK ME! FUCK ME HARDER!" Lisa screamed as she dug her long nails into my back. Those damn shits felt like the talons of a fucking falcon.

I came to an abrupt stop.

I couldn't do this. I had to get to work. And all I could see at the moment was a vivid picture of that no good ass Mrs. Washington laughing at me, telling me she was getting away with cold-blooded murder. Nah, fuck that! You weren't getting away with shit! Not on my mothafuckin' watch!

"What's wrong?" Lisa asked the second I stopped. I opened my eyes and looked at her. "I gotta go."

She smacked her teeth. "What the fuck?!?"

"Sorry," I said as I rolled up out of her and then hopped my fully naked ass out of the bed. My dick was already limp. I'd probably just beat my shit later to go to sleep.

"Wait one mothafuckin' minute! You're not finished yet! You gotta finish what the fuck you started!" demanded Lisa as she scrunched herself up in the bed and pulled the sheets over her to cover up her titties.

Lisa was this chick I knew from high school. We'd recently got back into touch with one another after our twenty-year high school reunion. She was the type of chick who I had longed to fuck when I was in high school. She was what these young niggas nowadays would call a "slim-thick situation". In fact, all the niggas used to drool over her ass. She still somewhat looked the same, but with three kids, all by three different men, and a job paying her no more than $35,000 a year, you can tell stress and drama somewhat took a toll on her face. She kind of reminded me of Vanessa Williams. She had the same round light green eyes, yellow complexion and bronze hair. The only difference was Vanessa Williams had money and Lisa's ass was broke as shit. I didn't even know why I let myself go down this road with her because she never even used to talk to me like that when we were in high school.

"I'm really sorry but you gotta leave. I just...I got this case I'm working on and it's stressing me the fuck out. Maybe we can link up later?" I told her as I proceeded to put my clothes on. Yeah, perhaps the case was *officially* closed, but in my eyes, it was far from closed. Shit was more open than a fresh, sore wound on the side of nigga's face after he got punched by Mike Tyson's bare knuckles.

"Ughhh! I don't even know why I even started fucking with you!" Lisa bellowed. She sounded as if she was suddenly disgusted with me. "I mean, you got a big dick and all, but damn, does it even fucking work?"

I took a deep breath and shook my head. Now this bitch was about to make me fucking go off on her if she didn't heed to a fucking simple instruction. "Look, please...I'm really sorry. I'll make it up to you. I promise," I lied.

"Yeah, yeah, yeah, nigga! I don't even know why I started fucking around with you! You were lame as fuck in high school and it's obvious you still lame as hell! No wonder your wife left you! WACK ASS!" With full-on anger, she threw the covers off herself and jetted out of the bed. "Now that was fucked up. Was that even necessary?" I muttered and took a quick glance over my shoulder, getting a good look of her body. As she quickly slipped on her panties, she said back to me, "I'm just fucking upset right now! I'm fucking horny and I'm on my lunch break and I just wasted an hour with your ass! That's foul as fuck!"

Lisa still had a nice shape to her and in any other situation I would've definitely been ripping that cooch apart. But like I said, with more pressing matters on the mind, I couldn't concentrate on shit else, not even my own well-being, until I figured out what was really going on with Mrs. Washington.

I suddenly managed to cool my nerves, preventing myself from cursing Lisa out. I get it though. It was truly my fault and I should've never invited her over knowing good and goddamn well I wasn't in the right state of mind to do shit.

Now fully dressed, I walked over to her and said, "You ever been to Ruth's Chris?"

"Nigga, I don't wanna hear anything else coming out of your mouth!" she barked as she pushed me out of her way and then marched over to my bathroom. I went over to my dresser and quickly pulled out something that I knew would suddenly change her tune. I then strolled over into the bathroom and watched her run water through her hair. She started back at me not saying a word. My hands were behind my back because I knew this surprise coming would instantly shift the funky ass attitude she had. I took a few steps toward her then reached out my right hand toward her, revealing a rectangular black box in the palm of my right hand. Suddenly she froze. "What's that?" "Open it," I told her. She looked so disarmed and caught off guard. With this slight caution she reached out and grabbed the black box. She opened it and instantly her entire gaze lit up like a little kid in a candy store. "This can't be…This…Wait. What is this for?"

"I bought this for you the other day, actually. It's a bracelet I got from Zale's. I know I've been busy lately and had been blowing you off here and there but I truly care for you," I lied. "But if you still think I'm lame as fuck then by all means we can stop what we are doing. But just know, I really do have feelings for you and wanted to take things to the next level."

She clutched her mouth and her eyes began to water. "I'm...I'm so sorry...I just—"

"No, it's cool. I get it. But do you understand now? I'm not blowing you off. It's just work has me bogged down."

"How much did this even cost?" she asked, wiping her eyes free of tears. "Now I feel so bad. I didn't mean what I said about you and your ex-wife. I'm so sorry. I'm just frustrated, that's all..."

I lightly chuckled as I grabbed the fake diamond-studded bracelet out of the box and helped her put it on. "Like I said...This is just a symbol of my feelings for you."

"Oh my God! This means so much to me!" she cried. See, I knew this *gift* would persuade her simply, semi-sloppy, tired-looking ass to re-think this situation we had going on. Truth be told, the bracelet was a gift I was planning on giving to my daughter, Natasha. However, since the little bitch wasn't speaking to me at the moment, I decided not to give it to her. Last time we spoke, she cursed me out for not being supportive of her choice to study dance in college. She told me I was such a shitty father and that she was glad Natalie, my ex-wife, cheated on me with one of my best friends. Tasha was a junior in college, so she was old enough to know what the fuck her words would do. Aside from not giving her the bracelet, I was also gonna stop those payments on her car note. Although the car was in both of ours names, I was paying note. I didn't give a fuck about my credit either because it was already jacked. Oh well...

Without hesitation, Lisa threw her arms around me and gave me the tightest hug. She planted kisses all up and down my neck. You would've sworn by the way she was kissing me and how her mood suddenly shifted that I had proposed to her raggedy ass. I felt like somewhat of a shitbag for giving her a gift that I clearly intended to give to my daughter but hey, guess the universe had different intentions for it.

Although I was pressed for time, I was taken back a bit by the fact that it was so crazy to see how easy it was to use a piece of jewelry to distract a woman's mind. "So, look, I really gotta head back to work but what is this Ruth's Chris place?" she asked as she couldn't keep her eyes off the fake ass bracelet. It was actually cubic zirconium and it was on sale for $75.

"Damn, you never heard of Ruth's Chris? It's a nice steakhouse," I said giving her a fake ass smile. "They have a location in Downtown, right off the river. I wanted to treat you to a romantic night."

"Oh wow! Wow! This just really made me feel so differently about you!" she said as she stared at herself in the mirror, swaying side from side as if she were a model. I grabbed her and began to make out with her as if we were two teenagers about to fuck in the backseat of a car for the first time.

We kept kissing but then Lisa then suddenly pulled back away from me. "Damn! DAMN! Where was all of this just a moment ago?"

"Shit, I don't know," I replied shrugging my shoulders. "But look, let me do what I gotta do and then I'm gonna swing by the crib later tonight and pick you up. Can you get a sitter for your kids?"

"Yeah, I can. I'll just call my sister. She ain't got shit else to do anyways," she said. We chatted for a few more minutes and then I led Lisa to the door to see her off. "I'll call you when I'm done, okay?"

"Okay, baby!" she smiled as she strolled out of the door. I

quickly locked it and then flew over to my living room where I had a small office setup. I yanked my phone out of my pocket and dialed Candace, another homicide detective who worked in my unit. I didn't want to bother with Jake and I didn't want him prying into my shit. Candace and I were cool. Real cool. We actually used to fuck around with each other but we had to stop because she was actually married. What a shame though because her pussy and head game was spectacular. I ain't never met a woman in my life who could suck a dick the way she did. I had to snap out of a daze I found myself in, reminiscing about our good ole times. The phone kept ringing until she finally answered with, "Hey, what's up Colvin?"

"Detective Whitaker. What's up with you. Feel like I haven't seen you in a minute? You've been avoiding me?"

"Haha. Funny you should mention…I was meaning to talk to you."

"Why is that?" I asked with a curious brow.

"My husband is away for two weeks on a vacation. I was, umm, wondering if you wanted to hang out."

I chuckled. "We'll see about that. But are you sure though? Remember the last time?"

"Yeah, well, I'll make sure we have a bit more privacy."

"Okay, well, let me know. But in the meantime, I need your help with a pressing matter."

"And what's that?

"Don't tell Jake either…"

"Uh-oh. What the hell you got going on?"

I scuffled through some notes I had sitting on my desk. "So, you know I just closed out that crazy rape case."

"Yeah, I heard. Still kind of fucking crazy that woman was able to kill that motherfucker like that! How in the world was she able to do that?!?"

"You know, sometimes I wish you were my partner. I told

Jake the same thing. The old bitch's story isn't adding up at all. It's...It's just too sketchy for me. You won't even believe what we found in her hamper, too."

"What's that?"

"The woman had a fucking pair of stocking filled with tangerines. The end was tied up."

"Damn. Like some Thin Line Between Love And Hate shit?"

"Bingo."

"So, you are saying this woman may have beat herself the fuck up? But what about the rape kit?"

"Well, we haven't gotten back the lab results yet but the Lieutenant already had me to close out the case and move on."

"Oh God. But you aren't..."

"Yeah."

"I don't know about this. I know you are a good detective and all but is this case really worth your career if the Lieutenant finds out your doing sneaky shit behind his back?"

"You know...I really don't care at this point. I'm pretty sure once I put two and two together the Lieutenant might reopen the case."

"Okay, so what do you need from me?"

"This Percy dude...I didn't do enough digging but I want an employment history on this guy. I wanna know exactly how my victim, Mrs. Washington, met this man."

"Okay..." I then heard Candace typing away at her desk. "So, I'm pulling up the case now. His full name is Percival De'Andrew Jacobs."

"Yup."

"Okay, well, let me run his social and then I'll hit you back in about fifteen minutes."

"Okay, perfect. I'll be here at my desk waiting patiently."

"I can't believe you're doing this on your day off. You really owe me big time, too…"

I smiled. "I got you. Don't worry."

Candace and I chatted some more and then she hung up. Chicago Police contracted with an outside background check agency to get basic background information on suspects and victims. In this instance, I would've done so with Mr. Percy but since the Lieutenant wanted me to go ahead and get the investigation over with, so obviously I didn't have the time to do so. In fact, he'd already assigned me to a new case. While I awaited her phone call, I went and made me a quick breakfast then jetted right back to my desk. And just before I was about to sit down and devour a bagel, Candace was calling me on my cell.

"Damn, that was quick!"

"Yeah, well, Mr. Percy wasn't that hard to dig information on."

"Why is that?"

"Damn, did you not run his name or license first to see who this man was?"

"Nah…I didn't bother."

"Wow. Lazy…Anyways, he's an ex-felon. He spent some time locked up for armed robbery. But before that he worked at a nursing facility out in the suburbs."

"What's the name of it?"

"Mt. Sinai Long-Term Health…Out in Lombard."

"Lombard? Damn, that's all the way out in the western suburbs."

"Yeah…"

"Mt. Sinai Long-Term Health," I said as I jotted down the name on a piece of paper. "Do you know how long he worked there?"

"Quite some time. About six years. He was a CNA."

"A male CNA. That's interesting."

"Why?"

"Never thought men gravitated toward nursing careers."

"That's sexist as fuck. I got two male cousin nurses. And one them started off as a CNA. Shit, there's good money in nursing."

"True. Anyways, thanks Candace. I owe you a lot. I'm finne ride out to this nursing facility."

Candace and I chatted for a bit more. Once I got off the phone with her I googled this nursing facility. They were about a good forty minutes outside of the city in this suburb called Lombard. I'd been there a couple of times when I needed to go to the mall. Soon as I got the phone number to the location, I called them up and asked to speak with the director of human resources. Within seconds I was connected to this individual. "Dorinda Clark speaking, how can I help you?" the woman answered the phone. She sounded like she was probably black. The jazzy raspiness of her voice was a dead giveaway.

"Good Afternoon, Ms. Clark. How are you today?"

"I'm fine...Who do I have the pleasure of speaking with?"

"My name is Detective Michael Colvin. I'm with the Homicide Investigations Unit within the Chicago Police Department. I'm a lead investigator working on a case."

"Oh...Oh okay," she replied sounding a bit confused. "Well, how can I be of service to you?"

"An ex-employee of yours who used to work there – Percival Andrews."

"Yes? I just got off the phone with someone to confirm his employment history."

"Yes, that was our outside background investigations unit. I'm calling to follow up with some more information..."

"Oh, I just don't like the sound of this but ask away..."

"Well, not to disclose too much information, but Mr. Andrews is a lead suspect in a current murder investigation."

"Oh my God! Excuse me? Please tell something bad didn't happen to Percy! He was such a wonderful man when he worked here! Everyone loved him! It was just so unfortunate what happened to him!"

My eye brow raised out of curiosity? "Excuse me? Did you already hear what happened to him?"

"No…Not at all. What I meant was him getting locked up over that crazy crime! I just know he didn't do it. I still believe to this day he was framed! I can't just wrap my head around how he could do something like that! That just wasn't his personality. Percival was an outstanding person!"

"Well, I hate to break it to you, ma'am, but Mr. Andrews broke into a woman's house last night and raped her. The victim luckily found a weapon and killed him out of self-defense."

Ms. Clark gasped. "WHAT?!??"

"Yes, ma'am…"

"No! NO! NO! I just don't believe it! I don't believe it at all!" she cried. "Percy was a wonderful young man! He wouldn't harm a soul! Ohh, Lord! I just feel so bad for him! And for his partner…"

"His partner?" I was now confused. So perhaps he did have a spouse or girlfriend of some sort.

"He had a girlfriend or a wife?"

Suddenly weird silence came between us. Sounded like Ms. Clark didn't know how to muster up the words. "I, umm…Damn…"

"What is it, ma'am?"

"Not too many people knew this…But…"

"But what?"

"Percy is…he's gay. Or *was* gay…"

My eyes swelled with shock. "Are you certain about that, ma'am? How would you know that?"

"Oh God. I really shouldn't be having this conversation. I

could really get into a lot of trouble," Ms. Clark said. "How do I even know you're a police detective?!? This could just be anybody!"

"I can meet you at your office in an hour...."

She agreed and without hesitation I grabbed my wallet, keys, phone and stormed out of my apartment to go have a conversation with Ms. Clark.

29

VERNITA

hile, soon as I left the house to let them Mexican boys clean up my place, I headed straight to some random ass hotel over in the South Loop. It was so nice, too! I had no idea what the name of this place was but as soon as I hopped out of Paulette, I ran straight to the front desk and had them to put me up in the first room they had available!

The room was gonna run me like three-hundred a night but I didn't give a damn at this point. My sanity mattered more than money! Besides, I'd be damned if I was gonna stay up in some bed bug-infested shit. Baby, Vernita didn't fuck with no mothafuckin' motels. I'd let them young, raggedy hoes that sold their pussy for forty dollars stay up in those rat-and-roach motels!

Soon as I got off the elevator on the fourth floor, I scurried down the hallway dashed to my room – 408. Within seconds I found the room, swiped the keycard to let myself in and then stormed in, letting the door close behind me. I quickly locked the door and took a huge sigh of relief. "YES, LORD!" The lights weren't on but sunlight peered in through the windows. I walked over to the queen-sized bed and threw all my bags and shit on it. But suddenly, out of nowhere, those goddamn demonic visions of Clarence, Alice and Percy appeared again! I gasped and was just about ready to dash out of the room, however, at this point, I knew it was all fake! These visions were nothing but the devil! I was convinced! Satan thought he had one over on me but he didn't realize he was messing with an anointed and appointed child of God! I was too blessed to be stressed. So with that being said, I took a deep breath and flew down onto the navy blue carpeted floor, right on my knees, and went straight into deep prayer. "Father God! I come before you right now in a time of great need to get these visions out of my mind!" Swaying back and forth, I kept praying as hard as I could and as loud as I could to stomp out the craziness from my mind!

At this point it seemed like the only thing that was going to work was nothing but prayer! While I cried out to the Lord, asking him to help me get these crazy, demonic visions and voices out of my mind, I couldn't help but still see these mothafuckas laughing at me. Percy was laid up in the bed, fully naked, but his head was hanging onto his neck with a bare piece of flesh. I didn't wanna look because the site was so traumatizing and gory. Then Alice was sitting down rubbing her head while she ate sunflower seeds! What in the hell?!? And, of course, Clarence was standing in the mirror looking at himself. I closed my eyes shut and focused on nothing but the comforting words of the Lord. "Victory is mine, Victory is mine! Victory today is mine! Oh, yes! I told Satan, get thee behind! Victory to-day is MINE!"

I had keep singing my favorite gospel song to myself to simmer my nerves down.

So many crazy thoughts ran through my mind as I paced the hotel room floor. The entire room was dark but that didn't matter because bright, blinding flashes of the past kept dancing in and out of my head. The crazy, vivid visions and voices kept coming and going but for some odd reason now I was able to mute the hell out of them. "Thank you, Jesus! Thank you!" I wailed and began to cry. But I was crying the biggest ears of joy because a I began to feel a sense of calm again.

"Thank you, Jesus! THANK YA! I WANNA THANK YA! HASHIO-MAH-KOKO-BAH!" I started speaking in tongues and the Holy Spirit began cover me! "EIH KO BAH!"

Chile! I didn't know what came over me (well, I did – it was nothing but the HOLY GHOST) but I suddenly exploded into a praise break. The more I danced on the floor the more I could see that those crazy thoughts were leaving my mind. God was telling me my past was my past and I had a glorious future to look forward to. God was STILL in control. Nothing but the devil was after me and now the Holy Ghost was slaying him! "GET THEE AWAY FROM ME, SATAN! I REBUKE YOU IN THE NAME OF JESUS!" I kept yelling to the top of my lungs. Chile, I didn't care if the people next door heard me. I had to get these demons away from me, you hear me?!?

Tears swimming down my face, I calmed down once more. Standing frozen in the middle of the hotel room, I looked around. Nothing but serene quiet could be heard minus the distant sound of a vacuum cleaner in the hallway outside of my door. The voices were gone. The visions of those mothafuckas were gone too. Those demons left! "Yes, Jesus!" My hands then began trembling with a sense of freedom. My body began quaking with joy. "I need to call, Dr. Jackson! I'm done with her ass!" I had enough of her!

My purse was sitting on top of one of these nice mahogany oak dressers in the room. I dashed over, grabbed my purse and pulled my phone out. I had that funky, know-it-all, young bitch on speed dial too! She was definitely going to get an earful from me. Couldn't believe her pissy pussy ass had me on this crazy medication, making me see all types of weird shit!

Once I hit dial, the phone rang and then some seconds later, her ugly ass receptionist picked up. I didn't like that big bitch either! Fat ass always had an attitude every time I went up in that mothafuckin' office! "Dr. Jackson's office! How can I help you?"

"Yes, I need to speak to Dr. Jackson, please!" I demanded with utmost nastiness all laced up in my tone. I even wanted this big hoe to feel all the heat I had.

"Umm, she can't come to the phone right now but I can leave a message, dear?"

"Baby, put Dr. Jackson on the mothafuckin' phone right NOW!"

"Excuse me?"

"Yeah, hoe, you heard me right! I said put that raggedy ass bitch on the mothafuckin' phone right now! And I ain't playing!"

"Ma'am! I'm gonna need you to calm down and stop cursing at me! Are you even a patient?!?"

"Yes, why the fuck else would I be calling?!?"

"Ma'am! I am about to hang up!"

"Baby, if yo fat ass hang up on me, I swear on my dead husband's grave I'm gonna come up there and snatch that cheap ass dollar store wig off your neck! NOW PUT DR. JACKSON ON THE FUCKING PHONE RIGHT FUCKIN' NOW!"

"Goodbye, ma'am..." Then the bitch hung up.

"OH NO YOU DIDN'T! OH NO THE FUCK YOU DIDN'T!" I couldn't believe that heffa would hang the fuck up on me! Did she know who she was fucking with! I didn't have time for any of this shit today! But since this how these hoes wanted to play games, I was gonna run right down to that doctor's office and have a word face-to-face with Dr. Jackson along with that nasty fat bitch sitting behind that damn front desk!

It was already pushing two PM and all I wanted to do was rest my nerves before I went over to Alice's house to help Sharday and the rest of the family with funeral arrangements. The stress of even dealing with last night was still etched so deeply in my mind, but now I was over it. COMPLETELY OVER IT! Honestly, I was glad I had Percy out of my life and now all I wanted to do was just move on from everything and be there for Alice's family. More importantly, I really needed to talk to Lamar!

I rushed back over to the dresser, grabbed my purse and pulled out my keys. Just as I was about head out the door, my phone began buzzing. I pulled it out of my purse and saw that it was indeed Dr. Jackson's office calling me back. I quickly answered, "YEAH, BITCH! YOU GOT THE RIGHT ONE TODAY, HOE!"

"Mrs. Washington! This is Dr. Jackson! What is going on?!??" That was Dr. Jackson and she sounded very concerned and frightened by my tone.

"Baby, I'mma tell you what the fuck is going on. I was just about to run down to that office of yours and have a word with you about this damn medication you got me on!"

"Vernita, please, just sit down for a moment and take a deep breath. It sounds like you are having another break-down. Please, just relax. We don't want you to get all worked up, dear!"

"BITCH, DON'T TELL ME TO TAKE A DEEP BREATH!" I went off as I once again began pacing the bedroom floor. All types of hell was seething in my bones and now I didn't even want to have this conversation anymore with her ass over the phone.

"Vernita, please. Just calm down, honey! That's all! I'm here for you! Just tell me what's happening!"

Out of nowhere I couldn't help but cry. "That medicine... It's making me go crazy. It's making me see dead people!"

"What's wrong?!? Did something happen, Vernita?"

"I killed someone! I didn't mean to do it! But he pushed me! I killed him!"

Dr. Jackson took a deep gasp then said, "Vernita! Where are you?"

"I'm at a hotel room!" I cried. "He tried to rape me! I had to defend myself."

"Vernita, please! Just relax, dear, and please tell me which hotel you are at? Do I need to send someone to pick you up?"

Suddenly I stopped crying and got angry all over again! My eyes exploded wide with fury. "NO! NO! THAT NIGGA CROSSED ME THE WRONG WAY AND KILLED HIM! AND I'LL KILL ANYONE ELSE WHO CROSSES ME THE WRONG WAY! I'VE DONE IT BEFORE AND I'LL DO IT AGAIN! I SWEAR TO GOD!"

"Vernita! Honey, please, just throw away that medication! That's the firsts thing you should do right now!" Dr. Jackson demanded while she constantly tried to talk me down and get me to stay put.

But at this point I didn't want to hear anything else she had to say. I managed to get the voices and crazy images out of my head with the power of prayer and it worked! I didn't need not nair crazy pill or medication from these motha-fuckin' doctors anymore! They were trying to kill me! I was convinced now! THEY WERE ALL TRYING TO KILL ME!

"Mrs. Washington, I am here to help you! I just really need you to calm down and relax before you hurt yourself, honey! That's all I am trying to do at this point! I wanna know what's really going on, dear! Please, I love you and I wanna see the best for you!" she kept pleading with me. Still shaking and filled with anger, I ran over to the body mirror in the bedroom to take a quick glance at myself. The room was still dark although some sunlight peered through the bedroom window. I turned the lights on and stared at myself in the mirror. Oh, how I looked so terrified! What in the hell was going on with me?!? Why was I doing this to myself. I was losing all my damn marbles. Why was I even going off on Dr. Jackson needlessly like this?!? Why did I even curse out that receptionist like that?!? "You still there, Vernita?"

"Yes...Yes, I'm here, Dr. Jackson!" I slapped my forehead and closed my eyes. Shaking my head, I stood there for a moment in disbelief that I was experiencing all of this. Everything around me was so surreal and didn't even know if I was even in reality anymore. Everything seemed so real and fake at the same time.

"Vernita...Just take a few deep breaths and listen carefully. You are probably experiencing some sort of psychosis. We need to get you into a hospital as soon as possible. And you just mentioned some moments ago that you may have harmed someone. Is this true or is this a hallucination?"

"I don't know! I don't know anymore, Doctor! I...I gotta go! I can cure myself. I might be up in age but I can cure myself!"

"Vernita, please, it sounds like you are beginning to experience the first stages of dementia. Maybe even Parkinson's Disease. These types of psychotic breakdowns are common for people with neurodegenerative disorders!"

Hearing the doctor utter those words instantly fired me up all over again! "Oh, no, baby! Ain't nothing wrong with me! It ain't nothing but this goddamn medicine you gave me! All of this medicine! I was fine before I started messing with all of this stuff. The first medicine done made me a sex addict! Then this other medicine got me seeing dead folks!

Oh, hell no! I ain't trusting not a single word any of you doctors gotta say!"

"Okay, please, Vernita! I understand—"

"You don't understand shit, bitch! Now I said what I had to say! I gotta go! My friend's funeral is coming up and I gotta help with the arrangements!"

"What friend, Vernita?"

"Alice! My friend! I told you about my friend!"

"Vernita, please...We've talked about this before! We need to—"

"I don't wanna hear nothing you gotta say!" I interrupted her in a roar. And with that I immediately hung up! Young, dumb bitch had no idea what the fuck she was talking about! I swore they just be giving people degrees for any motha-fuckin' thing! What in the hell did she know?!? Talkin' 'bout Parkinson's Disease. Bitch, I ain't over here shaking and shit! She had me ALL the way fucked up!

I knew I had to be making so much ruckus and wouldn't surprise me if hotel staff or even security came running to my room to see what was going on. But I didn't give a damn! I tossed my phone back onto the bed and stood in the mirror for a moment. Beads of sweat ran down my face. My mascara was running down my face. My eyes were still watery but now they were intensely red from all of the crying and yelling. I looked a hot ass mess and I'd be damned if I was gonna let this foolishness get the best of me. "Bitch, boss up! BOSS THE FUCK UP, VERNITA! DON'T LET THESE MOTHAFUCKAS DRIVE YOU CRAZY! YOU ARE A BAD BITCH! BAD BITCH!" The biggest smile then came across my face. "You know what...I'm finne go get me some dick! Fuck this shit!"

30

DETECTIVE MIKE COLVIN

here's this feeling of looming joy you get when you *assume* you're close to solving some puzzle or some other game of mystery. It's that sensation rising deep up in you that's gives you slight confirmation you are just about done solving some shit.

But just when you think you are almost finished, almost done solving some shit that makes you feel like you're some Albert Einstein-level genius, there's always that one puzzle piece that suddenly derails your victory of solving some hard ass shit.

Well, that thrilling joy swam through my head right before I met up with Ms. Clark. However, after a probing thirty-minute conversation with Ms. Clark here at this nursing facility, my quest to solve the mystery to Mrs. Washington was derailed. I was more confused than ever. Why? This nigga Percy was gay. Yes, gay. Like, gay-*gay*. There was just no other way to describe it. And what was Ms. Clark's proof of Percy's sexual preference in men? Health insurance. When he worked at the nursing home, Percy had a conversation with her about putting his "partner" on his health care insurance plan. Seemed like after all Mr. Andrews did have a significant other. And his name is or was Markell Vickers.

Exiting through the double doors of the nursing home, my mind was drawing blanks as to what my next move was going to be. But something told me I needed to get into contact with this Mr. Vickers. Now Ms. Clark did tell me she'd met this Markell individual once. Said he was a "nice-looking young man" who was in great shape and worked as a fitness trainer. She couldn't tell me the name of the gym but she did tell me that it was probably a gym not too far away from where Percy was living at the time. When we initially ID'd Percy as the suspect the night he was killed, we found out he lived down in South Shore. However, when one of the other investigators within my unit went to the apartment building listed on his identification, the landlord of the building told us that Percy hadn't been living there in quite some time and that he was evicted. With no further trace of where this man could've been living or staying, we just left it at that.

I did explain to Ms. Clark in great detail what happened to Percy and she was just completely stunned. Told me she couldn't believe anything because Percy was such down-to-earth, caring and "praying" man who'd give his shirt off his back during the middle of a freezing blizzard if someone else needed it. Something wasn't adding up...

I trekked through the parking lot fiending for a square. The sun was still out yet the temperatures were dropping. Roaring winds were cutting through this leather jacket I had on. Shit, I probably should've put on a thicker coat but whatever. I didn't give a fuck about freezing. Only thing I cared for at the moment was cracking this case. Speaking of which, I needed to call up Jake and ask if those results came back from the rape kit. Hopefully some nicotine would probably put a blaze in my brain cells and make me start putting shit together.

But back to Mr. Andrews –

Other than the armed robbery record, which turned out to also be related to a home invasion, I had no reason to believe that this Percy guy was a violent rapist. Especially NOW considering that the man was gay. I mean, you couldn't put shit past certain people. Hell, everyone was capable of possibly committing some crazy ass crime, especially under the right circumstances. But so far, all I knew about this Percy individual was that he was a nice, unassuming closeted gay man who out of nowhere committed two crazy crimes. One related to robbery. One related to rape. Let Ms. Clark tell it, he wasn't capable of any type of conduct, especially the ones he was accused of doing.

I got back into my car and checked my cell phone for missed text messages. The first message I saw was from Candace. She texted me some more information about Percy. He had been in and out of the foster care system for all of his childhood. Never graduated high school but he had a GED. Other than serving a stint in prison, this man managed to hold down stable jobs all of his adult life. Why all of a sudden would he decide to get caught up with Mrs. Washington? What was the extent of their relationship? Then I saw I had missed a text from Lisa. "Are we still on for tonight?" she texted with an attached picture of herself smiling. I texted her back. "Yeah…I'll hit you up when I get done with work." I threw my phone in the passenger seat and chucked up the car's engine. Idling for a moment, I had the urge to call Jake and tell him what I found out. I also had the urge to dash back over to Mrs. Washington's place and ask her some more questions because I just needed to know the full details of her relationship with Percy. Yeah, yeah, yeah, I knew I wasn't supposed to be digging deep like this and I could possibly get in trouble if Lieutenant found out, nevertheless at this point with this new information, I had to ask these questions because not only was my *hunch* still there, but now on a scale of one through ten, that feeling was coming in at a strong hundred. Something was off…Big time.

Time was of the essence, so with that being said I quickly threw the car in reverse and headed out the parking lot, hoping to hit the e-way ASAP. It was close to three now and there was a likelihood traffic was going to be a bitch. But I just had to go ask Mrs. Washington some follow-up questions. Hopefully she was still home. Hell, she should be…that was if she was really a traumatized rape victim. Shit, most of the victims of rape or any other form of extreme trauma who I'd interviewed over the years barely left their house after they'd been through a horrible situation. It was something so revealing about that smile Mrs. Washington had earlier too. Although I was starting to feel very fucking tired since I hadn't been to sleep in nearly two days, I was energized more than ever. The truth was inching closer and closer and I knew this case was just going to get re-opened once I solved another piece to this crazy ass puzzle.

I made my way onto the expressway hoping rush hour didn't begin yet. To my luck 290 was virtually empty. Just that quick I forgot I needed to follow-up with Jake about those rape kit test results, so I reached over to the passenger seat, grabbed my phone and dialed Jake.

Within seconds he answered the phone with a laugh then roared, "What the fuck are you doing calling me, Colvin? You're supposed to be sleep!"

"I can't sleep," I said back to him. "I got something to tell you…"

"Dude, get a bottle of Jack, smoke a cigar and call it the fucking night. You're stressing yourself out, my guy. The job isn't *that* serious."

"Whatever…Something isn't right, Jake. Look, don't tell the Lieutenant this but I just left Mr. Andrew's last place of employment before he got locked up. Something's not right."

"Oh God! What the fuck are you doing, man?!? Do you really wanna get in trouble, brother?"

"Jake…The man was gay. I told you something wasn't right. My intuition never fails me. Dude, I'm telling you I can't be wrong about this one."

"What?!?" Jake shouted. "And how in the fuck would she know that?"

"When he worked at this nursing home, he tried to get his partner onto his health insurance plan but because they weren't legally married he couldn't do it. Crazy thing was she still had a health insurance application of his and the dude was even listed on it as a 'domestic partner'," I said chuckling. "I'm telling you…Something isn't right. I just know it…"

"Okay, well, how does this change much?" Jake asked as I could hear him tapping what sounded like a pen or pencil on his desk. "Besides, what the fuck are you doing man? You know you don't have the Lieutenant's permission to be going out of your way to have fucking conversations with individuals over a CLOSED investigations," he said, sounding as if she was whispering. I guess he didn't want anyone to hear what he was saying. That was his way of protecting me. If someone else in the unit would've heard this conversation, they probably would've marched right to the Lieutenant's office to snitch. And I wouldn't put it past anyone because I wasn't that much of a well-liked individual in our unit. Other than Candace and Jake, everyone else loathed the fact that I had an extreme work ethic. Sorry I couldn't help the fact that I did my job and did it with conviction.

"Listen, Jake…Our suspect spent years working at fucking nursing homes all throughout Chicago. Sure, he did a stint for armed robbery, which to a degree it starting to sound very off-character. I'm gonna look more into that, but this man knew our victim pretty well. Even she said it. She's not telling the full truth about this situation. I'm not buying her story at all," I explained. "Look, just do me a favor and just see if those test results came back from the rape kit."

"Okay, well, I am pulling the case notes back up. Let me see if lab added the rape kit results," Jake said. Speeding through traffic, I waited impatiently like a kid on Christmas' Eve. I just knew once he opened up those results we'd have all the evidence we needed to corroborate the fact that Mrs. Washington wasn't some all-out victim of sexual assault.

"Bingo. They added them to the case notes. Let's see what we got here," Jake muttered. "Bleh. Bleh. Bleh. Okay, here at the bottom at reads – there were no traces of the suspect's semen found in the victim's mouth or vagina, however, this is not conclusive that there was no attempt at sexual assault. The victim's bruising inside of her thighs is consistent that there was at least an attempt at rape."

"Hrrrm. So, essentially we have an inconclusive rape kit," I said.

"Yeah, but come on, Colvin, what the fuck does that even prove. You and I know that rape kits don't mean shit. And just because semen wasn't found doesn't discount the possibility of penetration. Hell, for all we know the suspect could've used a condom."

"But there were no traces of latex to suggest that, so a condom definitely wasn't used."

"Okay, but what exactly are you getting at here?"

"Add two and two together. Suspect goes over the victim's house and there's no screaming or yelling heard for the duration of the night. Nobody in the neighborhood, let alone the complex, hears anything. Her neighbors live close by. Then we discover our suspect was gay?"

"Yeah, but what about the old white guy next door?" Jake asked.

"Remember he said he didn't hear a word. He had no idea what was going on," I retorted.

"Right, but he did say he suspected something was off because he heard loud crashing here and there but he didn't want to get involved in the woman's business," Jake said back to me.

I shook my head. "Yeah, yeah, yeah, but come on. I'm going to get into contact with this significant other, too."

"Look, Colvin, just stop while you're ahead, okay? Why are you gunning after this 76-year-old woman so hard? Besides, so what if the suspect was gay?!? How do we even know that's even the truth?!? What if he was lying to get healthcare benefits for a friend? What if he was bisexual? We don't know the full-extent of this man's sexuality and we won't get that now because our suspect is DEAD!"

"Bro, I'm gunning after the truth. But now that you mention it, there's even a remote chance our victim may have actually been in some sort of relationship with the suspect," I said.

"Eww no. God no! That woman is literally old enough to be the suspect's grandmother! That would be horrible! Oh God that's fucking disgusting! A young, gay or bisexual guy having sex with an older woman? Dude, go to FUCKING sleep! You're losing your shit!"

"Jake, think about this for a moment. This woman drives a fucking high-powered Mustang. She's windowed. She has no children. Mind you, I don't know if you noticed, but the woman's house somewhat reeked of fucking weed. Did you also not notice some of the wardrobe she had in that hamper? Nothing about that woman's house gave off humble, church-going grandma vibes. This woman probably has a thing for younger guys. I put my money on it," I said.

"And even if she did, how does that change this already-CLOSED investigation? Like, you are really pushing it!"

"What if he didn't rape her. What if they had a huge argument and she ended up killing him?"

"And what evidence do you have for that?"

"I don't have any but I am sure a confession would suffice."

"Oh God. You are really fucking pushing it!" Jake barked. "So with no fucking evidence at all, you mean to tell me you are going to accuse this woman of outright homicide?!?"

"There's something deeper to this story though. I'm sure of it, bro. I can't just fathom why a young guy like Mr. Andrews would form this years-long *friendship* with a woman who is literally decades older than him. It makes no sense at all," I said. "But it actually makes all the sense…"

"Yeah, look, I am gonna start working on this new case. But Colvin, you really need to drop this shit and move the fuck on. You're really fucking pushing it, brother. Like you are asking yourself for more than a department move. You are asking to get fucking fired."

"Yeah, yeah, yeah. Look, go ahead and work on that case. I'm gonna continue digging."

"COLVIN! WHAT THE FUCK ARE YOU DOING?!?" Jake barked but before I could let him continue shouting his bullshit at me I ended the phone call.

Honestly, Jake was right though. I had no idea what I was really doing at this point and once again I could hear the words of the Lieutenant fire off in the back of my mind. *Let it go. Stop being so fucking obsessed.* But obsession was what made me good at my job. And a lack of obsession is what made some people just absolutely suck at good police work. With that being said, as crazy as it sounded, I was speeding my ass right back over to Mrs. Washington's place to ask that woman some more questions. In fact, I was going to ask her a million questions and if she didn't like it, then oh fucking well.

With the day fading into late afternoon I needed to get to this woman's house as soon as possible before Lisa started blowing my phone up again. Last thing I needed to do was run her some more game. That just would've been a complete asshole move on my part.

A good twenty minutes later I was now idling on the side street, right in front of Mrs. Washington's townhouse. The cleaning crew that she'd hired to clean up her place was still here but I didn't see her car parked out front. Perhaps she went to go run some errands. But who the fuck was running errands when their ass was just in the hospital not too long ago after being raped?

Looking out the front passenger window, a debate was going off in my mind if I should go inside and snoop around. That was definitely against the law but at this point I kind of didn't care. If she came back and caught me I'd just run her some crazy excuse. But the more I thought about the more I realized that just would've been stupid for me to do.

I couldn't just waltz up into someone's house without a warrant. Not only would that cost me my job but that would definitely land me behind bars. I had to think of something else but with time quickly passing and no idea where this woman was, I had to at least make an attempt. I sat in the driver's seat some more contemplating my next move.

Fuck it.

I turned the car engine off, yanked the keys out of the ignition and rushed out of the car toward the driveway but before I could make it to the door I heard someone yell out, "Sir, are you the police?"

I turned to my left and saw this older-looking white man cautiously make his way toward me. "Yes, I am" I responded to him. "How can I help you?" I asked as he got a foot away from me. I'd instantly recognized him. He was Mrs. Washington's neighbor.

"Hi, I'm Dan. Dan Kilpatrick. I'm Vernita's neighbor," he replied extending his hand toward me. I shook it saying, "I'm Detective Colvin. How can I be of assistance?"

"I'm concerned about Vernita...I've been meaning to say something for quite some time now but I am thoroughly concerned about her welfare. She hasn't been the same for quite some time now. I don't know what's going on with her."

Instantly my brow rose out of curiosity. "Care to explain?"

Mr. Kilpatrick, probably in his mid-to-late-seventies, gripped his waist and pursed his lips as if he was trying to fight back a confession. From the flat look on his face I knew this old ass white man was about tell me something that would help me further drill down just exactly who this woman was.

"I think Vernita has very bad dementia. I think she may even have Parkinson's Disease. I'm not quite sure. I've been trying to help her out here and there. We used to be really good friends but this last year and a half, I've noticed her entire condition has been changing. Then, I don't know if you all were made aware of this but she was recently hospitalized. I found her passed out after she almost burned down her house!"

My face instantly twisted with surprise. "Hospitalized? Do you know why she was admitted or what ended up being wrong?"

"No, I don't know at all, sir. But my suspicion tells me that Vernita either has Alzheimer's or Parkinson's. I think she's been diagnosed but has just been in denial. Earlier this morning when she came back from the hospital, I tried to spark up a conversation with her but she was going off on the taxi cab driver who'd dropped her off!" He continued on saying, "She told me everything was fine and just brushed me off but as I watched her go inside of her house, I heard her speaking to herself." "I tried my best to just ignore everything but everything just tells me that she's not well. At all. Everything she's doing just reminds me of my deceased wife." A frown came across Mr. Kilpatrick's face and then tears swam down his wrinkled cheeks. "Judy, my wife, died from Alzheimer's and I see the signs in Vernita. Something's just wrong and I know it. She needs help, sir. I just fear that she also might be showing signs of hallucinations."

I was truly taken aback and then my mind began to drift off into different possibilities of what may or may not have happened last night. "What do you mean?"

"Even before all of the craziness of last night, from time to time I'd see her talking to herself in the driveway. It was like she was having full-on conversations with people. Often I didn't want to say or interrupt her. I didn't tell anyone about this last night. I just felt…felt so bad that something could even happen like this," Mr. Kilpatrick said, sobbing between his words.

"I am glad you told me this, Mr. Kilpatrick. This is very helpful. Do you have an idea of where she could've gone?" I asked as all I kept thinking was how everything about Mrs. Washington was just so strange.

"No idea. All I know is I saw her storm out of her place with a bunch of bags in her hand. Looked like she was carrying some luggage. Then she hopped in her car and took off."

"Does Vernita have any friends or family members?"

"Not that I know of...," Mr. Kilpatrick replied as he wiped his face free of tears.

"So Vernita never talked about romantic acquaintances?"

"No. Not at all...Other than her husband...And I'd only met Clarence once before he turned ill."

"Interesting...So you never saw any male come by?"

"No...Not at all...Well...Actually now that I think about it, from time to time I'd see some young fellow come by. One time I saw him come by with another fellow. But when I'd see him, he'd carry dumbbells and other exercise equipment with him. Perhaps it was her fitness instructor something. I know Vernita often exercised at the health club over on 47th street."

A lightbulb instantly went off in my head. I had to get over to the gym on 47th street. "The LA Fitness...?" I asked.

"Yes... The LA Fitness..."

"Okay, thank you...Well, I have to get going. I came by to check up on her but I see she isn't home. But she left the cleaning crew here by themselves? That's interesting."

Mr. Kilpatrick shrugged his shoulders. "Well, I have to get going. My stomach is killing me and I got a roast in the oven. Thank you so much, Detective." Mr. Kilpatrick gave me a nervous smile then walked back over to his driveway.

I watched him go inside before I proceeded to make my way up Mrs. Washington's driveway and toward her front door. I rang the doorbell but I am sure the sound of what sounded like high-powered vacuum cleaner drowned out the chiming. I waited for a moment to see if someone would come to the door. I looked around then exhaled knowing I was possibly committing career suicide by entering this woman's house without a search warrant.

"Fuck it," I grunted, grabbing the doorknob and opened the front door. Guess it was my luck that the door had been unlocked. Once again that deep intuitive feeling began to fire off in my core. As I cautiously walked inside the house, the sound of the vacuuming became more pronounced, damn near cracking my ears.

Nonetheless, looking around the townhouse, I was amazed at just how lavish this place was on the inside. The woman had this place completely decked the fuck out. It didn't quite hit me just how much luxury this woman was living in when I arrived on scene earlier this morning. I glanced over into the living room, taking in the expensive leather couches, the high-end entertainment center and other pieces of furniture that looked like they were imported from somewhere in Europe. Shit was a tad mind-blowing. According to my notes, the woman was a retired DMV worker. I didn't know what her deceased husband did for a living. Nevertheless, nothing about this place screamed that it belonged to a woman who processed driver's license applications for a living. Perhaps her deceased husband was the one with more refined tastes. Who knew. But all of this was very much still a mystery. Here you have a woman married to a man for decades, but then he dies. Presumably from natural causes. They had no children. No identifiable next of kin. No family friends or associates. Mrs. Washington oddly enough was a lonewolf. But then again, she did mention a friend. And this woman was recently deceased apparently. Now that I thought about, Mrs. Washington was probably at her friend's wake or funeral. Perhaps she decided to spend some time with this friend's relatives. Who knew...

I made my way past the kitchen and laughed when I saw a fruit bowl filled with tangerines sitting on the countertop. Shaking my head and chuckling, I trekked down the hallway as I made my way toward the master bedroom. As I got closer toward the bedroom, I saw the two Mexican guys dressed in white jumpsuits furiously vacuuming the entire bedroom floor. Damn, now that the blood and gore from earlier this morning was gone, the bedroom looked completely different. Looked like a presidential suite up in the damn W or some other upscale hotel in Downtown.

I didn't want to disturb these guys 'cause they looked like they were deep into work and if they were anything like me, I hated to be fucking distracted but I had to know where Mrs. Washington went. So, I gently knocked on the side of the door and suddenly the two men turned around and looked at me. They both turned their vacuum cleaners off and then pulled N95 masks down from their mouths.

"Excuse me but who are you?" one of them asked.

They both looked like they were no older than thirty.

"Hey, guys, I'm Detective Colvin with the Chicago Police Department," I said as I pulled out my badge and ID and flashed it to them. "Do you know where Mrs. Washington went?"

The other young guy shrugged his shoulders. "Seemed like she took off to go stay with someone or something. Don't know but she told us to get her place cleaned up as quickly as possible and lock it up when we were done."

"She had bags and stuff with her?"

"Yeah…"

"Did she make mention of when she'd be back?"

"Don't know," the same guy responded once again shrugging his shoulders.

"Okay. Damn. Well…" I paused for a moment and then awkward silence filled the room. "Well, I'm gonna get going," I told them and began to proceed back down the hallway, however, a sudden thought came to a mind. Like damn, this lady really trusted these two guys to be here by themselves? "Wait, I'm confused..So she just took off and told you guys to clean the place up? How are you going to lock up?"

"She gave us a key," the other guy responded.

"Interesting…" My gut feeling began to grow in intensity.

"Really interesting. Anyways, I'll get going. Thanks for the information."

"Hey…umm, Detective…," one of the guys called out to grab my attention. "She's kind of weird, bro. Like fucking weird as shit. Before she left out we heard her talking to herself. It was almost as if she was having a full-on conversation with someone else in the bathroom."

"Was she on her cell phone or something?"

Both of the cleaners looked at each other then they looked at me as if they'd seen a ghost. "No. Not at all. She said she was on the phone but when she walked out of the bathroom she grabbed what looked like a cell phone off her nightstand. It was strange as shit. She might be crazy, bro. She didn't even tell us what happened."

"Really?" My eyebrow lifted with more curiosity.

"Yeah. So what happened…"

"I, ummm…. Well, I guess you all do have the right to know but she was raped last night and then she killed the alleged perpetrator…with an envelope opener…That's why there was blood everywhere. But looks like you guys did a pretty good job I see…"

"Fuck bro! I told you she was crazy as shit!" the other guy laughed. "Let's just hurry up and do this shit and peace the fuck out, bro. I don't get good vibes from this chick at all."

I chuckled. "I don't either…"

The two guys quickly turned their vacuum cleaners back on and went right back to work. This time they seemed to be putting in a hundred percent more effort to get the bedroom spotless as quickly as possible so they could get out. Interesting how even they picked up on the woman's crazy vibes. More proof in the pudding that Mrs. Washington was definitely missing a few screws in her head.

I exited out of the bedroom and made my way down the

hallway. A part of me wanted to check out the other rooms in the house.

Fuck it.

I opened the first door off to my left. It was a guest bathroom. Nothing of interest in there.

I took a couple more steps and opened another door that too was on the left. The door opened, I strolled into what looked like a guest room. Nothing but a single queen-sized mattress sitting on top of a wood-framed bed sat in the center of the room. Although the lights were off I noticed walls were painted baby blue. Odd color choice. Maybe at one point this bedroom was occupied by a young boy or kid. Then again Mrs. Washington didn't have any kids, let alone grandchildren...

I walked deeper into the room and then over to a sliding door closet with a body mirror attached to it. I slid the closet door open and quickly scanned the small closet up and down. It was completely empty. Not even a single hanger was in sight. I quickly closed the closet door then dashed out the room.

At this point I definitely was treading on thin ice by searching this woman's house with no warrant. And even if I wanted to get a warrant, I need a justifiable cause. And a justifiable cause I didn't have; only thing I had in possession was just this *hunch.* This *hunch* had better lead to me to a fucking pot of gold, otherwise I was going to be out of a pension.

Although my gut was telling me Mrs. Washington was going to be away for quite some time, there was a part of me that kept envisioning that at any moment she could come bumbling through her front door and catch me. It would definitely be over for me. Old ladies like her were professionals at complaining. And despite the fact that she'd have to call up a long chain to reach the Lieutenant, old people had all the fucking time in the world to get into contact with the right head person in charge to get someone fired.

Shit was indeed risk…but there was just…something…

Something that just kept compelling me to search the fuck out of this woman's house, even if it meant that I was committing career suicide.

I made my way to another door toward the end of the hallway on the right. Before I opened the door I looked down toward the master bedroom just to make sure I didn't have those two guys staring at me, wondering what in the hell I was doing going through the woman's shit. The last thing I wanted was for them to report back to her that I had come to her house unannounced and they witnessed me snooping through her shit. Then again, they probably wouldn't even give a damn given just how spooked out they seemed by her.

I cautiously opened the door and peered in the dark room. It was completely empty. I looked back down the hallway again one more time just to make sure I didn't have curious eyes on me. Clear. I strolled in and rushed over to another closet. I slid the door open and this closet too was empty. "Damnit," I grumbled and quickly slid the closet door back closed.

I rushed out of the room and then closed the door.

Shaking my head out of frustration, I zipped past the kitchen, making my way toward the door. However, my eyes caught hold of another door between the stove and another closet door that was probably a pantry. I froze. That wasn't a door leading to a garage. Maybe it was a bigger pantry? I didn't know but once again my curiosity was boiling over like lava from a volcano. A debate went off in my conscience as to what my next move was going to be. My unblinking eyes were enslaved to the doorknob.

"Fuck it." I dashed over to the door and opened it. Although the room was dark, bright light coming from the kitchen allowed me to get a partial glimpse of what exactly this room was, and indeed it was a pantry. Shelves were installed to the walls and they were lined with canned goods, boxes of cereal, paper towel and other typical dry goods. Mrs. Washington had enough food and other items up here to survive an apocalypse or a natural disaster. Her ass must've been one of those extreme couponers. People like that got on my fucking nerves, too. Muhfuckas like that were always buying unnecessary shit. Just because some shit was on sell for a penny didn't mean you needed to get it.

I quickly scanned the room and then to my surprise there was yet another door. Damn, this house was like a fucking maze.

I walked inside the pantry and I glanced up, noticing there was a small lighting fixture in the center of the ceiling. I looked over my shoulder and saw the light switch. I cut the light on and then walked over to this other door. I paused for a moment, debating whether or not I should yet again take another dive down this rabbit hole. "Damn, well, I've gone this far, might as well see what the hell this lady got up in her house!" I grabbed the doorknob, slowly opened the door and yet again, to my mothafuckin' shock, I stood staring down a dark staircase. I began to proceed down and then rubbed the side of the wall to see if there was a light switch. It was, and I turned on what was a small ceiling light that immediately lit up the entire staircase. Nausea growing within me, I descended down the staircase. The sound of my footsteps thumping against the hardwood steps echoed in my ears as I got closer and closer to the bottom floor. Once there, I stared off into nothing but a dark room. I pulled out my cell phone and turned on the flashlight app to illuminate my immediate surrounding area. Then I saw another light switch. I flicked it on and my eyes widened when I realized was in a virtually empty basement. The walls were painted a light sea green.

The only piece of furniture in the room was a single shelf that was lined with books.

I walked deeper into the basement wondering if there'd be another door to journey through. There was one, however, from the rumbling I could hear emanating from it, it probably was just a boiler room. I strolled over to the door, grabbed the doorknob to open it. But the door was locked. I noticed you needed a key to gain entry. That boiler room had a weird, putrid smell coming from it but the smell wasn't something similar to a dead body. Shit, I'd be able to recognize that smell from a thousand miles away. The smell was moldy, almost a bit fishy too. Perhaps there was some rotting wood up in there. Besides, if Mrs. Washington was some crazy serial killer – which I knew she wasn't – she wouldn't store no damn dead bodies up in her house. Nah, she was the type if she did do some killing, she was probably smart enough to dispose of the bodies in a vacant property somewhere. I didn't even know why I was going down that train of thought though because this woman was damn near eighty and so far I knew absolutely nothing about this woman. I didn't even know why I was even allowing my mind to think she was a murderer. I was really taking things too far now but, man, that hunch. It was just growing and growing the more I looked around this room. Something in here was trying to grab my attention. I could just feel it. I scanned the room and then my eyes landed on that shelf. I walked over and noticed the entire shelf was lined with books that were probably collecting decades' worth of dust. Scanning each section of the shelf, nothing really stood out to me…that was until I got to the second to last part of the shelf and I noticed a laptop, an expensive-looking Macbook at that, sitting vacant. But that wasn't what really stood out to me. What really set alarms ringing off in my head was a splatter of what seemed like blood on the laptop. The investigative gut feeling ramped up in intensity and my intuition was telling me to grab the laptop. All the evidence I needed was right there on that laptop! *Grab it, Mike! GRAB THE FUCKING LAPTOP!*

"This old bitch!" I grabbed the laptop and rushed over to the light switch to turn the lights off in the basement. I ran back up the staircase and before I exited out, I turned the staircase light off as well. Definitely didn't want to leave any trace that someone had been down in her basement. I exited out of the pantry, rushed out of the kitchen and just before I made my way to the front door, I looked down the hallway and noticed the two cleaners were still going at it. They were completely undistracted and probably didn't even realize I was still in the house. "Perfect," I mumbled to myself and then flew out of the front door. I popped open the back of the car trunk, threw the laptop on top of my shit. I then hopped in front seat, chucked the engine up and sped off and made my way back to the apartment. I didn't know how I was going to do it but I was going to gonna get forensics to check out the blood on this laptop!

"**M**Y NECK! MY BACK! LICK MY PUSSY AND MY CRACK!"

I popped my fingers as I screamed the lyrics to that song. Baby, this tune was my jam! I loved me some Khia. Her ratchet, snaggle-tooth ass. Baby girl shole needed some dental work but she knew she could make her some nasty music!

I had to get the hell up out of that hotel and get back to my old-new self. I'd be damned if I was gonna let all these crazy hallucinations drive me to insanity! So on that note, I was making my way through Downtown to go check out a bar or a tavern so I can get my mothafuckin' drank on and hopefully procure me some dick. And honestly, at this point, Vernita was willing to let a white boy get a feel for these here sugar walls.

It was almost five PM and that meant that pretty soon a bunch of good lookin' white mens were gonna be flooding all the bars and taverns for happy hour. Honestly, I was also tired of dealing with niggas. I mean, don't get me wrong, I loves my black men. But sometimes I just didn't want to have to deal with all the drama and downright fuckin' bullshit these niggas made you go through. Sometimes the dick just wasn't worth it. Especially considering everything I went through with Percy!

For right now, I just wanted to go a bar, drink some bourbon, meet me a fine ass white man that looked like Tom Cruise and get my fat, juicy pussy sucked and fucked on!

Although it was a tad chilly today, I had the drop top pulled back as I glided down the street. Light gusts blew through my hair. The streets were crowded with all sorts of people who looked like they were in a rush to make it to the train or bus. The sound of taxi cabs honking their horns filled the air. I usually hated driving through Downtown but I was just so relieved to know I wasn't hearing any of these crazy voices, let alone see those crazy apparitions! The devil was surely a lie and I'd be damned if I was gonna let him get the best of me. Although I knew what I was about to engage in some sin for the evening, God knew my heart and he knew I was a faithful child of his. I had to do what I had to do to make myself feel whole again!

I had no idea what bar I was going to go to, so as I slowly drove down Michigan Avenue, I turned off a random street and found the closest parking garage. That was something else I absolutely hated about driving in Downtown. Parking was so expensive! I pulled up to the gate and lo and mothafuckin' behold, some young, muscular, light-skinned nigga with tattoos running all up and down his neck and arms hopped out of a booth then walked up to the driver's side window. "Good afternoon, ma'am. How long are you gonna be here?" "Hey," I replied to his sexy ass, smiling and licking my lips. "Chile, I don't know. I'm thinking for a few hours." "Well, it's gonna be thirty dollars because there's an event going on." Just that quickly I became pissed! "Thirty dollars?!?" I spat back to him. "Now, young man, you and I know that is a rip off! What kind of event is going on?"

"Some concert over in Millennium Park," he said nonchalantly. Although I was angry as hell, I just went ahead and dug in my pocketbook, pulled my wallet out and handed the young, fine ass nigga two twenty-dollar bills. I took a quick scan of him as he fiddled with some notepad in his hand. Looking down at his jeans, I saw his fat, long dick resting on the side of his leg. Baby, that dick looked like a Coca-Cola bottle up in his jeans. I had no idea how old this boy was but he was probably pushing twenty-five at the minimum.

"Okay, here's your receipt and place this sticker in the window," he replied but as I looked up I instantly gasped. Some old, ugly ass white man with craters all up in his face was extending his hand out to me. "Who are you? Where did that other boy go?!?"

"Excuse me?" the old ass white man replied looking confused. "What young man? I've been standing here the entire time."

"No! NO! There was a young black man who was just standing here!"

"No, ma'am. No black man works for this parking garage. Is everything okay?"

Not saying anything back to him, I just yanked the receipt and decal out of his hand, rolled the car window up and then drove through the gate. Oh, Lord! My mind was playing tricks on me again! But perhaps because I was so horny, I was just imagining folks. Then again, I was deluding myself. I was getting a tad scared again because obviously that young man wasn't real. My heart thumped with anxiety and something deep down in me told me that I really need to slow my roll and check into a hospital as soon as possible. But I quickly deadened that dreadful though as I didn't wanna deal with these damn doctors anymore! They were the worse! The ABSOLUTE worse!

So, after burying the anxiety in the back of mind, ignoring the possibility that something truly was wrong with me, I slowly drove up the ramp leading me to the second floor of the garage. "Goddamn!" I grumbled when I kept seeing each parking spot was occupied. This entire garage was parked to the brim.

Now making my way up to the third floor, I continued driving until finally I found a spot all the way toward the back. But to my luck I noticed that the spot was close to the elevator. Thank God because I noticed earlier my hip was a bit sore and if I planned on getting some dick tonight, I couldn't fuck with no damn stairs! I needed all the strength in my ass and hip muscles to take a good pounding.

I pulled into the spot and for a second, I just sat back and closed my eyes. I began to drift off hoping that these hallucinations and voices were truly over. "Lord, please bring me through this fire!" I prayed, rubbing the side of my head. Just as I was about to turn the car engine off, my cell phone began ringing. My phone was connected to my Bluetooth system in my car, so I instantly saw Sharday's phone number flashing across the screen. Just then and there I became sad all over again. Damn, it just totally slipped my mind that Alice was gone. I didn't know how I managed to forget about everything that just happened. But I guess because I was so stressed out from my own situation, I just totally forgot about Alice. Oh, Lord. What in the world was I doing right now?!? I should've been over Alice's house helping Sharday and the rest of the family with funeral arrangements! The phone kept ringing and a part of me contemplated whether or not I should answer. I truly needed some nasty sex just to get my mind off of things. All of this happening was just too much for me. Just as I was about to ignore the phone call and get out of the car, guilt instantly slapped me in the face. I hit the *answer* button on the steering wheel. "Oh, Sharday, girl,

I've been meaning to call you! How you holding up? I was just out and about running errands and what not."

"Hey, Ms. Vernita. I was just calling to check up on you because I hadn't heard or talked to you in a while. Is everything okay?" she asked. I suddenly became confused. "Wait? What are you talking about? I just saw you a few days ago."

"Ms. Vernita, we haven't talked in a while. It's been a few months...What are you talking about?"

"Sharday, I know you going through it. It's gonna be alright. God is still in control..."

"Ms. Vernita...I'm so confused right now. I have no idea what you're talking about."

"Sharday, Alice is in a better place. Know that for sure. She was a praying woman. She loved the Lord. I know it's hard, baby, but she's looking down on us right now. Believe that. Do you pray?"

"I know Mama's looking down on us, Ms. Vernita. And yes, I pray..."

"Do you need me to come over and help ya'll out with the funeral arrangements? Who got the body? I don't want my friend going to any ole okey doke funeral home. Some of these people will put too much make up on the body. Damn shame. Will have folks looking like they in a circus or something. Oh, and what church did Alice belong to? Because some of these churches don't do people right!"

"Oh no! Ms. Vernita, is everything okay?"

"Sharday! Why you keep asking me that? I'm fine! Are you okay?"

"I'm fine, Ms. Vernita! But...But why do you keep asking about Mama? She's been dead for years, Ms. Vernita."

"What are you talking about?!? Girl, stop playing with me! Alice just died!"

"Ms. Vernita! I think you might be losing your memory. Mama's been dead for nearly five years!"

"WHAT?!?"

"Yes, Ms. Vernita!"

My mouth dropped. Staring off at nothing in particular, I was trying my hardest to register the words that Sharday just dropped on me but my mind began to go blank. I didn't know what else to think at this point. I couldn't even formulate the words. "I...umm...I gotta go, Sharday. I got errands to run. I'm fine. I'm fine. Ain't nothing wrong with me. You just take care of yourself, chile!"

"Ms. Vernita, do you want me to come by and help you out? It sounds like you might need some help around the house. Have you been going to the doctor?"

"Alice just died. Why you messing with me?!? She just died!" I yelled out as tears dripped down my cheeks. I started to get really nervous and then as I tried my hardest to ponder over what Sharday was saying, it was starting to make sense. Oh, Lord! Alice had been dead! Her funeral was years ago! This entire time I had been having full-on conversations with her and she really wasn't even there. Now that I thought about it, all the memories I had of her were all jumbled together. Hell, I didn't know what was the past or present.

"Okay, Ms. Vernita, just calm down. You don't sound too well! Let me come by and help you out. It might take me some time to get there but I can be there in two hours! I just gotta let Lamar and the kids know!"

"What are you talking about, Sharday?!? Lamar! You messing around with your mama's boyfriend?!?"

"No, Ms. Vernita! Lamar is my husband! Remember? You were even at our wedding on the cruise? Remember? I can send my brother over there to check up on you!" I could hear Sharday cry as she continued to plead with me that I needed help.

Why was she messing with me?!? I just knew I wasn't dreaming up none of this mess. I think she was fucking with me. I just knew it! I may have been hearing things and seen folks but all of this right here had to be some joke. But then again, maybe it wasn't. Oh, Lord….I looked at myself in my rear view mirror. Lord, I was ill. I was really losing my mind. Now silent, I just sat in my seat, thinking hard about everything. OH LORD! I was losing my mind! "Oh, Lordy! Lord! LORD! LORD! Make it go away! Make it all go away! They coming after me!" "Ms. Vernita, just make it home safely! I'mma be there soon!" Sharday begged as she started talking to what had to have been her children in the background.

I started to feel very nauseous and this wave of forgetfulness began to drown me out. I could hear Sharday keep talking to me but at this point her words were sounding all like mumbo jumbo. "Okay, I'mma go now, dear. I ain't feeling too well," I told Sharday and then hung up the phone.

I sat back in the car for a second just to try to gather my thoughts. Everything was so confusing. I looked in the mirror and for a second I didn't even recognize my own damn self. I didn't even know my own name. In fact, I didn't even know where I was even at. Why was I here? Why was I in this parking garage and not back at home?

In a daze, I didn't know what to do next. I was getting terrified. I took a glance of myself once more in the rear view mirror but instantly gasped when I saw my deceased mother in the back seat. "Mama?!?"

I shook my head and closed my eyes. I looked again.

She was gone. Oh, how I missed my mother. And my father. And even Clarence. Chile, I was ready to go home to be with the Lord!

Tears swelled in my eyes as I shook off the thoughts of dying.

"Okay, chile, I need to get home. But I don't even know how to drive this here automobile!"

I fiddled with the keys in the ignition and just as I was

about to pull out the parking spot, my phone began ringing. Just like that, I snapped back into reality and I knew exactly where I was at. I stared off and tried to recollect where I was at again just to be sure.

I was in Downtown, just about ready to go out to drink and meet up with someone.

My name is Vernita. Vernita Ernestine Washington. I was born on May 26th, 1943 at St. Luke's Hospital on the South Side of Chicago. Okay, maybe it was just that medicine making me forget who I was. It had to be. I didn't have no damn Parkinson's or Alzheimer's. It had to be the tumor.

The phone kept ringing.

"Oh hell!" I grunted out when once again caught myself in a daze. I stared over at the car radio console's screen and saw Mr. Kilpatrick's name flashing! How in the hell did his nosey ass even get my phone number?!? I didn't even talk to that man like that! Then again, I must've given it to him. The phone kept ringing and ringing and I sure as hell didn't want to answer the phone, let alone be bothered by him! But the phone kept ringing. He was adamant. I hit the answer button on my steering wheel. "Hello?"

"Vernita! Where are you?"

"Mr. Kilpatrick! How you get my phone number?"

"Vernita, the cops are back at your place again! A bunch of them! They found three bodies in your basement! The cops are looking for you!"

Bodies?

"WHAT?!? WHAT ARE YOU TALKING ABOUT, MR. KILPATRICK!?!? STOP MESSING WITH ME! I DON'T LIKE THESE HERE GAMES YA'LL PLAYING ON ME. FIRST, SHARDAY! NOW YOU! YA'LL MAKING ME REALLY UPSET!"

"Vernita! Please calm down! Please! The cops are all over

the place! Where are you?!?" he asked as he screamed into the phone.

"I can't take this shit no more! I SWEAR I CAN'T!" My mind was beginning to see flashbacks of my life. Everything was all jumbled together once more and then I drew blank...

I got out of the car and just began to aimlessly roam around the dimly lit parking garage.

32

DETECTIVE MIKE COLVIN

It was almost close to six when I finally made my way to Lisa's apartment. After I left Mrs. Washington's apartment, I jetted straight home and threw on the nicest outfit I could scrounge up without needing to iron. I was tired as fuck but gassed up on knowing that I had what I knew to be this final puzzle piece in putting everything together with Mrs. Washington. That old bitch was going down for sure!

I sent her a text and told her I was outside, ready to pick her up for our date tonight. Some moments later, I saw her come rushing through the front door of her apartment building. My mouth flung wide open when I realized she was dressed like she was about to go to the fucking Mayor's Ball or some shit. Damn. I felt kind of bad because it was obvious that she'd never been to a really nice restaurant before. Cladded in this very revealing red dress, I had it in me to tell her she was a tad overdressed.

Lisa stayed over in Washington Park, which wasn't too far away from my crib over in Woodlawn. Although this part of the South Side was a bit safer compared to other parts,

Washington Park definitely had its rough spots, and unfortunately, Lisa and her kids stayed in the roughest. Once she hit the sidewalk, she took deliberate steps toward my car. I could see she had on some tall pumps and one misstep would've had her collapsing to the ground. I got out of the car and then opened the passenger door for her. "You like nice," I said smiling as I helped her in. I took a quick glance at her hand and noticed she had the bracelet on her wrist. Damn. Now I was started to feel a bit bad. "Oh wow! Really?" she said. "Why do you have that smirk on your face? Am I overdressed or something?" "Nah, not really," I lied. The last thing I wanted to do was make her feel out of place and then we'd have to possibly waste another hour for her to find a more *appropriate* outfit. Fuck it. Yeah, Ruth's Chris was a nice restaurant but it damn sure wasn't some fancy-schmancy place. I've seen plenty of hood niggas wine and dine at that place.

I got back over to the driver's side, hopped in the car, and began to put my seatbelt on. "

"Oh my God! I meant to tell you but I looked up Ruth's Chris and that place is so nice! I ain't never had a man take me here before! You are truly different!" Lisa commented as she stared at herself in the visor mirror, making some adjustments to her glued-in lashes. Honestly, I was a bit underdressed. I had on a pair of jeans, a polo, and some basic ass black dress shoes. "Damn, so you really never been there before?" I asked, feeling kind of bad that in all the years she'd been dealing with the niggas in her life, none of those clowns ever took her to a nice restaurant. "No, I haven't! But I am glad you are the first though," she said smiling right back at to me. She leaned over and began planting kisses all up and down my face and neck. I looked at her and then both of us began to make out like two horny ass high schoolers. Now my dick was starting to get hard and a part of me wanted to just scrap this date night, take her back to my place and finish what we started earlier. "Damn, baby, you making dick so hard right now," I moaned as I ran my hand between her thighs. "Yeah, well, feed me and I'll fuck your brains out!" she laughed. "Oh, for sure," I laughed back.

We continued to make out and I didn't even give a fuck that we were out on the side street where a bunch of people could've been observing us. Just as I was about to pull back and take off, my cell phone began vibrating in my pocket. I wanted to ignore it and keep making out with Lisa but I just had the urge to answer the phone. "Sorry," I quickly apologized as I pulled away from her and snatched the phone out of my pocket. When I saw it was the Lieutenant calling me, I knew I had no other choice but to answer. I swiped right to answer the call and before I could greet the boss, I heard him yelling, "COLVIN! WHERE THE FUCK ARE YOU AT?!?"

"Sir?"

"COLVIN! You need to get your ass down to this old lady's house RIGHT fucking now?!?"

I gulped. Fuck! I just had a feeling I was in trouble. But how and why? "Sir, what happened?"

"Three bodies, Colvin! THREE! All in Mrs. Washington's basement! GET DOWN HERE RIGHT NOW! I DON'T CARE WHERE YOU'RE AT AND WHAT YOU'RE DOING BUT YOU NEED TO GET DOWN HERE ASAP!"

"WHAT?!?" My eyes exploded with surprise and terror. "Sir, say that again?"

"Yes, you heard me mothafuckin' right! THREE FUCKING BODIES! Just get your ass down here RIGHT NOW! Where are you?!?"

"I'm right around the corner. Over in Washington Park. I was about to—"

"I DON'T CARE! GET HERE NOW!"

I looked over at Lisa. She had a look of disappointment

etched on her face. "Okay, I'm on my way…," I told the Lieutenant then hung up the phone.

"You know what, Mike. Fuck it! I'm done with you," she growled and quickly snatched the bracelet off her wrist then threw it at me. "I'm sorry, Lisa!" I yelled out. "Nigga, whatever!" she said shaking her head. "And don't buy the next bitch some cheap ass jewelry. Fucking clown. And your dick is little too," she spat as she quickly opened the car door and rushed out, quickly making her way back inside of her apartment building.

Although Mrs. Washington's townhouse was literally a six-minute ride right around the corner from Lisa's apartment building, seemed like she lived an hour away. Time was slowed down. My mind was completely empty. How in the hell did I miss three bodies?!? What the fuck?!? I had a million questions swimming through my mind. I was trying so hard to piece everything together but I couldn't. Nothing was making sense. AT ALL.

I pulled down the block near Mrs. Washington's townhouse and was completely stunned to see that half the damn force was out and about. There were at least fifty cruisers parked down the block. Half of Hyde Park's residents were on the street as well. I got closer and parked near a Deli. I hopped out and noticed everyone literally had looks of curiosity painted on their faces. Walking closer to the row of townhouses, I noticed some unmarked brown vehicles were parked off to the side. That had to be the Feds.

I approached a group of officers, ones who I had recognized from being here earlier in the day. They were standing guard in the intersection of the street. The entire area had literally been roped off…once again. "There's the man of the hour," one of the officers said to me. "Where's Lieutenant at?" I asked as I kept my eyes glued to the townhouse. "He's inside...," the officer, some tall, lanky white dude, uttered. I didn't know his name. He was just a regular beat officer.

Taking my time, I strolled over to the entrance of the driveway. Although by now it was getting darker, nothing but blue light emanating from all of the patrol cars illuminated the entire block. Nausea bubbled within me as I took cautious, deliberate steps up the driveway. I looked over to my right and saw Mr. Kilpatrick talking to some other officers. He was crying like he just found out his wife had been murdered or something. All of this shit was so surreal. Just as I was about to walk through the townhouse door, Jake and the Lieutenant just so happened to be walking out.

"There he fucking is," Lieutenant growled shaking his head out of disgust. "Let's have a conversation in private, *Detective* Colvin."

I looked at Jake and he just lowered and shook his head as he walked away not saying anything. Goddamn it! What in the fuck did he tell the Lieutenant! Boss and I walked over to his squad car and got in. Once the lieutenant slammed his car door shut, he looked over at me and asked, "Why were you over here earlier?"

"Sir?" I gulped.

"Just answer the fucking question...Why were you over here, Lieutenant? You were supposed to be off. I gave you explicit instructions to take your crazy ass home. You closed out a case and you were supposed to be off for a week. Why were you using department resources for your own private investigative purposes?"

"Sir, I already told you that this case wasn't a done deal. I know this isn't what you want to hear but I—"

"Don't say another fucking word, you fucking retarded

motherfucker," Lieutenant interrupted. "You think you can solve every fucking thing but you can't. You don't know shit"

"Sir. Please let me explain—"

"DON'T EXPLAIN SHIT TO ME!" he interrupted again. "I got three badly decomposed bodies found in this woman's house. And worse of all, you were seen coming in and out of this woman's place when you were supposed to be home. I wanna believe you don't have shit to do with those bodies, but now you got Internal Affairs all over my shit and your shit now. Are you fucking stupid?"

"Sir..."

"DETECTIVE! Get the fuck out of my car and stay as far away from the station for the next two weeks. You are suspended pending an investigation!"

"But sir..."

"AND DON'T TRY TO CONTACT NOBODY! Not even your lousy ass partner! Truth be told, I should've had you and Candace fired for fucking on the job!"

I immediately went silent.

"Sir...Please..."

"Yeah, you didn't think I knew about your violation of our fraternization policy, huh?

"Please sir, if you would just let me explain...," I begged but from the look on his face I knew I couldn't say shit else at this point.

"GET OUT!" he barked pointing toward the door.

With nothing else to say at this point, I followed the Lieutenant's stern instruction and got out of his squad car. "Fuck this fucking job," I grumbled to myself shaking my head. I quickly made my way through the thick crowd. A few officers tried to start up conversations with me but I didn't want to hear shit. I kept my eyes laser-focused on the sidewalk as I headed back over to my car. I hopped in and sped home within fifteen minutes. Once I got parked on the side street, I popped the car trunk open, grabbed Mrs. Washington's laptop, and swiftly made my way inside my building. Once I got inside my apartment, I stormed over to my desk and sat Mrs. Washington's bloodied laptop on my desk. Then it hit me… "FUCK!" I didn't have the charge for the laptop! I flipped the computer open and tried to power it on but the laptop was completely dead. "FUCK! GODDAMN IT!" I couldn't just let her get away with this shit. I had no idea why those bodies were discovered, let alone where Mrs. Washington was at, but all I knew her ass was guiltier than a mothafucker and needed to be strapped to an electric chair ASAP!

These last two weeks had felt like two months. Time moved slower than molasses oozing down a tree. I spent most of my days locked up in my bedroom catching up much-needed sleep. Hell, there wasn't even anything else for me to do but to sleep. Lisa wasn't fucking with me no more. No one from the station was returning my phone calls. Even Jake wasn't talking to me. The only person I'd managed to talk to was my daughter, and our brief fifteen-minute conversation didn't even go over well.

Today, however, I was hoping to get some reprieve. I got a phone call from the Lieutenant earlier telling me that today I was scheduled to have a meeting with our unit commander along with a commander from Internal Affairs. I was nervous as shit because this sounded like this was the end of my run in Homicide. As much as I was dreading this awful meeting, I was actually relieved because a transfer out of the department was probably what I needed in this particular juncture in life.

The lieutenant didn't give me much input on the exact

nature of the meeting but all he told me to do was make sure I dressed as if my job depended on it. So that being said, as I stood in my bathroom mirror, I scanned my black suit jacket making sure I didn't have a single trace of lint on it. I adjusted my maroon tie, making sure I had tied it correctly. I couldn't even remember the last time I put on a tie. I checked myself one last time in the mirror then made my way out of the apartment to my car.

Some twenty minutes later, I arrived at the station, ready to get this shit over with. As I made my way out of the car, I threw some sunglasses on, adjusted my suit, and slowly walked through the parking lot already envisioning a future in traffic enforcement.

It was a somewhat warm Wednesday afternoon and the heat beaming from the sun was making my underarms sweat profusely. This was exactly why I hated dressing up in professional attire. Shit was very uncomfortable. I didn't understand how other detectives and other higher-ups dressed this way all the time.

My meeting with the Lieutenant, the unit commander along with Internal Affairs was scheduled to start in five minutes over in the east wing of the building where the Internal Affairs division was located. I strolled into the office and made my way over to the conference room. I walked inside and was immediately hit with the presence of everyone. "Good morning, gentlemen," I greeted them and then tightened my lips.

"Have a seat, Detective," Commander Orwell replied back enthusiastically with this Joker-like smile. He was an older white man, probably in his early sixties. Everything about him was tight. His face. His stiff hair. The weird slits he had for eyes. Even his posture. Everything about him reeked asshole and I knew he was going to tear me a new one. I glanced over at the Lieutenant along with our unit commander, Commander Jenkins. They didn't say shit to me. Both men, two stern-looking brothers, just gave me a menacing stare. That was my cue to not say shit else, sit the fuck down and let the bullshit begin.

Soon as I sat down, Commander Jenkins, a nigga who almost reminded me of Denzel Washington, cleared his throat and said, "Detective Colvin, we brought you in because we want to discuss a number of things, principally your future with the Chicago Police Department. This is another reason why Commander Orwell from Internal Affairs is here."

"I understand, sir," I replied somewhat nervous.

"Good. I'm glad you do," Commander Jenkins said. "But before we get started, we wanted to give you some updates into the situation with Mrs. Washington and the three bodies discovered in her residence."

"I'm glad to hear. Is she a lead suspect?" I asked.

"No. Not at all, Detective Colvin. And for that reason, this is why you are here. You broke a number of laws and department protocols. One of them being using department resources to conduct your own outside investigation...an investigation that netted absolutely nothing of value." He continued, "In your absence, the rest of our *law-abiding* police detectives along with the assistance of the FBI conducted some very awesome investigative work. And in an hour, we are announcing that we have a suspect, actually several, in our investigation."

Although I couldn't see myself, my face fell flat and the anxiety I already had in me was now turned up to level ten.

"Detective, the suspect in your original investigation – Percival Andrews...I understand you were convinced that he was an innocent man...and that Mrs. Washington, who unfortunately now is hospitalized and whose health is rapidly declining, must've killed him. Do I understand this correctly?"

I didn't like where any of this was going and this motherfucker was already drawing up several conclusions that I hadn't even yet arrived at. "Sir, I had an inkling that Mrs. Washington wasn't telling the full truth about what happened that night that she alleged that Mr. Andrews physically assaulted and raped her. I would've further pursued the case based on several details but..." I looked over at Lieutenant. "But, my superior officer informed me that I needed to close the case out. And yes, I admit that I overstepped my boundaries but I was getting closer to the truth."

"Well, with all due respect, Detective, you were far from the truth. Mr. Andrews, along with his long-time *partner* and confidante, Markell Jacobs, were part of a large burglary ring. And, unfortunately, they took advantage of Mrs. Washington."

"How?" I was confused.

"Were you aware that Mrs. Washington had recently been diagnosed with a severe neurological complication?"

"No...No I wasn't aware."

"Yes. Mrs. Washington suffers from stage three dementia. She had no real relationship with Mr. Andrews other than the fact that he'd check on her from time to time while he and others took advantage of her. She also suffers from severe hallucinations. Family friends would come and check on her from time to time but for the most part, Mrs. Washington had no idea what was going on behind her back. She's a completely innocent victim in all of this..."

"I'm confused, sir. She seemed very lucid to me when I spoke to her. How did her condition just suddenly deteriorate?"

"Detective, let me make this very clear. Mrs. Washington has nothing to do with what I am about to tell you. The three bodies found in her basement were also associates of Mr. Andrews and Mr. Jacobs. Rhodessa and Ricky Clark were a married couple. They were well-known drug traffickers from the Memphis area and had recently moved to Chicago some years ago. Also, another associate of theirs, Juan Gonzalez, was a part of this burglary ring. We were able to use forensics to ID all of these bodies luckily. Mr. Gonzalez used a moving company to stakeout houses. We've also arrested several individuals associated with the moving company. As for our lead suspect, Mr. Jacobs, the FBI apprehended him in Atlanta. He is on his way back to Chicago as we speak," Commander Jenkins explained.

"Wow. I…I am shocked. I just don't know what to say…," I replied. I was stunned. I didn't see any of this coming. I just… I was just at a loss of words. "So…I assume then this is case closed?" I asked.

"Yes. This case is officially closed. Great work done, of course, by our law-abiding homicide detectives," Commander Orwell replied. "And on that note, we need to segue this conversation to your future with the Chicago Police Department, Detective Colvin. Can we please have your badge and gun?"

My mouth flung wide open. "Why?"

"Because effective today you are terminated from the Chicago Police Department," uttered Commander Orwell. "And you are also ineligible to receive your pension. Just count yourself lucky that you aren't sitting up in a jail cell…"

33

DETECTIVE MIKE COLVIN

A YEAR LATER...

"*M*ike, this is the third time telling you that you have to get all in the corners. You have to dig deep and pull back ALL the equipment. This shouldn't be that difficult! I found a roach in the corner this morning. If the regional manager would've come by and did an inspection, you would've costed me my job!"

Rachel, this nasty, fat white bitch, was once again grilling me for not doing an effective job at cleaning the kitchen. A year after I got fired, I had an extremely difficult time finding a place that would hire me. In exchange for receiving at least a partial pension, which I wouldn't have access to until I turned 60, I had to agree to not use the police department as a reference. That pretty much disbarred me from getting security gigs and shit. So, with no other real experience, I ended up working as a line cook at this wack ass, hipster vegan barbeque restaurant up on the North Side. Such a silly ass concept. I hated this fucking place with a passion, too.

Only reason why I took a job here was because these crackas were paying close to twenty-dollars an hour. Their food tasted like shit. Muhfuckas had the audacity to

"Sorry, Rachel, I'll do better next time," I apologized as I stood there feeling pathetic as fuck.

"Unfortunately, Mike, there isn't a next time. I'm gonna have to let you go. Can you please go ahead and clock out for me?"

"What?!? All because I missed one spot?"

"Mike! That one spot could've gotten us in trouble with the city! And please, lower your voice! We have customers in here now!"

I looked around and did notice that a few muhfuckas were now staring at us. I didn't give a fuck though. This fat bitch was just looking for any excuse to get rid of me. I knew her chunky, spoiled milk-smelling ass didn't like me from the moment she laid eyes on me. "Man, fuck this job and fuck you!" I yanked the hat off my head and apron off my shoulders, balled them up and threw them onto the floor. "Make sure you send me my check in the mail, too!"

"Mike! Get out. NEOW!" screamed Rachel as she pointed toward the exit of the restaurant.

"Bitch, you ain't gotta tell me twice. This place sucks any fucking damn way! Who the fuck eats vegan barbeque?!? Weird ass white folks!" I stormed around the kitchen counter and made my way outside toward my piece-of-shit Elantra. Since I got let go from CPD, I sold my Charger and down-graded to a used Hyundai with 80,000 miles on it.

I hopped in and chucked up the engine. I needed a fucking cigarette to cool my nerves. I slapped a Newport in my mouth, lit up and sped out of the parking lot. "Bitch ass mothafuckas."

An hour later, I was back at my apartment. Once inside the building, I walked up to my unit and saw I had a seven-day notice from my landlord. I was late on rent once again. I checked my bank account earlier and only had five-hundred to my name. Ain't no way in the hell I was gonna be able to come up with $1200 to pay my rent this month. I needed to hit up someone to borrow some cash but I didn't even know who I was going to bother to call. I virtually had no one to rely on. In fact, no one from CPD was fucking with me anymore. A part of me wanted to call my ex-wife and ask her if she could help me out. She came to my help not too long ago for some other stuff but her new bitch ass husband, Mark, gave her grief. I yanked the notice off the door then rushed inside my apartment.

I couldn't believe this was my life. All because I simply was trying to do the right fucking thing. Every day I woke up, I relived the entire day those bodies were discovered in that old bitch's house. I just couldn't believe that I was so fucking off. As crazy as it sounded, I just still had that *hunch*.

Something wasn't adding up.

But I had to shake that shit out of my head and figure out a way how I was gonna get this money to pay my rent this month. So, with no other choice and no time to waste, the next best thing I could do was sell a few electronics I had up in the house. Hopefully that would put hundreds of dollars in my hands once I listed these shits on Craig's List. I had a flatscreen TV in the living room. Another one in my bedroom. Then I had two old laptops that I currently wasn't using. I also had two old iPhones. I flew into my bedroom and began looking for the laptops. Last I remembered, I put them up in my closet. I dug through boxes tucked away in the back of the closet, but soon as I pulled out the two laptops, my eyes widened with surprise when I realized I still had Mrs. Washington's Macbook. I forgot I even still had this shit up in my house. Shit, how did I even forget though? Then again, since the day I was fired, my life had went through so much turmoil that the last thing I had on my mind was the fucking laptop. Then on top of that, with all those guys that got busted for that burglary ring, there was really no point in digging any deeper into Mrs. Washington. But there was just something about everything I couldn't let go. *There was something...*

Pausing for a moment, I looked at the side of the laptop and thought maybe I could find a charger on Amazon or an electronics store to power this shit on. I pulled out my cell phone, went to Amazon.com and searched for a charger that may have been compatible. To my luck, I found one, a used one that was going to take about three weeks to get here if I ordered it now. A debate went off in my head. Just let it go, Mike. Let it go. The case is over. You are not a cop anymore. The case is CLOSED. Nah, nigga. This is the case of a lifetime. That bitch is shady as shit!

"Fuck it," I groaned once I hit the order button. Now back to other personal business – I scrambled to get all the electronics I could sell. An hour later, I was getting hit up left and right from muhfuckas off Craig's List. Thank God because getting evicted would drive me over the edge...

Two weeks later the package from Amazon came on a sunny Thursday afternoon. Soon as the driver dropped off the package, like a manic man, I rushed downstairs to the stoop, grabbed the package and then ran back up to my unit. Once inside, I quickly opened the package and then made my way over to my desk where I kept the laptop at. The blot of blood was still visible on the back of the laptop and that was still very much evidence in the event something useful was on this laptop. I plugged the charger into the laptop and pressed the power button, hoping the Macbook would turn on. The keyboard lit up. "Yes!" Within seconds the desktop popped up. Damn, Mrs. Washington didn't even bother to password-protect her damn computer. Then again, that wasn't surprising. And there probably was no need for her to do that.

The desktop was virtually empty. She had two folders – one titled, "FINANCES" and another was titled "WEBCAM".

I clicked the FINANCES folder and immediately a bunch of .PDF files popped up. I opened them one by one. It was a combination of bank statements, credit card statements, bills and receipts she saved just to have electronic documentation. Damn, for an elderly woman, I didn't think the old hag would be technologically inclined enough to keep everything on a laptop. Then I stumbled upon three separate life insurance policies. My eyes widened with shock when I saw the amount of money that had been paid out to her. She had as much as three, one-million dollar policies. I jetted back over to her bank statements and became even more surprised once I took a deeper dive into her bank statements. This woman was rolling in some serious cash! Shit was making so many damn angry. Here I was, my entire life ruined over her ass, and apparently, she was languishing away in some nursing home sitting on millions of dollars. Such fucking bullshit.

With nothing else of importance to look at it, I closed out of the folder then scrolled over to the WEBCAM folder. I opened it up and was immediately slapped with what looked like thousands of recordings. All coming from the small camera embedded in the top center of the laptop screen. I chuckled wondering what in the hell this woman was recording. I clicked on one video and let it play. Twenty seconds in, all Mrs. Washington was doing was clicking away at the computer screen, talking to herself. Nothing important. She was just rambling to herself. "Hrrrm…" There had to be something in these videos, so now that I was unemployed and not really thirsty to begin another job search just yet, I made it up in my mind that I was gonna spend however long possible to go through all these videos. They all went back to 2015. Why was she recording herself though? Seemed kind of odd but then maybe she clicked on something inside the computer that turned the camera on she was unknowingly recording herself.

Two days later, and virtually getting little sleep, I was now about six hundred videos in. Every day, Mrs. Washington had the same routine. She'd log in, and just stare away at the computer. She'd talk to herself. Every now and then it seemed like she was talking to herself. It was about ten AM in the morning and I was fucking starving. I got up out of the bed holding the laptop in one hand as I trekked down the hallway into my kitchen. My eyes glued onto the computer screen and the volume cranked all the way up, I made myself a bowl of cereal with one hand then went into the living room. With nothing on but some boxers, I sat the computer down on the coffee table and slowly ate my Fruit Loops, hoping one of these videos would give me some deeper clues into this woman's life. I clicked the next video and this time, she seemed different. Looked like she was crying. But she didn't seem sad or depressed. She seemed enraged. Like she had just got done cursing someone out. She was rocking back and forth in her computer chair mumbling to herself. I could barely make out what she was saying, so I quickly placed the bowl of cereal down on the coffee table, grabbed the laptop then held my ear up to the speaker. *"Don't feel bad, Vernita. Don't feel bad. Just calm down...It had to be done. It had to be done. That nigga slept around and fucked your best friend. Fuck him. FUCK HIM! He was gonna die anyways."*

I gasped. "What the fuck?!?" I sat there in complete shock.

"And yeah, I killed that hoe, too. Both of them mothafuckas can

be together now. In hell! Fuck Clarence and fuck Alice! Gon have a
mothafuckin' baby behind my back! All this time I trusted that
mothafucka and this is what he do to me?!? Fuck them both! And
fuck Sharday! Fuck 'em all! And she ain't gettin' not nair a dime
out of me! NOTHIN'! Bitch can get all the money she can from her
sorry ass husband, Lamar. Sorry ass nigga. Couldn't even survive
in the NBA!"

I had to go back rewind everything she just said. Once I
confirmed everything I just heard, I shot up from the seat,
grabbed a pen and piece of paper and wrote down the
names Clarence, Alice, Sharday and Lamar. I clicked off the
video then searched her computer for each individual name.
Clarence's name was found in several documents – most of
which related to money and life insurance. That was
obvious though since that was her husband. But who in the
fuck was Alice? She said this was her best friend. Hrrrm. I
looked up Alice in the search bar and the only thing that
came up were two .PDF files. I opened it and it turned out to
be Southwest Airline tickets. One was for Mrs. Washington.
The other was for an Alice Brown. Made sense. They were
friends and were probably going on a vacation together. I
looked closely. They were flying to Ft. Lauderdale. I opened
the second .PDF file. This time I was staring at cruise tickets. But then something else struck me as odd. I further
scrolled down the .PDF file and saw there was another
cruise ticket attached. It was for a Jarquayrious Miller.
Hrrrm...I wrote down that name as well. I looked back at
the video and jotted down the date of the video. It was from
September 5th, 2014. I pulled out my phone and typed in
"ALICE BROWN OBITUARY CHICAGO". A few results
came up. I clicked on the first result and was taken to a
website belonging to R&R Funeral Home right here in
Chicago. I saw a picture of an older, fair-skinned woman
who looked like she was probably in her mid-to-late sixties.

The obituary read, "Brown, Alice, 67 years. Peacefully passed into eternal life on September 5th, 2014. Loving mother of Sharday Thompkins, Paul Thompkins and Janice Thompkins. Dearest grandmother of several grandchildren. Alice was a life-long resident of Bronzeville, Chicago, Illinois. An avid Bingo player, she loved her trips to the Bahamas, Jamaica and Florida. She will be greatly missed but we know she is resting in the sweet arms of Jesus."

"OH SHIT! OH SHIT! I KNEW IT! I KNEW IT WAS SOMTEHING TO THIS FUCKING OLD BITCH! SHE FUCKING KILLED HER FRIEND!" I couldn't contain myself as I started pacing the living room floor. I didn't know what it was but my gut-feeling told me to look into this Jarquayrious Miller name. I typed his name into my search bar on my phone and the first fucking thing that popped up was an article from ABC7. Then everything fucking gelled together! This little nigga was charged in an armed robbery and home invasion that resulted in the death Alice Brown. There was video evidence of him pushing him down her stairs inside of her house! Then it hit me — I remembered this case! I didn't work this but everything was coming back to me. In fact, this was a case that Candace herself had worked on! "FUCK!"

I had it in me to call Candace but unfortunately both of us were fired and she stopped talking to me. I glanced back at my phone and saw another article. "Inmate killed in riot at Joliet Prison." I clicked it and read this nigga was killed in prison.

Joliet Prison.

Joliet Prison.

Joliet Prison.

There was someone else who went to Joliet Prison.

Then this entire puzzle came beautifully together. As mysterious as it sounded, it all pieced together in my head.

This had to make sense. It sounded crazy. But I could see it all playing out in my head now.

Percival Andrews was at Joliet Prison, too. He was there for five years. Mrs. Washington probably found out her husband was sleeping around on her years ago with her best friend, Mrs. Alice Brown. She probably found out and commissioned Mr. Andrews to kill Alice Brown. Mrs. Washington probably then used Jarquayrious to kill Alice. But why would they go on a cruise?

Oh...because he was going to push her over the cruise ship. But then that fell through. So he broke into her house and pushed her down the stairs. He was probably going to snitch on Mrs. Washington but Mr. Andrews decided to take matters into his own hands...That was why Ms. Clark said he was such an outstanding citizen. He fucking set himself up to get arrested and serve time in prison to get at Jarquayrious.

I stood in the middle of the living room, stunned, completely stunned that I may have just solved the craziest crime ever. And this all made sense. Mrs. Washington didn't want Sharday, the secret love child, to get her hands on Clarence's life insurance money.

Either I was completely crazy or the smartest man alive.

Silent, I stood there thinking about everything that happened over the year. My eyes became watery. I lost so much thinking how my detective hunches were both blessings and curses. I solved a lot of cases. I brought closure to a lot of families. But there were times I was wrong. Completely wrong. In this case, even with a video confession of Mrs. Washington, was this even real proof she committed a crime? I had no other evidence. Shaking my head, I grabbed the laptop off the coffee table, clicked out of the video and then scrolled through what had to be at least a hundred more videos. I clicked a random video and let it play. I saw Mrs. Washington once again at her computer, clicking and typing away. She had reading glasses hanging over her nose. Then out of nowhere I could hear a deep voice shout out, "Where you at, bitch? You ready for some dick?"

I gasped once I saw none other than Mr. Andrews walk into the room in the background. This nigga was complete naked and dick was already hard.

"Hell yeah, I'm ready for some dick!" Mrs. Washington laughed. "Bring that dick over here!"

"What the hell?!?"

Mr. Andrews got closer and closer and once he was a few inches away from Mrs. Washington's face, she spun her head around, grabbed his dick and stuffed down her mouth. "OH SHIT!" Without thinking and completely blown away from what I just saw, I dropped the computer onto the ground.

I blanked out for a second but then I quickly looked down and saw that the computer literally shattered into three pieces. "FUCK! NO! NO! NO! NO! NOOOOOOOOOOOOOOOO!"

34

DETECTIVE MIKE COLVIN

J couldn't let this shit go.

I refused to just let this woman get away with multiple murders. Blood was on her hands. I didn't give a fuck if she was damn near eighty either. Wrong was wrong and she was going to pay for what the fuck she did!

Call me paranoid. Call me delusional. Call me whatever the fuck you wanted. But I had everything solved. Unfortunately, no proof.

Two weeks later, I was gonna get proof though. I knew what I was about to do would get this woman to confess.

I knew this was a crazy idea I was about to embark on but I knew I was going to get my mothafuckin' proof.

On a semi-sunny late Sunday morning, I strolled through the Orland Hills Nursing Home to pay my dear *friend*, Mrs. Washington, a visit. I checked in at the visitor's desk and was told Mrs. Washington was currently at the chapel for church service. From the sound of it, I thought the chapel would've been some separate space on the nursing home's ground but I was told it was just a conference room on the opposite side of the building. Once I got directions to the chapel, I made my way over there. As I walked closer and closer, I could hear the rumbling of gospel music pour out to into the corridor.

"I'm coming up on the rough side of the mountain! I must hold to God. His powerful hand. Oh yes! I'm coming up on the rough side of the mountain! I'm doing my best to make it in!"

Now that song right there was some old school country gospel music I ain't heard since I was little boy when my grandma used to drag my crazy ass to church. Boy, I missed those days. Didn't have a care in the world. Not even a single responsibility. I'd spend my summers down in Mississippi fucking all the country hoes.

I stood near the frame of the door and peered in. There were about a good five or six people in attendance. I scanned the room and there Mrs. Washington was, slightly bobbing her head as she sat in a wheelchair. A voluptuous black woman with a jheri curl dressed in a purple polka dot dress was at the front of the room near a podium blowing her pipes to the gospel song. Gosh she sounded so horrible but she was good enough to get the elders in attendance moving to the tune.

Soon as the woman finished the song, she prayed then concluded the church service. A young Latina woman dressed in nursing scrubs who sat off in the corner walked over to Mrs. Washington and began to roll her out of the room. Mrs. Washington looked completely gone; she was just a mere shell of herself. The nurse wheeled Mrs. Washington closer to the door and I just stood there hoping this woman would instantly recognize me. Feet away, Mrs. Washington lifted her head and her eyes instantly widened. Although apparently her dementia by now was severe, that look in her eyes let me know she still remembered who the fuck I was.

"Nathaniel! It's my brother, Nathaniel!" Mrs. Washington cried out as she reached her arms out toward me.

"No, Mrs. Washington. That's not your brother," the nurse laughed then looked at me. "Sorry about that. She does that from time to time."

"I'm actually kin to her. I can take her back to her room if you want," I told the nurse.

"Oh, you are? How are you all related?"

"I'm actually her brother's grandson. I'm Mike. Nice to meet you," I said extending my hand out to the nurse. "I'm Dominique. I'm so glad Mrs. Washington has company today! Her goddaughter just stopped by not too long ago. And she brought these good brownies. They were so good! You just missed her actually! And yes, you can take her back to her room. But actually, after church, I usually take Mrs. Washington for a walk outside in the park."

"Oh...Okay, well, I can do that, too," I said producing the fakest smile.

"Oh, great, because I need my lunch break already. I'm hungry! Thank you so much!" the nurse said then took off down the hallway. I leaned down into Mrs. Washington's ear and whispered, "Let's go for a walk, my favorite Great Aunt Vernita. We got a lot to discuss, don't we?"

"Nathaniel! You brought some of them ribs for me? Boy, you know I loves me some rib tips! How is Pauline doing?" Mrs. Washington squeezed out through her parched lips.

Not saying anything back to her, I rolled her down the hallway and then we made our way outside into an open courtyard park. The nursing home had a nice, well paved trail with a quaint Japanese garden centered in the middle. A few other nursing home residents were outside and they too were accompanied by nurses and others who were probably friends or family members.

As I kept pushing Mrs. Washington, she kept rambling off at the mouth, talking about people who I didn't know nothing about. We got toward a part of the trail where there was a cement picnic table along with matching stone chairs. I rolled Mrs. Washington next to the table and then sat down in one of the seats. "Pauline make some good chitlins too! She make em spicy! I want some hoghead cheese! Did you bring any with you, Nathaniel?"

"Bitch, stop playing fucking games with me. You must think I'm stupid."

"Pardon me? Don't use that language around me, Nathaniel! I'mma tell Mama!"

"I know you killed your husband. And you killed Alice. You killed Percy, too. You even had Percy to kill that boy in prison."

"NATHANIEL! Stop it! Stop right now!"

I pulled out a flash drive and stuck it in Mrs. Washington's face. "Bitch, you thought you were slick. You don't have fucking dementia. You're faking it. The moment those bodies were found, you started faking it. I know you are. Bitch, you are really fucking slick."

Mrs. Washington's eyes exploded with shock and her mouth hung open. "What's that? I don't know what you talkin' about!"

"Oh, yeah! You know what the fuck I'm talking about now, bitch!" I laughed. "This is what we call a flash drive. I got a hold of your laptop down in your basement and went through all those webcam videos. I spent weeks combing through your shit and then discovered all of your videos. I went through each fucking video and stumbled upon that video confession of yours. Then I saw the airline tickets. The cruise tickets. Bitch, it didn't take me long to figure it out!" I dug my index finger into my temple. "Bitch, I'm a genius! I'm good at what the fuck I do. From the moment I laid eyes on your crazy ass I knew you were on some other shit. Yeah, you may have some health issues, you might be hallucinating here and there, but your ass ain't demented. You are very much conscious of what the fuck is going on."

"Take me back to my room right now!" Mrs. Washington screamed out then she started yelling for help but her cracking voice could barely get loud enough to grab someone's attention.

"You can scream all you want, Mrs. Washington," I growled as I stood up and began to walk away. "But I'm sending this over the police ASAP."

Truth be told, the flash drive was completely empty. I was just using it as a rouse to see how she'd respond

"Okay, so you got me. You figured it out. Yup! I killed Clarence. I had Percy to poison him! And then I had one of my other lil boo thangs to kill that fat ass bitch, Alice! I'd be damned if her and her raggedy ass daughter were gonna get their claws on my mothafuckin' money. Especially considering all the shit I had to put up with Clarence! And yeah, I killed Percy's ass! After I found out what he and Markell were doing behind my back! Those slick niggas thought I was dumb! They were playing all sorts of games on me! So what the fuck you gon' do? Have me arrested? Put me in prison? You're a bitch ass nigga for even digging through my shit like that! But who would believe you? Baby, I gots the dementia! I have a tumor in my brain. I have had psychotic hallucinations. Nothing that comes out of my mouth can be trusted! Shit, sometimes I don't even trust my own self. I don't even know what's real or not real!" she exclaimed.

I slowly turned around, mouth dropped out of shock. I just kept shaking my head. "Yeah, see, I knew it. Honestly,

Vernita, I don't wanna put you in prison. You've already lived out your life."

"So what the fuck you want from me then, you hoe ass nigga!" she barked. "Let me guess. Money? Because I know yo dumb ass lost your job. Meddling in places where you didn't belong!"

"Now that you mention it…" I chuckled. "You damn right I want money!"

"How much?"

"I want $250,000. That's all I need to get up out the current jam I'm in. I don't even wanna go back to work. Fuck that bullshit ass job."

Mrs. Washington's went quiet and her breathing became hard. "Fine then…But on one condition…"

"What's that?"

"Give me some dick!"

I instantly scrunched my face with surprise. "What? From who?" Oh yeah! This bitch was really out of her fucking mind. Fuck this shit! I needed to walk the fuck away right now and just drop everything.

"Yeah, Detective Colvin. You heard me right. I'll scratch yo back and you scratch mines. You give me some dick and I'll give you all the money you need. Besides, since you seen the videos, you know what I'm capable of. I want some dick. I've been up in this nursing home now for a year playing with my pussy at night and I'm sick of it! I. WANT. SOME. DICK!"

"Bitch, you crazy!" I scoffed at her idea.

"Baby, this is all an act. I still got some sense in me. Now look here, if you want the money, you gon have to do right be me and give me some dick. So what the fuck you gon do?"

I stood there for a second shaking my head. "Are you serious right now? That's all you want? And you will give me the money?"

"YES! I'm serious, mothafucka! Now what you gon do?"

"I…Um…I don't know…And all I would have to do is fuck you once?"

"Yup! Not playing either. From the moment I laid eyes on you I knew you was working with some serious wood. I just knew I was gonna ride that mothafucka one day, too! And wow, looks like the Lord works in mysterious ways," she laughed her ass off as she sat in that wheelchair. Now that I thought about it, did this old bitch even need a wheelchair? Was this all a part of her act?

Shaking my head in silence, disgust gripping my insides, I knew I really didn't have absolute proof of her crimes other than now this verbal confession. And even if I wanted to use what I found on her laptop as evidence, the truth was I technically stole the laptop out of her house. And any evidence found on the laptop would've been thrown out of court. However, Mrs. Washington didn't need to know that. And she didn't need to know that the laptop was broken. And if all I had to do was fuck her once to get this cash, then goddamnit, I might just take her up on her offer. *What the fuck are you doing, nigga?!?!? Really, you're that desperate for money?* My conscience was eating me the fuck alive. I couldn't even believe I was really considering this as an option. But with no real job prospects and bill collectors calling me all the fucking time, what the fuck did I have to lose?

I took a deep stare at Mrs. Washington and almost wanted to throw up knowing that I had to put my dick up in her just to get some money. This was some worthless ass shit but at this juncture in my life a nigga had to do what a nigga had to do. So, fuck it. Besides, who was going to know about this any damn way? "Okay, well, where you do this then?" I asked, ready to get this party started. I probably needed to get high as fuck and drunk just to even do this shit.

299

"Sign me out of this nursing home and we can get a room at the Holiday Inn up the street. I pass by it every day when they take us on our day trips," she said.

"Okay, let's go then…," I replied. "But I just wanna know one thing though. Just tell me though. Was I right? Ever"

Mrs. Washington tilted her head to the side then smiled. "You got it right, sweet heart…" She continued saying, "Now go on head and roll me back to my room so I can get my belongings. You smoke reefer by the way?"

"I might just start today," I told her.

"And when we get in the car, I wanna stop by the liquor store to get me some Hennessey."

I walked over to her and began rolling her down the trail. "Good. 'Cause I'mma need to get fucking drunk to do this."

"Boy, don't do me like that. Don't knock what haven't tried yet."

VERNITA

*C*hile, life was so crazy!

After Mr. Colvin agreed to break me off some dick in exchange for minding his mothafuckin' business, he snuck me out of the nursing facility and now were making our way over to this Holiday Inn not too far away from the nursing home. It shole was nice outside today too! God was showing up and showing out, you hear me!

After we hopped in the car, as I requested, we made a first stop at a nearby liquor store so I could get me a bottle of peach Hennessey and a pack of Russian Crème Backwoods. Soon as we got in the car, I popped that bottle open and went straight to drinking. I couldn't even wait to get some of that brown liquor down my throat. Baby, I hadn't had me a good drink in nearly a year! And chile, I had a big bag of reefur I was gonna light up once we got inside the room. From time to time I'd convince Jarvis, one of young boys who worked up at the nursing home, to buy me some green. He was reluctant at first but I paid him extra to help poor Ms. Vernita out!

Looking out the window, I was starting to feel like I was on cloud number nine! I was feeling so good right about now. I couldn't believe how it seemed like everything fell into place. Although this Mr. Colvin was one shady mothafucka, I couldn't help but take advantage of the situation. He just better do right by me and give me what I want. If not, I already had a back-up plan for his ass. If he backed out on me or if the dick ended up being trash, I was gonna accuse him of raping me! Nigga thought I was dumb but I was pretty sure he had a back-up plan in case things didn't quite pan out the way he expected.

"These brownies sho is good! I really didn't even think Sharday's ugly ass could even bake like that," I mumbled as I tore through these gooey double chocolate fudge pecan brownies she whipped up for me. I re-opened the Tupperware container sitting on my lap and then asked Mr. Colvin if he wanted one. Sitting behind the steering wheel of the car, he looked over at me and gave me a firm, "No."

"You sure? You might need to put a lil *somethin'-somethin'* in your stomach before you dig up in these juice box! Baby, I can fuck for hours!" I told him.

"I'm sure," he responded nonchalantly, keeping his eyes attached to the road. He better change up that mood real quick and get some pep in his voice!

Since we'd been in his car, he had been pretty silent. I could tell he was so uncomfortable with the idea of giving me some dick. But he was gon learn today that an old, nasty bitch like me can suck and fuck just like any of these young hoes out here in the streets! And since he was going to get this money from me, he better be ready for a fuck-a-thon!

"Okay, then, well, I'mma finish out the rest of these brownies 'cause that food at that nursing home is nasty as shit!" I said as I pulled out another brownie and began munching away. I was just so surprised Sharday could bake.

Since I had been up in the nursing home, Sharday had been visiting me more often to check up on me. I felt kind of bad because obviously I had to play up that I was really out of my mind. We couldn't have normal conversations and talk about her life, her kids and what she had going on with Lamar. Gosh, these brownies were so good too. Too bad her mammy wasn't alive because I just knew her fat ass would've loved these! Chile, that heffa was capable of eating an entire pan of brownies by herself. Rotten ass hoe. To this day, I still couldn't believe she and Clarence fucked around with each other behind my back then the bitch got pregnant. That was so hurtful, especially considering I couldn't have kids. That would drive any woman to go crazy. That type of betrayal would never leave my memory. I thought about what they did to me every goddamn day. And that was probably why I kept hallucinating all that shit despite the fact that I got rid of her ass and Clarence years back. Mothafuckas.

"So, you just gon keep faking it until you die?" Mr. Colvin asked.

"Why does it matter to you?"

"How do you live with yourself knowing you did what the fuck you did?" He came to a stoplight then looked at me. "You better not try to off me too," he said as he pulled up his shirt and revealed his gun.

My eyes widened out of fear. I should've seen that coming. "I don't wanna hear none of that right now, Mr. Colvin! I just wanna feel good! I haven't felt good in nearly a year! Now, please, no more of that negative talk. You killin' the vibe."

"Yeah, whatever, you just better make sure I have my money!"

"Hush up now! You'll get your money!" I told him.

"Yeah...But I still wanna know why. Just because your husband slept behind your back with your friend? And what about Mr. Andrews?"

"Yeah, I done did some things, crazy things at that, but

that was only when you crossed me the wrong way. Now, please, I don't wanna talk about none of that right now!" I shouted. He just shook his head and kept his eyes on the road.

Baby, let me tell you something...

Life was surely a roller coaster! I have had my fair share of ups and downs. I've had plenty of good times, and obviously, a lot of bad times. Nevertheless, nothing wasn't going to ever stop me from living my best life!

Now, I knew something wasn't right with me. Turned out the tumor had grown a bit bigger. The hallucinations I had been experiencing had become more intense. And even my memory went to shit. Those medications weren't helping either. However, by the grace of God, I knew deep down inside nothing was seriously wrong me.

That day I passed out in the parking garage, I swore my life had descended into absolute chaos. Once again, those doctors got their hands all over me and began diagnosing me with all sorts of ailments.

I would've fought my way out of that hospital but when I found out that the police and FBI had been all up in my home, it was best for me to play into being sick and demented. And I had been doing just that for the past year to keep those mothafuckas out of my business.

Obviously except for Mr. Colvin...

And now that Mr. Colvin knew about all the skeletons buried deep up in my closet, I'd be damned if I was gonna go out spending the rest of my days shacked up in some prison cell. No, ma'am! Ain't nobody got time for that.

Mr. Colvin could try to guilt-trip me all he wanted but I had not a single bone of remorse in my body. Like I said before, they should've never did what they did to me. How dare Clarence sleep behind my mothafuckin' back and have a baby with my best friend. And as far as that raggedy fat hoe, yeah, I paid this little boy to push that fat bitch down the stairs. And when his little dumb ass got slick and threatened to snitch on me, I had Percy to get his ass!

And Percy – well, honestly, some things I just couldn't remember in great detail. I think that night I killed him I had been hallucinating. Honey, my memory was shot to shit now. But I could tell you right now though, the only thing that was real was the prospect of getting my walls tore up!

"You seem a tad nervous? You nervous?" I asked chuckling. "I won't bite…I promise. I might be almost eighty-years-old but this pussy don't act like it. You ever been with an older woman?" I asked Mr. Colvin. He shook his head no. "Well, there's a first time for everything," I said to him.

Some minutes later, we pulled into the parking lot of the Holiday Inn. Mr. Colvin found a spot close toward the entrance. Just before he turned the car engine off, he looked over at me and said in an angry voice, "Like, I'm really not playing. I want my mothafuckin' money, Vernita. You ruined my life and I ain't got shit now. If you're fucking with me, please believe I will run straight to the cops and show them everything!"

"Whoa! Whoa! Whoa! Look, you ain't getting nothin' from me until I'm done! You understand me?" I spat back at him. "Just fucking relax! You acting all irate right now for no fucking reason! Are you you a mothafuckin' faggot or something?"

"BITCH! Don't call me no faggot!"

"Well, what's the problem then?!? Pussy is pussy!"

"Man, fuck this shit! I'm not fucking you! That's some nasty shit! Got me all the way fucked up! Don't even know what the fuck I'm thinking! I'm in such a bad place right now but this shit right here and ain't worth it!"

"Well, bring me back to the nursing home then, nigga!"

"Yeah! I sure fucking will! And bitch, you going to jail! FUCK THIS SHIT!"

"Nigga, they ain't gonna believe not a goddamn thing you saying! Besides, I'm calling your bluff. Mothafucka, you don't have the balls to run down to that station and run your mouth. First of all, you broke into my house and stole that laptop. Besides, nigga, I've been diagnosed with late-stage dementia! I got medical records to back it up, hoe. Ain't no prosecutor in their right mind gon' believe yo weak, punk ass!" Soon as I said what the fuck I had to say to his bitch ass, he lowered and shook his head. "Yeah, bitch nigga, you think I'm dumb or something? Now what you gon do? You want the money or not?"

"This ain't right," he howled out like a hoe ass nigga. "This ain't right at all!"

"Stop all that fussin'! Boy you don't even know what my body look like! Don't let that wheelchair fool you. My hip might be giving me some issues now but I keeps my body in shape. My body looks better than the rest of these scalawags on the streets!"

"Oh God! This is fucking disgusting. I ain't fucking no old ass lady!" Mr. Colvin cried out, punching the steering wheel of the car.

"Stop making all that mothafuckin' noise! Fuck is wrong with you?!?"

"I'm...I'm about to throw up." He quickly grabbed his mouth, opened the car door and leaned out into the parking lot. Then I heard the sudden sound of him barfing up whatever the hell he had up in his stomach. This nigga was doing the most right now. Some seconds later, he slid back into his seat and wiped his mouth.

"It ain't that serious, Mr. Colvin. Just drink the damn Hennessy and when we get inside, I'll roll up this reefer. Jarvis got some good shit, too!"

***

After Mr. Colvin got us a room for the night, we quickly made our way to the second floor and down the hallway toward the room. I threw my Louis Vuitton travel bag down onto the bed and then went over to the window to close the blinds. Of course I didn't want the world to see all the nastiness I was about to unleash. I marched back over to the bed and opened my bag. It was packed with a change of clothes, some soap, perfume, toys and even some lingerie. I was gonna show this nigga what the fuck I was capable of once I got in the mood!

"Give me that liquor," Mr. Colvin barked as he stood near the bed. "Where's it at?"

The bottle was inside a plastic bag next to my bag. I grabbed it handed it to him. "Won't you go get some ice, make yourself a drink and just relax. I'mma change and then roll this reefer up," I told him.

"I'mma just drink this shit straight to the head," he said and without hesitation he popped the bottle open and took a huge swig. My face twisted with disgust. "Damn, save some for me at least. I'm not even that tipsy yet."

He screwed the cap back onto the bottle and then sat it on the table. He got in the bed, laid down and covered his eyes with is forearm.

Shaking my head, I let out a chuckle as I grabbed the pack of cigars from out of my purse and grabbed the ziplocked bag of weed from my Vuitton bag. I placed the cigars and reefer on the desk near the television.

Before I opened up this reefer, I needed to make sure no one in the damn hotel smelled this stuff. Baby, this shit Jarvis got for me was loud as fuck! I flew over to the bathroom, grabbed a towel and then rushed over to the front door of the room. I tucked the towel deep into the bottom of the door to ensure no smoke would escape the room. I marched back over to the desk, sat down and began cracking the cigar open, dumping the guts out into a nearby trashcan. Then I broke that weed down and stuffed it into the cigar. I rolled up the nicest, fattest blunt I could. I shot up from the seat and went over to my pocketbook still on the bed. I pulled a lighter out and immediately lit up the blunt.

"Damn, you really gonna smoke in here? Are you fucking nuts?" Mr. Colvin asked sarcastically, staring at me as if I were crazy. Still laying on the bed, he just shook his head as if I was out of mind.

"Boy, stop being pussy!" I said back to him as I took two strong pulls and then reached over to pass him the blunt.

"Fine," he uttered as he leaned over, grabbed the blunt from my hand and placed it between his lips.

"I thought this was your first time smoking reefer. You lied to me?" I said.

"This is my first time," he replied.

"Well, slow it down, partner! You gon be spaced the fuck out!"

He took a long pull then immediately started coughing. Pounding his chest, he wheezed like he was having an asthma attack.

"Told you," I laughed. "Pass it back to me."

He passed the blunt back to me and I took another three pulls. I passed it back to him and said, "I'm gonna get changed. Be right back." I rummaged through my Vuitton bag and quickly grabbed my lingerie, hairbrush and makeup kit and then made my way into the bathroom.

Once inside, I quickly took off the blouse and jeans I had on. Then I unhooked this bra and slid out of these big ass panties. I didn't need to take no bath either because my pussy stayed fresh and clean. I made sure of that!

I then slid into this sexy ass lace hollow steel prop bra. Although I hadn't worked out in quite some time, baby, my titties were still sitting upright and were still firm. I guess that jazzercise and water aerobics did something! My areolas were looking nice and right too. Hopefully Mr. Colvin was a titty sucker 'cause I shole wanted my nipples sucked on. Then I slid into this matching thong. Luckily, I just shaved. This thong was exposing my bare fat ass pussy lips! I spent the next ten minutes or so doing my makeup and my hair. Once I got done, I double-checked myself in the mirror. "Showtime!"

I danced out the bathroom, making my way into the center of the room floor. "You ready, Mr. Colvin?" I asked when I saw that he was still laid out on the bed almost as if he was napping. "Ain't no time for sleeping! Wake the fuck up, nigga!"

He took his arm off his eyes and then spun his head around at me. He sat up in the bed, his mouth was now flung wide open. "Damn…"

I stood there for a second perplexed by the look on his face. I didn't even know if he was saying that because he was disgusted or because he liked what he saw. "Damn what?" I had to ask.

"I, umm…," he gulped. "I…Wow. I just…I must be tweakin' or something. Damn Hennessey got me buggin' out."

Suddenly I smiled. "Nah, nigga. You ain't trippin'. What you see is what you *see*. Now stop playing and get out of those clothes so I can gobble on that dick!"

He cautiously stood up and then proceeded to take his shirt off. His eyes glued to me, I just stood there with my arms folded as I analyzed his torso. He was a bit on the thick side since the last time I saw him. But I didn't mind me a little thickness. Sometimes those skinny boys ain't nothin' but bones. And bone on bone was some uncomfortable fucking! He didn't have any tattoos. His chest was full of hair.

Then he slowly unbuckled his pants and slid them down along with his boxers, instantly exposing his long, yet soft dick!

"Damn! You ain't even hard yet and that's all you?" My mouth flung wide open.

"Yeah…"

Baby, his dick was so beautiful. It was long, uncut and matched his skin tone. He had some long, big balls too! Baby, I was about to be sucking on those nuts all night! Thank God he didn't have much pubic hair either! I hated it when these negroes didn't trim their shit! I didn't like sucking dick while public hair was getting all up in my mouth, cutting up my lips and whatnot. "Well, lay down 'cause I'mma show you how a dick is supposed to be sucked!" I exclaimed as I strolled up to the bed.

He laid down and covered his eyes again with his forearms.

Now in the bed, I slowly crawled in between his legs. My eyes were glued to the dick. Once I arrived at the dick, I planted my head in between his legs and began to dance my tongue from his taint, up his balls and then up his shaft. I held his dick in my hand and began to stroke it as I licked on his nutsack. "You like the feel of that?"

"Hell yeah," he moaned, his words a bit slurred. Sounded like that reefer and liquor had his ass gone, chile! Then he chuckled.

"What's funny?"

"Damn, I can't believe I'm doing this."

"Well, believe it," I said and without hesitation I began to slurp on his shaft, soaking it up with as much saliva as I could. Mr. Colvin thought this was just gonna be one time affair but once I blessed him with this nasty, sloppy head I knew he was gonna be crawling back to me for seconds, and thirds, maybe even fourths. Ya'll already knew how Vernita put that magic on these young boys. They couldn't resist…

***

Three hours later...

"You like that, baby? How them walls feel?" I purred as I slowly rode Detective Colvin's long, thick pipe. This was just the medicine to bring total healing to my body.

Baby, I swear I had been struck by lightning because electrifying tingles shot down my spine as I took in all of his eight inches. Chile, I was just assured that my coochie had done dried up but baby, my juices were soaking up this here hotel bed! That maid was gonna have to change out this mattress, you hear me! I couldn't keep a count but I knew I had to have cum at least ten or eleven times.

"Hell yeah? Shit, keep ridin' that muhfucka," groaned Mr. Colvin as he bit his lip and kept his eyes closed.

See, I knew I'd turn his ass into a believer! Look at this nigga! His ass was enjoying every single mothafuckin' second of this pussy.

He and I both were enraptured in so much bliss. In fact, his fuck game was so on point that it was making me quite dizzy actually. I would've never thought some dick would have me feeling like this. Damn near psychedelic. If I died today, chile, this was truly the way to go, you hear me!

Grinding harder, I wanted him to knock my uterus back. My hip was a bit sore but luckily that reefer and Hennessy was making my mind ignore the slight pain. I was creaming so much on his dick and I wanted to get a taste of myself, so I hopped off the dick, got on my knees and began to slurp up all of my cum off his veiny dick. "Oohh! Ohhh! Ooh! Slow down!" Mr. Colvin barked as he tried to pull my head up off his dick.

But just like that, suddenly something wasn't feeling

right. I started to get kind of nauseated. I clutched my chest. Felt like my heart was quivering...

"What's wrong?" Mr. Colvin asked as he immediately shot up looking at me with concern.

"Oh...I'm just a tad dizzy...I gotta use the bathroom," I told him as I got up out of the bed. I took a few steps. I stopped and looked up at the ceiling. Then everything became dizzy. The light in the room suddenly became blinding. I stumbled a bit more and then just fell out. I couldn't produce no words. Then a bright white grew in intensity in my eyes and I felt beckoned to it. This had to be it. I was dying. Baby, I done got me some dick then died. What a way to get called on home to glory! I felt myself going up to yonder!

I tried to make out the words but I couldn't say anything. My mind was beginning to draw blanks. Half my body felt numb. But then the light, which was so warm and welcoming turned dark. Dread set in. I knew I was gonna die. No! I couldn't die. My chest felt tighter. I had to live!

Everything was starting to blend together and I could feel life slowly fade away.

I looked over to my right and saw Mr. Colvin rush over to his pants pocket and pull out his phone and began dialing a number. Hopefully he was calling 9-11!

He stood there and when I was able to focus in on his face, right then and there something was off. His eyes became evil slits. He looked at me and said, "Sorry, Vernita..."

I tried my best to formulate words but I couldn't say anything. The tightness in my chest increased in intensity.

"Hey, Sharday, it's me Mike...I think the brownies worked," I heard him say. "Once she's out I'm gonna dress her up and then bring her back to the nursing home, put her up in the bed and lock her room door from the inside. Let me get going though because I gotta get here there ASAP so that way her body doesn't start to look crazy."

My eyes exploded with terror.

They set me up. They killed me! I knew it! I knew something was off!

Mr. Colvin hung up the phone and tossed it off to the side of the bed. "FUCK! I gotta fucking piss! Shit! Hurry the fuck up, Mike!" He then stormed passed me and dashed into the bathroom.

I didn't know what came over me but I suddenly mustered up the energy to move. I slowly crawled toward his jeans in the center of the floor and grabbed a hold of them. "That mothafucka…" To my luck, that shady nigga's small pistol was resting comfortably inside the right pocket. I pulled the gun out, cocked it back and then turned over on my back.

The moment he rushed out of the bathroom, he froze like he'd just seen a ghost.

I raised my arm, aimed it at Mr. Colvin.

"Shit!" he blurted out and before he could take cover I pulled the mothafuckin' trigger.

POW!

The sound of the gun shot popped in my ears and for a second, I blacked out. I reopened my eyes and saw Mr. Colvin now lying in the floor, completely motionless.

"Ya'll ain't gettin' shit from me…," I managed to squeeze out. A sudden heaviness overcame me and darkness swept me away.

"*V*ernita...Vernita..."

I slowly opened my eyes to the sound of a soft angelic-sounding voice. My vision was hazy. I couldn't make out anything. Then I heard the sound of what had to be hospital machines chirping.

I WAS ALIVE! The Lord done spared me!

As my eyes adjusted to the brightness of the cold hospital room, I saw a young black woman hovering over me. "How do you feel, sweetheart?"

"Where...Where am I?" I painfully squeezed out through my parched lips, my voice scratchy.

"You're in the hospital, dear. You're a survivor! You are an incredible woman!" said the doctor as she gave me a wide grin.

"What happened to me?" I asked as I scanned the room and noticed that the doctor wasn't the only person in the room. That trifling bitch Sharday, her husband Lamar and her kids were also in the room as well. A police officer was also standing guard.

Some tall, handsome Denzel Washington-looking man

walked over to me and said, "Mrs. Washington. I'm Commander Jenkins with the Chicago Police Department. I deeply apologize about everything that happened. We believe that—" "Sir, with all due respect," the doctor interrupted. "But I don't think it's the right to have this discussion right here and right now. Mrs. Washington suffers from late-stage dementia and what you say may end up being very traumatizing. We also need to conduct some more routine tests."

"Oh…Oh, I deeply apologize," said Commander Jenkins. He looked over at Sharday and Lamar. "Folks…I'll be out in the waiting area to follow up with the Orland Park Police Department. I'm so sorry for everything." Then he walked out that room.

"On that note, now that Mrs. Washington is awake, we're gonna need to run these tests on her now. So if you folks don't mind, can I have some privacy with her?" the doctor said.

"Sure thing, doctor," Lamar said and then grabbed his kids. He glanced over at me and his entire face was flat with expression. Sharday stood up and stared at me. "Can I just have a brief moment with her, doctor? I'll make it brief. I just wanna pray for her," she said. My eyes turned to slits knowing that bitch was lying right through her mothafuckin' mouth.

"Okay, but please, make it quick. The neurologist will be coming soon," the doctor said and then made her way out.

Now it was just Sharday and I in the room by ourselves.

Awkward silence filled the room.

"So, you're not gonna say anything, bitch? After all the shit you put me through?" Sharday growled.

I looked at her and said with boldness, "Baby, I'm like that Tupac. *I ain't a killa but don't push me. Revenge is like the sweetest joy next to getting pussy*…But I'm strictly dickly, hoe."

315

Sharday suddenly exploded out of her seat and rushed out of the room without saying anything else.

"Yeah, that's right, bitch! Ole raggedy, nasty ass bitch!" I barked.

I couldn't even believe she even had the audacity to be up in this hospital room, acting like she was here to look after me in a time of need. Even though I resented the hell out of her, she didn't have to kill me. Especially when you consider the fact that her no good ass mammy set me off to do what I did in the first place.

I didn't know what she put in those brownies but I guess the Lord wasn't gonna let the devil have his way with me. God wasn't through with me just yet.

But I'd tell you this right fuckin' now; if that whore thought she was gonna get her claws on my money, then she better think again. She wasn't gonna get shit and I'd already done seen to that.

Why?

Because just when I thought I was gonna die when I was falsely diagnosed with the cancer, I had got all my affairs in order and left a secret will in my safe.

All of my shit was going straight to one place and one place only – my church - Mt. Moriah Missionary Baptist Church where the Reverend C.N. Miller, III is the presiding pastor. So whatever fucking shenanigans Sharday and that mothafuckin' Mr. Colvin had up their sleeves weren't gonna work any damn way.

Although by now Sharday was probably seething with rage, contemplating her next move, I just sat up in this hospital bed and increased the morphine drip running through me. A big smile came across my face because for the first time in a long time I felt a sense a relief. All my burdens were lifted off my shoulders.

Why?

Well, for some odd reason, my memory came back in full focus.

Everything was so clear now.

And I had one thing on my mind that was so vivid. It was clear that I could see it like it had happened yesterday! And that was that night of Sharday's wedding on that raggedy ass Carnival Cruise. Baby, I didn't even fuck with Carnival Cruises like that. I was a Royal Caribbean Cruise-ridin' type of bitch.

"Uh-huh. Yeahhhh, Sharday. I ain't like shit about your raggedy ass wedding, but I'm glad I did what I did. That's right, hoe. I'm so glad I fucked your husband on your wedding night," I laughed to myself. "And now that I think about it, his dick wasn't even all that. So have at it, hoe. With them ugly ass kids of yours…Uhh-huh! But you know what, that Lamar could eat the hell out of some pussy! I know that for sure!"

The nice black doctor strolled back into the room and this time some short white man with a bald head was to her side. "Hey, Mrs. Washington. I'm Doctor Schilling. We're gonna run some tests on you now!"

"Pauline! PAULINE! I want some hoghead cheese and saltine crackers. Run up to the store and go get me some!" I blurted out, faking like I done had the dementia.

"Don't worry, Mrs. Washington, we're gonna take really good care of you!" the doctor said and all I could do was lay back and just laugh.

But just when I thought I was feeling good, my mind began to draw up blanks once more. Everything became fuzzy again. "Where am I? Where's mama?"

THE END

317

ABOUT THE AUTHOR

QUAN MILLZ is the profound and prolific writer from the sizzling streets of Miami, Florida. Now residing between Chicago, Illinois and Los Angeles, California, he's known for his gritty, graphic and gut-punching urban tales that depict the real and rawness of black urban life. His deeply detailed and visual storytelling talent gives readers a view of the rollercoaster of emotions that many endure when trying to climb their way out of dark struggles in the inner city. He's the author of the Project Hoe Dreams, This Hoe Got Roaches In Her Crib, Mama's Tears, The Coldest Thug Ever and many more!

Made in United States
Orlando, FL
01 September 2023

36625395R00200